An Endeavour to be Worthy

The Montford Cousins: Book 1

By

L.L. Diamond

An Endeavour to be Worthy

By L.L. Diamond

Published by L.L. Diamond

Cover and internal design © 2022 L.L. Diamond
Cover design by L.L. Diamond/Diamondback Covers
Cover photos: Regency Woman wearing a white muslin dress and long spencer by Kathy SG, Roses at Chatsworth by Ida Wikne courtesy of Shutterstock

ISBN-13: 978-1-960057-00-6

Facebook: https://www.facebook.com/LLDiamond
Instagram: @l.l.diamond
Twitter: @LLDiamond2
Blog: http://lldiamondwrites.com/
Austen Variations: http://austenvariations.com/

Chapter 1

"Lizzy!" Without pausing to curtsey, Amelia rushed forward to kiss Elizabeth's cheek and embrace her. "I am so pleased you could come, but where is Jane? Was she not to join us as well?"

"She is with the Gardiners on Gracechurch Street."

"What? Why? I thought she was excited at spending Christmastide with us."

Elizabeth took Amelia's hands. "She was quite excited, but Mama has been pressing her towards the young man who let Netherfield Park."

Her cousin's cupid's bow lips pursed, and her deep brown eyes flashed with a look Lizzy knew well. "I beg you not to call that woman Mama. I may not remember your mother, but from the stories I have been told and her portrait, she was a lady of beauty and, I am certain, a lady of sense. Your father's wife possesses naught to recommend her but her physical beauty and, if you ask me, her demeanour renders her most unappealing."

She sighed and squeezed Amelia's hands. "I cannot disagree with you, Cousin, but she has been married to Papa since I was five—"

"And you do not remember your mother." Amelia huffed, and her tiny figure sagged a little. "Forgive me. We have spoken of this often enough, but I cannot accept that you have not one memory of my aunt."

"I do have the stories my grandparents have shared as well as an image and feeling I cannot quite remember with perfect clarity." She opened her reticule and withdrew the piece she never allowed parted from her. "And Papa gave me a miniature he had painted of my mother. He had copies made for Jane and me that he gave us on our birthdays."

"Mrs. Bennet allowed that?" Amelia's eyebrows were raised and her eyes wide. She was well aware through their letters how rarely Papa spoke of her mother, not to mention defying Mama's wish that his late wife never be spoken of at Longbourn.

"Mama was not told. Papa brought us into the library to give us our gift. Did you know he keeps his miniature in his desk drawer? I have caught him staring at it more than once since I found it." She had been searching for a piece of paper when she happened upon the likeness of her mother, nestled in a soft piece of heavy velvet to protect it from damage.

"Lizzy!" Before she could react, strong arms wrapped around her and lifted her in the air. "Little Busy Lizzy. Grandmamma said you would come to stay, but I never thought your father would truly part with you for so long. Where is Janey? I thought she was to arrive with you." Why could Nicholas never greet her without startling her and calling her that ridiculous name?

"Mrs. Bennet is forcing her to pursue some young man," said Amelia with a hand to her hip. "So, she has forsaken us to stay with the Gardiners."

A bark of laughter escaped before Lizzy could stop it. "Forsaken? Really, Amelia? Is that not an exaggeration?" Her cousin had always allowed her emotions to rule her sensibilities. Though a petite young lady, Amelia's fiery temperament could overwhelm even the tallest of gentlemen.

"I think not," said Amelia. "Over the past few years, your father has so seldom allowed you to visit us. We should like to see both you and Jane. We have missed you. Grandmamma and Grandpapa have missed you too." Amelia glanced at her brother then lifted an eyebrow. "Anyhow, you wrote of two gentlemen who resided at Netherfield, yet you never mentioned their names."

Nicholas chuckled and crossed his arms over his chest. "Can you not imagine why? If we are not acquainted, we would ask all our friends of their characters—do all in our power to determine if they are worthy of our beloved cousins. Would we not?"

"I would be mortified," said Elizabeth while shaking her head. "'Tis bad enough Mama proclaims her plans for Jane to marry one of the gentlemen with no regard for who hears. I do not even wish to discuss Lydia and Kitty's behaviour when they came to call. I am certain this gentleman's sisters and friend persuaded him to depart Netherfield for London, and while those ladies are affected and condescending, I cannot blame them after the spectacle put on by Mama at the ball. When she learnt of his departure, Mama rushed to send Jane to the Gardiners in the hopes Jane will call on the sisters and be thrown into the gentleman's company again by happenstance."

Nicholas rolled his eyes. "Ah, the most common scheme of the matchmaking mamas: the hopeful call. Well, never fear. We shall entertain you and make Janey green with envy that she missed out on passing Christmas with us. Come, I was sent to the hall with explicit instructions to bring Lizzy to the drawing room." Her cousin held out his arm for her to take.

Before Lizzy set her hand upon her elder cousin's forearm, she pinched the back of his shoulder. "I thought we agreed you would cease calling me Busy Lizzy."

He laughed, his green eyes twinkling, as he brushed a shock of his sandy brown hair from his face. "Why would I ever do such a thing?"

"Oh, I cannot imagine. Maybe because it is embarrassing. You do remember when you addressed me as such before Lady Jersey?"

"You departed that morning for Longbourn," said Amelia from just behind them. "You missed Grandmamma haranguing Nicholas for doing so after you left."

"Amelia would come to the stables to giggle at my expense while I cleaned stalls." Nicholas's tone was far from amused.

"Grandpapa made you clean stalls? How did I never hear of this?" It was just the news Amelia would have included in one of her letters. They were as close as a brother and sister could be, but the two took great pleasure in teasing one another and regaling Lizzy of their successes. Amelia had said naught of him receiving such punishment.

"Did I not? I am not sure how I forgot to make mention of it."

Nicholas brought her to the green drawing room and ushered her inside. "Look who has joined us."

"Oh, Lizzybeth!" Her grandmother stood and clasped her hands. "I am so thrilled you could come."

Without hesitation, Lizzy rushed forward and let her grandmother wrap her in a warm embrace. She had missed this—she had missed them. Why had she let an entire year pass without visiting them? London was not a long journey, and Grandpapa would not have hesitated to send his carriage for her. He always had in the past. "I am happy to be here, Gran. Forgive me for not coming sooner." She turned and fell into her grandfather's waiting arms.

"Do not worry. We know your father well. I am certain he was quite insistent to keep you with him, and who could blame him?" Her grandfather drew back with a loving expression. "You resemble your mother, and you have her wit. Surely, he appreciates your good sense and humour. After all, he wed a lady with little sense and her daughters have little to recommend them in intelligence."

"Hugh," said her grandmother, swatting his arm. "You should not speak so of her sisters."

As he stepped back, he shrugged. "Have I told a falsehood?"

Elizabeth sighed and took his hand, patting the top. "Unfortunately, you have not." She could lie, but what purpose would it serve?

"Now, what is this nonsense of Janey staying with the Gardiners," said Grandmamma, gesturing to the sofa. After taking the place next to her grandfather, Elizabeth allowed him to take her hand and hold it securely in his. He had always enjoyed holding her hand and would hold Amelia's or Jane's hand if they were beside him. He was a staid, albeit affectionate man. Her grandparents never withheld their small displays of their affection—no one could doubt they wed for love and loved their family fiercely.

"Mrs. Bennet is pushing Jane towards the latest gentleman leasing Netherfield," said Amelia.

"Is she now." Grandpapa's bushy eyebrows drew together. "What has your father to say on the matter?"

"He laughs and ridicules her antics, but he has not indicated an unwillingness to approve of the gentleman." Papa never took his wife seriously. He would also benefit if Jane wed Mr. Bingley. As much as he cared for them, she would be one less daughter in need of gowns, ribbons, and other such frivolities.

"Hmm," said her grandfather. "Does this young man show an interest in our Janey?"

Nicholas scoffed and crossed his ankle over his knee. "What gentleman has not shown an interest? If we were to take her to a ball or introduce her to London society, she would be surrounded by her choice of suitors in a trice...as would Lizzy."

"Yes, but Henry would never wish to take part in those circles. A suitor with a nearby estate would suit him well. He would not need to be bothered with the events of London nor would he need to deal with the calls Janey would receive as a member of our family. Janey would also remain nearby after she was wed."

"Which would suit Mama."

Her grandmother narrowed her eyes. "Mrs. Bennet never seems to have a suitor for you. Why does she take such an interest in Janey?"

"She has always boasted of Jane being the most beautiful of her daughters. This gentleman has five thousand a year and is considered amiable by all our acquaintance. If Lydia had expressed her admiration for him, perhaps Mama would have pushed Lydia in his direction, despite her being too young to be out." Maybe Grandmamma would not notice that she skipped over the suitor query.

"Lydia is not quite thirteen. Besides, you said Lydia would never accept a husband unless he wore a red coat," said Amelia.

"That is true, and even at her tender age, she has been insufferable since the militia quartered themselves in Meryton. She has begged to be allowed to walk into town on her own."

Grandmamma pressed a hand to her chest. "Mrs. Bennet allowed that child to seek out officers?"

"Papa sent Lydia to her bedchamber, but Mama was put out. She saw no harm in letting Lydia see the officers. She believes Lydia wants to admire them from afar and does not understand that Lydia would flirt with them if afforded the opportunity."

Her grandmother shifted closer to the edge of her chair. "Lizzy, you have mentioned in the past of Mrs. Bennet pushing Janey towards this gentleman or that. Nothing has ever come of them, so we never worried, but what of you? Why does she not do the same for you?" She could have groaned aloud. Her grandmother was supposed to forget.

"Come, come. What warty, foul-smelling creature has Mrs. Bennet deemed appropriate for you?" asked Nicholas with a wide grin. He was insufferable.

Elizabeth bit her lower cheek and looked through the window to Hyde Park across the street. What she would not give to take a ramble after being locked away in the carriage for the journey here!

"Lizzy?"

Her shoulders slumped. Grandmamma's tone brooked no opposition. "Mama pressed me to accept the proposal of the heir of Longbourn."

"She what?" cried Grandpapa. "Why, he is no more than a parson with no connexions and no fortune until he inherits Longbourn. Moreover, I had the father investigated when I learnt of the entailment, and when he died, I have followed the son. You, the wife of Lady Catherine de Bourgh's parson. It is not to be borne. I would never approve of such an unequal union—and your father should know better than to allow so much as a hint of an engagement without my approval?"

"When I refused the proposal, Papa informed Mama he would not give his consent." She frowned and gave her grandfather's hand a wiggle. "Why do we require your consent to wed? I thought Papa's would be sufficient."

"We shall speak of it after supper. I wish to know of this gentleman Mrs. Bennet has set her cap at for our Janey."

"So, Lizzy, warty and foul-smelling?"

She let out a long exhale. "Mr. Collins was not warty."

Nicholas chuckled and rubbed his hands together. "So, he *was* foul-smelling. Excellent."

"No, you do not," said Grandmamma. "I am certain Lizzy does not wish to be teased over a proposal she neither sought nor desired. You will leave her be. Do you hear me?"

Nicholas flinched at their grandmother's stern tone. "Yes, Grandmamma."

At a tiny giggle, Grandmamma turned her pointed finger on Amelia. "And, I want to hear naught of you teasing either of them."

Amelia rolled her eyes. "Nicholas, I would most definitely tease, but not Lizzy. Mrs. Bennet prefers Jane over Lizzy and her own daughter Lydia to them both. I am not surprised she chose Lizzy to guarantee her a home after Mr. Bennet's death. Why are you?"

Her grandmother drew herself up in her seat, her spine stiff while Grandpapa lowered his chin and looked at her over his spectacles.

"She says I am headstrong and foolish. Jane could not be so beautiful for nothing, and Lydia is so agreeable—"

"You are beautiful as well, Lizzy," said Amelia. "If she knows you resemble your mother, could she not be taking her jealousy of your mother out on you?"

With a start, Lizzy drew her eyebrows down a little. "She has never mentioned my mother to me." Though Amelia could be right. Her mother was never mentioned at Longbourn except within her father's library.

"Amelia, that is enough." Grandfather squeezed her hand.

"But Mrs. Bennet is awful to Lizzy, yet she still calls her 'Mama.' She begged me not to mention what she has told me in her letters, but Mrs. Bennet oft times will purchase a new gown for Jane or her own daughters while not doing so for Lizzy."

"I have no need for new gowns when Grandmamma spoils me so."

Amelia stood and marched right up to Lizzy, who clenched her skirt in her free hand. Her cousin had never betrayed her trust. Why was she doing so now? "What of the gown Grandmamma gave you for your birthday?"

"Amelia," she said, tears making her vision cloudy. "Pray, stop."

"What happened to the gown?" Her grandmother stood and sat on her opposite side, turning her chin so she could not escape her grandmother's insistent gaze. "What happened to the gown, Lizzy?"

"I hoped to wear it to the assembly, but when Mrs. Bennet saw it, she made me wear a different gown, then gave it to Lydia."

"Who was not even out and tore it before the night ended, did she not?"

She could not look at Amelia while she nodded. "It was too tight in the chest, and the seam gave under her arm while she danced. I tried to repair it, but..."

"Oh, dearest," said her grandmother. "I planned to take you to Madame Morisot for gowns on the morrow, so do not worry about that one. The pattern was more appropriate for the country than London anyhow."

"Grandmamma, I do not require new gowns." She scrunched her nose. "You know how I detest fittings."

"Well, that is too bad since I have already scheduled the appointment. Amelia helped me select fabric for you, and we delivered it to Madame Morisot, who has your measurements that Jane sent me for your birthday present."

"You will love the patterns I selected. Grandmamma did."

"See, all you need do is let Madame ensure the fit is precise, and you will be ready to attend the events and concerts we have planned as well as the Twelfth Night ball."

"You need not go to such trouble. I am simply pleased to be with you again." Her grandparents usually spent Christmas in Yorkshire at Richmond Castle. Had they changed their plans to accommodate her visit?

"We would have attended balls and parties in Yorkshire had we remained, but we have a number of friends in town. We shall simply be in London instead of Yorkshire for Christmastide then remain for the Season. Perhaps we shall find a wife for Nicholas this year."

Nicholas groaned and slouched in his chair. "I shall do so when I am ready."

"I am certain some young lady is in search of a young viscount for a husband," said Elizabeth. Thank goodness the attention of the room had turned to someone else!

Her grandmother nudged Elizabeth's shoulder with her own. "Particularly, such a handsome young viscount."

He wagged a finger in her direction. "Careful, Cousin. You may come to regret your teasing ways."

"I have it on good authority that I am merely tolerable, despite what my adoring relations may claim." She glanced at Amelia. "I am certain to remain a spinster, embroidering cushions and teaching Jane's ten children to play the pianoforte very ill indeed."

Grandpapa smiled and patted her hand. "I must say, Lizzybeth, if a young man said you are merely tolerable, he must be a simpleton indeed."

Mr. Darcy was no simpleton, but his insult at the assembly stung more than it should from such a trifling acquaintance. His constant staring caused an odd sort of tremble in her belly. Why had she reacted so whenever she was in his presence? "He is prideful and the most disagreeable gentleman I have had the misfortune of meeting."

"More disagreeable than this heir Mrs. Bennet was adamant you wed?" asked Nicholas.

"Mr. Collins is a simpleton, cloying, and trying to bear in company. I suppose one could say he has a certain amount of improper pride. He insisted I would accept him upon his second application since the established custom of my sex is to reject a man on the first application."

Nicholas let out a great guffaw. "An imbecile indeed."

"You should have heard his reason for marrying, not to mention, the qualities he felt recommended him because my portion is so small. After all, it is by no means certain that another offer of marriage may ever be made to me." She said the last in the oily tone Collins had employed while restraining a shudder.

Her grandfather rose from the sofa and started across the room.

"Grandpapa, where are you going?"

"After all you have told me, I require a brandy. I believe you could use one as well."

"Hugh, young ladies do not drink brandy."

Elizabeth bit her cheek as she exchanged a look with Nicholas. She, Nicholas, and her grandfather had a tradition of sitting in his study and drinking a glass of brandy after supper. Her grandmother knew of her joining them in the study, but little of their conversations or that Grandpapa gave her brandy while they spoke.

"Come, Lizzybeth," said her grandmother. "I am certain you wish to refresh yourself before dinner. By now, Tate has your trunk unpacked and a bath prepared. She does know your preferences so well."

She kissed her grandmother on the cheek. "I can see myself to my chambers, Grandmamma."

"I shall walk with her," said Amelia, linking her arm with Elizabeth's. Before she could utter another word, her cousin dragged her up the stairs while she spoke of her excitement to spend the next six weeks with her.

It was good to be back at Richmond House. While Longbourn had always been home, her father's house had ceased to be that for several years. Richmond Castle and Richmond House were for all intents and purposes, home. This house, and moreover, her family here brought a peace to her heart that had been missing for some time. It was indeed good to be back.

Chapter 2

"Nicholas, Lizzybeth, should you like to join me in my study?"

"Really, Hugh, this is hardly appropriate," said Grandmamma in the same tone and fashion she used every evening when her grandfather invited her to his study.

Her grandfather was undeterred. "If Amelia enjoyed chess, I would request her presence, but neither of you take pleasure in the game, so I leave you to your pursuits. Do not forget that Lizzybeth has joined you some evenings." He neglected to mention that those occasions were rare, but he was good about not raising her grandmother's hackles.

Grandmamma gave a low growl while she stood. "Very well. I suppose we shall be spending the day together tomorrow shopping so I can have no reason to object to an hour or so with you tonight."

He only nodded in her grandmother's direction with a small slip of a smile, barely discernible unless you knew him. "I am pleased you see the matter from my perspective, my dear."

Elizabeth took his arm while she bit her cheek to keep from laughing or grinning. Her grandmother and grandfather always bickered when it came to her joining the men for talk and brandy, not that her grandmother knew Grandpapa gave her brandy. He occasionally slipped as he had this afternoon, but he always followed with his claim to have misspoken. Her grandmother could not have fallen for his falsehood, could she? She was not usually so easily deceived.

Upon reaching his study, Elizabeth plunked down in her usual chair and tucked her feet under her while Nicholas sat on the small settee and spread his long arms across the back. He had been a thin but tall child and remained so until last year.

Now, he had shed the last of his boyish face and appeared much more a man of five and twenty years than the youthful boy she had once known.

"So, are you to search for a wife this season?"

He scrubbed his face with his hand. "Grandmamma is relentless. She started speaking of young ladies last season, and her insistence has only grown."

"You are the future of the Richmond earldom, Son. We want to ensure that future is secure." Grandpapa handed Nicholas a glass of brandy, then one to Elizabeth. "If you had a younger brother, we could delay matters to your schedule, but we have suffered too much loss amongst our own children. We fear—"

"I understand your position. I do, but I have yet to meet a lady who can hold an acceptable conversation without falling into a discussion of fashion or the state of the roads. Is it so terrible to want more than an acceptable match?"

"No. Of course it is not." Elizabeth leaned against the arm of her chair. She would hug Nicholas if she could, but he would never accept her coddling him. Not that she could. He was far too tall with his over six-foot height, and he was also a grown man. Besides being five years her senior, he had not shown an inkling of allowing such an embrace since his parents were killed in a carriage accident ten years ago. While as good natured as ever, Nicholas seemed to wall a part of himself off after his parents' deaths, which pained her to see. "Do anything rather than marry without affection."

Her grandfather set a hand on Nicholas's shoulder. "I agree with your cousin, but would you take a turn about the library so I can speak to Lizzybeth?"

"What? Why?" At a dip of Grandpapa's chin, Nicholas stood with a grumble. "I do not understand why I must leave for you to speak to Lizzy. Precious little happens in this household without my knowledge."

Her grandfather neglected to react to his grandson's protests. He simply patted his shoulder. "Never you mind. Just do as I ask."

Elizabeth grinned at Nicholas's sour expression and gave a small wave while he closed the door behind him. "What do you want to ask that you do not want Nicholas to know?"

"I desire the identity of Janey's suitor. If Nicholas is acquainted with the gentleman, he may conduct his own enquiries, which I would prefer not to happen."

She nodded and sighed. "I do not know if I would call Mr. Bingley a suitor—"

"Bingley you said?" Her grandfather blinked several times, and his forehead creased.

"Yes, Mr. Charles Bingley. Do you know him?"

"I am not personally acquainted with him, but I know of him. Your grandmother detests his sisters."

Elizabeth laughed and covered her mouth to keep from choking while she swallowed. "I cannot find fault with her feelings for those ladies, but Grandmamma and I often share similarities of opinion on most matters."

"Except for the idea of ladies drinking brandy." One corner of his lips curved upward.

"And who is to blame for that? Besides, she surely knows I drink with you and Nicholas in the evenings."

"Hush, child. Your grandmother would have my guts for garters if she ever had proof. You notice I never offer you more than wine or sherry when Amelia is with us, do you not?"

That had not escaped her attention. "Amelia would not tell our secret."

"No, but with how close she is to your grandmother, I feel it unfair to expect her to keep the confidence."

She pursed her lips. "But you feel no such qualms of Nicholas?"

"If I did not offer you brandy, Nicholas would. I consider him as much a conspirator as I do you." With a smile, she took another sip of her drink while Grandpapa peeked through the door to summon Nicholas.

"Well? Has all been settled to your satisfaction, Grandpapa? I enjoy the library, but I am able to spend all day every day in its confines should I wish."

"We have finished our conversation."

Nicholas looked back and forth between them. "Did you discover the name of this mysterious suitor?"

She sighed and relaxed into her chair. "I would not call him a suitor. He has shown Jane a prodigious amount of attention, but he took possession of Netherfield at Michaelmas. While Jane likes him a great deal, I cannot be certain of his intentions. His sister mentioned the possibility of him being matched with a friend's younger sister. While I do not believe her claim, I cannot discount the possibility."

Her grandfather furrowed his brow. "Interesting, indeed. Do not fret. I shall know how to act."

"I am not reassured. Mama will never forgive me if I am responsible for ruining her hopes."

"If the gentleman is unworthy, then you should not face any wrath," said Nicholas.

"After the debacle with Mr. Collins, I am tempted to keep you with us." Her grandfather sat in his favourite chair while he groused.

"You know Papa would never allow—"

"Oh, he would. I would give him no choice in the matter." Before she could enquire further, he held up a hand. "Do not ask me for particulars. Just trust that I shall do what is best for your happiness."

"I knew I should not have told you." She set her glass on the side table and crossed her arms over her chest. Why were they so obstinate? She could manage Mama.

"Yes, you should have told us," said Nicholas. "He cannot simply marry you off to any gentleman, cleric, militiaman, or tradesman who believes you worthy. You deserve to find someone who loves you. I would not have you wed without affection either, Lils."

"You have not called me Lils in years." Surely, her mouth was agape.

"An oversight on my part, I am certain. I use the name often enough in my head, but I have supposed of late that you have far too many nicknames for one young lady. Perhaps I began addressing you as Amelia does to make things simpler." He cleared his throat. "Pardon me. I believe I require some air."

As soon as he departed the room, she turned to her grandfather. "What have I said?"

"I do not know, but you are right, he has not called you Lils in several years."

"When I visited that Easter, he had changed so. I hardly recognized him." He had seemed to grow up overnight. The transformation saddened her.

"He appeared much the same."

"But he was not as open as he was before."

"No," said Grandpapa with a sigh. "He has been the same in some ways but different in others. Despite his young age, he had responsibilities thrust upon him because of James's death when he was five. I had not intended to burden him, but I fear

I made a mistake in trusting what he could manage at his age and after such a tragedy. An error I shall not make again. My grandchildren will be protected."

"Grandpapa, we are well and loved. We could ask for little that you have not provided."

"Do not think I am unaware of what occurs at Longbourn. Your father locks himself away in his library and allows his wife to do as she pleases. Your mother, God rest her soul, would be heartbroken to know what he has become." Her grandfather had not stepped foot in Longbourn for years. How could he know so much of what occurs within its walls?

"Oft times I wonder if he married Mama for no other reason than to break the entail."

"Why else would he marry a lady he held no affection for? If the babe had survived, then I doubt he would have spared a second glance for Fanny Gardiner, but the poor boy was born too early. You were too young to remember, but when we received word of Sophie's early confinement, we travelled from Yorkshire without stopping other than to swap horses at the inns. When we arrived, your father had locked himself in his library, bereft, while Hill managed the household. She ensured you and Jane were fed and cared for and found a wet nurse for the babe. Sophie was laid out and prepared for burial. Your father, however, was inconsolable. He refused to emerge from that blasted library. He drank port and whiskey and mourned your mother the only way he understood. As soon as the babe died, we put him in your mother's arms and had the bodies taken to Richmond where they are interred in the chapel. You would not remember much, but you and Janey spent almost two years with us after their death.

"Hill, meanwhile, refused to buy your father more liquor unless he ate and managed to keep him from drinking himself into an early grave. According to her, about a year after Sophie died, he requested a bath and a shave and gradually began to pull himself together. No one is sure why he proposed to Fanny Gardiner, but your grandmother and I believe he wished to have you and Janey with him, so he wed Fanny to care for you. Foolishly, we allowed your return."

"You knew how Mama behaves towards me before you asked, did you not?"

He sat with his elbows upon his knees, turning his glass in his hands, while he nodded. "Your grandmother corresponds frequently with Mrs. Hill. We have debated over the years whether it was prudent to bring you and Janey to live with us, yet we considered how Sophie would feel. Would she wish us to raise you ourselves? She loved your father with her whole heart, and we thought she would want you to remain with him."

"You let her love for Papa guide you." It was the only explanation that made sense.

"Yes, but your mother would want you to marry for love—as she did. I shall not allow that woman he has wed to foist some unworthy gentleman upon you. At least your father kept his word and never mentioned yours and Janey's fortunes. His wife's avarice would know no bounds if she knew."

"My fortune?" No one had mentioned a word of a fortune. Why had she never been told? All these years, it was assumed the five Bennet ladies had no more than Mrs. Bennet's five thousand pounds to sustain them after her father's death.

At her question, her grandfather's eyes flared. "He never told you?" He ran his fingers through his greying hair. "I suppose that was a wise decision. Janey is too soft-hearted and would have mentioned it in front of Mrs. Bennet at some point."

"And after Mama insisted her daughters receive their share, she would not stop until she told the entire neighbourhood." Her grandfather was correct. As much as she loved Jane, she thought too well of everyone. She would never believe Mama unworthy of complete trust. "Mama would consider me undeserving of such a sum." Her grandparents knew what happened at Longbourn without her, so what point was there in hiding it?

"Lizzybeth, pray, remember. That woman is not your mother. Allow us to now act as we should have so long ago. Your mother's fortune of thirty thousand pounds was split between the two of you, and I have added to that sum over the years. You each have the same fortune as your mother, and I control the funds. Regardless of what your father or Mrs. Bennet claim, you cannot wed without my approval—neither can Janey for that matter."

"Would you withhold consent from Mr. Bingley?"

He shook his head with a grim countenance. "I am unsure. I should like to see him court her before I decide. Nicholas and I shall pay a call to the Gardiner's home on the morrow. She should spend Christmastide with us. If Mr. Bingley is a worthy young man, he will call upon her here."

"Miss Bingley does not know of our connexion to you. She would have pushed her brother in Jane's direction if she had heard word of it." That lady would surely consider the granddaughter of an earl appropriate for her brother, would she not?

Grandpapa's shoulders jerked with a silent chuckle. "If she has her sights on who I believe, the young lady is the granddaughter of an earl as well and boasts a fortune to match yours. Not only that, but Miss Bingley also has her sights on the young lady's brother.

"I do know that when your father brought Sophie to Longbourn as a new bride, they enjoyed keeping her connexions a secret. They found the assumptions of the neighbourhood amusing. To this day, I do not believe anyone has heard word of us. Your father drank too heavily to receive condolences, so when people came to the door, Hill told them a relative paid for the funeral in their home county."

"Well, I have never heard mention of the Earl of Richmond or your surname in Meryton, and Papa told us to never tell anyone of you or Grandmamma." She could only imagine how entertained her father would be by hiding his late wife's heritage. He truly found humour in the oddest of things.

He exhaled heavily and shook his head. "I have to believe that after your mother died, it was his way of protecting you and your future. He is unwilling to control his wife so he controls the information she can use to make his life miserable. The amusement he derives would be an added inducement."

Elizabeth downed the last sip of her brandy. "I beg you. No more." Fanny Bennet was the only mother she had ever known—that she could remember, anyway. Her father was not perfect, and neither was Mama, but they were all she knew. More than ever, her heart yearned for some remembrance of her mother, but she had been three when her mother died giving birth to her brother. No matter how hard she tried, naught of her mother remained in her memory. All of this was too much. She wanted nothing more than to bury her head in her pillow and not awaken until morning.

"If you would like more brandy, I can make your excuses to your grandmother."

"You would give me a second glass?" He never offered her more than the small serving he doled out when they first sat down. At his lift of the decanter, she held up a hand. "I should spend some time with Amelia and Grandmamma first. Perhaps when I retire."

"I shall have Nicholas bring you a glass."

With a nod, she stood. "Thank you."

"Lizzybeth?"

She turned back to him just before opening the door. "Yes?"

"Forgive me for speaking so freely. Your grandmother and I have considered bringing you and Janey to live with us many times over the years, but I never felt the urgency to do so then as I do now. We shall never prevent you from writing your father or your younger sisters, and your father will have the ability to visit you at Richmond House or Castle—"

"Papa will not stand for it. He will demand our return."

"After your mother's death, he signed documents making me guardian of you and Janey. I allowed him to take you when he married Fanny Gardiner, but according to the law, you both are still my wards."

"How is that possible? Papa is not dead."

"We thought, at the time, he would drink himself to death. With the right documents and the aid of a solicitor, the Court of Chancery made me your guardians. Janey will do as she is told, but you are more forthright, just like your mother. I want you to understand I am doing what I believe to be best."

Elizabeth walked forward, kissed her grandfather's cheek, and lifted on her toes so she could hug him. "I have always trusted you, Grandpapa."

"I love you, my sweet girl."

"I love you, too." Her eyes burned, and she buried her face into his shoulder, inhaling the sweet peppermint scent that she associated with him. How could such a simple odour provide such comfort? After one last kiss to his cheek, she dabbed her eyes with the back of her hand.

"You are tired. Retire. I shall make your excuses to your grandmother."

"I do not want to disappoint her."

"Do not worry. I shall speak with her after Amelia retires. She will understand."

She slipped from the study and made her way to her chambers. When she entered, Tate curtseyed and began unfastening the back of her gown. "How was your evening, miss?"

"Lovely. It is good to be with my grandparents again."

"I can imagine. It has been a long time—over a year now by my recollection."

"Too long." Elizabeth glanced over her shoulder. "You are here early. I do not usually retire until later."

"If you will forgive me for saying it, I noticed the dark circles under your eyes when I dressed you for dinner. I thought you might retire earlier than is your wont."

Tate made quick work of readying her for the night, then curtseyed and departed through the servants' door a moment before a light knock came from her sitting room. Elizabeth hurried through and opened the door just enough for Nicholas to squeeze through.

"Grandpapa asked me to bring you this," he said, handing her the promised glass of brandy.

"Thank you." She glanced to the glass he held in his other hand. "Are you joining me?"

"I thought you may wish for company. I should also like to hear more about this proposal of marriage." He sat on the sofa and crossed his ankle over his knee. "Was Mr. Collins on one knee?"

"Good Lord, Nicholas. I told Mama he had nothing to tell me which I needed to hear, but she insisted. Even after I refused, she demanded I accept him. If Papa had not told me I would be a stranger to Mama if I refused and a stranger to him if I accepted, I would have cried. The man is every bit ridiculous." She sat beside him and pulled her legs under her. "His first night at Longbourn, he read Fordyce's sermons to the family and spoke of his patroness, Lady Catherine, and the cost of the windows and the chimneys and the chamber pots at Rosings Park...Oh! At the ball two nights ago, he approached Mr. Darcy and introduced himself—"

Her cousin jumped a little. "Did you say Darcy?" Ugh! She had not meant to mention him by name—ever.

"Yes, he was a guest of the neighbour letting Netherfield."

Nicholas's eyes went wide, and he straightened. "Tell me this gentleman Janey is so enamoured of is not Charles Bingley."

"What—?" She had been afraid he would deduce who the gentlemen was if he knew enough, and she was right.

"Good Lord. I wondered when you mentioned the sisters, but the income you stated, a newly leased estate, Darcy being a guest, all of it makes sense." He took a sip of his drink, baring his teeth when he swallowed. "Lizzy, we cannot allow Janey to marry him."

"Why on earth not?" Her grandfather's grim visage upon learning Mr. Bingley's identity was not reassuring, but now Nicholas? What could he possibly know?

"Bingley is a friendly and cheerful man, but he is also spineless. I cannot imagine him changing his small clothes without his sisters' permission. Miss Bingley likely tells his valet what he is to wear each day, how to cut his hair, how snug to fit his breeches. No, Janey would be marrying a child in the guise of an adult. She deserves better."

Elizabeth watched the fire for a moment, the flames winding up to points and disappearing into the smoke. "Mama will be quite put out." Mama would be livid and blame her, yet she did no more than tell her family Mr. Bingley's name. She was not preventing him from proposing.

"You told Grandpapa of this, did you not?"

"Yes, he asked you to leave us for that purpose." She should not have mentioned Mr. Darcy's name! She could slap herself for letting the name slip, not that it would be of any aid now.

Nicholas downed the last of his brandy and rose. "Forgive me. I should speak to my grandfather." With his glass in hand, he peeked out the door before disappearing through.

She sagged into the corner of the settee and sipped her brandy. Mayhap remaining with her grandparents, Amelia, and Nicholas would be best. Obviously, Mama was too fearful of what would happen to her should Papa die, making her far too eager to marry her daughters to men of questionable worth—if Nicholas and her grandfather were to be believed. She sighed, set her glass on the table, and rose to go to bed. Enough for tonight. She would worry about it on the morrow.

Chapter 3

"'This perfect, Madame," said Grandmamma as she took a turn around Elizabeth. "The pleating on the back is exquisite. What do you think, dearest?"

"The colour is lovely, but is it not rather extravagant? Few of my morning gowns will match a ruby redingote." The coat was stunning, though she was accustomed to a practical amber or silver that would match most of her clothes.

Amelia clasped her hands with a dreamy expression. "But it will be perfect for Christmas. The colour almost perfectly resembles that of a holly berry." Unlike Elizabeth, Amelia adored shopping and fittings. By her excitement, she seemed closer to Lydia's age, despite being the same age as Jane.

"The measurements you provided were impeccable, Lady Richmond," said Madame Morisot in a heavy French accent. "Your purchases will be sent to Richmond House this afternoon, and the redingote and the sprigged muslin can be worn home as you requested. The gown she wore upon arrival will be sent with your delivery."

"Merci, Madame. I also require more appointments. We shall have three granddaughters partaking of the Season this year, and they will all need gowns—many more gowns."

A pang tore through Elizabeth's chest. After the conversation with her grandfather last night, she should not be surprised her grandparents would send for Jane today, but the confirmation was still a shock. How would Jane's tender sensibilities handle the removal from her uncle's home?

"Bien sûr, Madame. How lovely for you." Madame Morisot waved her grandmother over to a large book on the counter. When Gran returned, she was tucking a card into her reticule. "Thankfully, we ordered your new slippers and boots this morning, Tate will purchase your stockings and ribbons today—I would take you, but Grafton House is always a crush—Amelia and I selected some new gloves for you last week, so I suppose our last stop is the milliner's."

"If you have not looked, Madame Giry across the street has a wonderful selection," said Madame Morisot. "She also received some beautiful scarves and shawls a few days ago."

After another dizzying number of purchases, they loaded into the carriage, and Elizabeth sank into the squabs, dropping her head back against the rich, cushioned interior. "Gran, I truly do not need so much. The gowns alone were more than I tend to have for a year."

Her grandmother folded her hands in her lap and sat tall. "This is London, not Hertfordshire. You will require every gown we purchased and more for the Season. Besides, how can I not enjoy spoiling you? That sprigged muslin you are wearing with the tiny holly leaves and berries precisely matches the ruby redingote, which is lovely with your complexion and dark hair. I always envied your mother her ebony curls, and yours are the same shade and texture. Selecting the best fabrics for her was more pleasurable than selecting them for myself. I do not bemoan your dislike of shopping since I enjoy the diversion immensely. You and Janey both will be well appointed for the Season. It will be important for you to look the part of an earl's granddaughter. You will see."

"I do not object to you selecting my fabrics or patterns. You have excellent taste, Grandmamma, but white?" She laughed and held up her new gloves. "I would never purchase white kid gloves. Mark my words, I shall ruin them. Not intentionally, mind you. At some moment, I shall not consider my actions when I pet a dog on the street, or who knows what else, and they will be ruined."

"Then I shall buy you a new pair." Her grandmother clasped her hands, clearly pleased with herself.

Amelia took Elizabeth's hand. "Grandmamma has never been able to shop so freely for you before. Allow her to do as she sees fit."

She exhaled. "Forgive me. I am simply unaccustomed to the extravagance. I feel wasteful." She had never been allowed to be wasteful.

"Dearest," said her grandmother. "This is not Longbourn or a small market town in Hertfordshire. Now, shall we go to the drapers and purchase fabric for Janey after luncheon, or would Janey prefer to select her own? Madame had an appointment available for tomorrow, and we shall require her gowns to be completed as soon as possible."

"Janey can borrow some of my gowns. I believe our complexions are similar enough that mine should suit." Amelia and Jane were of similar height and figure as well. Their hair colour was their most striking difference: Amelia's was a dark auburn while Jane's was chestnut.

Her grandmother opened her reticule and began digging within its confines. "Very kind of you. I am certain that will be of help to us. My good friend Lady Vranes is having an exhibition of contemporary art at her home in Mayfair on Thursday evening. I thought we would attend. It would be a small gathering, yet enough for you to be introduced to a number of people. You enjoy art, Lizzybeth. Lady Vranes takes a prodigious interest in young artists and their work. You may enjoy her company greatly." She withdrew a card, read it for a moment, then placed it back in her bag.

"I look forward to making her acquaintance then," she said as the carriage pulled to the kerb at Richmond House. When the servant placed the step, Elizabeth alighted and entered the house, nodding to Mr. Gideon, the butler, as she entered.

"How was your shopping, miss?"

"My grandmother selected fine fabrics and fashionable patterns, but I am thrilled to be home. If I had to put on another gown, I might have been devilishly unladylike and screamed my displeasure."

Mr. Gideon, who was about her height and had the darkest skin she had ever seen, smiled and nodded as she handed him her bonnet. "You have been sorely missed at Richmond House this past year, Miss Elizabeth, sorely missed."

"Thank you, Mr. Gideon. I am happy to be with my family here once again. Have you read any interesting books of late?" Her grandfather allowed Mr. Gideon free rein of the library, and the two had discussed their opinions of everything from poetry to histories over the years.

"I just finished *Les Liaisons Dangereuses*."

French was Mr. Gideon's first language, and when at Richmond House, her grandparents often had her practice her French lessons by conversing with him, often speaking of Africa and his life before journeying to England. He once explained why he had chosen to be called Mr. Gideon. His name was in actuality Jabari, which meant brave and fearless. The missionaries he met in Africa had told him Gideon meant brave and strong. "*Les Liaisons Dangereuses?* How scandalous of you. What did you think of it?"

"I thought it a great deal of scheming, and some of the characters who were good met a sad end."

"Those who were evil paid for their manipulations, do you not think?"

"They did, though I would have enjoyed the Marquise de Merteuil receiving more of a reckoning for her duplicity." While they chatted, her grandmother and Amelia handed off their coats and hats to a couple of maids.

The drawing rooms appeared empty and quiet from where she stood. Had her grandfather and Nicholas returned with Jane yet or had they waited until the afternoon? "Where are my grandfather and Viscount Hatton?"

"They arrived a half hour before you," said Mr. Gideon. "They took your sister into your grandfather's study."

"Thank you."

"Lizzybeth, they may require time to speak with Janey alone." Her grandmother called after her as she hurried down the passage. The murmur of voices carried through the door as she rapped lightly.

"Come," called Grandpapa.

When she entered, Jane sat in a chair with Nicholas on the sofa. "Lizzy!" Her sister rushed forward to embrace her. "Did you know Grandpapa and Nicholas would remove me from Gracechurch Street this morning?" Upon further study, Jane's eyes were red rimmed. She had been crying.

"I suspected after speaking to them last night. How are Aunt and Uncle?"

"They are well. The children missed you, little Emily in particular. She cried when you were not with me."

"She is a dear, sweet child." She squeezed Jane's hands. "Forgive me for not joining them, but Gran had made an appointment for me with the modiste and insisted I accompany her."

"I understand. I am certain Grandmamma will have an appointment for me before long."

"Yours is tomorrow," said Elizabeth with a smile.

"Are we truly not returning to Longbourn?" The weakness of her voice tore at Elizabeth's heart.

When she glanced at her grandfather, he shook his head in a slight motion. "No, I believe we are to remain here for the foreseeable future. Will it not be nice to spend so much time with Gran and Amelia? We have not spent time with them in more than a year."

"I *have* missed our grandparents, Nicholas, and Amelia. This is just so sudden. Aunt Gardiner and I were to call on Miss Bingley and Mrs. Hurst this morning."

"I understand you believe them to be amiable, Janey, but they are not well regarded amongst our friends," said Nicholas as he shifted beside her and took one of her hands in his. "They are spiteful gossips, who surely would have nothing good to say of you and Lizzy. When they realise you are a Montford, they will behave with false sincerity for the connexion to an earldom and no more. I have witnessed them curry favour with the daughter of a peer, then insult her when her back is turned. You should not trust them."

Grandpapa sat behind his desk and leaned upon his forearms. "Those two would also attempt to gain favour with Nicholas in the hopes of forwarding a match between him and Miss Bingley. I have yet to meet this Bingley fellow, but your grandmother has made the acquaintance of his sisters. She abhors their behaviour to such an extent that she would never invite either of them to an event we hosted. This young Mr. Bingley is the head of his household, yet he needs to exert his authority over his sister lest she bring him to ruin—and I promise you she will insult a person of rank one day and pay the price. She is too full of herself to take heed of her surroundings."

Jane's eyes were wide, and her jaw was slack. "They seemed so kind. I am certain they are simply misunderstood."

"I wish I could say they are," said Nicholas. "You must trust that if we thought Mr. Bingley the best match you could make, we would have let matters be. Perhaps during the Season, you will make the acquaintance of a gentleman who will appreciate you more than Mr. Bingley."

"He did depart Hertfordshire without taking his leave of the neighbourhood." She remained silent for a moment and waited for Jane to react. When her sister did no more than frown, Elizabeth cradled her sister's cheeks in her palms. "Janey, do you love him?"

Jane's eyebrows drew together ever so slightly, and a line appeared between them. "I do not know. He is agreeable and handsome. I enjoy his society and would anticipate his company."

"Do you miss him?" She pressed a bit when she repeated the question, but Jane needed to know what was in her heart.

"No, not as I would you or Mama." Nicholas winced behind her. At times, she wished they would better conceal their dislike of Mama.

"Since they have returned, why do you not greet your grandmother and Amelia?" suggested Grandpapa. "I know they are eager to see you."

"Yes," said Jane smoothing her gown. "Lizzy is right. We have been away for too long. I should appreciate the time I am afforded with them before we return to Longbourn." After another quick hug, Jane departed, closing the door behind her.

"She has been crying."

"We surprised her," said Grandpapa. "Mr. and Mrs. Gardiner were gracious and understanding. They are not ignorant of the character of Mrs. Bennet. They send their love and best wishes to you and hope you can call upon them while we are in London."

"I would enjoy that. They are people of sense and education."

"I agree." Her grandfather gave a crooked smile. "I am concerned that Janey mentioned a return to Longbourn. Nicholas and I made clear the two of you were to remain with us indefinitely."

"Do not push her to accept that just yet," said Elizabeth. "I fear pressing may do more harm than good."

Her grandfather nodded while he sat back into his chair. "I agree. Is this one of the gowns your grandmother selected for you?" He pointed his finger, moving it up and down her clothing.

"Yes, she chose well. I cannot think of one I dislike."

"I do like the pale green and the pattern." He pointed to her throat. "Your mother's cross does not match so well as it should." He opened a cupboard to his left and a safe hidden within, then withdrew a small box. "Your grandmother has more of your mother's jewels in her possession, but this was tucked away in here. I gave it to Sophie for her seventeenth birthday." Carefully, he lifted a necklace of jade-coloured beads. "They are nothing extravagant, but I think they will complement your gown."

"What of Jane?"

Grandpapa smiled and stepped around his desk. "Your grandmother and I separated your mother's jewellery a long time ago. Jane has pieces set aside for her as well. This was to be your gift for St. Nicholas Day, but I see no harm in giving it to you early."

He removed the cross, placed it in the box, and fastened the necklace while she touched the smooth beads at the base of her neck. When he finished, she stepped over and kissed his cheek. "Thank you."

He nodded. "Before you ask why we have your mother's jewellery, Hill packed your mother's belongings while your father was drinking so heavily and sent them to us. She feared of her ability to send them to us if your father died and the heir took possession of the estate."

Once again, she touched the beads. More than likely, Mama would have taken them for her own—not that Elizabeth would say as much out loud.

"I know you just returned from shopping," said Nicholas, "but Grandpapa and I thought to take a trip to Hatchard's. What do you say? Would you care to join us?"

"Yes, you need never ask. You know I cannot pass over a trip to the book shop."

"Wonderful. I shall have a carriage readied."

As soon as Nicholas departed, Elizabeth steeled herself. "Grandpapa, what did you and Nicholas mean when you said Jane is a Montford? Are we not Bennets?"

He sat on the edge of his desk with a great exhale. "I wondered why you had not asked me sooner. 'Tis unlike you to miss a detail such as that. To answer your question, when I became your guardian, you were made a Montford on the court documents. You are still Elizabeth Abigail Bennet, but your surname has been Montford since you were almost four years of age. When you returned to Longbourn, I saw no reason to change or mention such a trifling detail. The surname could only be of aid when the gentlemen came to call."

She turned and examined the portrait of her mother over the mantel. How she wished she could remember her! In the painting, she wore the same beads Elizabeth now wore around her neck as well as an arch smile with her eyebrow lifted just so.

"You are the same young lady you have always been, my dear, whether you are here or at Longbourn and your surname is Bennet or Montford. Your caring heart beats the same within your chest now as it did a week ago. Naught has changed but where you live. We will also never treat you with anything less than the respect you and Janey deserve—that you have always deserved."

"I know, Grandpapa. I never thought—"

"We have revealed a great deal since you arrived yesterday. I simply wanted to ensure you know you do have a voice. We can discuss what bothers you and solutions to those matters, but I am of the opinion that you are entitled to more than what you have received. While Hill told us of how you were treated by Mrs. Bennet, she also mentioned how close you were with your father. We never wished to come between you. That said, we have abhorred that he never did more to control his wife, and I cannot condone his being so lackadaisical with the gentlemen who call. Nicholas mentioned to me the ultimatum your father gave to Mr. Collins's proposal. The joke he made of the situation only reaffirms my belief that I am doing what is right for you and Janey. You *both* deserve more. You are worth every attention paid to your happiness."

"How can I fault you for doing what you feel is right? I am not upset or angry with you, if that is what you believe." She spoke the truth. He had her and Jane's best interests at heart. How could she find fault with motives that were born out of love?

He folded her in his embrace and kissed her hair. "Forgive me."

"I know of nothing for which you require forgiveness."

"I thought we were to Hatchards?" Nicholas leaned against the door frame when she drew back from her grandfather. "Unless you are to spend the day in maudlin pursuits, the carriage is in front of the house."

Grandpapa presented his elbow to her. "Then, let us be off."

Amelia laughed loudly and dropped back on the bed with a sigh, her dark auburn hair spreading across the rose coverlet. "If I could find a man who treats me as a rational lady, I shall be well pleased, but I have yet to meet one I can tolerate beyond a single call."

"Oh, you poor dear," said Jane before she took a sip of chocolate.

"The worst was Sir Percy. Such a fop! He was every bit ridiculous."

Jane elbowed Amelia's arm gently with a teasing grin. "But what of Sir Anthony? Did you not say he dances with you at all of the balls?"

Their cousin's head turned with a jolt, and she gave a dismissive wave. "Oh, we are no more than friends, and a familiar and welcome face in the crowd for each other."

With a laugh, Elizabeth pushed a biscuit across the plate to her cousin. "At least no gentleman has called you tolerable, but not handsome enough to tempt him." She lowered her voice, though it was not nearly as deep as Mr. Darcy's.

"I am all aghast. A gentleman said that of you and within your hearing?"

"He did. His friend attempted to persuade him to ask me to dance. Told the gentleman I was pretty, and that was his response."

"Would I be acquainted with him?"

Jane picked up a biscuit. "You may. He is a gentleman of consequence. The rumour around the assembly was he has ten thousand a year."

Her cousin bounced in her place. "Who is he?"

"Mr. Darcy," said Jane before Elizabeth could stop her.

"Jane!"

Her sister looked at her and covered her mouth with her hand while she chewed her biscuit. "Was I not supposed to say? You told everyone in Meryton of the slight. How was I to know you were suddenly keeping his identity a secret?"

"Well, Nicholas and Grandpapa knew of Mr. Bingley. I assumed they would know Mr. Darcy too, so I had not mentioned making his acquaintance."

Amelia, meanwhile, was clutching her stomach while she laughed. "Do you mean Fitzwilliam Darcy of Pemberley in Derbyshire?"

"Yes, I believe that is the name of his estate." Of course Amelia would know him!

"Lizzy, he is one of Nicholas's friends. His father and Grandpapa were friends until the elder Mr. Darcy's death. He is also a well-respected and a sought-after marriage prospect. Every Mama wants to garner his attention for her daughter. After all, who does not desire a handsome, rich, and good man for a husband?"

She balked. "I shall agree that he is handsome and rich, though I fear I cannot agree with good. I found him prideful and the most disagreeable man I have ever had the misfortune of meeting." An understatement at best!

"Mr. Bingley is not disagreeable and was liked by the whole of the neighbourhood," said Jane. "Why would he be friends with Mr. Darcy if the gentleman was so very bad? I still say his disagreement with Mr. Wickham was a misunderstanding."

Not likely! How could one with such a countenance and engaging manners give so false an account?

"You want everyone to be good and kind, Janey." Amelia wrapped an arm around Jane and hugged her to her side. "'Tis one of the many qualities we love about you. As for you and Mr. Darcy, Lizzy, you had best reconcile yourself to being in his company again. Our grandparents consider him very much a part of this family, and I am certain we shall be invited to the same balls and parties as him during Christmastide."

Elizabeth dipped her biscuit in her chocolate and shoved it in her mouth. Just what she needed: more time spent with Mr. Darcy. Whatever had she done to deserve him ruining her Christmas?

Chapter 4

A footman took Darcy's coat and hat, then gestured towards Lady Vranes's ballroom. "Enjoy your evening, sir."

He held his spine straight, and his neck was rigid as he followed the murmur of voices and the footmen stationed along the hall to the entrance. Lord, but he despised these evenings—avoiding the schemes of the matchmaking mamas while he tried to converse with friends and view the latest works from the artists in London. He stepped inside and drew his shoulders back.

"Mr. Darcy, so good of you to come," said Lady Vranes with a tilt of her head.

After he bowed over her hand, he drew himself back up as tall as he could. "Lady Vranes, I am pleased to be in your company once again and thank you for the invitation. This evening certainly seems a success." He glanced around at the people filling the room and viewing the many paintings that covered the walls from ceiling to floor.

"Take a look around, sir." Lady Vranes motioned to the room with her fan. "I have discovered several new artists who are exhibiting here this evening. Mr. Nash has a lovely view of Shoreham Harbour, and Miss Cosway paints some interesting portraits."

He nodded with as much of a smile as he could manage. "I shall be certain to look for them."

"Darcy," said a voice behind him as he stepped to the first set of paintings.

After he bowed to his friend, they shook hands. "Hatton, I should have known you and your family would attend one of Lady Vranes's gatherings." Nicholas Montford, Viscount

Hatton was the heir to the Richmond earldom, not that he was in any hurry to assume the title. His grandfather was still living and an excellent man. The earl had been a great friend to Darcy's own father for decades.

"I thought you at Pemberley."

"No, I recently returned from Hertfordshire. Bingley requested my aid with an estate he leased."

Hatton's eyes flashed for a moment. "You were with Bingley in Hertfordshire? I had been told he was there but had not heard of your presence." Nicholas glanced over his shoulder, making Darcy turn to look behind him. Was that? Good heavens! He spun around and stood with his hands clenched at his sides. How was this possible? Elizabeth Bennet was in London and at Lady Vranes's salon. How had she secured an invitation to such an exclusive event?

He had been trying with all that was in him to forget her since he departed Hertfordshire but with little success. Now, she was standing across the room, speaking with...was that Lady Richmond? With a shake of his head, he looked again. Elizabeth Bennet was in Hertfordshire at Longbourn. Was his heart so desperate for her that he was conjuring her up in the least likely of places?

"Come. You should greet my grandparents. They will be thrilled to see you." He barely registered the slight tug at his elbow, drawing him across the room. "Grandmamma, look who I have found."

"Fitzwilliam," said Lady Richmond. He shook himself in an effort to give the countess his full attention. "We have not had the pleasure of seeing you in nearly a year. You and your sister must join us for dinner this week. I shall not accept a refusal, mind you. It has been too long, and I know Hugh would feel as strongly as I do on the matter. Would Saturday evening be acceptable?"

"Lizzy, there is a landscape..." Miss Amelia Montford stopped speaking and stared, her eyes widening before she dropped a curtsey. "Mr. Darcy, forgive me. I had not noticed you there."

"Do not trouble yourself." He bowed, his gaze meeting Miss Elizabeth's as he straightened. "Miss Elizabeth Bennet, 'tis a pleasure to see you once again."

With a peculiar cough, Miss Montford covered her mouth with her gloved hand, her eyes crinkling at the edges. "I beg your pardon," she said between coughs. "I fear something...has become caught...in my throat."

"It is a pleasure to see you again, Mr. Darcy," said Miss Bennet with a curtsey.

"I must correct you, Darcy." Hatton placed a hand upon his shoulder. "She is not Miss Elizabeth Bennet but Miss Elizabeth Montford."

In his attempt to stifle a gasp, he joined Miss Montford in a fit of coughing. "I must beg your forgiveness, but Miss Elizabeth Montford? Why were she and her sister introduced as Miss Bennets in Hertfordshire?"

"'Tis a long story." At the deeper voice from his shoulder, Darcy stepped back to include Lord Richmond in their party. "The short explanation is that Lizzybeth's mother was my daughter, Sophie. She and Janey lived with us for almost two years after their mother's death. They became Montfords during that time. Lizzybeth, you never mentioned you were acquainted with Darcy."

Miss Elizabeth opened and closed her mouth twice. "We are but *tolerably* acquainted. I had no notion he was a friend of the family until last night when Amelia told me as much."

Miss Montford burst into another fit of coughing. Was she laughing? Moreover, was she laughing at him?

His mind spun. What could have happened to necessitate the earl taking such drastic action? A rumour had been mentioned of the elder Miss Bennets' mother dying in childbirth, but nothing of her family or connexions or them being wards of their grandfather. Heavens, not even Miss Bennet—nay, Montford—spoke of the family when she visited with Bingley's sisters at Netherfield. Miss Bingley and Mrs. Hurst surely enquired of her family: uncles, cousins, grandparents. How had she neglected to mention Lord and Lady Richmond?

"Janey, do you know Fitzwilliam too?" asked Lady Richmond.

Miss Benn...Montford stepped forward from beside her grandfather and curtseyed. "Good evening, Mr. Darcy." How had he missed that she was standing so close?

"Miss...Montford, I hope you and your family are well."

"Yes, sir. They were well when my sister and I departed Longbourn three days ago."

"Mr. Darcy," said Miss Amelia Montford. "If you will forgive me, I should like to show Lizzy a painting I believe she will enjoy."

"Of course." After a slight bow, Miss Montford pulled Miss Elizabeth across the room. He turned at Hatton's soft chuckles.

"You are the gentleman who called her tolerable."

He squeezed his eyes closed as his face burned. How could he have known who she truly was? His name was being bandied about with whispers of ten thousand a year. The situation had been intolerable. Bingley had forced him to attend the ridiculous assembly, and at any moment, he had expected some mother to shove her obsequious daughter under his nose in the hopes he would take an interest "I was in an ill humour that evening. I beg your forgiveness, and I shall apologise to Miss Elizabeth."

"My goodness," said Lady Richmond. "A great deal of begging forgiveness has occurred since we happened upon you, Fitzwilliam. I have known you since you were a boy, and you have never performed well in unfamiliar surroundings, balls and salons in particular. Once Lizzybeth knows of your discomfort, I am certain she will forgive you. She is not one to bear a grudge."

Hatton scoffed. "You cannot be serious, Grandmamma. Do you not remember when I put alum in her toothpowder?"

Lord Richmond's silent laughter could be discerned over the murmurs of the guests. "I do. Did she not take the piglets from the barn and put them in your bed? What a sight she was—wet through and filthy with a countenance so guilty, I knew she had been up to mischief before I could ask her so much as one question."

"I had forgotten that incident." Lady Richmond grinned and looped her arm through Hatton's. "Lizzybeth was incensed I made her help the maids clean the mud and the muck from Nicholas's room."

"I had to scrub the floors. Do you remember?"

Darcy bit his tongue to keep from laughing at Hatton's wide eyes and affronted tone.

His grandfather shrugged, though he still wore a wide grin. "Well, if you had not ruined your cousin's toothpowder, she would not have put the piglets in your bedchamber. You reap what you sow, my boy. Not that my punishments ever prevented you from playing tricks on Lizzybeth or Amelia for that matter. Your younger cousin proved to be more of an adversary, so you found yourself in more trouble as a result of those escapades."

Hatton straightened his topcoat. "What you say is true. Regardless of the repercussions, I take far too much enjoyment in stoking Lizzy's ire, which I have not done in some time, so if you will pardon me, I shall be pestering my cousin." With a crooked curve of his lips, Hatton strode across the room to where Miss Amelia Montford and Miss Elizabeth stood, the latter turning to face her cousin when their gazes met and she broke the connection as quickly as it was made.

"You should join us for a light supper after the exhibition," said Lady Richmond, drawing his attention.

"My sister expects my return before long, but I thank you for the invitation. We shall attend that dinner you spoke of earlier, if the invitation still stands."

"Of course, it does. I shall be delighted to see Georgiana. We have not spoken since I called on her near Easter. Now, why is Nicholas beckoning to me? I shall add to the begging for the evening. Forgive me, I should see what he wants." After a curtsey, she crossed to join her grandchildren.

"You said my granddaughter is tolerable?" said Lord Richmond near his ear, making Darcy wince. "I can only imagine there must be more by Amelia's reaction to you. I thought she would choke trying to disguise those chuckles. You have a history of being quite intolerant to ladies who throw themselves at you, yet I know my granddaughter, and she would never throw herself at any man."

With an exhale, he clasped his hands behind his back. Lord Richmond was as much a father or grandfather to him as his own father and grandfather, but now was not the time for familiarity. "No, my lord, Bingley implored me to dance and singled out your granddaughter as an excellent prospect. I was in a foul temper, so when she looked at me, I said 'she is tolerable I suppose, but not handsome enough to tempt me.' Her reaction I shall never forget. She rose, joined her friend Miss Lucas, and after a moment with their heads together, laughed at me. At once, I was intrigued and regretful. No lady of our acquaintance would behave as your granddaughter did in those circumstances."

"I now understand why her eyes were shooting daggers from the moment she saw you."

"I should like to apologise if she will give me the opportunity. My words were not true. I have long considered her one of the handsomest ladies of my acquaintance." He could not stop thinking of Miss Elizabeth, and the constant preoccupation with her was maddening. Nothing could distract him—not his ledgers or a book or even a night at an exhibition could rid his mind of her.

She approached a painting and tilted her head while she examined the work, her grandmother at her side pointing and speaking. He could just imagine her brows drawn down a hair and her lips barely pursed while she studied the scene before her. For the most part, she was the same Miss Elizabeth as in Hertfordshire with the exception of her gown. The deep green bodice contrasted with the white silk that fell in an elegant line to the floor. Jade-coloured beads adorned her graceful neck, taking the place of her usual yellow topaz cross that had always sat nestled just below the base of her throat. Lace gloves covered her slender arms and ended just above the elbow and gave a peek of pale skin between the seam of the glove and the bottom of her sleeve. What he would not give to trail his finger along that line, hear the hitch in her breath at his touch, and taste her pale pink lips that, even now, called to him from across the ballroom.

"Darcy? Are you well?" He started at the earl's voice.

He had thought her family and situation unsuitable, but all this time, she was more than a Bennet from Hertfordshire. She cared not for connexions or fortunes or she, not to mention her sister, would have bandied about her grandfather's name and title to ingratiate herself to him and the Bingleys. Instead, they never said a word. Blast, he was an addle pate. She, no doubt, thought him prideful and arrogant, and she would be right. "I am quite well. I thank you. Only considering how ashamed my father would be of me at the moment."

Lord Richmond set a hand upon his shoulder and squeezed. "We all say things we regret from time to time. 'Tis how we make amends for the wrongs of a moment that define us for our lifetime. Come to the dinner my wife mentioned. Introduce her to Georgiana. Bring the colonel if he is in London; he can sing your praises as well. All is not lost."

After raking his fingers through his hair, he chuckled ruefully. "Sir—"

"Do not tell me falsehoods or deny what is written as clear as day upon your face when you watch my granddaughter. I am no fool. Your father wore the same expression the first time he set eyes upon your mother. You are an excellent man, as your father was before you, and if you can earn my granddaughter's forgiveness and respect, I would be more than pleased if you joined our family even if, in some fashion, you have been one of us since you were born. You stayed with us during your mother's illnesses and when she died."

He cleared the sizable lump that had risen in his throat. "You and your family journeyed to Pemberley after my father's accident and were all of great aid. You, in particular, taught me to be the master I am. I have never forgotten. I do not remember much of my grandparents, but you and Lady Richmond were as much my grandparents as they were." Lady Richmond and Miss Amelia Montford had run the house while Lord Richmond and Nicholas aided him in his father's study. They had saved him after his father's death. He could not even consider what might have occurred if they had not come. Would he have succumbed to Lady Catherine's entreaties to wed his sickly cousin Anne?

Lord Richmond sniffed and blinked. "Thank you, Son. Now, while I do enjoy your company, I suggest you spend the rest of the evening with my grandchildren. Should you do so, you may find an opportunity to apologise without Amelia or Nicholas too close to overhear. You do not want them to tease you as mercilessly as they are sure to be teasing Lizzybeth tonight."

With a deep inhale, Darcy nodded. "I cannot but try."

Elizabeth's insides were a turbulent mess. The butterflies flying in maddening circles seemed to create a wave that travelled through her. She had clenched her hands around the top of her reticule to keep from trembling when Mr. Darcy approached as well as during the ensuing conversation. Amelia had warned her they would cross paths, but how could she have known it would happen so soon? The worst part was she kept catching herself staring at him while he spoke to her grandfather. In some ways, his expression was as it always was, stern and forbidding, particularly when she found him watching her, yet at times, it softened, such as when he looked at her grandparents.

"Lizzybeth, stop staring at poor Fitzwilliam."

"I had not meant—" She glanced about them. "Where are Nicholas and Amelia?"

"Your cousins have sought out the refreshment table." Her grandmother patted her forearm. "I have never seen such a sight as your countenance when you first noticed Fitzwilliam. Child, what has he done for you to dislike him so?"

"Grandmamma, Amelia mentioned he is a friend to this family, but you must know that he offended the entire neighbourhood while staying at Netherfield. His manner was prideful and disagreeable. He could hardly be bothered to speak to anyone outside his party, and I cannot abide how he stares at me to find fault."

Her grandmother glanced over her shoulder. "You believe he watches you in that manner to find fault?"

"Why else would he do so? He said himself I am tolerable but not handsome enough to tempt him. His disdain for me was quite plain." What else could be said?

"Oh, dearest," she said, linking their arms. "As someone who has known Fitzwilliam Darcy since he was a babe, I can tell you he is not as you describe. In smaller parties where he has friends, he can be amiable, and you just may see him smile." Her grandmother tugged her around. "Do you see those ladies behind him?"

A mama and her two daughters stood approximately five feet behind Mr. Darcy; their hands cupped over their mouths as though telling the most secret of secrets while watching him. "They are speaking of him?"

"For the moment, but give them time. One will stumble into him or the mother will devise some way to force an introduction by the end of the night. If he had not spoken as he had at the assembly and flattered you instead, how would Mrs. Bennet have reacted?"

Elizabeth winced. "She would have done all in her power to throw us together as she did Jane and Mr. Bingley."

"I do not know the whole of your acquaintance, though I daresay, knowing *you* as I do, you have held his initial comments and behaviour against him and allowed your wounded pride to judge him unfairly since that first meeting."

She could not be blamed for doing so, could she? And what of Mr. Wickham's charges against him? Mr. Darcy would not have told Grandmamma of his denying that young man's inheritance. An elbow to her ribs jolted her attention back to the room.

"He is coming this way. Do not do him the disservice of holding to your former prejudices. Be the Lizzybeth your grandfather and I know and love."

"That was laid on with a trowel.¹"

Her grandmother winked with a grin. "I should mention that Fitzwilliam is very fond of Shakespeare. You should use that quote with him."

As the gentleman approached, her grandmother tapped her on the shoulder. "What a stunning portrait," she said loudly. "Pardon me, my dear. I wish to take a closer look."

"Grandmamma!" she said in a loud whisper reminiscent of Mama. Why would she abandon her to the disagreeable nature of Mr. Darcy? Yes, she should allow him to make amends, yet her grandmother had no need to depart for that purpose. He could very well apologise with Gran present.

"Miss Elizabeth."

She had been glancing about her when she jerked her attention back to the gentleman who had crossed the room to speak to her—to the gentleman her grandmother hoped she would find agreeable. He would certainly be invited to dinners and balls over Christmastide, not to mention during the Season. If they managed a truce of sorts, those events would be more pleasant. She would never enjoy a ball with him staring at her as he had in Hertfordshire. That constant scrutiny was unnerving.

"Mr. Darcy, I hope you are enjoying the exhibition. Lady Vranes has a unique eye for art, does she not?"

Before he could respond, a lady stumbled into him, prompting him to grab Elizabeth by the arms and draw her to one side.

Chapter 5

Darcy shifted Elizabeth out of the way and hastened from the interloper in a frantic dance. She was not the first to almost knock him to the floor in an attempt to force an introduction, and to his great misfortune, she would not be the last. His married cousin, a viscount and heir to the Fitzwilliam earldom, was still plagued by the occasional scheme, but usually by married ladies hoping for a tumble. Marriage could not even save a man from this ridiculousness!

"How terribly clumsy of me," said the older woman who had hit him from behind. "I tripped on my own feet." When the ornately dressed woman lifted her face, her expression overspread with the widest of affected smiles. "You are Viscount Milton's cousin, are you not? Mr. Darcy?"

As was his wont in these situations, he executed an abrupt turn, and with a gentle hand to Miss Elizabeth's elbow, steered her in the direction of the hall. "I hope you are in need of refreshment. My conscience would not allow me to leave you when I made my escape."

"Do not trouble yourself. I am uninjured, and after that spectacle, I cannot fault you for your manner of leaving. My grandmother claimed she would attempt such a manoeuvre, but I would not have believed it if I had not seen it with my own eyes. Thank goodness Mama was not here to witness her scheme. No gentleman of means would be safe in Hertfordshire, not as long as she had daughters to marry off."

"While we are not in company, allow me to beg your forgiveness for the comment I made at the assembly."

Miss Elizabeth's merry laughter surrounded him, enveloping him in a warmth he had never experienced before. "Grandmamma is correct. Our entire evening thus far has been spent begging others for forgiveness. We are a sorry lot indeed, though not as sorry as the lady who tried to use you as a target for lawn bowls."

A smile tugged at one corner of his lips. No one teased him but Georgiana and Richard, and her willingness to make light of the situation alleviated some of the tension. When they reached the table, Hatton and his sister were not to be found. He handed Miss Elizabeth a glass of punch. "Do you know how long you are to remain in town?"

"We were to stay with my grandparents through Twelfth Night, but it seems we are to remain for the Season as well."

"Will this be your first Season?"

"I spent a month of the Season with my grandparents two years ago, though I only attended two theatre performances and a private concert. My grandfather was not well at the time, so we spent most of our time with him."

"He had an episode with his heart, did he not?"

"The physician claimed it to be so. He was put to bed and on orders to rest. I spent the month reading to him."

"I am certain he was grateful for your efforts." He all but shook himself to cease the image of her doing the same for him. Why could he not control the direction of his thoughts when in her company? She invaded his mind, her presence lingering in every corner and tempting him beyond reason.

"Grandpapa?" she asked with a grin. "No, he despises being read to. He humoured me while he was the most ill before he demanded the book to read for himself. My grandfather detests even the slightest notion of being helpless."

"My sister and I dined with Lord and Lady Richmond before they departed for Yorkshire for the summer that year. We were all greatly relieved at his recovery."

She nodded while she swallowed the sip of her punch and puckered her lips in the most adorable fashion. "Oh, my."

"Is it sour?"

"No, the liquor is quite strong." She cleared her throat while he tasted his glass of the concoction.

"'Tis no wonder. I believe this is Regent's Punch.[2] My aunt served it for a ball last year. I am uncertain of the receipt, though due to the champagne, madeira, and brandy in the mixture, my uncle complained of the expense."

After one more sip and more twisting and pursing of her lips, she held the back of her hand over her nose, handing him the glass. "I should stop. Otherwise, I fear I may lose my wits."

Good Lord, he should like to see her lose her wits. With a cough, he set down his glass and took hers, placing it next to his. He needed to get a hold of himself lest he do something to embarrass himself. "We should find Hatton, Miss Montford, Miss Benn...Mont—. Forgive me. I never stumble over my words so."

"Do not trouble yourself. I had not known of my grandfather giving us the Montford surname until two days ago. If I had to mention Jane as you do, I would have a similar difficulty. I am not accustomed to Montford for myself yet much less addressing Jane in such a way." She winced. "I should not have spoken as I have."

He held out his arm. "Do not worry over it. You have said nothing that your grandfather has not already told me this evening. Since neither of us wishes to chance more of the punch, I do believe we should find your family."

Upon their return to the ballroom, Lady Richmond and Miss Amelia Montford were speaking with Lady Vranes, so he stepped up to the closest painting and leaned a little closer to Miss Elizabeth. "What genre do you favour?"

"Oh, Amelia wanted to show me the landscape, there, which I do like. The prospect resembles Netherfield, I think."

The great house set back with a sprawling lake and cows grazing peacefully along the banks was indeed similar to Netherfield. "I do see why she wished you to see it. The view is well done. Is there another work you have enjoyed?"

"I have looked at so few. You arrived before us, sir, thus have had more time to view the exhibition." That one eyebrow arched, and her lips curved upward on one side, making an alluring sight. "I am curious to know your favourite."

He led her across the room. "I believe I arrived but a moment before you and your family, but thus far, I am partial to this one." With a lift of his hand, he gestured to the landscape before them.

"'Tis beautiful. I have never seen the like. Do you know the prospect, or could it be painted from the artist's imagination?"

"I have stood near that very spot at Stanage Edge in the summer and taken great pleasure in the bluebells as I ride through that area of the Peak." He glanced away from the work to find her staring with rapt attention at the scene. Her head tilted ever so slightly, and she scraped her teeth along her bottom lip. Had she no idea how that little gesture tortured him? He squeezed his hands into fists to keep from reaching for her. How was he to resist? She would make him mad if she continued as she was.

"Lizzy," said Hatton, who walked up beside her. "Grandpapa desires your opinion on a possible gift for our grandmother. And the last time he asked Amelia, she told Grandmamma."

"Where is he?"

Hatton pointed to the far corner. "Behind Lord Rutledge."

Miss Elizabeth sank down with her face screwed into a frown. "Lord Rutledge?"

Her cousin grinned. "Just slip behind the rotund lady near the fireplace and follow the wall until you reach him," he said near her ear. "He will never see you."

"Pardon me, Mr. Darcy."

Hatton shifted to his side while Miss Elizabeth wound through what had become a crush. Rather than use the lady Hatton had mentioned to shield her from Rutledge's notice, she made a wider berth before she disappeared behind the guests near the wall.

"Why does she dislike Rutledge?" The young earl was known as a boor and for his officiousness in their circles, but had she a different reason for her avoidance?

"Lizzy attended a dinner with my grandmother at Sir Walter Elliot's in Grosvenor Square where Lord Rutledge was also a guest. He must have considered her pretty as he remained as close to her as possible for the entirety of the evening. You know his demeanour well enough to understand how he behaved. She thought him a bother and never left my grandmother's side. Thankfully for her, he attempted to call while she was calling upon Mrs. Bennet's family the next day, but he tried again for several days."

"He never managed to see her?"

Hatton chuckled. "No, our butler in town, Mr. Gideon, told Rutledge she was making calls. Gideon has known us all since we were babes and had not missed the obvious distaste etched upon Lizzy's face when he mentioned the first call. He would do all in his power to protect Amelia, Janey, and Lizzy."

"Lady Vranes has some lovely landscapes in this exhibition," said Lady Richmond as she stepped to her grandson's side. "I believe I have viewed them all. Your grandfather has indicated his desire to return home. Do you wish to stay or depart with us?"

"I shall join you. Other than Darcy, I see no one I wish to speak with." Hatton tipped his head towards the door. "Will you not join us for supper?"

He glanced at Miss Elizabeth, who skirted the edge of the room on her grandfather's arm. Miss Jane Montford walked behind them arm in arm with Miss Amelia Montford. He shook his head. "I promised Georgiana I would return before long, and Richard is to return from Dover tonight. He has been on the coast for the past week on business for the army."

"If the colonel has no prior engagements, bring him with you for dinner," said Lady Richmond. "Hugh and I enjoy his company immensely. We shall see you, shall we not?"

"Yes, I shall be pleased to accept your offer on behalf of Georgiana and myself, and I shall pass along the invitation to Richard. Thank you." After the formality of bows and curtseys, he shook Hatton's hand as they made to leave.

He sought out Lady Vranes, and after a few words, sought out his own carriage amongst the throng along the square. Once his driver navigated through the crowd, the ride to Darcy House was quick. When he alighted, he peered down Park Lane to where Richmond House stood proud and tall on the far end.

How could he have been so foolish as to insult the granddaughter of Lord Richmond? He let out a low groan. How could he have known Miss Elizabeth Bennet was in actuality Miss Elizabeth Montford? The earl and countess knew well his demeanour at balls and the like and did not seem to bear a grudge over the matter. What of Miss Elizabeth? What was her opinion of him? He sighed and went inside, following voices to the music room where Georgiana was sitting down at the pianoforte while Richard sat with a sizeable glass of brandy resting upon his knee.

"Brother! How was the exhibition?"

"As is her wont, Lady Vranes amassed a variety of talented artists and interesting works. Lord and Lady Richmond were in attendance with their grandchildren. They have invited us to dine with them Saturday evening. You were included in the invitation, Richard, should you care to attend with us."

"I do not have any prior commitments, and I do enjoy an evening spent with the Montfords. Richmond and Hatton possess an irreverent wit I find entertaining."

"What of Miss Montford?" asked Georgiana with a teasing lilt. "She is a handsome lady, and you often say you cannot wed a lady without fortune in mind."

"Poppet, I have no desire to marry. I am content with my life as it is and much prefer friendships to romantic entanglements. Miss Montford and I are fond of each other's company and are pleased to have a willing and able dance partner, but we are no more than amiable acquaintances."

"Lord and Lady Richmond have two granddaughters who are staying with them who I should like to introduce to you, Georgiana. I met them while at Netherfield and happened upon them at the exhibition tonight."

Georgiana frowned and tilted her head. "The only ladies you made mention of in your letters were the Misses Bennets—Miss Elizabeth, in particular."

"Did he?" Richard turned his gaze on him with a crooked grin. "And what had he to say of Miss Elizabeth?"

"She takes pleasure in reading, she takes great delight in walks, and she is not intimidated by Miss Bingley. Why do you ask?" Had he truly mentioned Miss Elizabeth so much in his correspondence? He must have since Georgiana noticed.

"Your brother so rarely has much to say of any lady, much less giving one a compliment, which he seems to have done with Miss Elizabeth. Shall I hear wedding bells, Cousin?"

With a giggle, his sister came forward and kissed his cheek. "I know very little of her, but I believe I should enjoy such a sister."

"I have not even courted the lady, and the two of you are speaking of weddings." Would he object to Miss Elizabeth as his bride? By the infatuation he had held for her since Hertfordshire, he would be willing. He had been unable to get her out of his mind.

"Ha!" Richard slapped his leg and sat up straight. "So, you are thinking of her as a potential bride."

How to tell his loud and overly inquisitive cousin that he had no wish to discuss Miss Elizabeth with Georgiana present? He made a pointed glance to his sister. "I have not said that."

"What have you neglected to tell us?" asked Richard while Georgiana looked back and forth between them.

He scrubbed his face with his hands and exhaled long and heavy. "When I met Miss Ben...Miss Montford and Miss Elizabeth, I was not aware that they were Lord Richmond's granddaughters, and I may have made a comment within Miss Elizabeth's hearing upon our first acquaintance. When I saw them tonight, Miss Elizabeth claimed we are 'tolerably acquainted,' making Lord and Lady Richmond as well as Hatton realise that I made the unfortunate remark."

His sister sat on the sofa near Richard with a tiny crinkle between her eyebrows. "I do not understand. What could you have said with tolerably acquainted to make it unfortunate?"

"Yes, Darcy, what could you have said?"

Why was Richard wearing that insufferable expression? Truly, his cousin had no need to ask since he had witnessed, on far too many occasions, his foul humour at a ball or dinner. His cousin knew him too well not to have some idea of what he could have said."

He stared hard at Richard. "I said she was tolerable but not handsome enough to tempt me."

Georgiana gasped. "Brother! What an unfeeling statement! Does Miss Elizabeth still speak to you?"

Richard's shoulders were shaking while he covered his face with one hand, the sound of his mirth escaping and grating on Darcy's nerves. He should have waited until Richard was absent to mention Miss Elizabeth to his sister.

"Miss Elizabeth and I conversed for a time tonight. Why?"

"Because if a gentleman said that about me," said Georgiana, "I would do my best to keep from being in his company. Even then, I would speak to him as little as possible. Miss Elizabeth was either being polite since you are friends with her grandfather, or she is the most generous and forgiving lady I have ever heard of." She yawned and rose from the sofa. "While I would love hearing more of this singular lady, I am fatigued and was awaiting your return to go to bed. If you do not object, I should like to retire. Good night."

After they bid her good night as well, Richard took a sip of his brandy with an absurd smile. "You mentioned her to Georgiana, yet you returned from Hertfordshire in one of the worst tempers your sister has ever seen."

"She told you?"

"She did. You also told her Bingley had formed an inappropriate entanglement. You said that you had no idea of Miss Elizabeth's and Miss Jane Montford's connexion to the Richmond earldom until you saw them tonight. Between your sister's mention of Miss Elizabeth in your letters, and your recent boorish behaviour, I do wonder if you are the one who formed an inappropriate entanglement—on your side anyway—and you fled to London to protect yourself from her."

"Richard, her younger sisters from Mr. Bennet's current wife behave with no decorum, and his wife is worse, allowing the youngest who might be thirteen in the drawing room with company as well as pushing the eldest shamelessly towards Bingley. Even Mr. Bennet was improper at times."

"You thought her beneath you until you knew her to be a Montford, and now, I wager you are considering courting her."

"Lord Richmond gave his blessing, and I begged her forgiveness for what I said."

His cousin scoffed and rolled his eyes. "'Tis not the point, Darcy. You considered her below you in Hertfordshire, but now that you are aware of her family name and connections, you are no doubt relieved. She is suddenly an appropriate match, and you feel justified in giving yourself leave to like her."

"Should I not feel as much?"

"Darcy, she is the same lady this evening as she was in Hertfordshire, and you are an unconscionable ass." Richard stood and stepped closer to him. "You have the funds and independence to marry as you please. Lady Catherine will surely disown you for not marrying Anne, but you have said for years you would never wed her. Is this Miss Elizabeth the daughter of a gentleman?"

"Yes, he has a small estate, though it is entailed to Lady Catherine's vicar."

"That is a disappointing connexion indeed," quipped Richard. "Yet, Mr. Bennet still possesses an estate—"

"A modest one."

"Most of the gentlemen you have had as friends since Oxford are masters of modest estates. Can you imagine how one of them would react if you insulted their daughter or even their sister because you felt the young lady beneath you? What if an earl's or a duke's son made such a remark about Georgiana? How would you behave?"

He cringed. Few of his friends were married or had children as yet, but Crowley had struck Thorpe for commenting that Crowley's sister was pretty albeit not a proper choice for his wife due to her small fortune.

"I know you are in essentials an excellent master and gentleman, as does Richmond and Hatton, otherwise one or both of them may have blackened your eyes and been justified in the action. Out of curiosity, what was Miss Elizabeth's reaction to your insulting description of her?"

"She laughed," he said almost in a whisper.

Richard blinked while one side of his mouth tugged upward. "If she found humour in what you said of her, I look forward to meeting her. She must be a truly singular lady." He clapped him on the shoulder. "I had a long ride from Dover today and want to retire."

"Goodnight."

As soon as his cousin departed the room, Darcy sank onto the settee and dropped his head against the back. The set down from Richard was unavoidable, but in light of his behaviour, he could not deny that he deserved the harsh reminder that he was a gentleman. He had hardly behaved as one when in Miss Elizabeth's company in Hertfordshire. Tonight, he made amends or seemed to. She had accepted his apology, but had he deserved her forgiveness? How was he to know?

Chapter 6

Elizabeth stood as Mr. Darcy, his sister, and Colonel Fitzwilliam were announced. Since the conversation with Nicholas, she had managed to avoid the topic of Mr. Darcy with her family, though truth be told, they had not mentioned him as much as she would have expected after Lady Vranes's exhibition, which had been a tremendous relief. Though how to account for Nicholas's lack of teasing? Since he was a boy, he lived to find humour in not just the absurd, but in hers and Amelia's follies. Why was he not enjoying himself immensely at her expense? The silence on his part was disquieting as was his ardent defence of Mr. Darcy.

When Mr. Darcy and his party entered, all present greeted one another as was the custom before her grandfather strode forward and clapped Mr. Darcy on the shoulder and shook his hand. "Darcy, I am pleased you could come. Fitzwilliam, you are quite welcome." He repeated the gesture with the colonel, then kissed Miss Darcy's hand. "My, you have certainly grown since we were last in company, my dear. You resemble your mother so much I would require a second look should I see you across the room.

"Georgiana, Colonel, you know Nicholas and Amelia, but allow me to introduce my granddaughters, Miss Jane Montford and Miss Elizabeth Montford. They have come to live with us and are to remain through the Season." He stepped beside Jane. "Girls, Colonel Fitzwilliam is Mr. Darcy's cousin, and Georgiana is, of course, his younger sister."

Grandmamma took Miss Darcy's hand and brought the girl to sit beside her. "Pray, come be seated."

"If you will give me one moment," said Mr. Darcy, disappearing through the door, then reappearing a moment later with flowers in his hands. "I took the liberty of bringing you each a small bouquet." He handed a nosegay of roses to Grandmamma, whose cheeks pinked and gushed a thank you, then to Amelia and Jane. When he finally stood in front of Elizabeth with the last cluster of roses, her heart beat so hard and fast. Why? It was no more than flowers. Why should that cause such a flutter? Good heavens, what if she fainted?

She looked down to the flowers before her. Each nosegay was different, whether the colour or the appearance of the rose. Where had he found such variety in December? "Miss Elizabeth, I am certain you are partial to wildflowers, but I hope you enjoy roses as well."

She wrapped her hand tightly around the ribbon covered stems. "They are stunning. Thank you." Her voice was so soft. Why was that?

He stepped over to sit near Nicholas and her grandfather while she continued to stare at the roses. He brought her flowers—Mr. Darcy had brought them all flowers.

"Lizzybeth?" Her head popped up at her grandmother's voice. "Georgiana has expressed a desire to get to know you. Would you come sit with us?"

Somehow, she managed to nod and sat on the sofa beside Miss Darcy, her grandmother on the young lady's opposite side. "I am happy to make your acquaintance, Miss Darcy." She glanced over at Jane's nosegay.

"Miss Elizabeth?"

Her head whipped around to Miss Darcy's raised eyebrows. "Forgive me. I was wool-gathering. I was curious of the roses since some of ours are different colours."

Grandmamma held hers forward. "Some are different varieties of roses, not just colours. Mine are pink, which can mean the beginning of a relationship, but I believe here means grace, sophistication, and elegance since they are also China roses, which represent grace or lasting beauty.

"Jane's are burgundy, which means simplicity and beauty, and are Damask roses, which stand for purity. He selected the same for Amelia.

"Now, yours—"

"Are pink," said Miss Darcy with a grin. "As your grandmother mentioned, pink can mean grace, sophistication, and elegance as well as the beginning of a relationship, but they are also Provence roses..." The girl's cheeks reddened, and she stopped. Why? She had not said what a Provence rose meant. Now, she had to know.

"I do not understand. I know a little of the language of flowers, but I never knew roses could have meanings for colour as well as variety."

Her grandmother leaned behind Miss Darcy. "Provence roses mean my heart is in flames." She spoke in hushed tones.

Oh, my. Her own cheeks were in flames. The bouquet could not possibly mean what her grandmother said. It was a coincidence. Surely, a coincidence. That or her grandmother was mistaken.

"Fitzwilliam and I selected the roses ourselves in the hothouse. I hope you like them."

Her stomach plummeted at Miss Darcy's weak tone. "Yes, they are lovely, but your brother would never mean...his heart could not possibly..." This was the end. She would die of mortification right where she sat.

"Lizzybeth," said her grandmother, "breathe."

A maid stood before her. "I can put those in water for you, miss, and Tate will put them in your bedchamber."

"Thank you." She released the small bouquet, though her gaze followed them until they disappeared through the door.

"Miss Elizabeth, I hope my brother did not shock you with his nosegay. He mentioned what occurred the evening he made your acquaintance, and I know he regrets what he said, though I am certain he wishes to apologise to you himself." The poor dear spoke with hesitance and could barely meet Elizabeth's eye. Miss Darcy was shy? Had not Wickham made the claim of her being proud like her brother?

"Perhaps we should have selected a different variety. Fitzwilliam feared being too bold," said Miss Darcy in a soft tone near her ear. "Forgive me. I convinced him to choose the Provence roses." She had almost shrunk into the settee and stared at her hands.

"Do not trouble yourself, Miss Darcy. The roses are beautiful, and I thank you for the thought you put into them. I assure you, the time and effort makes them a welcome gift." The girl relaxed and a smile began to spread upon her face.

"Dinner is served."

Upon the call for dinner, her grandmother stood and took her husband's arm while Colonel Fitzwilliam approached with a wide smile and a deep bow. "Miss Montford, Georgiana, would you do me the honour?"

When she was the sole person left on the sofa, Mr. Darcy stepped before her. "Miss Elizabeth, would you do me the honour?" She took a deep inhale. Her courage rose with any attempt to intimidate her. While Mr. Darcy had likely not intended to intimidate her, she would treat it with the same manner. She would not let it intimidate her.

She set her hand in his as he helped her rise. Even through their gloves, a current travelled between them and penetrated his topcoat and fine lawn shirt when she placed her palm upon his forearm. "You look lovely this evening." Again, her gown was not one she had worn in Hertfordshire. Silver silk was overlaid with a white gauze with silver embroidery accents. The style was still simple and elegant and complemented Miss Elizabeth's complexion perfectly with amethyst ear drops hanging from her delicate lobes.

"Thank you. I fear my grandmother enjoyed visiting the modiste far too much, and I have yet another appointment with Madame for next week."

"Your grandfather indicated you were remaining for the Season. You will require a great many gowns and such for the events."

She gave him a side-long look. "Gran has persuaded you to convince me, I see."

"No, I am merely familiar with what Georgiana requires, and she is not yet out." Miss Elizabeth's arched eyebrow brought a smile to his lips. "You were teasing me."

"I confess I was."

When they reached the dining room, his heart dropped in his chest like a stone when Georgiana was seated to one side of Miss Elizabeth and his cousin the other. He should have liked to speak with her during the meal, but for some reason, Lady Richmond placed him almost opposite between Lord Richmond and Hatton.

"How is Pemberley faring?" asked Lord Richmond while the footmen served the first course.

"Quite well. On a suggestion, I had clover sowed into the hayfields, which increased our harvest. This year, I intend to do the same in some of the pastureland."

"I had heard mention at White's of this practice but have not tried it myself."

Hatton attended the discussion with his eyebrows drawn slightly to the middle. "My steward had clover sown into the pastures at Hatfield but not the hayfields. I should be curious to know his reaction to your success."

Miss Elizabeth's merry laugh rang out across the table, and Darcy stopped. Her wide grin reached her eyes as Richard leaned a bit closer, though not enough to be improper, and said something that made her cover her mouth with her hand. Blast it! His cousin had all the good fortune to be placed in the very seat he coveted. He wanted to sit at her side and make her laugh—not that he had ever amused her in such a way. Well, in some fashion, he had when he said she was tolerable. He grimaced.

Georgiana bent forward some over her plate and joined their discussion, her shoulders shaking at his cousin's antics.

"Fitzwilliam," said Lady Richmond. "Do you plan to attend the ball held by the Duke of Dorset next Friday?"

"Yes, I thought to make a brief appearance."

"You should join us for a light supper beforehand and the carriage ride over. We would be pleased to have your company, would we not, Hugh?" Lady Richmond looked to her husband who nodded.

"Indeed, we would, my dear."

When he glanced to Miss Elizabeth, she met his eye for a moment, one side of her lips curved, then she was distracted by Georgiana. Gah! Now, he was jealous of his own sister. This was maddening. He had never been so eager to be in a lady's company—to bask in her attention. How could he have known at the assembly that he would come to regret his actions so acutely?

At the conclusion of the meal, Lord Richmond stood. "Gentlemen, if you would accompany me to my study." He walked around the table and held out his arm. "Lizzybeth, would you join us."

"No, absolutely not," said Lady Richmond with a wag of her finger. "Really, when it is just you and Nicholas, this habit is one thing, but to expose her to whatever it is you men discuss is wholly inappropriate. I do know what you are about, Husband, but I am putting my foot down."

"Well, then lift your pretty slipper back up. We never speak of inappropriate topics, so Lizzybeth's presence will not alter our evening one jot. She will be with us for but a short time. We may talk of politics, the roads, or even the weather, and my granddaughter's opinions are intelligent and welcome. I promise."

Miss Elizabeth wrapped her arm around her grandfather's but rose to her tiptoes and spoke in hushed tones near his ear, making him shake his head. "No, I should like you to be with us for a time. As I told your grandmother, we never discuss subjects inappropriate for a lady, or I would not insist so." Without further argument, he steered her from the dining room to his study, saw her seated in a chair, and brought her a glass of brandy.

"Thank you," she said.

Hatton served himself, while Lord Richmond passed glasses to Darcy and his cousin, who held up his glass. "A lady who is not only in possession of wit and intelligence *but* also drinks fine brandy. If I were not so opposed to marriage for myself, I might consider you an exceptional prospect, Miss Elizabeth."

"I am flattered, sir." Her gaze met Mr. Darcy's for a moment, then diverted to the brandy in her hands. His heart could not truly be in flames as the rose meant, could it? He had said she was tolerable, though he had apologised for the comment at Lady Vranes's exhibition. He had been all that was amiable since they met again a few nights ago, yet what of Mr. Wickham's accusations against him? How could she believe that man's words against Miss Darcy now that she had met her? How could she reconcile Wickham's claims with the living, breathing girl she dined with this evening?

Her grandfather sat in the chair beside hers and took her free hand. "My granddaughter often joins Nicholas and me for brandy in the evenings, though I tell my wife she drinks sherry. Lizzybeth has never joined us when we have company for dinner, but I feel we should clear the air once and for all. Though not by blood, Darcy is a member of this family through the long association and close friendship I possessed with his grandfather and later his father. In my heart, he is as much my grandson as Nicholas." He cleared his throat and levelled a hard gaze at Mr. Darcy. "With that said, I must say I was not pleased at hearing of your behaviour in Hertfordshire, Darcy, but I could not censure you at the exhibition, now, could I? I did, however, mean the opinions I expressed of your character that evening. You are an excellent man, but by your own admission, you did not show yourself as one in Meryton."

Mr. Darcy stood tall and rigid, watching her grandfather with a tight expression. "I have begged Miss Elizabeth's forgiveness, and I assure you, every word of my apology was in earnest. When I spoke to my cousin and Georgiana upon arriving home that evening, I mentioned some of what occurred with Miss Elizabeth and was given a well-deserved chastisement from them as well. I was intemperate with those of the neighbourhood and made no pains to disguise my unwillingness to be there. I know I shall need to prove myself to her, but I can only hope Miss Elizabeth will forgive me in time."

Her grandfather turned to her and lifted his eyebrows. "Well, Lizzybeth?"

"I beg you. Do not flog poor Mr. Darcy on my behalf—"

"No, no," said the colonel with a dismissive wave of his hand. "Flog him. He can be an irritating prig when the mood strikes him. May I enquire how your neighbours in Hertfordshire described him?"

Poor Mr. Darcy! She had forgiven him the night of the exhibition. Why should he be made to apologise again? "Pray, stop. As he said, he apologised, and I willingly forgave him. But, if I may, I should like to ask a question."

"Of course. You may ask anything you wish." Mr. Darcy set down his glass and clasped his hands behind his back as though bracing for a severe hit.

"I should like to know your association with Mr. Wickham."

"Wickham?" chorused Nicholas and Colonel Fitzwilliam in rough voices.

"How do you know that reprobate?" asked her cousin. Good Lord, his voice had never held such venom. What had Mr. Wickham done to inspire it?

Mr. Darcy shifted and moved in a way that suggested he was stretching his neck. "He is quartered with the militia in Meryton."

Colonel Fitzwilliam stood. "Is? So you have done naught to protect the local girls and shops from his schemes? You know well his proclivities. How many tradesmen should lose money before you act? What of the young ladies he defiles?"

"He claimed Mr. Darcy refused to bestow the living his father set aside for him."

Mr. Darcy's head jerked so their gazes met, his intense gaze boring into hers. "And you believed his preposterous tale of woe?"

"At the time, you treated everyone in Meryton as below your notice. You were generally thought to be proud and disagreeable. Why would I have doubted Mr. Wickham's claims? Naught of your character inclined me to think well of you." When he flinched, her cheek seemed to sting. She had begged her grandfather not to flog him further, yet she had delivered a decisive blow.

Grandpapa set his hand on her shoulder. "Darcy, your father thought well of young Wickham, though I remember what occurred after your father's death and was disappointed George was so deceived. My granddaughter had only Wickham's appearance of goodness, and her first impression of you to guide her. May I suggest you enlighten her to your history with Wickham so she may understand why you are distressed?"

Mr. Darcy picked up his glass of brandy, downed the remainder, then cleared his throat. "As he may have told you, George Wickham is the son of my father's steward who, like my father, was an excellent man." As Mr. Darcy continued, Elizabeth's stomach clenched in a most unforgiving manner. He squandered four thousand pounds in three years? How could one waste such a sum? Her dinner and the brandy stung at her throat.

When he finished his recitation, the colonel, who leaned against the armrest of his chair, was gritting his teeth. "Tell them of the tradesmen's daughters, tell them of the Kympton innkeeper's daughter. Hell, tell them of Ramsgate."

Elizabeth gasped, and the colonel rubbed his hand across his forehead. "Forgive me, Miss Elizabeth. I cannot be calm where Wickham is concerned. No one should fall prey to his depravity."

With a frantic shake of his head, Mr. Darcy accepted another glass of brandy from Nicholas. "I cannot speak of Ramsgate, Richard. You should know better than to ask it of me." Her head shifted back and forth as they argued. What was so significant about Ramsgate?

"You cannot overcome your discomfort—even for Miss Elizabeth's protection?" The colonel held his cousin's gaze with a steely countenance.

"What on earth happened to cause such a reaction?" asked Nicholas. "Wickham had finished Eton with the two of you and left Oxford before I started my studies, but I am still aware of his reputation. His exploits were spoken of for some time. Honestly, Darcy, I cannot condone you keeping what you know of him to yourself. He wreaks havoc wherever he steps foot with little effort and with the neighbourhood believing him to be all that a gentleman should be until the results of his actions are realised." Her stomach continued to tense as more and more was said. Had she truly been so deceived in Mr. Wickham's character?

"I cannot risk what happened in Ramsgate becoming gossip." Mr. Darcy spoke through clinched teeth, his tall frame rigid.

"Darcy," said her grandfather in a low tone. "None in this room will say a word of what you divulge, and you know it.

What has you at sixes and sevens, young man? If you do not speak of it, you will burst by the looks of you."

As ill as Elizabeth had thought herself, it was nothing to the churning in her stomach at what Mr. Darcy revealed next. The gall of that man, to call Miss Darcy proud when he had convinced her to elope for her fortune. He was a vile, disgusting seducer, and she had fallen for his easy manner.

"Thank God no one in Hertfordshire knew of yours and Jane's fortunes," said Nicholas.

"He would not have stopped until he had somehow wed one of them." Colonel Fitzwilliam rested his elbows upon his knees, turning his glass in his hand. "May I ask when Wickham told you of my cousin refusing the living?"

She had the urge to squirm under the colonel's unwavering stare. "We made Mr. Wickham's acquaintance about a week before the ball at Netherfield—"

"The 19th of November," said Mr. Darcy. "Bingley and I rode into Meryton that day. You and your sisters were standing in a group with Mr. Collins. I saw you speaking to Wickham but could not confront him before the entirety of Meryton. What if he spoke against Georgiana? He could ruin her."

She took a fortifying breath. "Yes, that was the very day. My aunt Philips had a card party the following evening. I never considered how readily he offered the information on such a slight acquaintance or questioned his claims until I made the acquaintance of Miss Darcy." How could she have been so gullible?

"Why would meeting Georgiana cast doubt?" asked her grandfather.

"He claimed he devoted hours to her amusement when she was a child, but she had become very proud." She swallowed hard. Her utter stupidity made her nauseous and her face burn. "The young lady who entered this house tonight has no improper pride. She is exceedingly shy."

"Her reserve has grown since the debacle with Wickham," said Mr. Darcy. "Before, she would accompany me on occasion to the theatre or for performances and exhibitions. She would have taken great pleasure in Lady Vranes's exhibition, but when I attempted to persuade her, she refused my invitation with vehemence."

Elizabeth's eyes blurred, and she stifled a sob. "I never questioned the ease with which he told me that story. How blind I have been!" She choked back her emotions. "But what of those in Meryton. What of the debts he owes the shopkeepers? What happens to them when the militia decamps and departs town?" She grabbed her grandfather's hand. "Lydia, despite her tender age, is enamoured of him and spoke of him incessantly after seeing him in Meryton that day. From what the colonel and Mr. Darcy have told us, he would not think twice about ruining her. Mrs. Bennet indulges her, and she is a spoilt child who will see nothing amiss in her actions. Our respectability would be in tatters. Meanwhile, Lydia would see it as her scheme to be wed before the rest of us—a grand adventure."

"Lizzybeth." Her grandfather knelt before her. "Calm yourself. We shall speak of this further and make arrangements to protect those in Meryton." He lifted her hand that held her brandy. "Take a sip. It will be of aid." A dampness on her cheek made her sweep a tear from the corner of her eye. When had she started to cry?

"Miss Elizabeth, pray, do not distress yourself," said Mr. Darcy, standing directly behind her grandfather. "Wickham is a practiced deceiver. You are not the first he has charmed into believing his tales. I have sorted many of the messes he has abandoned over the years. If he has done nothing but tell you a few lies, you should count yourself as fortunate."

She buried her face in her hands and wept. Had she been in love, she could not have been more wretchedly blind. Till this moment, she had never known herself.

Chapter 7

Asudden, cold dampness on Fitzwilliam's cheek made
him straighten with a start. What the—?

"Good morning, Darcy," said Richard standing
beside him with a glass of what appeared to be water.

After a glance about the room, he cradled his aching head
in his hands and groaned. He must have fallen asleep on his
desk. He smacked and attempted to lick his dry lips. His mouth
was like cotton wool. With a sway, he belched.

"Darcy?"

Before he could protest, his cousin shoved his face in a pail
while he cast up his accounts. Secluding himself in his study
and drinking had been a mistake—an enormous mistake. He
heaved again and again until he could finally pull himself free
from Richard's grip. "Pray, enough. There is naught left in my
stomach to lose."

Richard handed the bucket to Jameson, his valet, with a
crooked grin. "I have not seen you this ill from a night of
drinking in some time. You had two glasses of brandy at
Richmond House. I should have known when you shut
yourself in here upon our arrival you would put yourself in
your cups, yet you do so rarely overindulge. How much did you
drink?"

"I am not certain. A few glasses of port and another two of
brandy I think." He pressed his hand to his stomach. Just the
mention of it made his stomach revolt.

"Miss Elizabeth has you at sixes and sevens, Cousin."

He rubbed his throbbing head. "Coffee. I require coffee
and toast."

"Perhaps some willow bark?" asked Jameson. "It may be of
aid."

"If the coffee and toast do not settle my stomach and help with this head, then I shall try it. You know I detest the flavour."

"'Tis better than laudanum, sir."

As soon as his valet departed, Richard opened a window. "The air of the city is not much of an improvement, but this room is quite stale." He sat in the chair opposite and crossed his ankle over his knee. "If I had known you wished to be in your cups, I would have joined you. You are always an amusing sort when you overindulge."

"Are you enjoying yourself?" His fingers pressed his temples, but that only made the pounding intensify.

"Oh, immensely, Cousin. These moments are so few and far between I must take advantage when I am so privileged to happen upon one."

"You are an ass."

"I have not heard that name in quite some time. I believe you last called me that when I dared you to run naked through the gardens at Pemberley."

He removed his hands from his face. "I must have called you that since. We were but sixteen when that happened, and you *were* an ass. You knew my father was walking the rose garden with Lord and Lady Richmond. I had never before seen my father so angry."

"Yes, well, you never overheard him and Lord Richmond laughing about it a few days later. I was in the library, and they could be heard through the door leading to the study. Apparently, Lady Richmond had turned her head as soon as your bare chest came into view, so she bore witness to nothing more or perhaps the earl would have been more upset. They both recognised it for the prank it was or I would not have been summoned to your father's study to be given my punishment."

"I was made to clean the stables until we returned to school, but I knew naught of any repercussions for you. What punishment did you receive?"

"Do you remember the tenant who broke his leg that spring?"

He nodded, then grabbed the sides of his head. Moving it was a terrible idea. "Yes, that was Mr. Lewis. He was in dire straits as he had ten children to feed, and the eldest four were girls. The boys were not yet old enough to tend his fields."

"I ploughed his fields. The poor man must have been terrified I would not have them ready in time for planting since it took two tries to get the first field right. His wife and daughters helped him sow the seed."

Jameson entered and set a tray on the desk with coffee and toast as well as a smaller pitcher. "I took the liberty of bringing the willow bark, sir. Would you care for a bath?"

He picked up a piece of toast while his cousin nodded with a pinched expression. "I believe I should if my cousin is to be believed. I shall ring you when I am ready."

"Of course, sir."

Once Jameson closed the door behind him, Fitzwilliam relaxed back into his chair. "I always questioned how Mr. Lewis harvested a crop that year. I wonder if my father or Lord Richmond thought of that solution."

"I am not certain. The entire affair seemed sorted by the time he spoke to me. I remember shaking in my boots terrified of being meted some horrific punishment. He told me I was fortunate I had not dared you to jump from the roof or a more dangerous feat, which I would not have done. Wickham would have, but I never considered such a foolhardy scheme.

"So, by your state this morning, I assume you spent the night castigating yourself for your treatment of Miss Elizabeth while in Hertfordshire, not to mention leaving that neighbourhood vulnerable to the likes of Wickham. You appeared as though you had been slapped when she began to cry."

"Are you saying I should not feel responsible? While I heard yours and Georgiana's chastisement after Lady Vranes's exhibition, I do not know that I understood how little regard I gave to those of Meryton—to most outside of my friends and family—until last night. I have been unfeeling and arrogant."

"For what it is worth," said Richard after a tip of his head back and forth. "I have told you for the past three years that you have become insufferable. Yet, how many times have I warned you of some scheme to entrap you? I do have some understanding what you have been through, even if I have not experienced it myself, but you made yourself more and more unapproachable. I recall mentioning that you would come to regret your forbidding temper."

"Yes, yes, you were right."

"Well, yes, I was. I am not denying that, but I do not mean to flog you with it."

"No?"

"No. Ladies like Miss Elizabeth and Miss Jane Montford are not in the common way. For whatever reason, Miss Elizabeth's and her sister's connexions were kept secret in Hertfordshire, and you had no reason to think them different than what you have experienced in the past."

Fitzwilliam dropped his head back against the supple leather of his chair and closed his eyes. Perhaps that would be of aid to his aching head. "Except they *are* different, it seems, and I allowed my pride to rule my heart. Last night, I sought to be in Miss Elizabeth's company. Despite the initial shock of her presence, I was as you said—relieved she was acceptable. I had offered my apologies, she had claimed to have forgiven me, so I believed naught amiss in pursuing her. My father would be ashamed of me."

"Have you ever spoken to my father of his days as a young man? He and your father had similar experiences to you and my brother. They were pursued just as vigorously. I believe your father would understand, but at the same time, he would hope you learn from your mistakes."

"What have I to learn but that I am insufferable?" He groaned. "You saw me last night, bestowing those nosegays to the ladies as though I had every hope in the world. Can you imagine how she must have felt? If she knew the meaning as Georgiana did, no doubt, I shocked her to her core. I do not deserve her."

Richard chuckled and shook his head. "I do not believe I have ever witnessed such a profound case of self-pity. What was it your father always said of Lady Anne? 'She is the loveliest of ladies, and I endeavour every day to be worthy of her.' Perhaps you should adopt your father's philosophy."

He lifted his head and swallowed, closing his eyes with the motion then reopening them. The toast had helped settle his stomach a little, but not completely. "I do remember my father speaking so. My mother would simply smile and call him a sentimental fool."

"You and your father are not so dissimilar. Talk to Lord Richmond. He will certainly have a host of stories to tell you of your father's experiences, not to mention, some notion of his granddaughter's feelings."

"At the exhibition, he had all but given me his blessing, but after last night, he has surely changed his opinion." How could he blame him? If a suitor treated Georgiana thus—well, that thought was what made him forgo the Port and pour that first glass of brandy.

"He gave no reprimand at Lady Vranes's because you were in company, but he knows you are an excellent man who has struggled to deal with Pemberley, Georgiana, and all that was heaped upon you when your father died. Do not assume he has been so capricious over what occurred last night. Wickham is a tricky bastard. After Ramsgate, you could not act without discretion lest Georgiana's reputation be called into question. The earl, Hatton, and Miss Elizabeth surely recognise that."

"You were appalled I never exposed him."

"Yes, but you could have sent word to me. If he is in the militia, a well-placed order or a word with his colonel could have him moved to a more remote location. He would not have known you were involved, and the people of Meryton would be safe."

"He would not be ignorant of the possibility you arranged it."

"I suppose he is clever enough for that."

"He would also wreak havoc wherever he was moved."

"That would depend on the colonel. I know a couple who could keep a tight grip on his reins. He would have little to no freedoms from his duties to create mischief. Whether Miss Elizabeth returns to Hertfordshire or not, we should consider the best way to remove him. Her sisters are at risk, and she would not want them to be injured." Richard was correct—again. Perhaps Lord Richmond would have some thoughts on the best method.

"Darcy, Miss Elizabeth would be quite fortunate if you single her out. Obviously, she has captured your heart, else you would not berate yourself as you are. If you have feelings for her, then do not hesitate to court her. You do require a wife."

Fitzwilliam shook his head. "No—"

"We all make mistakes. That you recognise yours and feel guilt is admirable. Do not make things so cut and dry. You make mistakes as does every man, woman, and child. You have made your apologies. Make them again if you feel it necessary and endeavour to be worthy of her as your father did your mother. Goodness knows she is the first to attract your attention, and who knows when another may come along who creates this much upheaval?" Richard chuckled at his own joke. "That must have some meaning, do you not think?"

He swallowed a sip of coffee and breathed. "You make this sound so simple."

"Do I? I am not certain how. You still need to win your lady fair. If she is disposed to think ill of you, you may have some difficulty there."

"I do not know how she feels. She was agreeable enough at the exhibition as well as last night. I apologised, and she accepted. That was before she enquired of Wickham, of course."

"Well, there is half the battle won already."

He sighed and scratched a tiny dent in the top of his desk with his nail. Was half the battle won? When he had noticed Miss Elizabeth at the exhibition, his heart had leapt in his chest. He had wanted her desperately before departing Hertfordshire, and nothing had changed except her circumstances. He could not be blind to that.

Even had she not been with Lord and Lady Richmond, he would have remained by her side for as long as she would have allowed it. Yes, he wanted her—he needed her, but that meant he needed to further redeem himself in her eyes, but how? He did not deserve her, but perhaps his father had the right of it: he may not deserve her, but he could endeavour to be worthy of her every day of his life.

"You should also consider that another gentleman will not overlook her connexions. He may enjoy her company and think her handsome, but her relation to Lord Richmond will not be unknown to him and *will* have bearing upon his decision. You can provide her with felicity in marriage. Of that, I am certain. If she is all you claim, does she not deserve a love match?"

Nicholas walked into the library and dropped next to Elizabeth on the settee. "You are down early for a Sunday."

"I slept poorly and had no wish to continue staring at the canopy. What of you? Since when do you rise with the sun?"

"Since I began riding out at Richmond with the steward some mornings. Grandpapa was pleased I wished to take the responsibility. He and Grandmamma now take a walk every morning down and around the lake."

"I am certain my grandmother enjoys having more of his time."

He nudged her with his shoulder. "I have been meaning to ask you since the exhibition: why did you not tell us Darcy was the gentleman who insulted you?"

With a groan, she placed a scrap of ribbon in her book and closed it with a snap. "Because if you were acquainted with him, I knew this would happen. I also had no desire to suffer your wit. Amelia's laughter was enough. You found humour in that I was called tolerable. Why would I suffer the indignity of telling you who said it?"

He chuckled and propped his elbow on the back of the settee, his head propped on his hand. "I have teased you often since we were children, but have I ever made light of your appearance?"

"Yes," she said, turning to face him. "I seem to recall you saying I had the nose of a squirrel. I was fourteen."

"Squirrels are not ugly, Lils. I was so confused as to why you were insulted. Grandpapa was as well."

"You meant that to be a compliment?" She lifted her one eyebrow.

"No, not necessarily. You kept twitching and rubbing your nose."

"You blew a dandelion in my face."

He frowned and blinked a couple of times before a curve spread across his lips. "I had forgotten about that. Still, would you have preferred a mouse or a rabbit?"

She shook her head. "You are nonsensical. What has this to do with not telling you of Mr. Darcy?"

"I do not know," he said with a laugh.

"Amelia said you are friends with him. You are a few years younger. How did that come to be?"

"He is seven and twenty, and I am four and twenty, so not too great a difference. Darcy and I were acquainted through his father's and grandfather's friendship with Grandpapa, not to mention he and I crossed paths at Eton and Oxford. Most of my friends were of his circles until he finished his studies and returned to Pemberley. His father died not long after. He assumed his place as master and as guardian of his much younger sister. If you judged him based on his quiet and staid demeanour, you must know he is more responsible than most his age. He does not enjoy the card rooms or often drink to excess. He is also one of the most dependable and loyal of friends."

"Would you call an unknown lady tolerable but not handsome enough to tempt you?"

He chuckled, then coughed and stifled his grin. "No, but I *have* ignored ladies vying for my attention at balls and other events. Just last night, I slipped through the crowd to avoid a Mama who was heading in my direction."

"Was she the same one conspiring to obtain an introduction to Mr. Darcy?"

"She wore a green gown with so much lace she resembled a meringue?"

Elizabeth held up a finger. "I thought it similar to one of Mama's confections. 'A gown is not completed until it is decorated with enough lace to be the envy of your neighbours.'" She used the shrill tone Mama often used when lecturing her.

"Heaven forbid the seamstress miss one inch!" he said with this hand to his chest and finishing with this mouth agape. "What did you think of Darcy's behaviour last night?"

"He was all that was agreeable and amiable. I admit I feel guilty for enquiring of Mr. Wickham after the reactions to the mere mention of the man's name. Poor Mr. Darcy for the censure he received from all three of you, and poor Miss Darcy for what she endured." She gave him a side-long look. "Are you hoping I shall set my cap at him?"

Nicholas lifted his head from his hand and shook it. "No, I do not mean for you to change your opinion of him with such haste." She arched her eyebrow again. "Well, I suppose I do hope you will come to like him but not necessarily for marriage, though he needs a strong lady who can stand up to him and help him. Pemberley is a great estate, and he has spent the years since his father's death learning to manage it. We have attempted to be of as much aid to him as possible since that day. His experience makes me appreciate every moment I can spend with grandfather, learning from him. I do not anticipate the day I become earl any more than I look upon the day I became a viscount with fondness, yet when the time comes, I shall be more prepared than Darcy was."

"You speak of him as though he can do no wrong."

Nicholas grinned with a slight bark. "No, Darcy can do wrong. His behaviour in Hertfordshire is proof of it. He is not perfect. After all, there can be only one of me."

"Thank heavens for that," said Lizzy with a roll of her eyes.

Chapter 8

Darcy lifted the knocker and rapped against the door of Richmond House, then tapped his foot in a fast, staccato rhythm while he waited.

"Good morning, Mr. Darcy," said Mr. Gideon when he opened the door. "I am afraid the family is at church this morning. May I pass along a message to the earl or Lord Hatton?"

Sunday! Of course, it was Sunday. He should have known. How could he have become so caught up in his own thoughts that he had completely overlooked the day? "No, thank you. I wished to assure myself Miss Elizabeth was well this morning, but if she attended church, I am certain she—"

"Good morning, Mr. Darcy." His head jolted to Miss Elizabeth who stood near the bottom of the stairs.

"You did not go to church." Why had he stated the obvious?

"No, I slept poorly, so my grandparents allowed me to remain behind. If you should like to talk, I can call for tea...or coffee if you prefer." She gestured towards the drawing room, and his traitorous legs followed of their own volition.

"Mr. Darcy, I can take your coat and hat," said Mr. Gideon, making him need to turn back for a moment before joining Miss Elizabeth.

After she rang and requested coffee, she offered him a seat by the fire and took the chair across from him, folding her hands in her lap. Her eyes were a little puffy, but their vivid blue still stood out against her ivory skin and black hair. "It is kind of you to call," she said in a soft voice.

"You were beside yourself last night, and I could not allow you to shoulder any blame for your belief of Wickham's lies.

He is quite practised at the art; I assure you." A rustling of skirts drew his attention to a servant entering the room.

"I see Mr. Gideon requested Tate join us," said Miss Elizabeth with a crooked curve of her lips. "Tate is my abigail."

He should not be surprised a chaperon would arrive. This was not Longbourn, but Richmond House, and did not Hatton mention that the butler was protective of the ladies? "His consideration does him credit."

"Mr. Gideon has been a butler here since I was very young. He helped me with my French and taught me much of Africa, where he is from. The entire family is fond of him, and he has always treated us as he would his own family. We are blessed to have him."

A maid delivered the tray of coffee and biscuits, and Miss Elizabeth served him, her graceful fingers inadvertently touching his then retreating with haste when she passed him his cup.

"I enjoyed meeting your sister. Would you mind if I called on her this week?"

"You would be most welcome to call." His body came to life at the idea of Miss Elizabeth in his house—sitting in his drawing room or joining Georgiana at the pianoforte. She would be a welcome sight indeed! What was he doing? He needed to bring himself under regulation before he embarrassed himself before her. "I am certain Georgiana would be overjoyed to welcome you. She spoke of naught but you and your sister for the entire walk to Darcy House last night."

"Walk? Are you so close?"

"I am eight houses down in the direction of Hyde Park Corner." The proximity to Richmond House was why, after his head ceased that infernal throbbing, he had not thought twice about hastening down to ensure himself Miss Elizabeth's state had improved. He could kick himself for upsetting her as he had.

He cleared his throat and shifted in his seat. "I plan to journey to Hertfordshire tomorrow to speak to Colonel Forster. Should I inform the colonel of Wickham's history, I am hopeful he can prevent him from committing too much harm."

"What of Miss Darcy's reputation? You cannot risk him speaking of Ramsgate." Her wide eyes and the way her hand paused in lifting her cup spoke of her concern. She was too good.

"I shall not take any chances. I assure you."

She set her cup on the table beside her. "Grandfather has spoken of journeying to Hertfordshire for business. The two of you could travel together. An earl expressing his concern over Mr. Wickham's vicious propensities may be of aid in keeping him from causing further mischief."

"I was unaware your grandfather intended to go to Meryton."

"I suppose since our families are so close, I have no need to dissemble." With a sigh, she crossed her arms over her chest. "My grandfather is not best pleased with my father, and Jane and I are to remain with my grandparents."

"You will not return to Longbourn?"

She shook her head. "My father is permitted to visit us here at Richmond House or, after we quit London, at Richmond Castle, but we shall not return to Meryton."

Heavens! What must have occurred for the earl to take such an action? "I am sorry to hear there has been such difficulty that your grandfather believes your removal necessary."

"I do believe your suggestion regarding Wickham has merit. I shall consult with Lord Richmond this afternoon."

After glancing at the clock, her arms relaxed, and she retrieved her coffee from the side table. "If you remain for about ten minutes, you may speak to him yourself. Grandpapa rushes Gran to the carriage after the service since he does not care to linger. They shall not be much longer."

Miss Elizabeth was inviting him to wait with her for the earl. Her invitation was one he could no more refuse than he could cut off his own foot. "I am sorry for distressing you so last night. My sister was disappointed in me when I told her of the assembly, and my cousin chastised me for my arrogance. I do heartily regret what I said."

"I should like us to remember the past as it gives us pleasure, which means I should like us to begin again if you agree."

His knee bounced, so he pressed his hand upon his thigh to stop the motion. Given their past, beginning again would be ideal. "Would I be permitted to call on you?" There, he had said it. Now, he need only pray she say yes.

"You wish to call on me?" Her tone was higher. Had he surprised her? Had she not understood the roses? Georgiana had been certain she would be flattered.

"Yes, I should like to," he said with a jerky nod.

"Why?"

He sucked in a large breath. He should have expected her to ask. Once he cleared his throat, he tugged at his collar. Had the room warmed since he entered? "Despite what I said at the assembly, I find you more than tolerable. I actually consider you one of the handsomest ladies of my acquaintance."

The cup rattled on Miss Elizabeth's saucer. "I beg your pardon." Her eyes were wide, and she stared at him with her face turned away a bit.

"If you recall, I asked you to dance at Lucas Lodge and at Netherfield. I singled out no other lady from the neighbourhood."

She stiffened and tilted her head. "You stared at me to find fault."

His head hitched back. To find fault? Could she truly mean that? "I had not known I was staring so, but no, not to find fault—certainly not to find fault."

"So, the nosegay of roses yesterday...the meaning...was..." Blast! Perhaps he should not have listened to Georgiana's advice on the roses. What did a sixteen-year-old know of courtship? She read gothic romances and, at the insistence of her companion, Shakespeare. Shakespeare was not romantic. Either the heroes met a horrible end or their relationship was meant as a comedy. He had no wish for either.

He scratched his cheek then ran his fingers through his hair. "I had not meant to cause you a shock, but yes, Georgiana was of great aid, ensuring the roses were appropriate for each lady. Yours were meant to hint at my feelings."

"Your feelings," she said softly. "With all that you told me in my grandfather's study, I had not given what my grandmother told me about the roses further thought until now."

"I—"

A commotion filtered in from the hall, and Miss Elizabeth glanced at him before she set down her cup and rose. No more than a moment passed before her grandmother entered and, without a pause, clasped her hands in front of her. "Fitzwilliam? Were we expecting you this morning?"

"No, Lady Richmond." He stood and joined his hands behind his back. "I had forgotten the day and had called to speak to the earl. Miss Elizabeth has been kind enough to offer me refreshment until your return."

"Excellent," said Lord Richmond as he entered with Hatton just behind him. "I heard you say you desired a word. We have breakfast after church on Sundays. You should join us. We can talk after." He offered Miss Elizabeth his arm, motioning for Darcy to follow them to the breakfast room.

"The children have the same seats they have had for years," said Lady Richmond, "but we do not stand on ceremony for most family meals. Pray, sit where you like."

Every muscle in his body leapt at the empty seat beside Miss Elizabeth. "May I?"

"Of course. I do not require an extra chair this morning." Her crystalline eyes sparkled, and she possessed an alluring curve of her lips. Thankfully, with the arrival of her family, she did not appear so uneasy with his company, but she had not answered his request to call. What if she refused him? Before yesterday, he would not have considered such an eventuality. Richard would say he had exhibited another side of his arrogance.

"I never had the opportunity to thank you for the roses, Mr. Darcy," said Miss Jane Montford. "They are lovely. Your sister said they came from your hothouse?"

"Yes. When my grandfather had Darcy House built, the parcel of land was large enough for a hothouse. We have a couple of small citrus trees, herbs, and Georgiana keeps several varieties of roses so we have fresh flowers in the house during the winter. I am certain my sister would be pleased to show you should you wish to see it, Miss Montford."

Miss Amelia Montford giggled and covered her mouth with her hand for a moment. "Oh, how odd. Even though he spoke to you, Janey, I startled at my name. Mr. Darcy, I must insist you address us as younger sisters lest we never know to whom you are speaking. I shall not be offended at being addressed as Miss Amelia. What of you, Jane?"

"I agree. Under the circumstances, I should prefer the simplicity," said the other Miss Montford. "You must call me Miss Jane else we will have a great deal of confusion."

He nodded. "The confusion will be less on my part as well. I thank you."

"So, Fitzwilliam, now that is settled, does your dear younger sister have any roses to spare?" asked Lady Richmond. "Four nosegays must have taken a good number."

He peeked at Miss Elizabeth. "When I told her of my plan, she insisted. She was happy to make the sacrifice."

The food was placed in the centre of the table, and Miss Elizabeth started with the sausages, taking one, and holding the serving dish in his direction. "Mr. Darcy?"

"Thank you." He wrapped his hands under the plate, but his fingers covered hers and the dish tipped. Miss Elizabeth gasped, and he grabbed the edge, righting it before any of the food fell to the floor.

"Well done, Darcy," said Hatton.

"How clumsy of me." Miss Elizabeth turned to face the table, the cheek facing him as red as a beetroot.

"I am certain it was my fault."

"Do you remember when Lizzy broke the jar of black butter on Grandmamma's best tablecloth?" said Miss Amelia with a giggle.

Miss Jane grinned. "Mama once insisted Lizzy help Hill bring dinner up from the kitchens. As she was entering the dining room from the servants' entrance, she tripped on a loose floorboard, which sent the gravy flying over the table and splattering Mama and Lydia. I shall never forget the expressions upon their countenances." She gave this exaggerated gasp.

With a whimper, Miss Elizabeth covered her face while Nicholas and Miss Amelia burst into laughter. Lord and Lady Richmond peered at Miss Elizabeth but showed no hint of amusement. "I was sent to my room and had to wash Mama's and Lydia's gowns if you remember, Jane," she said.

"I thought Hill or Tate scrubbed them for you."

"No." She shook her head. "Mama insisted Hill was needed upstairs, and Tate was sent to Meryton on an errand. Though, Lydia's reaction at the gravy covering her face was worth the chapped hands." A slight smile broke through the serious set of her mouth before she lifted her hands and gasped, seemingly mimicking Miss Lydia at that moment. "Since you brought up that debacle, perhaps I should mention when you sneaked into Mama's room to use her perfume and spilled it all over her dresser."

"Lizzy!" Miss Jane covered her mouth with her hands.

"Do you remember who you blamed?"

"Wait! She told a falsehood to cover her misdeed?" asked Nicholas loudly and with no little surprise.

"She did. You see, Mama had a preference for a white barn cat she named Miss Petunia. Well, Miss Petunia was sleeping in Mama's bedroom window when she discovered the spilt perfume, so guess who Jane incriminated?"

"Oh! Do not remind me!" Miss Jane shook her head. "I felt so guilty. Poor Miss Petunia was never allowed upstairs in the house again, and she would cry at the door to the kitchens, begging to come in."

"Did you ever confess the truth?" asked Darcy.

"After two days, I could take no more and told Mama the whole of it, but she refused to believe me. For the rest of Miss

Petunia's life, I allowed her in my bedchamber at night. She was the sweetest cat, and I wronged her in the worst of ways. It was the last time I lied."

Lady Richmond tsked. "Mrs. Bennet never discovered her?"

Miss Elizabeth held a finger in the air. "Jane has an old oak tree beside her window and a large limb was close enough for Miss Petunia to come and go as she pleased."

"Eventually, she stopped waiting at the stairs, and I would find her outside the window."

As a much older brother, he had no similar experiences but had oft times wondered what it was like to have siblings closer to his age. Despite Miss Amelia and Hatton being cousins to Miss Jane and Miss Elizabeth, they acted much as Richard behaved with him or his own sisters and brothers. He would wish his children to have these sorts of happy experiences—children with ebony curls and a teasing smile—but first, he had to prove himself to the lady, should the lady see fit to allow his calls.

The moment Mr. Darcy disappeared through the door behind her grandfather and Nicholas, Elizabeth let out a heavy breath and let her shoulders drop. He had requested to call. *He had requested to call.* How was she to respond? Before meeting him again in London, she had not desired to spend time with him if she could avoid the imposition. Now that she had learnt more of him, what did she want?

"Lizzybeth?" asked Grandmamma, sitting down beside her. "Do you know the reason for Mr. Darcy's call this morning?" She glanced about the room. Where had Amelia and Jane gone? "Lizzybeth?"

"Initially, he wished to ensure I was well after last night."

Her grandmother let out a "Hmph. When your grandfather informed me of what occurred in his study, I told him he should not have pressed so, but he never listens. That man is as obstinate as a mule when an idea gets into his thick skull."

"No, Gran, what was said needed to be revealed. I was foolish and let Mr. Darcy's insult influence my judgement. It was a lesson I needed to learn. Being so quick to judge is a fault I should seek to change."

"You must admit, it was kind of Mr. Darcy to come." Her grandmother leaned forward to catch her eye.

"I agree." She concentrated on her fingers fidgeting as though they were a book that was impossible to put down.

"Lizzy, I shooed Janey and Amelia away because while you were as open as always with your sister and cousins, you almost dropped a plate of sausages when I assume Mr. Darcy touched your hand. The two of you have had nothing but misunderstandings since you first met, and I know the meaning of his roses came as a shock—"

"That is an understatement. I meet him again in London, and he apologises for the remark at the assembly, gives me roses saying his heart is aflame, then requests to call—all in a matter of a few days. How am I supposed to respond? I am not sure what to make of what has occurred much less my own feelings."

"He asked to call?"

"Yes, this morning after I offered him coffee." She needed to get out of the house. A walk! She could walk in Hyde Park. "I believe I should like to take a walk through the park."

"Dearest, have you looked outside? It had just started raining when we arrived home from church. You would catch your death in the cold and damp."

She hurried to the window and bit back a groan. Not only was it raining, but a light fog had rolled in. Even if she insisted upon going, no footman or maid would agree to accompany her.

"My, you are beside yourself." Her grandmother turned her around by her elbow. "If you are unsure of your answer, then tell him. If you want, your grandfather can speak to him. We have not meant to burden you by promoting him, but your grandfather and I agree that he would be an excellent match for you. Should you find another suitor you would prefer, of course, we shall not stand in your way, but you require a gentleman who will challenge you and make you see reason when you adamantly refuse. Do remember that granting a gentleman permission to call is not tantamount to an acceptance of his hand. If he calls and you do not suit, you both can choose to become friends and go on to pursue other prospects."

Elizabeth scraped her teeth along her bottom lip. "I suppose I see your point. When he asked, my mind rushed to think of it as an obligation."

"You will spend much of Christmas at the same dinners and parties. Become further acquainted and listen to your heart—it will tell you if he is meant to be your friend or your husband. Those feelings are vastly different, and the latter, in most cases, press to be recognised, though I have known a few people where they were caught unawares by their own feelings. You, however, are too open not to notice."

"Did you know right away that Grandpapa was your match?"

Gran almost giggled and waved her hand in a dismissive fashion. "Oh, that man. He was the most infuriating gentleman I had ever met, but he could make my heart beat so fast I thought it would burst from my chest." She leaned against Elizabeth's shoulder with her own. "He still can." Her weathered fingers tucked a curl away from Elizabeth's face. "Do not worry about what is to come. Our hearts tell us what to do and who we love. We just have to listen."

Chapter 9

The familiar shops of Meryton and the assembly rooms passed and faded away as Lord Richmond's carriage passed through the small market town, a number of people turning and watching the expensive carriage as it drove through.

When they took the fork in the road that would take them to Longbourn, Lord Richmond gave a low growl and shifted in his seat. "I do not anticipate this, but I see no other alternative."

"You know this is the best course," said Hatton. "I have questioned why they remained at Longbourn for years."

The earl lifted his bushy eyebrows. "You never said."

Hatton shrugged one shoulder. "I trust your judgement, even if I felt the choice here was clouded by your affection for my aunt."

"Forgive us," said Lord Richmond to Darcy, who had joined them for the journey. "I suppose this seems as though we are speaking in riddles."

Darcy closed his pocket watch and returned it to his pocket. "Miss Elizabeth mentioned she and her sister would be residing with you in the future. I know no more, but obviously, you need not justify your decisions to me."

The earl sniffed. "I have naught to hide. In fact, I would see your presence when we confront Bennet as a benefit. You witnessed the impropriety of his family sans my granddaughters, of course. Mr. Bingley's changeable nature is well known to you as is the characters of his sisters. Your testimony could be useful if needed."

He frowned and straightened his cuffs. They would be alighting soon. "I was unaware Bingley was a factor in your decision." What could Bingley have done to offend Lord Richmond?

"Come," said Hatton. "I know he is your friend, but surely, you know of his propensity to fall in and out of love. Can you assure us his infatuation with our Janey was or is more than a whim on his part? And, if he was to be serious in his attachment, what of his sisters? It is known Mr. Hurst and his wife live in Bingley's London home, and the sisters rule the roost. Janey is too complacent and believes in the good of everyone. His sisters are manipulative enough to use the connection to us to their advantage while making Janey's life a misery. You would not allow Miss Darcy to be used so, and we cannot allow it either."

He looked at the passing forest. They were right. When Bingley had been needed for business in London, his sisters departed Netherfield with the intention of keeping their brother in London indefinitely. As soon as they learnt of Miss Jane's connexions, they would be salivating for the match, but they would reduce her role from mistress of the house to no more than a bragging piece—a method to gain invitations to more exclusive events. His gaze met Hatton's. "I understand." How would he tell Bingley when the time came? Bingley would see Miss Jane at an event at some point. He did not relish the idea of that conversation.

Lord Richmond's voice brought him back to the conversation at hand. "You should know Lizzy claims Miss Bingley has hinted at a match between her brother and your sister."

His entire body gave a start. "I beg your pardon? She mentioned this to Miss Elizabeth?" When would Miss Bingley have had the opportunity or the gall to do so?

"She sent a letter to Janey the morning they departed Netherfield. In it, she said they were particularly excited to be in Miss Darcy's company again, and how could they not hope for a union that would bring happiness to so many? If she wrote the truth of her feelings, his union with Georgiana would also bring her closer to the possibility of marrying you."

"Blast! That woman is a menace." How many times had he insisted to Bingley that he would never consider Miss Bingley? Bingley would chuckle and nod and say the same thing every time. "I could tell her as much again, but she will never listen." Had Bingley even told her the first time? Probably not.

"I must admit relief to hearing that from you," said Lord Richmond. "My wife has overheard Miss Bingley at parties, speaking of your close association with her family. She implies enough to cause gossip. Thus far, we have yet to hear a serious rumour and all who speak of it seem to believe her to be suffering from delusions. Ah, here we are."

When he turned back to the window, they had just pulled up to the front of Longbourn. A servant placed the step and opened the door, allowing the men to alight. The door opened and the housekeeper stepped onto the portico and dropped a curtsey. "Lord Richmond, 'tis good to see you, my lord."

"Mrs. Hill, I have come to speak to Mr. Bennet. Is he inside?"

"He is in his library as is his wont most days."

"Thank you, Mrs. Hill. A cart will arrive soon. If you still wish to leave, you and your husband may pack your trunks and journey to Richmond House. You will be made comfortable there until arrangements can be made for your return to Yorkshire."

The woman's eyes became shiny with tears. "Thank you, my lord. We are exceedingly grateful for your generosity."

The earl placed a hand upon the Mrs. Hill's shoulder. "You have been loyal and trustworthy to me and my granddaughters, and you will always be cared for by us. My steward has seen to a cottage on the grounds of the castle where you are free to live for the rest of your days as a reward for your excellent service. Should your husband wish it, he is welcome to work with the horses since he has a way with them. We would never turn away the help of a man with his skill." Mrs. Hill grasped Lord Richmond's hand and kissed it before bustling back inside the house. Darcy would do no less for a servant who was as much of an asset to his household, so the earl's generosity was not surprising. Lord Richmond and his father had both taught him to appreciate and care for those in his employ, particularly those who were as faithful as Mrs. Hill seemed to be.

"Come. We must see Bennet."

Darcy tamped down the disquiet in his gut. "Are you certain you desire my presence?" What if he only inflamed the situation? That would not be of aid to anyone.

Without a servant, Lord Richmond walked through the hall and down a corridor that ran alongside the staircase. Loud giggles and Mrs. Bennet's strident voice came from the drawing room, making him wince. The earl opened the last door on the left and stepped inside. "Good morning, Bennet."

The master of the house looked up from the book he was reading and stiffened. "How did you come to be here? Where is Hill?"

The earl stopped in front of Mr. Bennet's desk and clasped his arms behind his back. "Did you expect my own servant to bar my entrance to this house?"

"*Your* servant, sir? She has been in my employ since the housekeeper quit after my wife died. I had no need of an abigail in this home, and she required employment. Should I have turned her out?"

"So, instead, you offered her a pittance of a salary to become housekeeper. Yes, I know it all. Mrs. Hill, being broken-hearted over Sophie's death, refused to let you drink yourself into an early grave and remained in the hopes of saving you—for Sophie and for the sake of your children. When Lizzybeth and Janey returned to this home, I asked her to remain and be my eyes and ears in this house, which she has done faithfully since. She has been paid handsomely for remaining and putting up with your wife and her nervous complaints."

Mr. Bennet's countenance became pinched, and his lips pressed together. When he opened his mouth, his eyes darted behind the earl to Nicholas and Darcy. "Why are they here?"

Lord Richmond cleared his throat and adjusted his shoulders. "It has come to my attention that your wife has been seeking suitors for Janey and Lizzybeth—and inappropriate ones at that."

"I see no issue with that Bingley fellow. He may be a bit too cheerful for my tastes, but he suits Jane. Besides, once my wife has an idea in her head, only a strong blow could remove it. I prefer not to bother, though I did make an exception for Lizzy. She is a great deal too good for Mr. Collins."

"Yet you allowed your wife to push the match until Lizzy was forced to refuse an unwanted proposal as well as your wife's attempts to force her acceptance," said Nicholas, his eyes hard.

"Why should I rob myself of the amusement? The little toad pursuing Lizzy when she found him ridiculous was comical."

Darcy stepped further into the room as he stiffened and clenched his hands into tight fists. "You found entertainment in your daughter's unease?" The growl that had come from him made him pause. He had that same voice when he dealt with Wickham. Was Mr. Bennet as horrible as Wickham?

With a lift of his eyebrows, Mr. Bennet looked between him and Lord Richmond. "I should have known the two of you would be acquainted; although, why he should care for Lizzy's comfort is beyond me? He insulted her at the assembly, and all in Meryton know they both heartily dislike each other. You have no business here, Mr. Darcy. You may leave. Go. For you are not wanted in this house."

"I requested his presence, and he has made amends with Lizzybeth. They have spent a couple of evenings in company together. Darcy even introduced his sister to your daughters and gave them both nosegays at dinner two nights ago."

"Janey," said Mr. Bennet, shooting to his feet. "She is supposed to be at the Gardiners. Why would she be at Richmond House?"

"I came here to inform you that due to your lack of care or concern over the fate of my granddaughters, I have taken custody of them. They will remain with me until they find suitable gentlemen."

"And should they never wed, they will never want for a home. They will be welcome to remain in mine, or I will establish a household for them should they wish it." Hatton stepped beside his grandfather while he spoke, towering over Mr. Bennet, who remained behind his desk.

"This is preposterous! You cannot object to a gentleman of five thousand a year."

Hatton scoffed. "A man who constantly falls in and out of love and allows his sisters to lead him around by his nose. Miss

Bingley and Mrs. Hurst do not want Jane Bennet to marry their brother. Why do you think they no longer reside at Netherfield?"

"He speaks the truth," said Darcy. "Since Miss Bingley has no knowledge of Miss Bennet's connexion to the Richmond earldom, she has belittled your estate, your daughters, and your wife's family. She spoke of little else after your daughter dined with them. They then complained bitterly at being made to house both of your daughters while Miss Bennet was ill." While her name was no longer Miss Bennet, Mr. Bennet could become more incensed if he referred to her as Miss Montford. Perhaps it was better to take heed of that possibility.

"Did Bennet visit his daughter while she was ill at Netherfield?" asked the earl.

"No." He pulled his shoulders back and released them in the hopes of relieving some tension in his neck. "Mrs. Bennet came and brought the three younger daughters who are not yet out. She proclaimed Miss Bennet too ill to be moved, then stayed for tea while complimenting Bingley and the house at every opportunity. Poor Miss Elizabeth was visibly embarrassed, though she attempted to disguise it. The youngest then cajoled Bingley to give a ball, even though she is too young to attend such an event."

The earl shook his head. "If your wife's greatest fear is supporting your daughters after your death, I am happy to relieve her of the eldest two. They should not be victims of your lack of foresight and lackadaisical manner towards your family's situation and eventual fate. I will not stand aside and allow what occurs in this household to take its toll on my granddaughters."

Mr. Bennet's nostrils flared, and his complexion was turning redder by the moment. He slammed his fist on the desk and stood. "You have no right! When you return to London, you had best have them prepare to travel for I shall be reclaiming them."

With a step forward, Lord Richmond placed a finger upon the desk. "Do not forget, Bennet, that Janey and Lizzybeth became my wards after Sophie's death. You wallowed in your misery in drink. When each of Mrs. Bennet's daughters were born, you sent Lizzybeth and Janey to us, then left them for six months to a year. We never complained, but you have shown a willingness to abandon your daughters at your wife's whim. As it stands, you have no claim to them and have not had one for most of their lives.

"Aside from the situations with Collins and Bingley, I long ago received word of your wife's dislike and disregard for Lizzybeth, but I thought of Sophie and how she would hate for me to remove them from Longbourn, from you. After hearing of that imbecile Collins's proposal—and from Darcy's description as well as that of Lizzybeth, I can call him an imbecile—and your wife's insistence of Janey following Mr. Bingley to London, I can no longer turn my back on them. My love for my daughter and granddaughters will not allow me to ignore what is happening in this house. Mr. and Mrs. Hill are resigning their positions with you. They have likely already loaded their trunks onto one of my carriages and departed for London.

"I must also warn you that my financial aid to your household is now at an end. Since the girls returned, I have provided funds for their educations. My money has, no doubt, gone to fulfil more of your wife's desires than my granddaughter's needs. You will no longer receive a single farthing from me. Good day, Bennet."

"Now, see here—"

Darcy required no further invitation to depart Longbourn. While he understood why the earl wished his presence, he did not want to remain any longer than necessary. Before he could reach the hall, the door to the drawing room burst open and Miss Lydia stumbled through, her raucous giggles echoing off the walls.

"Mr. Darcy! What are you doing here?"

"Darcy? Where?"

His teeth ground together as his jaw clenched and released. Wickham called on Longbourn? What business would he have here? None of the daughters remaining were yet out. Surely, an easier prey existed in this county than one of the Bennet girls.

"Wickham," said Hatton, almost as if he were happy to see him. "What brings you to Longbourn? There is no fortune to be had, so you must be seeking young ladies to ruin."

"And just who are you?" asked Miss Lydia with a hand to her hip.

Hatton never spared her a glance. "You do know what became of Miss Hattie Miller, do you not?"

Wickham shrugged. "I do not know of whom you are speaking?"

"Mr. Jeremiah Miller was two years behind you at Oxford. While his family visited one weekend, you somehow managed to seduce his younger sister. She died in childbirth."

"Since I do not know her, I am certain she had me confused with another gentleman," said Wickham in that tone that never failed to convince all to his claims.

"What of Harriet Bond?" Darcy struggled to grit out the name. "You ruined her without a second thought. They could not bury her in the chapel graveyard with the way she died, but you are well aware since her brother called you out. As I recall, you fled Derbyshire to avoid the duel."

"Why should we believe you?" cried Miss Lydia with Mrs. Bennet nodding at her shoulder.

"Because I have paid his debts and cleaned up his messes since I was old enough to do so. If you think the two ladies we have mentioned are the sum total of his debauchery, then you are mistaken. I know of four of his by-blows that survive. Miss Bond was overwrought at realising she was with child, which was what brought about her death." Miss Lydia and Miss Kitty were far too young, but since Mrs. Bennet thought them old enough to entertain Wickham, why should he refrain from speaking so freely?

"Do not forget your precious sister," said Wickham with a deep chuckle. "You would not want to see her ruined."

"No, he would not." Lord Richmond stepped from behind them and pulled a piece of paper from his coat pocket. "But I doubt those in debtor's prison will care much of your lies."

"Debtor's prison? I owe you nothing, old boy." Wickham dropped the charm in his voice and began speaking like the snake he was.

"Oh, but you do. You see Darcy sold your debts to me, and I intend to see you removed from all polite society." He opened the front door and ushered in four large men. "Pray, put him in the carriage. We shall take him to the camp and inform the colonel, then you will deliver him to whichever debtor's prison will have him, Fleet or Marshalsea. Take your pick. I care not."

Before Wickham could react, the four men grabbed him and threw him into the back of a small carriage while Miss Lydia and Mrs. Bennet clutched their chests and wailed at the injustice. They hurried out and beat at the door of the equipage while one of the men climbed to the top to drive, another climbed onto the back, and the last two rode inside with Wickham, ensuring he was unable to bolt from the door.

Mrs. Bennet's gaze returned to the earl and Hatton, and she sidled forward. "Mr. Bennet did not mention we were entertaining guests."

Lord Richmond never so much as looked at the lady. He glanced back to a gaping Mr. Bennet, nodded to Hatton and Darcy, and led them directly to their own carriage. "Well, I suppose that is the end of that unpleasantness."

"Grandpapa, you said Mr. Bennet was welcome to visit Janey and Lizzy, but after that confrontation, do you truly believe he will?"

"Even without the words we exchanged, I doubt he would exert himself so. He is quite altered from the young man who requested my Sophie's hand in marriage. I liked him then. He loved your aunt beyond reason, and his estate was immaculate and brought in three thousand pounds per annum. In his grief and laziness, he has since let it fall into ruin. My biggest regret is that I did not remove Janey and Lizzybeth sooner."

For the first time since laying eyes on Wickham, Darcy relaxed. "You cannot fault yourself for considering what your daughter would have wanted."

"Why should I not? Janey was treated well enough, but it would have broken her heart to see Lizzybeth disregarded as she was. She deserved better."

He could not argue. If it was up to him, he would give Elizabeth all she desired and more.

Chapter 10

T he chandeliers twinkled and the freshly polished silver gleamed while footmen in their best livery were stationed around the room, some weaving through the crowd carrying trays laden with silver goblets. She was not standing amidst an assembly in Meryton, that was certain.

Elizabeth tugged at the top of her gloves while Jane stood beside her, her pale-yellow gown with its sheer overlay glowing in the candlelight. "Do you think we shall be asked to dance?" she asked, leaning closer to Jane's ear.

"Of course, you will." Her grandmother stood to Elizabeth's other side with her grandfather, Amelia, and Nicholas continuing down the line. "You are granddaughters of the Richmond earldom and Montfords. You will not be snubbed."

Nicholas bent forward so he was seen from the end. "Which means, if no one asks, I shall be sent around the room to persuade my friends to do so."

"I despise when you do that," said Amelia with her nose wrinkled and her lips pinched.

"Ah!" Her grandfather lifted a hand. "I see Darcy and Colonel Fitzwilliam." Grandmamma took his elbow, and he led their party across the ballroom. "Dorset does prefer an overstated affair, does he not?" said Grandpapa while they greeted Mr. Darcy and the colonel with bows and curtseys.

"Do you know what is contained within the goblets?" Elizabeth craned her neck to see over those around her.

"It changes every year," said Nicholas. "Last year, it was champagne. You there!" He waved over a nearby footman with a tray. "What is being served this evening?"

"I have Constantia wine, but the trays vary. Champagne and orange wine are also being served. The punch tables have negus, rum punch, and mulled wine as well."

Nicholas took glasses from the tray and passed them to each of their group, including the colonel and Mr. Darcy. "Thank you, good man." After a slight bow, the footman departed with an empty tray.

After Elizabeth smelled the contents, she swirled the liquid around the glass. "I have never had Constantia wine." She took a small sip, letting the fresh notes of citrus, honeysuckle, and ginger wash over her tongue. "Oh, it is lovely."

"It is also quite dear." Her grandmother took a sip of her own. "And this is a very good vintage."

"How did he acquire enough to serve at a ball?" asked Nicholas.

After swallowing his own taste, Mr. Darcy shrugged. "He likely stored what he could find all year unless he intends to serve the few bottles he has until they are empty. I have tasted it once or twice before but have never purchased any."

"The Prince Regent and the royals snatch it all up before the rest of us can purchase it," said her grandfather. "The shop where I buy my brandy and port has stocked some in the past. The proprietor sets aside a bottle here and there for me from time to time, but I do not open one unless it is a special occasion."

"Miss Elizabeth." Mr. Darcy stepped closer to her side. "May I request a set with you this evening? If you have any free dances remaining, that is."

She smiled. "We just arrived, and I know so few here that I have yet to give away a dance. Which dance would you prefer?"

He fidgeted in his place. "I would be pleased to take the first. May I request a second as well?"

"A second?" She drew her head back a little and arched her eyebrow. "Would that not be gossiped about, sir?"

With a shrug, one side of his lips twitched. "I thought you may prefer to have your supper set reserved. Lord Rutledge is in attendance, and I am certain you do not wish him to claim that set." His eyes held an unusual gleam. He was teasing her!

She covered her mouth to keep from laughing loudly. When she removed it, she wagged her finger at him. "That is not fair, Mr. Darcy. After the exhibition at Lady Vranes's, you know I would do anything to avoid Lord Rutledge's society, so I find myself at a disadvantage, as I do not know *your* weakness."

"I believe you could guess more than one." He turned to Jane. "Miss Jane, if the second is not already spoken for, may I claim that set?"

"You may, sir. The colonel was kind enough to request my first."

"I did," said the colonel, "and I would be pleased to claim Miss Elizabeth's second. Then, I must speak to Miss Amelia before her dances are all taken."

Her grandparents watched the happenings with smiles upon their faces until the ladies' initial dances were spoken for, Amelia having received a request for her first from Sir Anthony Greene, a baronet with an estate in Nottinghamshire.

When the first dance was announced, Mr. Darcy offered his hand, and Elizabeth set hers atop so he could lead her to the line. The music began, and they each honoured their partner before the first steps. "You must forgive me for not saying so earlier, but you look stunning tonight."

She smiled and looked at him over her shoulder as they turned. "This will not do. If we continue, we shall be as Grandmamma once said and begging forgiveness for the entirety of the evening. I do thank you for the pretty compliment. I shall pass along your praises to my maid as well."

The pattern brought her to take a turn with the colonel, who grinned. "I do hope my dour cousin told you how beautiful you are tonight."

"My, you are full of pretty words too. Have you been giving your cousin lessons?"

He gave an amused bark. "That depends. Were they truly pretty or are you being kind and humouring him?"

She returned to Mr. Darcy and could not keep her good cheer from flowing forth. Between the dancing and the amusing conversation, her heart was well satisfied. She was happy. If someone had asked her a fortnight ago whether she would enjoy a dance with Mr. Darcy, she would not have hesitated to scoff at the notion, yet here she was.

"Dare I ask what my cousin said?"

"He simply asked if you complimented my looks tonight. I assured him you had."

He narrowed an eye. "With my cousin, more had to be said."

"I defended your ability to please a lady with your words. Does that suffice?"

His cheeks turned a little pink, and he practically beamed. "Yes, that will do very well. Thank you."

"Now, I have no wish to ruin your good temper this evening, but I know you accompanied Nicholas and my grandfather to Hertfordshire on Monday. As much as I have asked, they will not tell me what occurred. I do not suppose I can convince you to do so." She hated to request the information from him, but her grandfather and Nicholas had been exceedingly stubborn about the whole affair. Why was she to be left in the dark when the whole of the visit concerned the future of her and Jane?

Mr. Darcy glanced about them. "I would prefer not to discuss such happenings at a ball. My sister requested your presence for tea later this week. We could speak of it then, or if the weather is agreeable, we could take a walk in Hyde Park before your visit."

"Either of those schemes will suit, Mr. Darcy. Thank you. May I say how handsome you look this evening?" His countenance had fallen so when she enquired of their trip to Hertfordshire. Why had she felt the need to repair the damage?

He chuckled and after bowing at the end of the dance, stepped forward, much closer than he had been thus far. "I thank you, and I shall pass your compliments on to my valet."

"And will he be satisfied by them? Tate does enjoy hearing of her successes."

With a shrug, he bowed at the beginning of the second dance. "I have never spoken to him of the praise of others. Gentlemen are not like ladies. We do not receive those delicate compliments with the same frequency."

As she walked around him following the pattern of the dance, Miss Bingley stood along the edge of the dance floor, her narrowed eyes glaring at Mr. Darcy. When Elizabeth pivoted around and stepped closer to him, she bent just a little closer. "Miss Bingley is watching you."

He flinched, but his eyes remained trained on her. "I wonder how she secured an invitation. The duke has boasted of the exclusivity of his invitations for years. Bingley's wealth is too new, and he has yet to purchase an estate."

"Could she be an acquaintance of the duchess?"

"No, the duke and duchess are of the same mind. I received an invitation due to my connexions to the Fitzwilliam and Holderness earldoms and the Leeds dukedom, and because Pemberley has been in the Darcy family since William the Conqueror gifted the land to the first Darcy in England. Bingley has no such associations."

She swallowed hard. Her grandfather had mentioned the Fitzwilliams, but he had neglected to mention Mr. Darcy's other connexions or was he unaware? No, he had known the last few generations of Darcys. He had to know.

With this new knowledge, it was no wonder he had attempted to warn her off in Meryton. Miss Elizabeth Bennet had no such titles or fortune in her family to be a suitable match for Mr. Darcy of Pemberley. Without her grandfather and Nicholas, she would be considered beneath him—and that was without Mama's and Lydia's mortifying behaviour. Without taking part in much of her grandfather's world, her view was narrow and short-sighted. She was a simpleton, indeed.

As soon as the dance concluded, she swapped partners with Jane, who drew her close as they passed. "Mr. Bingley is here. Did you see?"

"I did. If he approaches, Grandpapa and Nicholas will speak to him. We can only wait and see what happens." Would Jane welcome Mr. Bingley's attentions after all Nicholas and Mr. Darcy had said? She had been at Richmond House for almost a fortnight. Would their words and the time spent considering their opinions have made for a change? Jane was so tender hearted; it was difficult to be certain.

Darcy frowned while he watched Miss Elizabeth dancing with Sir Anthony. She had been quieter since spotting Miss Bingley in the crowd. Had he made her uncomfortable in some way? Miss Bingley had certainly never intimidated Miss Elizabeth in the past. Why would she do so tonight? No, he must have said or done something to disquiet her, but what could it be?

"I say, Darcy! I did not expect to happen upon you here," said Bingley as he approached. His usual cheerful visage pasted upon his countenance.

"I am surprised at that since Miss Bingley saw me dancing the first set."

His friend started. "She did? Why, she never said a word." He rubbed his cheek as he watched the dancers for a moment. "Perhaps she thought herself mistaken. After all, you never dance the first." There was the biddable and believing Bingley he knew. How had that never irked him before, and why did it suddenly do so this evening?

Bingley's head shifted forward, and he squinted. "I say. Is that Miss Jane Bennet? How did she procure an invitation? If you recall, my sisters claimed the family had no connexions to speak of."

"As it turns out," said Darcy, keeping his voice as even as he could. "She is not Miss Jane Bennet. She is Miss Jane Montford. Her grandfather is Hugh Montford, the Earl of Richmond and her cousin is Nicholas Montford, Viscount Hatton."

"'Tis impossible," said Bingley with a chuckle. "Someone is mistaken or playing a joke on you. Caroline and Louisa would have discovered the tittle tattle of their origins if they were truly so."

"I assure you. I am close friends with the family, and I dined with Lord Richmond's family on Saturday. Miss Montford and Miss Elizabeth are his granddaughters. After their mother's death, they lived with their grandparents. At which time, he changed their surnames to Montford. He has brought them to London for Christmastide, and they are to remain for the Season."

Bingley gave a sort of twitch. "How could no one in the neighbourhood know of the relation?"

He withheld a sigh. Why were Miss Bingley's statements like scripture to her brother? It took entirely too much convincing for him to believe her incorrect. "From what Lord Richmond has told me, his daughter, Lady Sophie, and Mr. Bennet enjoyed withholding the knowledge from their friends and neighbours. They thought it a great joke."

"Mr. Darcy!" Miss Bingley turned to squeeze between two groups, rushing up to attach herself to his arm. "I thought my eyes were deceiving me when you were dancing the first, but you *are* here."

"I was not aware you were acquainted with the Duke of Dorset," said Darcy.

"Oh, I am not. My brother managed to be invited as a guest of his daughter, Lady Jemima."

"Lady Jemima?" What was Bingley thinking? The duke would never give consent to that union, and if Bingley somehow affected her reputation, the duke would not think twice about ruining him.

"We met at a musicale after our return to London. She is an angel."

While watching the dancers, Miss Bingley's eyes flared, then she gasped. "Is that...? It is! That is Miss Bennet. If that horrid family is invited, I was deceived as to the exclusivity of this event." The lady's face was puckered as though she had sucked on a lemon.

"Take great care, Miss Bingley," said Hatton as he approached from her other side. "The lady you called Miss Bennet is Miss Jane Montford, my cousin. The Richmond earldom will know how to act should one of our own be insulted."

With another more affected gasp, Miss Bingley clutched her chest. "Why, Jane is a dear, sweet girl. I would never do such a horrible thing."

Hatton did not appear the slightest bit convinced. "I am certain you would not." As he passed behind Bingley, Hatton clapped him on the shoulder. "Good to see you again, Bingley."

Not a moment after Hatton disappeared into the throng, Bingley turned, his eyes wide. "You spoke the truth. She is a Montford."

"When have I ever lied to you, Bingley? Now, if you will pardon me, Miss Elizabeth promised me the supper dance."

"But you danced the first with her!" Miss Bingley's expression was most unattractive, gawping at him like a fish.

He had been certain she dissembled about doubting it was him standing up for the first. With her outburst, she not only gave away her falsehood but also revealed her knowledge of his partner for the set. If not for Bingley, he would cut her. Her very presence set his teeth on edge. "Yes, she honoured me with two sets this evening."

"How fortunate for you," she said through her teeth. "I am certain her *fine eyes* are brighter and more attractive in town than in Hertfordshire. Her gown is a vast improvement but still not the latest fashion."

Darcy shook his head and chuckled. "You have complained of not securing an appointment with Madame

Morisot. If you do not care for Georgiana's or the Miss Montfords' gowns, perhaps you should find another dressmaker since theirs are the Madame's designs. Lady Richmond's is as well. I believe Madame Morisot is the sole modiste for the Montfords. I know Georgiana will use none but her." Without another word, he turned on his heel to claim Miss Elizabeth. He would much prefer her company to Bingley's or that of his sisters' for that matter. Now, where had Sir Anthony taken Miss Elizabeth? He rose to his toes. Ah, there she was, in the far corner with Lord and Lady Richmond.

Her eyes brightened as he approached, making his heart stutter in his chest. She was happy to see him. Could her opinion of him have changed so soon?

"Miss Elizabeth, I believe you promised me this dance," he said when he approached. A current travelled through his glove and up his arm when she set her delicate hand upon his. She was beautiful this evening, her blush pink gown complementing her rosy cheeks, and the lower cut back providing a tantalising glimpse of her shoulder blades. Her maid had expertly woven seed pearls into her hair, and a pink topaz and pearl necklace adorned her graceful neck.

"Is aught amiss, Mr. Darcy?"

"No, why do you ask?"

"You are staring, sir." Despite her words, her tone and the alluring curve of her lips was anything but accusatory.

"I was admiring your beauty," he said as close to her ear as he could manage. "I would beg your forgiveness, but I am not sorry."

She laughed as she took her place across from him in the line. "Pray, no more forgiveness." Her smile faded. "Miss Bingley is glaring at us again."

"I am not surprised. Her brother approached and began asking questions about your presence here. He was insistent I was mistaken on Lord Richmond being your grandfather." He bowed to her curtsey as the music began. "Miss Bingley then joined us and was not at all charitable. I have no desire to cause you worry, but if she approaches, be warned. She will not be kind."

"Oh, I am certain every sweet word will be laced with a great deal of venom, but I shall not allow her to disturb my equanimity. I only worry for Jane. Her generous heart would be injured if she understood Miss Bingley's more veiled insults."

"Is your sister dancing the supper set?"

"Yes, Sir Anthony requested it of her."

Hopefully, they would be seated close, which would allow them to protect Miss Jane should it be required. "Sir Anthony will not allow Miss Bingley to abuse your sister. He is an excellent man."

"My grandfather said as much, but I am relieved to hear it from you as well." Her eyes darted, looking past him. "Oh, Nicholas has been ensnared to dance. What fun Amelia, Jane, and I shall have on the carriage ride home."

Chapter 11

Thankfully, at supper, their large party managed to sit together. Miss Elizabeth was to Darcy's left with Miss Jane on her opposite side. Sir Anthony, of course, sat between Miss Jane and Miss Amelia, which meant Bingley could not do so if he tried. Lord and Lady Richmond and Hatton sat across from them.

The duchess planned a sumptuous and elegant menu, the extravagance continuing through dessert when a luscious ice cream was served with gingerbread and other sweetmeats. The duke always celebrated the approach of Christmas with so lavish a ball that all who were in London clamoured for an invitation.

"I have never seen the like," said Miss Elizabeth. "Do you think they eat like this every day?"

He shrugged. "I do not know. I cannot claim a friendship with the duke. In fact, I have not attended this ball in three years."

Their gazes held for a moment before she inhaled and looked across to where her grandparents were speaking with Miss Amelia's supper partner. "Do you know who he is?" she asked softly.

"Lord Pitt. I am not acquainted with him, but he is a member at White's."

"Lord Pitt?" She whispered the name then tilted her head. "Are you teasing me?"

"No, I assure you." He drew his brows down.

"How unfortunate," she said.

He ran a hand over his mouth. Why was he surprised she would consider the title in such a manner?

"Miss Benn...Montford."

Darcy's head shot up at Bingley's voice.

"I was wondering if you had a set available."

Miss Jane glanced around at them, then clasped her hands in her lap. "Mr. Bingley, 'tis agreeable to see you again, but I am afraid my dances are all spoken for. I am sorry."

His countenance fell for but a second before his cheerful demeanour was restored. "Ah, I see I waited too long to ask. That is my fault. I should not have tarried. Miss Montford." With a slight bow to her, then Lord Richmond, he departed, heading in the direction of the card rooms.

"Even in Meryton, Jane was never without partners. Why would he believe she had a set still available?"

"He approached me before the supper set. When he noticed you dancing, he expressed his shock you would be invited. I informed him of yours and Miss Jane's relationship to Lord Richmond. Hatton happened upon us and confirmed the two of you are his cousins. If he wished for a set, he could have made the request before the supper set or even before the meal. I am uncertain why he waited."

She peered over her shoulder, but Bingley was already gone. "Did you enquire how he had procured an invitation?"

"He claimed an acquaintance with the duke's daughter Lady Jemima."

Hatton began coughing and spluttering. "Forgive me."

Miss Elizabeth watched him for a moment before she turned her gaze back on him. "I am unaware of some knowledge Nicholas possesses, but I wonder if you also know why he has reacted so."

The reason for Hatton's coughing was known to most, but he was not about to tell Miss Elizabeth. Explaining how the spinster daughter of the duke was rumoured to have taken a number of lovers since she first came out was not an explanation he was willing to provide. If they were married, perhaps, but not as they were now.

Miss Jane whispered a word or two to Miss Elizabeth, who stood. "My sister and I shall return in a moment."

After they departed, Darcy caught Hatton's attention. "Bingley went to the card rooms. When the ladies are dancing, I wish to see what he is about."

The viscount straightened and lifted his eyebrows. "What do you suspect?"

He shook his head. "I do not know that I suspect anything, but in my experience, he does not frequent the card rooms."

Not long after the ladies returned, the dance was announced, and their partners claimed them for the next set. "My grandparents will not let them out of their sight. Come." Hatton led the way into a dimly lit room, hazy with cigar smoke. The stale air made his eyes sting and his chest tighten, forcing him to cough. He never entered the card rooms, even if they were an easy escape from the ladies vying for his attention. This was an even greater hell than the ballroom.

"Is that him?"

He followed Hatton's gesture to a table in the far corner where Bingley sat wearing an immense frown—quite unlike his usual cheerful visage. While he scowled at the cards in his hand, he had a paltry sum in front of him. How much had he started with?

"Darcy, I have not seen you since last Season," said Henry Parr, the second son of the Earl of Essex, as he approached. He shook Hatton's hand. "What brings you into a card room of all places?" He had befriended Parr at Oxford, but while Darcy had an estate to manage, Parr, who had become a barrister, remained in London.

"I saw Bingley enter and was curious."

"Ah, yes. Did you not know he frequents the card rooms?"

Darcy's eyes surely flared for a moment. "I have never known him to do so. When did this start?"

"Since you try to avoid these things, I suppose I should not be surprised that you were unaware. Last Season, he spent a prodigious amount of time in the gaming rooms at White's as well as some of the card rooms. I am uncertain of why he frequented some and not others, but I can tell you that he has lost a significant sum."

"I do not suppose you know how much," said Hatton.

"No," said Parr, "but I do know he owes Lady Jemima approximately forty thousand pounds."

Darcy nearly choked on his own spit. "You cannot be serious."

"I was unaware Lady Jemima was allowed in the card rooms," said Hatton.

"Her father began bringing her two years after she came out." Parr gestured to a lady with her back to them, sitting at Bingley's table. Even from the back, her appearance spoke of wealth; her gown was crafted of the finest silk and her turban was bedecked with a costly jewelled pin and an ostrich feather. "She is an accomplished card player, though it is no wonder she has remained unwed. Most of the gentlemen have seen her play cards, smoke cigars, and drink brandy as though she were one of us."

"I should tell my grandfather," said Hatton.

Darcy shook Parr's hand. "I thank you for the information."

His friend pulled him a little closer. "I believe Lady Jemima invited him tonight in the hopes he would pay his debt, but he is down again—by a great deal last I could tell."

With a wince, Darcy nodded. "I understand."

"What will you do?"

He held up his hands in a sort of shrug. "I can speak to him, but he is a grown man. I can do little else."

Parr clapped him on the shoulder. "Someone needs to set him straight before he loses everything."

After one last nod, Darcy followed Hatton to the ballroom, then walked towards the corner where Lord and Lady Richmond stood, watching their granddaughters dance. Richmond's forehead furrowed. "By your countenances, I shall not like what I am about to hear."

"We should wait until tomorrow to discuss this," said Darcy. "I should not like to speak of it here."

Lord Richmond spoke near his wife's ear, then motioned for them to follow. They departed the doors to the terrace, and Lord Richmond led them away from two men smoking to the far corner of the garden. "What has you both looking so grim?"

"At Darcy's suggestion, we went to the card rooms to see what Bingley was up to. It seems he has been frequenting them at the balls and at White's of late, losing large sums of money."

The earl lifted his eyebrows. "How large?"

With a sigh, Darcy rubbed the back of his neck. "According to Henry Parr, he owes Lady Jemima forty thousand pounds."

"Forty—" Lord Richmond spluttered and covered his mouth. When his hand dropped, he stiffened. "Is it certain?"

"Bingley told me himself he was a guest of Lady Jemima this evening. It is being said she hoped he would pay his debt, but he is doing naught but increasing the sum."

"If Dorset knows of Bingley's indebtedness to his daughter, he will not be kind."

"He had one hundred thousand pounds his father left him to purchase an estate. I knew of two very reasonable estates for sale, but when I mentioned them, he hesitated and leased Netherfield instead. He claimed he wished to learn more of estate management before making so large a purchase. Could his reason be a lack of money? Could he have truly lost so much?"

Hatton gave a laugh that was anything but happy. "I would wager all I own that he is insolvent. He is broke. We shall need to be more vigilant about Janey since he may see her as a means of paying his debts."

"She has but thirty thousand," said Lord Richmond. "Her fortune would not be enough. If what Mr. Parr has told you is true, he is in dire straits. It is only a matter of time before he will lose all but the clothes on his back." The earl exhaled low and heavy. "We should return. I do not want to leave my wife to watch all three girls on her own."

"I agree." Hatton rubbed his hands together. The night held a chill, but Darcy had been oblivious. He had not considered the cold since he learnt of Bingley's predicament.

The ladies were returning from the dance floor when they joined Lady Richmond, and his heart beat a little faster when Miss Elizabeth came to stand at his side. "You and Nicholas have been rather mysterious. First, you disappear instead of returning to the ballroom, then you remove my grandfather from the room. I cannot help but be quite curious."

"We merely had information your grandfather should know."

"About Mr. Bingley?" she asked. "After he asked Jane to dance, I saw the way you watched him." She glanced over her shoulder at her family. "I should like to know if this involves my sister."

"This is not fair."

"What do you mean?"

He gave an incredulous bark. "I can deny you nothing; you tilt your head or lift that one eyebrow, and I am lost."

She flinched a little. "I had not intended to discomfit you or make you feel as though you were breaking a confidence. Should you not be able to confide in me, I shall understand."

Elizabeth bit her bottom lip while Mr. Darcy shook his head. "By the time we have the discussion we spoke of earlier, I should know more of this and whether I can share it with you. Would that be agreeable?"

"Yes, absolutely. Mr. Dar—"

"Miss Elizabeth! I was not aware you were in town."

Every muscle in her back tightened at the familiar voice, and she clenched her fingers around the ribbon of her reticule. "Lord Rutledge, I hope you have been well." He grinned widely as he bowed, and she curtseyed.

The earl glanced at Mr. Darcy but did not acknowledge him. "I was sorry to have missed you the last two times I called at Richmond House. You were visiting relatives on one occasion and had departed for the country on the second. My mother would have liked to have had you for tea if you had remained in London longer. May I enquire how long will you be with your grandparents? I should like to call upon you soon if you will allow it."

Ugh! He was clean, dressed well, and educated, but he caused an unpleasant shudder whenever he was near. He was slimy, and after the one occasion where she had stood up with him, she had almost begged for a bath upon her arrival home. "I am terribly sorry. My grandmother has made so many plans, I can hardly commit to another engagement. Between the shops and making calls, I am certain we shall be from home most mornings."

"Do not forget you promised my sister to take tea with her as well."

She took Mr. Darcy's arm. "I have not forgotten, sir. I beg your pardon, but Mr. Darcy promised to take me to the punch table after that last set."

"May I claim a dance with you this evening?" said Lord Rutledge with haste.

"I am sorry again, but my dances have all been claimed." She curtseyed. "Good evening, my lord."

Thankfully, Mr. Darcy showed no hesitation and whisked her to the refreshment table. "He is watching, is he not? I can feel his stare on the back of my head."

Mr. Darcy handed her a cup of something. She cared not what it was. "He is. I must admit to some relief that you are not fond of him. He has a poor reputation."

"My grandmother has mentioned as much to me. Should he become a problem, Grandpapa will deal with him, but I have managed to avoid his calls and any further dances thus far. I am frankly amazed he still wishes to call on me. He has not seen me in town in over a year."

"Perhaps he finds you difficult to forget."

Their gazes held until she could not take the intensity of the connection and broke it to sip from her cup. Why could she not hold his eye?

"I hope you like Negus," he said.

"You are well aware the trip to the punch table was a ruse. I owe you a debt of gratitude for following through. You could have denied the engagement and hied away."

One side of his lips curved. "I would never abandon you so."

"I have done nothing to deserve such devotion." What else could she say? She did not doubt the feelings he had professed, but her own were such a muddle. That intense stare of his made gooseflesh erupt across her neck and arms, and when he stood close to her, she had to keep her hand from reaching out and resting upon his arm. Why? And when he leaned in next to her ear to speak, it was all she could do not to turn her head and touch her lips to his. How was she to cope with such urges? Did they mean she cared for him, even if a little? It was all too confusing.

"Yet, you have it all the same." When he said such sweet words, she had to hold herself back from kissing his cheek.

Chapter 12

Grandpapa stood from his chair and motioned to Elizabeth. "Come, Lizzybeth. You promised me a game of chess as I recall."

"I did?" She stood and looped her arm through her grandfather's. "I do not remember such a promise, but you know I shall never refuse a challenge." Her grandfather had taught her chess at an early age, but she had also learnt a great deal from her father. Since her return, her grandfather had enjoyed a rivalry of sorts between them, though he had not won a single match.

"We always have chess tournaments after Sunday breakfast, though I need to see to a letter before I join you," said Nicholas, who excused himself from the table and departed the room.

As she and her grandfather walked towards the study, she squeezed his arm. "I have never been more thankful for your rush to depart church as soon as the service is over."

He kissed her temple. "I did not miss your reaction to Lord Rutledge when he called your name. If you wish it, I can speak with him."

"I know, but other than my general dislike, I have naught with which to accuse him. He has been polite. In some fashion, he shares certain traits with Mr. Collins. They both behave in a subservient manner towards a lady: Mr. Collins to Lady Catherine and Lord Rutledge to his mother, they both do not understand—or feign an ignorance—to a lady's polite refusals, and they both make me want to order a bath after speaking with them."

Grandpapa chuckled. "The dowager has always been a formidable lady as has Lady Catherine, and both do prefer a gentleman who grovels."

She shuddered. "I cannot respect a man who behaves as they do." How could any lady?

"That is just as well since I could never invite one of those men to my table, or if I did, I would have to find some way to avoid the engagement."

"Grandpapa." She drawled out the name, not that she could blame him.

The echo of the knocker through the house made them pause. The door opening and closing followed. "Good morning, Mr. Darcy," said Mr. Gideon, making her inhale quickly. Something inside her stomach fluttered.

Her grandfather elbowed her in the ribs. "I can guess who he has come to see." He spoke in soft tones, even though they were hidden behind a wall. His voice would not carry into the hall.

"'Tis Sunday."

"And he is a member of this family, not by blood but in affection. You seem to have forgiven him and are allowing yourself to know him."

She pressed a hand to her stomach in an attempt to stop the fluttering inside. "I am, even if he confuses me."

"How, may I ask?" After watching her for a moment, he drew her into his study and closed the door.

"What about Mr. Darcy? We shall be considered rude." She began to turn back, but a hand to her arm stopped her.

"Your grandmother, Amelia, and Janey will entertain him. What is it that bothers you? You cannot still be bearing a grudge for his past behaviour?"

"Oh, no. Since learning more of him, I have gone over our every interaction following the assembly and have come to the realisation that neither of us were without fault. He should not have made the comment, but I also let my wounded vanity colour every interaction with him. The truth is, when he entered the assembly, I was drawn to him. He is tall and handsome, and I caught myself watching him. When he insulted me, I laughed it off despite the pain that sliced through my chest. At occasions after, when he approached and spoke to me, my stomach would flutter, and when he watched me as he did, gooseflesh would prickle my neck. But I convinced myself it was my dislike of him that caused those reactions."

"And now you have forgiven him and have come to know him as a decent man, yet you still have those sensations?" Her grandfather dipped his chin down and looked at her over his spectacles.

"How did you know?"

He wrapped an arm around her shoulders. "Dearest, at our ages, your grandmother and I do not have those reactions as often, but we do still have them—when we share a certain look, or I kiss her. Your heart recognises him as someone you can develop deeper feelings for. Your grandmother and I have given some nudges in his direction, but perhaps we should give you room to breathe. More than anything, we wanted you to forgive him and befriend him if possible. We do not want you to feel forced into a courtship you do not desire."

She exhaled and leaned her head on his shoulder. "I suppose I did feel forced in the beginning, more to accept his apology than to accept him as a suitor. But when he watched my family at the Netherfield ball, and even at the party at Lucas Lodge, his countenance reflected the disgust he felt for them."

"You know I love you, Lizzybeth, but Mrs. Bennet and her daughters are not appropriate in company. You and Jane have said so yourselves. You cannot blame him."

"I know. He just never showed an interest in me until he discovered you were my grandfather. What if it is because I am suddenly acceptable due to my connexion with you?" There, she said it.

Her grandfather pulled her around to face him with a hand on each arm. "I can tell you he is not that sort of man, but if you want to know the answer for certain, you will need to ask him."

"How can I ask such an offensive question? It would be uncivil, would it not?"

He smiled and drew her into a hug. "If anyone can manage it without giving offence, it is you."

The peppermint scent he always carried flooded her senses and made the tension in her neck release. "I am not reassured, Grandpapa."

He chuckled and kissed her forehead. "I do have to let you figure some things out on your own. Perhaps we should see why that young man of yours has called on a Sunday." After he wrapped her hand around his arm, he led her from the study.

"He is not my young man."

"Oh, if you let him, I think he could be," said her grandfather close to her ear. When they entered the drawing room, Mr. Darcy stood with his hands clasped in front of him. "Darcy! What could bring you to Richmond House today?"

Mr. Darcy turned and bowed to her grandfather, who strode straight up to him to shake his hand. "I do understand it is Sunday, but at the ball, I promised Miss Elizabeth a walk in Hyde Park if we had favourable weather. Today is unseasonably warm, and the sun does a great deal to keep one from developing a chill. I thought she may wish for the exercise."

"I would. Thank you. I should fetch my coat."

Elizabeth hurried from the room, running up the stairs when she could no longer be seen. He had mentioned the possibility of a walk, and he was here. He remembered! When she burst into her bedchamber, she hastened towards the dressing room, but Tate emerged and startled. "Miss Elizabeth, I had not expected you, and what is amiss? You are panting?"

"I am well, but I require my redingote, a bonnet, and gloves so I may take a walk with Mr. Darcy."

Tate smiled for but a second, but she sucked her lips between her teeth and returned into the dressing room. She returned and held out Elizabeth's new boots. "May I suggest these?"

An almost giggle escaped before she could stop it. "You are right. Thank you." Once she wore her boots, her maid helped with her coat and handed her the gloves and bonnet. "Have I forgotten anything else?"

"You look lovely and ready to walk in the park. Enjoy the fresh air, miss."

"Thank you, Tate."

Upon her return, Mr. Darcy stood in the hall, wearing his coat and holding his hat in his hands, a footman standing close by. "If you are ready, shall we go?"

She tugged on the white leather gloves she was sure to ruin and the bonnet that her grandmother insisted perfectly matched her new redingote. "Yes, I have not had the chance to walk since I arrived. The weather tempted me as we rode home from church, but I could not upon our return since we had yet to have breakfast."

"Of course," he said as they stepped outside, and he placed his hat on his head. He held out his arm, and she set her hand in the crook of his elbow, her heartbeat picking up at the contact. Matthew, her grandparent's footman, thankfully did not walk too close behind them, lagging back a little.

"You wanted to know what occurred when we journeyed to Hertfordshire. I am uncertain if you wish to know what happened when we visited Longbourn or with Wickham, but since it is difficult to tell the first story without starting the second, I..."

"You are not certain how to separate the two? Do not worry. I should like to know as much as you will tell me."

As he spoke in those low tones that hummed through her body, she turned her attention to the mistletoe growing in the barest of trees and the birds that had remained for the winter flew around their branches. By the time they approached the Serpentine, he spoke of Mr. Wickham's presence at Longbourn and Mama's and Lydia's vehement defence of the man. Her face burned and she squeezed her eyes closed. "What you must think of me," she said when he paused.

"What do you mean?"

She shook her head and opened her eyes. "My family's behaviour is mortifying, particularly Mama and Lydia. Their lack of decorum certainly reflects upon me."

"At one time, I confess I would have viewed your situation thus, but your behaviour was always beyond reproach. You and Miss Jane carried yourselves with dignity and grace, despite the chaos that sometimes surrounded you."

"While Jane was ill, Mama called at Netherfield and exposed herself as well as all of us to ridicule, do you not agree?"

"Do not forget the ball. Your mother all but announced an impending betrothal between Miss Montford and Bingley."

She winced. "Amelia has never met her, but between what Jane and I have said, Amelia does not like when I call Mrs. Bennet Mama. I feel hateful to express my feelings, yet I have often wished, after such horrifying behaviour, that I had never called her Mama. Such wishes make me feel guilty."

"I imagine Mrs. Bennet is the only mother you remember."

"She is." With a squeeze to his arm, she wiped a dampness near the corner of her eye. "Pray, tell me of Mr. Wickham. He emerged from the parlour—drawing room as you called it—and a scene ensued."

"Yes, but little did Wickham know that your grandfather had purchased his debts from me. I was unaware of two carriages that followed us to Longbourn. One of which contained four huge men who dragged Wickham from the house. Your grandfather spoke with Colonel Forster and explained Wickham was being jailed for his debts, and he was taken to London. I understand they took him to Fleet Prison where he has been ever since."

She furrowed her brow. "What of the second carriage? You said two followed you to Longbourn."

Her jaw hung lax as he explained her grandfather's conversation with Mrs. Hill. "Mr. and Mrs. Hill are here? In London?"

"They are likely in the servants' wing of Richmond House, unless he has arranged for them to journey to Yorkshire."

"Why would he not tell me? He said Hill kept him apprised of our well-being and the happenings at Longbourn. I do not understand. Why would he keep *this* a secret?"

"Perhaps with your move to Richmond House and the revelation you would not be returning to Hertfordshire, he thought to protect you."

She huffed. "I am not a fragile flower. I could understand keeping such knowledge from Jane, but me? We have often spoken freely on many topics—politics, agriculture, business. He knows I am not a simpleton."

"He has spoken of your wit and intelligence often," said Mr. Darcy, offering his arm once more. "Maybe he had not thought the information important."

"Maybe."

"I must say that when we met, I never connected the Jane and Elizabeth your grandfather mentioned with you and your sister."

After taking his arm, she began to follow him again along the edge of the water. "Why would you? Jane and Elizabeth are common enough names. You could travel almost anywhere in England and find a family with one or both names amongst their number."

A deep sigh came from her, and he stopped and faced her. "Are you well? Perhaps I should not have told you the entirety."

"No, I am glad you have told me. I should not go on as I have. You are too good to listen to my childish complaints."

"I do not see them as childish at all."

She lifted that eyebrow he said he could not resist and smiled. "What of your visit to the card rooms Friday evening?"

He groaned and turned them around, heading back towards the path. "You do not forget a thing, do you?"

"Whatever you learn of Mr. Bingley can affect Jane. You must tell me."

With a deep chuckle, he looked down at her with raised eyebrows. "I must, must I?"

She broke the connection of their gazes. Two swans glided across the water, their paths creating ripples that travelled along the surface.

He nudged her with his elbow. "I am teasing. Forgive me. I am not certain what to make of what I learnt of Bingley. He seems to be someone I do not know."

"What do you mean?"

"A gentleman I knew from Oxford was in the card rooms when Nicholas and I found Bingley. He claims Bingley has been gaming at White's as well as some of the private balls he has attended and has accumulated a generous debt."

Her shoulders stiffened. "How much debt? Were you told?"

"The rumour is he owes the Duke of Dorset's eldest daughter a sum of forty thousand pounds."

Elizabeth tripped on her own feet, only her hold on Mr. Darcy's arm saved her from falling on her face. "Forty thousand! How can one owe even half that sum?"

"He was at the same table as Lady Jemima and was down to his last few pounds. I cannot be certain, but he must owe others too. How could his debt be all with one lady?"

"Could she have covered his losses, which is why he owes her such a sizeable amount?" She had heard the name Lady Jemima before, but where and when? What was it about her that had been mentioned?

"She would have to have a reason to pay his debts, and I cannot think why."

"Oh, my," she said and covered her mouth with her hand.

"What is it?"

"When you mentioned Lady Jemima's name, I knew the name, but I could not remember where or why. During my last stay in town, my grandmother once took me to return a call to

Lady Jersey. Five or six other ladies had happened to call at the same time, and one of them was Lady Jemima. She is a tall lady with dark brown hair and a dimple in her chin. I overheard her whisper to another lady—a widow—of her new...she...I cannot speak of this to you." Her cheeks burned all the way down to her chest.

"I have heard of the lady's reputation. When did this call take place?"

"When my grandfather was ill. At that time, Lady Jemima had just started a...a tryst with a new man. She gave no name, but her description could have been Mr. Bingley—a boyish complexion, cheerful, and...eager. Other descriptions were given that I would prefer not to repeat. I had to press my lips together and bite them closed to keep from gasping. What if she introduced him to gaming so they could be together in a public setting without being together?" What other explanation could exist?

"I do not doubt what you overheard, but without a name we cannot be certain. If he is entangled with the duke's daughter in such a way, he is an imbecile."

Her stomach plummeted. "What if he pursues Jane to pay off some of his debt?"

"Hatton was present and aware of all I learnt. Your grandfather and cousin will protect her."

Her shoulders unwound, and she breathed easier. "Thank goodness."

He started back along the path that returned them to Park Lane. "Now that we have discussed that unpleasantness. My sister requests your presence for tea on Thursday. Your grandmother, sister, and cousin are invited as well."

"Jane has fittings with Madame Morisot, so she and my grandmother may not be home. I am uncertain about Amelia. I promise to send word to your sister by tomorrow."

"She will be pleased. She is eager to know you better."

"Miss Darcy is a dear, sweet girl."

As they approached the gate, Tate called out to them and hastened forward. "Lady Richmond sent me to keep you from the house for a time or to sneak you through the servants' corridors to your rooms."

"What could possibly have put you into such a state? You appear to have been running." She had never in her life seen Tate do more than walk at a brisk pace.

"Lord Rutledge is in the drawing room with the family. After seeing you in church, he decided to call in the hopes of catching you at home."

"Come," said Mr. Darcy, leading them down a different path. "We shall exit through the Stanhope Gate, which is closer to Darcy House. You can have tea with Georgiana and me while we await word from your grandparents that Lord Rutledge has departed."

"One moment." Tate hurried over to Matthew. After the footman nodded, he took the gate in front of them.

"Matthew will tell your grandparents where you are," said Tate when she returned. "In the meantime, I shall accompany you as a chaperon."

"Though I appreciate your willingness to offer me refuge, Mr. Darcy. I can return and simply remain in my sitting room until he goes."

"Nonsense. Why spend that time alone and cornered in your rooms when you can have tea and biscuits and enjoy yourself?"

Whyever indeed.

Chapter 13

He was trapped in a bizarre form of torture with no escape. Since their walk on Sunday, Miss Elizabeth was either at Darcy House for the afternoon or he walked Georgiana to Richmond House for her to spend the afternoon with Miss Elizabeth and the Miss Montfords.

The earl had caught him in the hall on one such occasion and invited him for an afternoon of chess, which he accepted. After calling checkmate on Lord Richmond, the gentleman fetched Miss Elizabeth as his next opponent—a manoeuvre that muddled his brain. How was he supposed to concentrate with her sitting across the table, her impish grin tormenting him while she waited for his next move. The only thing worse was how she scraped her teeth along her bottom lip as she contemplated her next play. He had no way of combating the distraction she presented. Needless to say, she had defeated him with a swiftness that had him reeling.

Today, Miss Elizabeth and Miss Amelia were playing duets with Georgiana, the proof of their efforts carrying into his study through the adjoining door to the library, which was located directly across from the music room.

The torture was self-imposed. He would freely admit it if asked. When the footman had alerted him to the arrival of Miss Elizabeth and her cousin, he had left the door ajar, and every giggle and chord of happy laughter pulled at him, enticed him to stand and follow the sound—much like a siren's song. How much longer could he resist?

"Mr. Darcy," said Higgins, his butler. "Mr. Bingley has called and requests an audience with you, sir."

"Yes, show him in." Finally! He had called at Bingley's every morning this week but was told the younger man was not at home. Although, on the second attempt, when the butler invited him in to visit with Bingley's sisters, Darcy claimed a forgotten appointment with his solicitor and hastened from the house as though it were on fire.

His friend entered with his usual jovial countenance as Darcy stood. "Darcy, I must beg your forgiveness for missing your calls. Urgent business has kept me quite occupied."

"Thank you, Higgins." He sat and gestured for Bingley to take the seat across from him. "I hope nothing serious."

"No, no. I am selling my mill in Manchester. It is the only mill I own outside of Scarborough and inconvenient when I want to oversee the management in person."

Was that not his largest and most profitable mill? "I thought it a great asset."

"Oh, it is. It is. It will also bring more money when it is sold."

He leaned back in his chair and steepled his fingers in front of him. "You already have enough to purchase an estate. Those mills were excess you said you would use for your future daughters' fortunes and to establish any sons born after your heir. Your plan was sound. Why change your mind?"

"Because I have, Darcy." Bingley's more authoritative tone gave him pause. That tone had never come from Bingley in his presence, not even when Miss Bingley was at her most trying. What nerve had he struck? Before he could speak, Bingley shook himself a little, bringing the return of his cheerful countenance. "It is of no matter. I did not come to discuss business, but to request an introduction to Lord Richmond. Would you mind?"

Darcy's eyebrows shot up, and a bark of something escaped him. "Why do you desire an introduction to the earl? You are acquainted with Hatton. He possesses a more direct connexion than me." Yes, he could have simply agreed, but would Bingley reveal more when pressed?

"You know that Hatton does not think well of me. I am certain it is as a result of my fortune being from trade, but he has never said as much. He would not arrange the meeting."

"What do you wish to discuss with the earl?"

"What difference does it make?" asked Bingley. Only someone who knew him well would notice that barely perceptible edge to his voice.

"What difference does it make?" He laughed and straightened. The muscles of his back were winding tighter by the second. "What if you wish for Lord Richmond to invest in one of your mills? I arrange the introduction without the knowledge of why, and you press him to commit to a venture. Then, I have used a man I consider family to further your business. That I shall not do."

"I have no wish to conduct business with the man. I should like to call on Miss Benn...Montford."

"Miss Jane Montford? You are acquainted with her. Why do you not knock on the door of Richmond House? The knocker is up most days." Bingley was unlikely to be admitted but had he even tried?

Bingley nearly writhed in his seat. "The butler does not even let me in the door. He requests my name, says Miss Montford is from home, then takes my card."

"Why the sudden interest in Miss Montford?"

"Sudden interest? I showed her particular attention in Hertfordshire. She is an angel, and I should never have returned to London without taking my leave of her and the Bennets." His pitch was a little higher, and he had stopped moving so much, stiffening and turning a bit red.

"As I recall, you agreed with your sister that her lack of fortune and connexions were not what you required. That morning, you agreed to depart Hertfordshire with Miss Bingley penning that letter so as not to cause offence. Now, you claim to have preferred Miss Montford all along? All that has changed is her connexions." After Richard's chastisement, he withheld a cringe at asking Bingley of what he had been accused of himself.

"Her newfound connexions are precisely why I am seeking her out. I favoured her in Hertfordshire but was misled about her family. The granddaughter of an earl would have a fortune, do you not think?" His hands clasped together. He would appear a villain from a pantomime if he began to rub his palms together.

"I have heard rumour that you are enjoying the card rooms and gaming at White's of late."

"There is nothing amiss in some friendly wagering."

"Not if you can pay your losses" he said, dipping his chin. "Is that why you are selling your mill? Do you have unpaid debts?"

Bingley stood with his hands clenched at his side. "I can manage my own affairs, Darcy."

"Forty thousand is no small sum." It was time to lay his cards on the table and test Bingley's reaction.

"'Tis not so great a sum." His gaze darted to the side as he spoke, making Darcy's stomach clench. He was dissembling. How much could he really owe?

"When Lady Jemima tires of you, how will you manage? She will demand her money, and if you do not pay her, you may face the wrath of her father. What will you do then?"

"Lady Jemima and I ceased our agreement before I departed for Hertfordshire. Regardless of the debt I owe her, she will keep my confidence." Bingley's voice had gone deeper and darker.

"She is not the only person to know of your entanglement."

Will you arrange the introduction or not?" His friend's face had since darkened and his tone had become curt.

"Lord Richmond will never consent to an acquaintance. He knows of your interest in Hertfordshire, and your, for all intents and purposes, abandonment of his granddaughter. Hatton has, no doubt, informed him of your debts and tryst with Lady Jemima. You will not gain an audience with Miss Montford, and if by some scheme, you manage to wed the lady, he would ensure her fortune never reached your coffers."

"How do you know?" Bingley's hands clenched into fists at his sides.

"His daughter was married to Mr. Bennet, and when she died, he saw to it her settlement was split and set aside for her daughters. He would ensure he remained in control of those funds, and would also ensure that when he dies, Hatton will control them. You would never see so much as a farthing of her money."

Bingley's face screwed into a glower the likes of which Darcy had never witnessed upon his face. "Damn you, Darcy," he said before he stormed from the room.

With a heavy sigh, Darcy cradled his forehead in his hands. His suspicion was confirmed and possibly worse than expected. Bingley looked to the side when he was confronted with the number of forty thousand. Good God, how much could he owe in truth?

"Are you well?"

When he lifted his head, Miss Elizabeth stood with her hands resting on the back of the chair Bingley had just vacated. "I am not ill, but I would not say I am well."

"We could hear Mr. Bingley yell from the music room. Your sister was alarmed, but I assured her nothing serious was amiss. She and Amelia are now practicing Silent Night."

He nodded. "I had forgotten the door was open, and I suppose Bingley never noticed. Did you hear much of what he said?"

"I waited until he slammed the door to leave the music room, so I heard very little. Was this regarding Jane?"

"He requested an introduction to your grandfather."

"Grandpapa would never agree, and you told him as much."

"Yes," he said rubbing the tension in his own shoulder. "And I confronted him about what he owes Lady Jemima."

Her eyes widened, and she stepped around the chair. "You did? Had he any defence of himself?"

Darcy pushed himself out of the chair and paced before the fire. "No, and when I mentioned the amount, he diverted his gaze as he defended the sum. I am certain he owes more. He would not be trying to sell his most profitable mill if he was solvent. I can only guess that he has lost most of his wealth."

"And he is now seeking a betrothal to Jane for her fortune."

"Yes, when he would never have done so before. His sister convinced him of the ills of the match and hatched the scheme to remove him from Hertfordshire before he was obliged. I mentioned that many at the ball were already speaking of an engagement. Miss Bingley claimed she had heard naught of the rumours. He took her part and left."

"Poor Jane," she said with a sigh to her voice. "Her spirits have rallied since he left Hertfordshire, but to be considered only for her fortune and no other inducement..."

"Not the only consideration. I do believe he enjoys her company, and I know he finds her beautiful." Why was he defending him? Yes, they were friends, but he could not agree with Bingley's current behaviour—he could not agree in the least.

Miss Elizabeth crossed her arms over her chest. "An amiable friendship and admiration of one's beauty is not love. My sister deserves better."

"I agree. I do not know why I am justifying his behaviour."

"It must be difficult to see a friend alter in so drastic a way." She stepped closer and placed her hand on his forearm. He covered her hand with his, lifting it and running his thumb along each individual finger. She shivered and shifted back. "I should return to the music room. Amelia and your sister will be waiting."

He followed her through the library, but she paused in the corridor and turned so they were facing one another. Her turn was so abrupt, they were impossibly close, the orange blossom fragrance of her perfume tickling his nose. "Mr. Darcy, if you still wish it, I would be honoured to receive your call."

"Lizzy, you are under the mistletoe with Mr. Darcy," said Miss Amelia while she pointed to the ceiling above them.

He looked up. How could he have forgotten the mistletoe? His superstitious housekeeper had wanted to wait until Christmas Eve to decorate as to avoid bad fortune, but Georgiana had been overeager. The 21st was not so early, after all. But would Miss Elizabeth allow his kiss?

As he lowered his chin, a soft cheek caressed his and a delicate kiss was placed near the sensitive flesh of his ear.

Before he could reciprocate the gesture, Miss Elizabeth had disappeared, and Miss Amelia's laughing filtered out of the music room. He placed his hand to his cheek. The sensation of her lips against his skin had yet to fade. If only it would never disappear!

Elizabeth straightened the skirt and pressed a hand to her stomach in an attempt to still those ridiculous butterflies. "Tate, I do not know. Are you certain this is the gown I should wear?"

"Gracious, Miss Elizabeth, I have never seen you thus. If you remain so harried, how will you wed him? You may not survive the courtship much less a betrothal." Tate's crooked grin belied the statement.

"Stop it. I am serious." There was also the matter of the kiss. Mistletoe may have been involved, but what had he thought of her being so forward? How would she even approach him this evening without her face overspreading with a deep blush?

"Miss Elizabeth, you are exquisite. The crimson velvet your grandmother found complements your rosy cheeks and dark hair beautifully. Mr. Darcy will need to gather his wits to keep from losing them when he sees you." At a knock on the dressing room door, Tate bustled to open it.

"You look lovely, Lizzybeth," said her grandmother once she entered. "But your mother's topaz necklace will not do for tonight. She held out a box as Tate removed her cross and replaced it with a long gold chain from her grandmother's offering, then a pin that was placed upon the velvet between her breasts, just below the white crepe-lissé that accented the gown and helped preserve her modesty.

"'Tis too much, Grandmamma." She would never become accustomed to such finery.

"Nonsense. I purchased the gold necklace after I saw that gown on you at Madame Morisot's shop, and the pin was my mother's. Now, they are both yours. I have waited too long for you three girls to be old enough for this. I shall brook no opposition."

She took her white lace gloves from Tate. "Yes, Gran."

"Come. We are all waiting on you in the hall, even Mr. Darcy." Her grandmother said his name in a sing-song fashion while she departed. When Elizabeth peered over her shoulder, Tate's shoulders shook at her grandmother's antics. Her face heated. This was ridiculous! She was blushing and she had yet to be face to face with Mr. Darcy, so what would occur when she was? She straightened her spine. Whether he was offended by her gesture or not, she would survive. She would just have to ignore whatever reaction she had to his presence.

As she descended the stairs, Mr. Darcy's impressive figure stood out from Nicholas's and her grandfather's. All three were tall, but her grandfather and cousin were of a thinner frame while Mr. Darcy's shoulders were broader.

He looked up as she reached halfway, his chest swelled, and his hand clenched the brim of his hat. His countenance showed no revulsion nor apprehension, so she released some of her stiffness. "Good evening, Mr. Darcy," she said as she approached. While everyone began putting on their coats and hats, she leaned forward just a little. "Take care, sir. You might crush the felt."

With a start, he looked down and released his grip on his hat. "I had forgotten I was holding it. You are stunning. You take my breath away."

"Thank you, sir. You are quite handsome yourself." Tate appeared and helped her with her white cape—another of her grandmother's impractical purchases. Perhaps she would need to start shopping for her own fabrics and selecting her own patterns lest her grandmother clothe her in nothing but white, pearl, and the palest of fashionable coats, gloves, and bonnets.

Two carriages awaited them at the kerb. Jane entered the first with her grandparents, and Mr. Darcy steered her to the second, with Amelia and Nicholas joining them.

"Do you know how Lord Gower persuaded Mrs. Maria Dickons to perform a private concert?" asked Nicholas. "She is a reputed soprano, and I have heard rumour she is to sing in The Marriage of Figaro this Season. She is quite in demand to perform at a private party."

Mr. Darcy shook his head. "Whilst in Hertfordshire, Miss Bingley mentioned Mrs. Dickons name in the gossip sheets. The claim was her husband had lost a great deal of money trading, and she now lives separately from him. Perhaps she needs the funds."

"With her popularity, she could demand a large sum," said Amelia. "We heard her sing at the King's Theatre last Season. Grandmamma was impressed. She spoke very highly of the performance."

"Have you heard her sing, Miss Elizabeth?"

"No, I have not had the pleasure, but after hearing of her reputation, I am eager to experience her voice for myself."

The trip to Belgrave Square from Park Lane was swift, and when the equipage pulled to the kerb, she alighted with Mr. Darcy's aid. Once all were on the pavement, he placed her hand in the crook of his elbow and led her inside behind her grandparents.

"Have you ever met Lord Gower?" He spoke in low tones near her ear, causing a prickle as his breath caressed the tender flesh at her nape.

"No, I have not." Before she could enquire of his reason for asking, she stood before a rather short and stout gentleman with a quizzing glass that made his one eye appear three times its size. Her grandfather introduced their party, to which the earl nodded and welcomed them before urging them into his ballroom for the occasion. Chairs were set up in rows, and her grandfather selected seats near the middle of the room.

"Miss Darcy did not wish to join us tonight?"

"Since Ramsgate, she seldom attends even these smaller events. I have tried, but she will claim fatigue and retire."

"I must tempt her to join us for some occasion, even if no more than for a walk in the park." The poor dear should not remain shuttered away for the rest of her life. "What of the colonel? We have not seen him since the Duke of Dorset's ball."

"He was called back to Dover. I hope he will return before Christmas, but of course, I have no guarantees."

The crowd quieted when Mrs. Dickons was announced, and the lady took to the small area left free of chairs for a stage. She clasped her hands as the pianoforte began, and when she opened her mouth, it was as if her voice had descended from heaven above. "Beautiful," said Elizabeth in a whisper.

She glanced at Mr. Darcy, but he was not watching Mrs. Dickons. His gaze met hers and held, his expression much the same as in Hertfordshire. Something grazed her knee and her pinkie finger, making her look down to where Mr. Darcy's knee was barely touching hers, which had brought his finger into contact with hers.

Her grandfather coughed, Mr. Darcy swiftly righted his knee, and the spell was broken. What a strange turn. If Charlotte had asked her before she came to London if she would ever welcome Mr. Darcy's suit, Elizabeth would have laughed. Now, her hand itched to take his and bring a smile to his usually serious visage. Not only that, but she would kiss him again if afforded another opportunity. Her cheeks burned. She was shameless. Thank goodness Amelia could not read the train of her thoughts, otherwise Elizabeth would never hear the end of her cousin's teasing.

Chapter 14

W hen Mr. and Miss Darcy were announced, Elizabeth stood and smoothed her gown. After Mr. Darcy's reaction to the red velvet gown she wore for the performance of Mrs. Dickons, she persuaded Tate to have it ready for her to wear again for Christmas Eve. He and his sister entered, and his gaze landed directly on her and lingered before he greeted her grandparents and Nicholas.

Miss Darcy hastened to her and clasped her hands. "Miss Elizabeth, is this the gown you wore Monday evening? My brother mentioned the colour and how well it looked on you, and I must say he did not exaggerate. Madame Morisot's work is incomparable. Do you not think?"

"When have I ever exaggerated?" asked Mr. Darcy, stepping to his sister's shoulder.

"I never claimed you had." Miss Darcy looked up at him with an impish smile. "I should greet the Misses Montford." She crossed the room to where Jane and Amelia spoke with Grandmamma by the fire.

"She has become more animated since spending time with you and your cousin. I appreciate the time you both have taken with her."

Elizabeth's gaze returned to him. Her insides full of flutters. How many butterflies could take flight within the confines? If she could somehow count, she would estimate in the dozens, at least. "We could do no less. I enjoy her company greatly as does Amelia. Miss Darcy has been a welcome addition to our party during the afternoons. I do not believe I have ever practiced the pianoforte so much in my life." Which was quite true. When she did not have the diversion of friends, Miss Darcy must have spent most of her days playing and singing. Her skill reflected the time and effort she had put into the endeavours.

"Georgiana said you would be performing this evening. I am eager to hear the fruit of your efforts."

Her head tilted, she looked up at him. "You have heard us play. I am certain the sound carried into your study. As I learnt when Mr. Bingley called on Saturday, your study is not far from the music room."

"No, it is not, though I do not believe I heard an entire completed piece. Without being in the room, I also could not know who was performing. I shall have the opportunity to match the lady to the piece this evening, which I am anticipating.

"I must also thank you for allowing my sister to help you decorate today. She has spoken of nothing else since she returned home."

She grinned and glanced at his sister who had giggled, drawing her attention. "Yes, my grandmother attempted to persuade her housekeeper to decorating on the 21st as it seems your household did, but Mrs. Taylor adamantly refused. She is of the mind we should all die a horrible, painful death if even one sprig of holly or mistletoe is hung before Christmas Eve." His low chuckle rumbled through her. Would she ever become accustomed to the sensation?

"My housekeeper attempted to delay, but Georgiana was adamant. She would brook no refusal. The younger maids were excited to help her, but my housekeeper refused to be a part of bringing bad fortune upon us or herself."

"Darcy? Lizzybeth? Dinner has been served," said her grandmother, waving them to follow. Mr. Darcy held out his arm, which she did not hesitate to take. Grandmamma had not put out place cards but allowed them to sit where they pleased.

Amelia and Nicholas sat in their usual chairs, and Miss Darcy sat between Jane and Amelia. The footman pulled out the chair Elizabeth favoured, and Mr. Darcy followed, sitting to her right, between her and her grandfather.

"I am pleased you could join us for Christmas this year, Darcy," said her grandfather. "Since most of society tends to depart town for their estates at this time, I have been pleasantly surprised at how many have stayed and have planned routs and fetes. I must admit that having you and Georgiana joining our merry party makes us feel as though we have the entire family with us."

Mr. Darcy nodded with a relaxed bearing. "We thank you for including us. Richard is still in Dover last I heard of him, and his parents and Milton journeyed to Yorkshire. They will not return until the Season. Georgiana has done so well with her piano master of late that I hesitated to remove us. When we learnt you and your family would remain, Georgiana and I thought London would be preferable to a Christmastide at Pemberley this year. My sister has enjoyed her time with Miss Elizabeth and Miss Amelia, and the relationship of our families has added a great deal to our contentment in town." He peered back at Elizabeth with a slightly crooked smile. He could not be saying she added a great deal to their contentment, could he? No, now *she* was exaggerating and reading more into his words than he likely meant.

Grandmamma had planned a lovely meal with beef and brawn and a sumptuous selection of sweetmeats with plum cake for dessert. As was his wont, her grandfather presented her his arm after the meal. You can join Miss Darcy soon but join us for a time first. I insist."

"Hugh," said Grandmamma with a disapproving drawl.

He only beamed and led her from the room with Mr. Darcy and Nicholas following behind. After her grandfather handed her a glass of brandy, he served Mr. Darcy before sitting in his favourite chair. "I assume you told Lizzybeth of what happened in Hertfordshire and at the Dorset ball."

Mr. Darcy's eyebrows shot up onto his forehead. "I beg your pardon." Her stomach clenched. Would her grandfather disapprove? He had told her little, though surely to protect her feelings. Had the housekeeper told him of seeing her in the servants' passages speaking to the Hills?

Grandpapa chuckled and turned his glass in his hands. "Do not get your back up. I expected it. I am not blind, you know."

If her grandfather knew that much, he may well know all...well, not the kiss. As much as she would wish for that to remain between just her and Mr. Darcy, Amelia witnessed her boldness. She could not force her cousin to forget. "I overheard Mr. Bingley's call at Darcy House as well. I had never heard a word spoken in frustration or anger from him until then."

Nicholas straightened with a jolt, and his head whirled around towards Mr. Darcy. "You never mentioned anything of this."

"He told me," said Grandpapa. "After Mr. Bingley's first attempt to call on our Janey, Mr. Gideon came to me. I ensured that man has never stepped foot inside this house. Thankfully, your cousin has not noticed the additional footmen your grandmother and I have had accompany them shopping. Men who owe large sums of money can become desperate, and a desperate man is a dangerous man. I shall take no chances." Her stomach twisted and something rose in her throat. Would Mr. Bingley truly attempt to take Jane for her fortune? Her grandfather would protect Jane with every resource he possessed so perhaps remaining with her grandparents was a better situation than Longbourn. Her father would never have taken this so seriously. He would have laughed and made sport of any concerns laid before him while Mrs. Bennet continued to welcome Mr. Bingley with open arms.

"I have not had a letter from Papa. Have you?" They had been at Richmond House over three weeks. Her father was not a faithful correspondent, but he never failed to send a response to her note informing him of her safe arrival.

Her grandfather shook his head with a grim set to his mouth. "Naught has been in the post from him. I would have expected a letter for you, at least."

He was well, or Mary would have sent word of any ill news. Her younger sister was not aware of the status of Jane and Elizabeth's grandparents, but she did have the direction. Anyhow, she would need to pen a letter to Charlotte. Her wedding to Mr. Collins would be soon. She suppressed a shudder.

"Are you well, Miss Elizabeth?"

She snapped from her thoughts of Charlotte's wedding and smiled and Mr. Darcy. "Yes, thank you. I was just thinking that Miss Lucas's wedding should not be long after Twelfth Night. I need to write to her to be certain. She has been a good friend for so long that I do not wish to miss it."

"I am certain you do not," said her grandfather. "When you tell me the day, I shall arrange for you and Janey to attend."

"I had not heard she was betrothed," said Mr. Darcy. "Who is her intended?"

"Mr. Collins, actually."

Nicholas spluttered on his brandy, then withdrew a handkerchief to press to his clothing and his mouth in an attempt to repair the damage. "That was badly done, Lizzy.

You had not mentioned your friend accepted the heir of Longbourn. If she is friends with you, I cannot imagine her tolerating his ridiculousness—unless he is not as ridiculous as you claim."

"No, he is ridiculous," said Mr. Darcy. "He approached me at the Netherfield ball and introduced himself to me with a scraping bow. I was then forced to hear him give me the current health of Lady Catherine as well as Anne. By the way he spoke of them, you would think my aunt was the queen herself."

Her cheeks warmed at the behaviour of such a relation, and her cousin snickered as he poured himself more brandy. "Would you care for more, grandfather? Darcy?" After they both accepted another helping, Nicholas returned to his chair, crossing his ankle over his knee. "I have not seen Lady Catherine in London in ages. Your cousin was always pale as I recall." Mr. Wickham had made mention of Miss de Bourgh's sickly state, had he not?

"My aunt keeps Anne in the country for her health, so rarely journeys to town. I believe Anne's ailments are more a product of my aunt's overtreatment, though I cannot be certain. If one physician finds naught amiss, she sends for another who then prescribes a tonic and bleeding."

Elizabeth pressed her hand to her chest. "How sad. Are you certain she does not have some malady?"

"I have spoken to two of the physicians my aunt consulted. Anne would be healthy if her mother did not cosset her so. The problem is Anne believes her mother's declarations, so she believes herself ill." What a shame. She took the last sip of her brandy, returned her glass to the tray, and kissed her grandfather on the cheek. "I have enjoyed my time with the gentlemen this evening, but it is time to join the ladies, I fear." As she passed Mr. Darcy on her way to the door, their gazes held. He held out a hand, so she placed hers in his palm, allowing him to kiss her knuckles.

"Miss Elizabeth," he said all low, making her knees knock together. Had he heard them when they hit or was that only in her imagination? When the door closed behind her, a murmur filtered through the door with Nicholas's laughter following soon after. Her cousin was teasing him. Nicholas needed to have a taste of his own medicine, but what to do?

"There you are, Lizzybeth," said her grandmother when she entered the drawing room. "We are playing snapdragon on the morrow, but is there a game you would wish for tonight? Miss Darcy and Amelia mentioned that the three of you have practiced the pianoforte for this evening. Would you prefer that to any games?"

"I thought you should perform first," said Jane. "Then, if Mr. and Miss Darcy are not tired and we have more time, we could play cards or charades."

Miss Darcy giggled, briefly covering her mouth with her hand. "My brother would never play charades." No, he would not prefer behaving in the silly manner charades would require.

Her grandmother sipped her sherry. "Very well. We shall see how the evening progresses. We could always persuade Nicholas to play. He sneaks in here to practice late in the evening, but I have heard him."

"I was not aware he played," said Miss Darcy.

"We all had lessons from the same master when we were younger," said Amelia.

The gentleman were not much longer with their brandy before they joined the ladies in the drawing room. Mr. Darcy sat beside Elizabeth on the settee while Amelia and Miss Darcy made their way to the instrument. Nicholas stood near the mantel while her grandparents claimed chairs near the fire, which were set to face the pianoforte, holding hands. They had always been affectionate at home with family by holding hands and sometimes kissing a hand or a cheek. Grandpapa had once confessed he had fallen in love with her grandmother the first time he saw her at a ball. They were still very much in love. What she would not give for a happy marriage such as theirs!

As Amelia and Miss Darcy began playing, Mr. Darcy bent near her ear. "Your grandparents' marriage is one to be envied, is it not?" He spoke softly so as not to disturb the others' enjoyment of the performance.

"Mayhap not envy but emulate," she said, turning her head to speak as he had to her. His proximity was making those butterflies take flight and soar in wide circles around her stomach.

When the first carol ended, Elizabeth stood and joined them singing *God Rest Ye Merry Gentleman* while they accompanied her on the pianoforte. She could not look directly at Mr. Darcy while she sang, lest she falter, but on those moments her eyes flitted over him, he watched her with unwavering attention. She clasped her hands together in front of her so she did not shake. Nicholas would be terrible should he notice.

Elizabeth played a duet with Miss Darcy while Amelia sang *The Twelve Days of Christmas*. Amelia's voice was richer and stronger than hers, which made her the soprano more proficient at that particular song. The entire party complimented her after she took her curtsey.

After their performance concluded, Elizabeth's eye was caught by something drifting by the window. She stepped closer and gasped at the snow showering down upon Park Lane as well as Hyde Park across the street. "'Tis snowing!" She rushed through the house to the breakfast parlour, opening the doors to the back garden.

"Lizzybeth! Wait!" called Grandmamma.

With a gasp, she stepped onto the terrace and dropped her head back, the snowflakes falling towards her from a pitch-black sky, then stuck out her tongue in an effort to catch one of the delicate flakes upon the tip.

At Mr. Darcy's characteristic low laugh, she spun around to face him. He wore his great coat and held her ruby red redingote over his arm. "You will give your grandmother an apoplexy. She is adamant you will catch your death."

"I am not cold." As she spoke, a cloud punctuated each word.

"Your pink nose and cheeks say otherwise."

He held out her coat, allowing her to slip her arms inside before he slid it over her shoulders, the tops of his fingers brushing lightly over the bare flesh where her neck and shoulders met. She inhaled and turned. Her gaze met his and his face dipped closer and closer.

"Lizzy! Grandmamma had me bring your boots."

At Amelia's voice, Mr. Darcy made an about face and looked up at the sky. Elizabeth's heart, meanwhile, pounded furiously against her ribs. He was going to kiss her. Nothing else would necessitate him drawing so close, would it?

She accepted the boots and put them on while Mr. Darcy's back was turned, though she left them unlaced and set her slippers just inside the door.

"It is so pretty," said Miss Darcy. She and Jane were bundled up against the cold as they came outside. Grandmamma must have caught them before they could follow.

Elizabeth glanced around. Her grandparents stood arm in arm watching and pointing at the white flakes, which became heavier by the moment, Nicholas leaned against the door with his usual wry grin, and Amelia held out both hands, letting the crystalline, white flakes land in her palms.

Not much had accumulated on the ground thus far, but Elizabeth grinned and bit her bottom lip as she gathered the thick layer on the railing and formed a ball, hurling it at Nicholas before he knew what she was about. Her snowball hit him in the side of the head, and she squealed and ran into the garden when he lunged after her. "No!"

"You will pay, Busy Lizzy!"

She managed to evade his first attempt to catch her, then ran back to the terrace. When she reached Mr. Darcy, she grabbed the arm of his great coat and swung around him to take cover behind his broad chest and back. Nicholas would not hit Mr. Darcy, would he?

Her breaths made white puffs in the air as she peeked around Mr. Darcy's side. Nicholas all but swaggered up the steps. "You think Darcy will protect you?"

Mr. Darcy took a step to the side, so Elizabeth shifted with him. Was he trying to get her pummelled by snow? She peeked around once more as Nicholas scooped a large amount of snow into his hands and began forming it into a ball.

"Run, Miss Elizabeth," said Miss Darcy while Jane stood beside her, her jaw lax. She had never attempted to match Nicholas and had never understood Elizabeth's attempts.

A high laugh came from Amelia. "You are in trouble, now, Lizzy."

Should she run? Should she remain? What if Mr. Darcy became upset at being wet by the snow? She was not quite close enough to gather another snowball from the railing on this side of the terrace, so she needed to make haste into the house. Nicholas would never bring snow inside. Grandmamma would ensure he regretted that decision. Before she attempted her escape, a nudge from Mr. Darcy's arm made her look down. His hand was wrapped around behind him, an enormous snowball in his palm. How did he—?

She took the packed ball of ice and peeked around his arm. As soon as her head emerged, Nicholas took aim and threw his weapon. She ducked behind Mr. Darcy as he shifted to the side to avoid the strike. Without delay, Elizabeth stepped around Mr. Darcy and let her snowball fly. Nicholas had been rushing to make a second when hers struck him in the shoulder.

When she tried to flee into the house, Grandmamma caught her by the arm. "That is enough. We shall return inside before we catch our deaths."

"I am not cold, Gran." Her cheeks hurt but that was surely more from smiling than it was the cold.

"Watch out, Lizzy! There will be retribution for your mischief tonight."

As Gran tugged her inside, she turned sideways so she could see Nicholas. "Do your worst, Cousin. I am not afraid of you."

Mr. Darcy chuckled while they returned to the drawing room. A maid brought wassail which they drank before the fire until Miss Darcy began to yawn. As they walked their guests into the hall, Grandmamma pointed. "Lizzybeth, you and Mr. Darcy are standing under the kissing bough."

They both peered up as Amelia began to laugh. Why did she always laugh? And why did they not look where they were walking? Her cheeks would hold a permanent tinge of red if this continued.

Gran began steering her cousins back into the drawing room. "Come, Amelia, children. It would not do to embarrass your cousin." After her grandmother forced her cousins, Jane, and Miss Darcy back into the drawing room, she looked at Mr. Darcy, who once again drew closer and closer. Just before he would kiss her cheek, she held her breath and turned, allowing him to place his kiss upon her lips.

His lips were soft, and she sighed as they cradled hers just so. His warm breath caressed her cheek, and his breathing hitched as he released her lips for but a second before reclaiming them again.

"We shall expect you tomorrow," said Grandpapa in a loud tone.

Mr. Darcy drew back and gave an awkward sort of nod and bow as everyone returned to the hall. "Will you sit with me at church?" The words were rushed.

"Yes." Her voice was still breathless.

"Merry Christmas, Elizabeth," he said before he turned, offered his sister his arm, and departed through the door.

She touched her lips. Who could have imagined a kiss could be so perfect?

Nicholas made a loud kissing noise near her ear. He made several more of the offending sounds before she let her elbow fly and hit him square in the stomach, making him grunt loudly.

"That is enough, Nicholas. You will not tease your cousin. Do you hear me?"

"Yes, Gran," he said, rubbing his stomach with a grimace upon his face.

Chapter 15

Darcy was in heaven and hell all at the same time. How was he supposed to sit so close to Miss Elizabeth, soaking in her orange blossom scent, and remain sane? When they shared the hymnal, his arm brushed against hers, which added to the exquisite torture. He could not so much as give one thought to the kiss last night under the kissing bough. Miss Elizabeth had tilted her face so as to press her lips to his. Had she done so intentionally? He could only assume she had. His heart screamed she had. His aim at her cheek was true, so how else could his lips have ended upon hers?

"Have you noticed the Bingleys are here?" she whispered near his ear when the parson instructed the congregation to take their seats. She gave an almost imperceptible dip of her chin to two pews in front of them on the opposite side of the church. Miss Bingley glared at them, and from beside her, Bingley stared at Miss Jane Montford, who by her countenance was well aware of the scrutiny. She sat primly with her hands clasped in her lap, her attention fixed upon the service, her jaw tight.

With the distraction of Miss Elizabeth beside him, he was not shocked he missed the Bingley's presence. When he looked back in their direction, Miss Bingley attended the service, but Bingley still watched Miss Montford.

An elbow to Darcy's side alerted him to the congregation standing for the final hymn. He joined them, though Georgiana placed a hand upon his arm. "Brother, why does Mr. Bingley stare so?" Thankfully, she asked in soft enough tones to be drowned out by the entire church joined in song.

"Later," he said softly. After one last glance at Bingley, his sister shifted closer to his side and joined in singing the hymn.

When the parson released them, Darcy glanced at the earl, who pointed towards the far side of the church, so they would avoid happening upon Bingley in the centre aisle. He took Georgiana's hand and followed Nicholas and Miss Elizabeth to the end of the pew where they hastened down the side aisle. At the rear of the chapel, Georgiana took his arm, and he offered the other to Miss Elizabeth, allowing Nicholas to await his grandmother and sister who were to the rear of their party and attend them from the church. The earl had Miss Jane on his arm nestled between the rest of their party where she was shielded from Bingley should he wish to make a scene.

Without difficulty, they reached the portico, started down the steps, and crossed the street. St. George's of Hanover square was on the corner of St. George's and Maddox Streets, and the earl had given specific instructions for the carriages to await them on Maddox to facilitate their departure. As expected, both equipages were near the corner. The servant popped to attention and opened the carriage door as they approached.

"Get Georgiana inside first," said Miss Elizabeth. "I am certain I heard Mr. Bingley behind us."

He handed in his sister, and as soon as the earl reached them, Miss Elizabeth pressed her sister in front of her. Without delay, he offered his hand to Miss Jane and Miss Elizabeth, who boarded the carriage with haste.

"Take them to Richmond House. We shall follow," said the earl.

"Miss Bennet!" Bingley had a hand in the air while he walked as quickly as he could.

Darcy hopped inside and rapped his walking stick to the ceiling. The servant did not tarry when Lord Richmond urged him to make haste. They pulled away from the kerb, and he looked back through the window to where Nicholas had his hands on Bingley's chest while the countess and Miss Amelia Montford entered the second equipage.

"If he just wishes to speak with me, I do not see the harm," said Miss Jane.

Miss Elizabeth leaned forward so she could take her sister's hands. "We have learnt a great deal about Mr. Bingley of late, dearest. He owes a very large sum of money, and we know he is now pursuing you for the fortune our mother left for us."

"But he knew nothing of our mother in Hertfordshire. How would he know of any fortune when I have never heard of it?" Miss Jane's wrinkled forehead spoke of her confusion.

"I knew nothing of it until grandfather told me the evening of my arrival in town. Grandpapa split our mother's fortune upon her death. With interest and what he has added, we each have thirty thousand pounds."

Miss Jane's eyes widened, and her hand pressed to her chest. "Why were we never told?"

"So Mama would never know. Could you imagine her reaction if she discovered we had such large fortunes and her daughters had only their share of her five thousand pounds?"

"If you will forgive me for being blunt, Miss Jane," Mr Darcy said, "Miss Bingley persuaded her brother against a match with you before he departed Hertfordshire. His not taking his leave of you and the letter she sent were planned. He came to me after the Duke of Dorset's ball and requested I facilitate an introduction to your grandfather. His desire was to court you, but when I told him your grandfather would not agree to the acquaintance—that he would protect you above all—Bingley became frustrated and angry."

"I heard him," said Miss Elizabeth. "He was so angry, Jane, his yelling could be heard in another room."

Georgiana gasped. "That was when we were practicing in the music room. I remember hearing the disagreement, but Miss Elizabeth closed the door so we would not be disturbed in our practice. I must say I am disappointed in Mr. Bingley. He is no better than Mr. Wickham." Her nose crinkled when she said the last.

"Mr. Wickham?" asked Miss Jane.

"Mr. Wickham attempted to court me for my thirty thousand pounds. Thankfully, my brother discovered his scheme and put a stop to it, else I would have fallen for his pretty words and charming smile. I am very sorry Mr. Bingley wishes to do the same to you. I could think it of Miss Bingley for she has had her cap set at my brother for some time, but her brother seemed more of a gentleman." Georgiana set her hand upon the sisters' joined ones.

"You should have told me sooner." Miss Jane's tone was firm with a decided frown levelled upon Miss Elizabeth.

"I knew the knowledge would bring you pain, Jane. Pray, understand. I wanted to spare you that."

Miss Jane removed her hands and crossed her arms over her chest. "While I appreciate your consideration, I am not a fragile flower in need of protection."

"I shall remember that in the future. I promise."

"I have met the Mr. Wickham you mentioned," Miss Jane said to Georgiana. "He can indeed be exceedingly charming and spoke of your brother while they were both in Meryton— spoke quite ill of him really. I am grieved to hear he is not as he seems."

The ride to Park Lane was not long, and upon their arrival, the door swiftly opened for them to enter Richmond House.

"Merry Christmas, Mr. Darcy," said Mr. Gideon when he opened the front door.

"Merry Christmas, Mr. Gideon." He and Georgiana happened to greet the butler in unison, making the man beam as they entered.

The man helped Darcy with his coat while several maids appeared to be of aid to the ladies. "I hope church was enjoyable." For the first time, Mr. Gideon's slight accent was noticeable.

"The service was lovely," said Miss Elizabeth. "My grandparents, Lord Hatton, and Miss Montford will be directly behind us. We shall await them in the green drawing room."

"Very good, miss. We shall be ready for their arrival."

Miss Jane wrung her hands. "Do you think they are well?"

"I am certain they will be here soon," said Darcy. Due to the delay, they may have been caught in traffic." Bingley had never been a violent man, yet he had never expected Bingley to fall into such debt either.

A commotion in the front hall announced the rest of their party's arrival. When Darcy peered at Miss Elizabeth, he could not miss the heavy exhale and the manner in which her body relaxed.

Lady Richmond was the first to enter the drawing room, making her way to Miss Jane and sitting beside her. The two spoke in hushed tones as the earl and Hatton entered. Georgiana joined Miss Jane and the countess and offered the latter her hand. Perhaps the similarity of their experiences would deepen their friendship. He had no objections. Georgiana would only benefit from such an association.

He stepped over to Lord Richmond and Hatton with Miss Elizabeth close behind. "I am not sure what Bingley hoped to accomplish."

"He surely hoped to force a meeting with Janey," said Lord Richmond. "Nicholas restrained him while we boarded our carriage. That Miss Bingley woman approached and attempted to ingratiate herself to Amelia, but Amelia and my wife cut her. Lady Jersey, as well as Lady Dalrymple and Miss Carteret were nearby and witnessed the exchange. I am certain those who are in London for Christmastide will know before the first of January."

"Enough!" When he turned, Lady Richmond was standing with her hands raised in front of her. "'Tis Christmas, and we shall not dwell any longer on the Bingleys but enjoy our day. Now, we have gifts for each of you. Fitzwilliam, I shall not accept a refusal."

He and Miss Elizabeth sat upon the settee as the countess distributed her packages. While she handed Miss Elizabeth a box, the earl handed him a bottle. "My wife charged me with finding you a gift. I hope you approve." The older gentleman wore a slight smile.

When he took the bottle, he turned it in his hands to view the label. "An excellent brandy. I thank you."

"Brandy, my lord," said the countess with her lips pursed.

"He purchases the latest books as soon as Hatchard's puts them on the shelves, and they had nothing newer than a month ago, which I am certain he already possesses. What would you have me buy?"

"Lady Richmond, I must admit your husband is correct. I do not require much, and this will be savoured since Richard drank my last bottle of this vintage six months ago, and I have been unable to procure more."

"For heaven's sakes, do not let the colonel near it then," said the earl. "I had no idea he was so intemperate."

"He does enjoy a good brandy, but I was at Pemberley for the summer while he lived at Darcy House, not long after he was assigned to Horse Guards." Richard could drink quite a bit and keep his wits about him, but he was not one to drink an entire bottle of brandy in one sitting.

Miss Elizabeth opened the lid of her box and gasped. "Grandmamma, you have given me so much jewellery since my arrival. I do not require so much." Nestled in velvet was a necklace with a pendant that resembled a snowflake. Diamonds set in gold with the larger stones in the centre and becoming smaller as they neared the tips.

"Nonsense. This is the last of your mother's jewels that was set aside for you, as is Jane's gift."

Miss Jane flipped open the lid on hers and inhaled swiftly. "Grandmamma, this is lovely." She turned it to show Miss Elizabeth the modest sapphire necklace and matching ear drops.

His sister held a stack of music sheets and a cashmere shawl sat upon her lap. "Fitzwilliam, what of our gifts?"

After he excused himself, he ducked out into the hall where Mr. Gideon happened to be passing. "Pardon me, but a servant from Darcy House was supposed to deliver some gifts while we were at church."

"Ah, yes," said Mr. Gideon. "Forgive me. I forgot to mention it upon your arrival." He stepped inside a doorway on one side and brought out a small trunk. "Where would you like it?"

"I can take it. Thank you," he said. When he returned to the drawing room, he withdrew two packages and handed them to Georgiana, who in turn, gave them to Miss Amelia and Miss Jane. Meanwhile, he passed gifts to Lord and Lady Richmond and Hatton. Lastly, he returned to Miss Elizabeth's side and passed her the last.

"'Tis from Georgiana and I both."

She gave him a side-long look, but her fingers trembled ever-so-slightly while she peeled away the silk paper. "How beautiful. Thank you."

"What is it Lizzybeth?" asked her grandmother.

With a careful touch, she lifted it from the wrapping. "A hair comb."

"Which will be lovely in your dark hair." Her grandmother admired the piece, then stepped over to sit close to her husband while she removed the paper from hers. "What gorgeous silk! Thank you, Fitzwilliam. I must admit I adore a trip to Madame Morisot's, and you have given me just the excuse."

"Yes, thank you Darcy," said the earl dryly.

Miss Amelia and Miss Jane thanked both him and Georgiana for the fabric in their packages. Hatton clapped him on the shoulder after expressing his appreciation of the journal he had received, and Lord Richmond gave a hearty laugh when he saw the bottle of brandy Darcy had gifted him. "Great minds think alike, do they not, Darcy?"

"I had just managed to find a shipment a few days ago." His attention returned to Miss Elizabeth, who fingered through the material that was beneath the hair comb. "You have given me fabric as well?"

Her grandmother chuckled. "He has selected well. You have always looked well in rose, and you will need a great many gowns for the Season."

"Lady Richmond, breakfast is served."

"Come. That tea and toast I had before church was not sufficient to last me until dinner," said the countess.

As was his wont, he offered his arm to Miss Elizabeth, but this time, also his sister. "If you do not like the fabric—"

She startled, and her eyes widened. "No! Forgive me for being remiss in thanking you. I should have done so when I first noticed the silk."

Georgiana gave a giggle. "Your sister says you do not enjoy fittings."

"That is true, but that does not mean I do not enjoy wearing a pretty gown. My favourite colour is that shade of pink, so I shall enjoy the gown doubly so."

"My brother selected the material all on his own," said Georgiana, making his cheeks burn. "I accompanied him to the drapers and selected all the fabric but yours. Fitzwilliam found that one and had it cut before I had any say."

Miss Elizabeth's gaze held his. "I would say he has an excellent eye for ladies' fashion."

He could not help but smile at Georgiana's giggle. She had laughed more since being in the company of the Montford ladies than she had since Wickham. They did her well indeed.

When they all sat around the table, Miss Jane placed her hand over Georgiana's where it rested on the table. "Miss Darcy, I must thank you for comforting me in the carriage."

"Oh! I am happy I could be of aid, though I cannot consider what I did so important."

"But it was. It is always reassuring not to be alone. I do wish what happened to you had not occurred, but I am thankful you shared your experience with me." Darcy's heart swelled. His sister had ladies she could confide in and trust. Had she ever found one such friend? He had never met one.

"Thank you. I hope you will call me Georgiana. I should like all of you to do so."

"Then you should call us by our Christian names too," said Miss Elizabeth.

In that moment, his little sister beamed brighter than she had in so long it was all he could do not to weep at the table. How ridiculous was he to be so sentimental?

After a generous breakfast as well as tea and cakes, a chess tournament between Lord Richmond, Hatton, Elizabeth, and Mr. Darcy followed. Elizabeth and Mr. Darcy were the last two to play with Elizabeth the victor. Not long after they returned to the drawing room, Lady Richmond whispered to a servant who brought out a large bowl with raisins, poured brandy over the dried fruit, and set it on fire.

Miss Elizabeth grabbed Georgiana's hand and pulled her up to the bowl. "I love snapdragon."

"I have never played," said the young lady. "More often than not, Christmas is just my brother and myself at Pemberley. We have a meal, of course, and play chess, and I perform on the pianoforte." What? She had never played Snapdragon? The game was a tradition at Richmond Castle and Longbourn, thus Elizabeth played regardless of where she spent Christmastide.

"'Tis simple really," said Amelia. "You attempt to take a raisin from the flames and eat it."

Georgiana's eyes grew to the size of horse chestnuts. "You put your hand in the fire?"

As she asked in a squeaky voice, Nicholas reached in, grabbed one of the raisins, and tossed it into his mouth. "See, simple, but you have to be quick about it."

Georgiana reached in but missed the raisin on the first attempt.

"You can do it." Elizabeth took her turn, grabbing her own, and eating it.

When Georgiana's turn came around again, she managed to grab a raisin and eat it with a grin. The rest of the party cheered. The game lasted but a quarter hour at most before Elizabeth returned to sit on the settee near Mr. Darcy.

"I must thank you for your kindness to my sister," he said. "I have not seen her so happy in a long time."

She shook her head. "I have done nothing but be her friend. I consider myself fortunate to have the company of such a kind young lady. You need not thank me for something I am pleased to do. I do think after their similar experiences, Jane may become more of a confidant of sorts for her. They are both reserved, though Georgiana is a bit more open with her feelings, but their tempers suit. Jane is six years her senior, yet Charlotte and I were close for a long time, and she is seven years older.

"Richard and I hoped for her to make friends when she attended school, but she was miserable and wrote of nothing but her fervent desire to return to Pemberley. While she has known your cousin for a while, making the acquaintance of you and your sister, and being in company more with Miss Amelia will only be of benefit to her."

Unable to hold his gaze another second, she looked back at Georgiana and Jane who conversed quietly near the fire. All day, she had attempted not to show how distracted she was by him. When they sat side by side in church, her arm prickled at his nearness and the cedar notes of his cologne flooded her senses. Her insides were a muddled mess. She had been uncommonly forward when she caught his lips with hers under the kissing bough. He did not seem offended at the time, but upon further reflection, had he considered her move too bold— too forward? She had fretted over kissing his cheek, and he had not thought ill of her. Was she being ridiculous once again?

She took in a deep breath. Her grandparents were engrossed in a chess match. While her grandmother had not taken part in their tournament earlier, she challenged her husband to a rare game, a challenge he accepted with an unusual glint in his eye. Jane and Georgiana were still occupied, and Amelia and Nicholas were arguing some such nonsense as they oft times would. She took a small silk paper-wrapped parcel from where she had tucked it into the cushion.

"I have this for you," she said as she held out her gift. Good Lord, she was trembling from head to toe. Their eyes met as he, with careful fingers, took the package from her palm. She clenched her hands together in her lap. "'Tis not much. Just a trifling really."

"No, I am certain it is wonderful." A dimple appeared on one cheek, and she clenched her hands tighter if that was possible.

"You have not opened it yet."

He untied the ribbon and opened the paper, revealing the small stack of four handkerchiefs she had embroidered since their walk in Hyde Park. She was not as accomplished with a needle as Jane, but she had managed a good "D" for Darcy and had finished the edge of the muslin so it did not fray.

"You need not use them if you do not care for them. I am not very skilled at embroidery."

After a glance around the room, he covered her fidgeting hands with his. "They are wonderful. I shall use them every day." He removed his handkerchief from his pocket and replaced it with one of hers. Once he had set the rest with the bottle of brandy from her grandfather, he leaned as close as propriety would allow in the situation. "You have, at times, been uneasy with me today. Have I done something to cause you distress?"

"No," she said turning her head quickly, so their gazes met. "I confess I have worried of your reaction to what I did under the kissing bough."

He broke into an enormous, dimpled grin that took her aback. "You need not fret as I consider that the best Christmas gift I have received thus far." He chuckled as a vicious heat crept up her chest and to her cheeks. How was she to respond to such a bold statement?

Chapter 16

Tate secured the last pin and stepped back. "Will that suit, miss?"

"You have never attempted this arrangement before. I believe it resembles one of the Greek statues in the British Museum. I do like it. Do you think Mr. Darcy will also?"

Her maid began storing the remainder of the pins and her brush in the dressing table. "With the way he looks at you, I daresay Mr. Darcy would not care if your hair stood on end. You have such perfect curls, as your mother had before you. Her abigail taught me when you were little how to care for them. You are fortunate. Most ladies sleep in papers every night to have the curls you have without effort."

"The curls come from my grandfather. You would not think it now to look at him, but in the gallery at Richmond Castle, the portrait of him from when he was one and twenty shows him with thick, black curls. My grandmother has said his great grandmother was Portuguese, and we inherited those dark curls from her." A few of those portraits also had gentlemen and ladies with the same sandy brown hair as Nicholas as well as one or two blondes, including her grandmother.

When she stood, Tate was gathering Elizabeth's redingote, gloves, and bonnet. Today, she, Jane, and Amelia were to spend more time with Georgiana at Darcy House. "Before I go, I have a gift for you."

"Miss, I have told you before, you need not—"

She pulled the basket from under her bed and set it on the mattress. "Besides being tradition, you deserve more than what I give you. I could not do without you, and I did enjoy shopping for this, which you know is a rarity for me."

With the same chiding look Tate always gave her, she stepped closer, withdrawing a bottle of lavender water, a new pair of tan kid gloves, and ribbons before she gasped. "You do too much, Miss."

"No, I do not. You have never received more than a trifling at Longbourn, which was less than what I wanted to do. In fact, when I told my grandmother of the gift I wished to give you, she heartily approved and contributed as well." Tate had always received a basket on Boxing Day, but Elizabeth had never been able to do as much as she would have liked with her pin money at Longbourn.

"The blue wool will make a nice coat, and there is fabric to line it. The sprigged muslin is for a gown you can enjoy wearing to church on Sundays, and the white muslin is for new chemises and shifts." Tate was removing each of the fabrics as Elizabeth explained. The last required no explanation as it was obviously fabric for two new gowns to wear when she worked. "Mrs. Gardiner has an excellent dressmaker who has a shop near Gracechurch Street. We have arranged an appointment for you for next week.

Tate blinked furiously. "Thank you, miss, and thank your grandmother too. I would never have expected—"

"Which is why I wanted to do it." That and she had never been able to truly show her gratitude. After she put on her coat and bonnet, she shoved her gloves into her pocket to pick up another basket. "Now, I must be going." Elizabeth carried the other basket down to the hall where Amelia and Jane awaited her. "Forgive me. I gave Tate her basket, but I have one more."

She held the gift in her hand out to Mr. Gideon, who furrowed his brow. "But, miss, your grandfather has given me my gift."

"I know, but this is one from me. You have done so much for us since we were children, and I wished to thank you properly. Do not argue. I insist."

He took the offered basket with some hesitance. When he peered inside, he shook his head. "'Tis too much, miss. Your grandfather was already very generous. He gave me a bottle of wine, a book, and wool for a new coat."

"Tate felt as though I did too much, but I am not of the same opinion, though I am glad I consulted with grandfather first so we did not purchase you the same book." She had discussed her idea with Grandpapa when they went to Hatchard's with Nicholas not long after her arrival in town.

"Thank you, miss. I am grateful for you and your grandfather's generosity."

She took his hand and patted it. "This is no more than you deserve, Mr. Gideon. Now, since I wore my coat and hat down, shall we?" she asked, turning her attention to Jane and Amelia. "I am certain Georgiana is wondering if we have forgotten her." After Mr. Gideon saw them out, they walked the short distance to Darcy House and were swiftly admitted by his butler.

Georgiana entered as they were removing their coats and hats. "You have impeccable timing. With the help of Mrs. Newnham and my brother, I just finished handing out our Boxing Day gifts. What have you planned for us to do today?"

"I have no plans," said Jane, who looked at a shrugging Amelia.

"What about a game?" Georgiana led them into the drawing room. "I enjoyed Snapdragon and have wondered what else I have missed. Fitzwilliam is so much older than me, and I never played many of the childhood games I know you did."

"We used to play Blind Man's Bluff, Hide and Seek, shuttlecocks—but that is better suited to the outside and warmer weather as is lawn bowls and skipping rope." Amelia counted each off on her fingers as she recited them.

Jane wrinkled her nose. "I have not played any of those for so long. I never liked Blind Man's Bluff."

"You need more than the four of us for that game to be enjoyable," said Elizabeth. "Hide and Seek is perhaps the best for inside. We are less likely to break an heirloom as well."

Georgiana rubbed her hands together. "Perfect. How do we play?"

"'Tis simple. One person searches for the rest who hide." After Amelia mentioned some of the finer points, she offered to count while the rest of them hid.

Elizabeth took Georgiana's hand and pulled her from the room. "Come."

When they reached the hall, Georgiana grinned. "I know the perfect place." She tugged Elizabeth into the library, opened a cupboard, and slid inside on the bottom with a giggle. "Will this work?"

"You are right. 'Tis perfect."

With Georgiana hidden, she hurried around the edge of the room in search of anything—a heavy drapery or a tiny alcove—but as she passed the study door, she was pulled inside, making her gasp and cover her heart with her hand. Only Mr. Darcy standing before her made her relax. "You frightened me."

"Am I to guess by Georgiana fitting herself in the cupboard, you and the ladies are playing Hide and Seek?"

She shrugged and nodded. "And I should find somewhere soon, or my cousin will not have a difficult search."

He took her hand and led her into the music room where a heavy drapery flowed to the floor. "The terrace doors are behind them, but we keep them drawn to help with the chill in the room."

When she stepped behind the draperies, she grabbed his hand and pulled him inside with her. What was she thinking? If Amelia caught them thus, she would be teased for days.

"You want me to hide with you?" His tone was a touch higher than was his wont.

"I do not know why I pulled you back here," she said with a wince. "Amelia will take great enjoyment at teasing me for it."

He shifted away from the edge. "If she enters the room, I can move to the other end and remain unseen." With a gentle grasp, he took her hand and brushed a soft kiss across her knuckles. His gaze bore into hers, and she bit her bottom lip while her insides took flight. Her eyes fluttered closed when his cheek pressed against hers. "You make it difficult not to kiss you when you bite your lip as you are."

Her lips suddenly itched for the softness of his. Yes, she had kissed him under the kissing bough, but that had been a whim. When had the urge appeared?

As his knuckles grazed her cheek, she rose on her tiptoes and claimed his lips. What was she to do now? Aside from pressing her mouth to his, what else was there to kissing?

His palm cupped her cheek as his lips moved, cradling hers and suckling. She followed his movements while she held his lapel to keep from falling into him. Every part of her burst to life, tingling and trembling, at his slightest touch as his hand wound around to her neck and down between her shoulder blades.

When his tongue flicked against the corner of her mouth, she all but gasped which allowed him to deepen the kiss, that clever tongue caressing hers. Her fingers tightened around his lapel, and her other hand grasped his topcoat at his shoulder as she pressed shamelessly against him. She needed to be closer!

She was lost—lost in every touch, every caress, and every staggered breath he exhaled against her cheek. This was a heaven she had never expected. The muscles of his shoulders tensed under her palms and his heart beat erratically under her hand on his chest.

He groaned, and she pressed herself closer, the sound spurring her on. Was it possible to burrow beneath one's flesh and join with them? She did not know but her body craved more. Was there more?

"Ha!"

They hurtled apart at the exclamation, and the whipping away of the drapery. Mr. Darcy turned his back to the intruder, and Elizabeth covered her mouth. How had she not heard anyone coming?

"Fitzwilliam!" exclaimed Georgiana, her mouth agape. "You must hide before Amelia comes. She found me first and is searching for Jane. If she finds you thus, she will tease Elizabeth mercilessly. She has done so ever since you kissed her cheek under the mistletoe."

"I found Jane!" carried in from the corridor.

Georgiana pointed with a fearsome glare further into the heavy drapery, dragged Elizabeth out, and let the panel fall. She then turned her and tugged at the back of her gown. "There, where he had bunched it is now not so obvious."

"Thank you." She rubbed her hand down her bodice and the front. "Is anything else amiss?" What was wrong with her mind? She never had such difficulty thinking.

"Your lips are red and maybe a little swollen, but I know naught of how to fix it."

She glanced around with a frantic motion for a mirror. Why was there no mirror? "Do you think they will guess?" Good Lord! Amelia would be relentless. At least she would not tell Nicholas. He would be amused but not nearly as forgiving. What had she been thinking? She had not. That was the problem.

"As long as they do not see my brother, I doubt it. We should find Amelia and Jane to lessen the chance of discovery." Her mind was still muddled as she began to step away, but her hand was taken, and she was drawn back around. Mr. Darcy had pulled part of the drapery back and kissed her hand. After he released her, she hastened to follow Georgiana from the room.

"There you are!" cried Amelia.

Amelia and Jane stopped, and Jane narrowed her eyes. "Why do you resemble John Lucas when he was stung on the mouth by a bee?" Her sister approached and reached for Elizabeth's face while Georgiana bit her cheek.

She swatted Jane's hands away. "I do not know. I was simply hiding behind some draperies. Perhaps I sucked my lips between my teeth to keep quiet and irritated them, but I was not stung by anything." Except Mr. Darcy's knee-buckling kiss!

Her sister continued to scrutinise her. "Very well." When Jane turned and started back towards the drawing room, Amelia lifted her eyebrows before she followed.

She squeezed her eyes closed for a moment while Georgiana tugged her forward by her elbow. What a relief! Unless, of course, Jane or Amelia mentioned this in front of her grandparents or Nicholas. They would be more apt to know what Elizabeth had been up to.

Nevertheless, she could not regret one moment. Even now, her chest pained her when she thought of not seeing Mr. Darcy again. Could that mean she was falling in love with him? Her opinion of him had changed drastically since Hertfordshire. Since he apologised for the assembly, she had begun to look forward to his calls—she longed to hear his voice and she craved touching him, his lips trailing a fiery blaze across her flesh. She clenched her hand into a fist to keep from fanning her heated cheeks.

One thing was certain: today was a hide and seek unlike any she had ever played but had been a most enjoyable diversion—the most enjoyable she could remember.

"Fitzwilliam!"

Darcy covered his face and sighed. After Georgiana had caught him and Elizabeth kissing behind the draperies, this set down could not have been avoided if he had tried. She could not understand the temptation of Elizabeth standing before him with that alluring expression. The only thing more tempting would have been if her tongue had peeked out to wet her lip. She need not have initiated their kiss if her tongue had done so. He would have been even more lost than he already was.

"Why are you in the library and not your study? Was this your attempt at hiding from me?" Georgiana strode in as though the house belonged to her and not him.

He managed to restrain the retort begging to burst from him. What he would not do to have Elizabeth in his arms, her tongue—those sorts of thoughts needed to cease before he embarrassed himself. He set his book in his lap and shifted in his seat.

Georgiana cocked her head a little. "What is that look for?"

"Nothing. I beg your forgiveness for finding us thus. We forgot ourselves—"

"Obviously," said Georgiana, planting her hands on her hips. She wore a fierce scowl, more resembling his father than his mother at that moment.

"Do not scold me so. I am not George Wickham. I intend to make her the offer of my hand." She could not think him so bad, could she?

"When?"

"I beg your pardon?" She could not possibly be doing this. He refused to propose until he was certain Elizabeth would accept.

"She is obviously willing to kiss you behind draperies, Fitzwilliam. Do you believe she will say no?"

"Has she confided her feelings for me to you?"

"No. We have become friends, but she has not shared much of her heart. And I would not expect it of her. Would you confide your feelings for Elizabeth to her brother if one existed—to Lord Hatton?"

His shoulders sagged, and he dropped his head onto the back of the settee. "No, I would not—not unless I required his permission. I should speak to Lord Richmond—"

"Not to tell him about the kiss? He would march you before her and order you to propose."

"No! I do not know. I thought perhaps gaining his permission before would be of some benefit, but perhaps I should ask Miss Elizabeth first. She is rather independent for a lady. I would not want her to think I made any plans without her." Was that the correct course? How was he to know? This was enough to make his head ache.

Georgiana giggled then walked around and kissed his cheek. "You *are* hopelessly distracted, Brother. I do hope you secure her soon. I should like to have such a sister."

"I am pleased you like her but do allow me to do as I see fit. It was not so long ago that she thought ill of me."

His sister nudged him with her elbow. "For what it is worth coming from me, I believe her feelings are quite the opposite. She may not realise what she feels as yet, but I do not believe her the type of lady who kisses gentlemen who hold no place in her heart."

"I agree," he said, turning his head so he could see his little sister. She became more a lady every day. His mother and father would be proud of her.

"I intend to retire. Do not stay up too late. What if Lizzy prefers your handsome face to your wit? You may send her running with those dark circles under your eyes."

"Pardon?" His head shot up as Georgiana giggled and scurried from the room. It seemed all the time with the Montfords had taught his little sister more than he had initially thought. With a groan, he rose and poured himself a generous glass of brandy. If he did not propose soon, Elizabeth would push him into an early grave. He would not survive if she became any more passionate and willing in his arms without the ability to fully reciprocate. But how to guarantee the success of his suit? He could not bear a rejection.

He took a sip and returned to the settee, letting his head rest against the back. With his eyes closed, he sighed at the remembrance of her in his arms. The supple skin of her upper back and her soft breasts pressed against his chest were enough to drive him mad without her innocent responses to his kisses.

When she had first placed her lips upon his, it was obvious she had not known what to do, though she was quick to learn. She had soon shredded his ability to think or even remember their precarious position. He had lost himself to the sounds of the room, everything but her lips against his and the feel of her in his arms. What would become of him if they wed? One night with her would ruin him. His mind would never recover. He would be lost—lost indeed.

Chapter 17

Elizabeth's small palm rested upon his arm as they strolled through Hyde Park in the lightly falling snow. He covered her hand with his, his heart fuller than ever right at that moment.

"I wonder if it will be cold enough for a Frost Fair this year." The last Frost Fair had been in 1789 as the Thames had not frozen over since. She would have not been born yet.

"My father told me of the last one. With the risk of the ice not being thick enough, he was adamant that he and my mother would not attend, but she insisted. He could deny her nothing. Thankfully, no mishaps occurred." His father's solicitous care of his mother was one of his fondest memories.

"They happen so rarely; I understand her insistence. The experience would be a once in a lifetime occurrence. To eat gingerbread and dance and skate upon the Thames would be something indeed."

She glanced over her shoulder at the footmen walking behind them. "Why does Grandpapa insist I require two footmen? He said Lord Rutledge was kind when he spoke to him—not that I wanted him to. The man is a nuisance, but I had managed to avoid him more often than not. As for Mr. Bingley, he has no interest in me. And you are hardly a threat." She looked at him with mischief in her eyes. What could she be about?

"If we are alone, you pose a very real threat to me."

With a laugh, she nudged him with her shoulder. "Me? You are a foot taller, and your shoulders are far broader than mine. What harm could I pose?"

"Well, when you lift that eyebrow of yours, bite your bottom lip, or wet that same lip with your tongue, you make it impossible for me to resist. I am in real danger of sweeping you behind some draperies, or that tree over there, and kissing you until your grandfather or cousin call me out. My preoccupation of you would be so great they would certainly win, which could mean you are forced to wed Lord Rutledge."

She stopped and tilted her head while she held his gaze. "With the exception of the comment on Lord Rutledge, I cannot tell if you are teasing me."

He started once again, tugging her back along the pathway. "What of Boxing Day when I was so swept up in your kisses that I failed to hear Georgiana?"

She covered her eyes before letting her hand drop. "Oh! Pray, do not remind me. Your poor sister, then Jane was insistent I was ill or a bee had stung me on the lips."

"Why would she believe a bee had stung you in the house in December?" What an odd assumption. He had heard of people dying of bee stings, but it was winter. Bees were not out this time of year.

"John Lucas had a bee sting his top lip when I was eleven. His lips turned dark red and became swollen. Fortunately, not so severely that he died. Mr. Jones had a young boy who died from swelling after a bee sting. I suppose Jane remembers the incident." She inhaled a deep breath. "I have waited for either Amelia or Jane to mention what happened to my grandmother, but thus far, I do not believe they have done so. Gran has not mentioned anything of it to me."

"Georgiana scolded me. She entered the library where I was hiding and upbraided me for stealing away behind the draperies with you."

"You should have told her I initiated matters."

He frowned. "I would never speak so when I had not the will to resist."

"Would it not be preferable that she think poorly of me rather than a brother she sees as more of a father?"

Did Georgiana see him more as a father? She remembered their father, though she was only ten when he died. "Regardless, I would never make mention of it."

"Why not? 'Tis my fault. I was the one who wantonly lured you into the situation. I should not behave so. I should behave more as a lady."

"No!" He peered behind them, but the footmen appeared to be attending their surroundings more than their charge. He took her hands in his and held them between them. "I think you no less a lady by what you have done—by what we have done. I want to marry you and would never consider my wife wanton for expressing her desire for me. Do you understand?" He had kept his voice low enough so the footmen would not overhear.

"Yes, you are saying you prefer me to be a wanton." She pressed her mouth tightly together, though the edges curled and twitched.

As he set her hand back upon his arm, he started walking at a brisk pace while he shook his head. "You will be the death of me, woman." Her tinkling laughter made him smile.

"Mr. Darcy?"

"Hmm?"

"If you wish to marry me, why have you not asked?"

"Because after all that happened between us in Hertfordshire, I know I must redeem myself in your eyes."

Redeem himself? She tugged at his arm, turning him to face her. "Do you not realise you redeemed yourself not long after your apology? I have not seriously thought of your insult for some time. We have been in company together almost every day and not for a mere call—either you are at Richmond House or I am at Darcy House for most of the day. Have I given you any reason to think I still hold your words and previous behaviour against you?" She stepped a little closer and leaned in. "I could not have allowed such a kiss if I held any sort of animosity toward you. Would you consider me respectable if I did?"

"Do you care for me?"

She lifted her eyebrows and crossed her arms over her chest. "Do you think I give my kisses to gentlemen I do not care for? My feelings have made such a change since we became reacquainted. I wake in the morning, anticipating when we will be in company—even if it is for but a moment while I call upon Georgiana—and when you depart, my heart does not want you go. My entire body comes to life when you even lean in as though you will kiss me, and I cannot describe how it feels when your lips touch mine. I may speak of being wanton, but I could not be so with another." Her eyes burned, and she swiped at a dampness on one. How could he ask her such a question?

She turned and started back towards the Cumberland Gate and Richmond House. Her grandfather's footmen frowned when she passed, but she paid them no mind. Before she could go far, a hand to her elbow made her pause. "Forgive me," he said near her ear without turning her around. "My heart is too full of you, and my mind becomes overrun and ceases to function. I do not think you bestow your favours upon other gentlemen, which is fortunate, since I would want to tear them limb from bloody limb if you had. You are all I have desired since you refused to dance with me at Lucas Lodge. These past few weeks with you have only made that desire more vivid and real. I love you. More than anything, I long to marry you and have been biding my time for any indication you would accept the offer of my hand. This waiting is torture, so if what you have described is truly how you feel, say you will be mine. Say you will marry me."

"Miss Elizabeth?"

She blinked in an attempt to prevent any more tears from falling and touched the back of her glove to her cheeks before she turned to the footman. "I am well, Matthew. We are just talking." The servant returned to where the other footman awaited him, and they turned their attention to what was around them once again.

"You are in earnest?" she asked.

"I would never tease about my feelings or yours. Marry me, Elizabeth?"

Her vision blurred, and she stifled a sob. "Yes."

"Yes?"

She laughed and nodded. "Yes, I shall marry you. I love you too." How had this happened so quickly? The moment the question was uttered, her heart began screaming for her to accept. She had not even understood that longing inside her was love until he had asked if she cared as though he assumed she held no feelings for him at all. Walking away had sent a pain through her that consumed her from head to toe, and the way her heart seemed to grow in her chest as he spoke of his feelings. Even now, she had to hold herself back from jumping into his arms.

He took her gloved hands and kissed them both before encasing them in his. "We should get you warm. You are trembling. Besides, I did promise Georgiana to bring you for chocolate after our walk."

"When will you speak to my grandfather?"

"May I do so when I walk you home? I should like to be considered your betrothed sooner rather than later."

"Yes, I should prefer that as well," she said almost breathless. Had she truly just accepted Mr. Darcy's hand in marriage? The notion seemed almost unreal, but she was about to burst from her skin and a smile was sure to be spread across her countenance.

After they walked through the Stanhope Gate and crossed the street, she let the footmen know she would be calling on Miss Darcy, so they watched her enter the house before returning to her grandfather's home.

"Where is my sister?" he asked as they handed off their coats and hats to the maid and footman who greeted them.

"She was in the music room last I saw her," said the footman.

They made their way to the music room, but it was empty. "Where could she be? I shall be but a moment." He stepped out while she made her way to the pianoforte and touched a key, then another. She trailed her fingers along the curve as she walked to a portrait over the mantel. The lady favoured Georgiana, but the eyes were reminiscent of Mr. Darcy. The room around her was comfortable yet fine. Her stomach tightened. She was to be mistress of this house. How was she to credit it?

"I found my butler, who was returning from the wine cellar. Georgiana went to Richmond House, at the invitation of your sister, for tea."

He glanced into the corridor. "We should not be alone."

"Would only a few moments be *so* bad?" He was correct, but she had just accepted his proposal of marriage. She ached to be in his arms.

He took her hand and led her into his study. As soon as the door was closed behind her, he drew her into his embrace and stole her breath with his kiss. One hand pressed her lower back until she was flush against him as the other curved up her neck into the back of her hair. His tongue grazed hers, and her knees weakened.

Her greedy fingers traced along his cheeks and threaded through his hair, which was softer than she would have expected. Was it possible for this to never end? Of course, it was not, but when it created such warmth within her, how could she not wish for it?

His lips found their way across her cheek to her neck, grazing the length before suckling under her ear. She whimpered and grabbed the shoulder of his topcoat in an effort to remain standing.

"We should stop," he said almost in a growl.

"In a moment."

As he sat on the settee, he drew her onto his lap, his lips and tongue still wreaking havoc on her ability to think. She could not breathe. Her breasts were too confined by her stays and the bodice of her gown, making her pant. How would she not faint?

A hand that had been bunching the gown at her waist lifted along her ribs until his thumb rubbed along the aching tip of her breast. She writhed as another ache bloomed between her legs. "I want to touch you."

He drew back and their gazes held. Would he be shocked by her admission? His fingers began to work at the knot of his cravat, and once it was untied, her shaky fingers untied the top of his shirt while he fumbled with the buttons on his topcoat and waistcoat. When his neck became visible, her fingers caressed from the nape to under his chin, eliciting a hiss before he reclaimed her lips.

"Fitzwilliam," she breathed as his fingers returned to her breast.

He kissed her again, hungrily, while his hands massaged over her sides, her thighs, and her back. After some time in that attitude, he gentled his kisses until he drew back, wearing a sweet smile.

She sighed and laid her head upon his shoulder. "Could we not just wed on the morrow? I do not want to move." Their current position was most agreeable. She would be pleased to remain in such an attitude forever.

"As much as it pains me, we must. One way or another, Georgiana or your family will discover you have not returned to Richmond House, and your footmen know where you are." Good Lord, he was right. Though everything in her resisted, she pulled herself from his lap and stood, her legs shaky, allowing them to steady for a moment while she adjusted her gown.

"A mirror would be of aid."

He stood and took her hand. "If it means we can enjoy such activities in my study, then I shall have one hung before we are wed," he said with both of his dimples peeking through. The latch of the door rattled, and they froze, their eyes wide.

"I say. Higgins, why is this door locked?"

Her stomach dropped at the colonel's voice, and Fitzwilliam pulled her into the library, across the room, and into a servants' passage. He peered around corners and hastened her up the stairs. When they reached the upper floor, she was led into a richly appointed bedchamber. "What room is this?"

"My bedchamber. You desired a mirror, and I did not want Richard to discover us together as we were. He would not tell, but I would not want you embarrassed as you surely would be."

She kissed him on the lips. "Thank you."

After he ensured his valet was not in his dressing room, he allowed her to enter. "A mirror, towelling, and water, which will be cold, but—"

"It is no matter. If you call for warm, I could be discovered." He kissed her passionately and left her to right herself, which took but a moment. Between kisses, laughs, and fumbling fingers that would prefer to remove clothing than put it to rights, she then helped Fitzwilliam button his waistcoat and topcoat while he tied his own cravat.

Once they were presentable, he pulled her to another door by her hand, then peeked through. "Go left and you will find the stairs. I shall follow soon. Await me in the music room. Should you be stopped along the way, you were told Georgiana was home, so you knocked upon the door to her bedchamber." A good excuse. Fitzwilliam was not told of Georgiana's departure until after he sought out the butler. After he peered once more through the door, he allowed her to depart. Thankfully, no servants lingered about, and she made her way to the music room without difficulty.

"Miss Elizabeth?" When she whirled around, Colonel Fitzwilliam stood in the door. "Mr. Higgins mentioned Darcy is here, but he never said you were calling upon Georgiana."

"Mr. Darcy and I were walking in the park. We returned to have tea with Georgiana and did not learn until after searching for her, that she is calling at Richmond House. Mr. Darcy wished to refresh himself before we walked over." She curtseyed. "'Tis agreeable to see you again, sir. I hope you have been well."

"Yes, thank you," he said with a bow.

"Richard! I am glad to see you in one piece. Will you be with us for a while?"

The colonel whirled around as Fitzwilliam strode into the room. "I am here through Twelfth Night at least." He glanced back and forth between them. Was there something amiss? She lightly placed her hand on her stomach. Had she missed some sign of what they had done?

"I hate to leave you so soon, but I must walk Miss Elizabeth to Richmond House and speak with the earl. Georgiana and I shall return for dinner, and we can talk over brandy after. What say you?"

"Of course." The colonel wore a crooked grin that made her stiffen. "Miss Elizabeth, I hope we shall have the opportunity to visit soon."

"Yes, colonel. I look forward to it." Why was he wearing that expression?

As soon as they had put on their coats and hats and were outside, she gripped Fitzwilliam's sleeve. "He suspects something; I am certain. The way his gaze shifted between us, and his grin before we departed gave me reason to believe he suspects."

"I agree."

"Did I miss something? Could he tell by looking at me?"

"Elizabeth, he surely saw no more than your reddened lips and a smile I could not contain. He will keep a confidence. Do not fret. You have nothing to be ashamed of. We did naught but kiss and touch a little."

"I am not ashamed, only mortified. As you knew I would be. Even if we were wed, I would likely blush to the roots of my hair." How would she manage then? She knew naught of what occurred between a man and a wife, other than he could do as he liked with her. Why did that make her as achy and breathless as when they were in his study?

"I enjoy your blushes," he said in a low tone that sent a shiver through her. That sensation would never grow old.

Chapter 18

W hen they reached Richmond House, Elizabeth followed the voices coming from the drawing room in search of Georgiana while he knocked upon the door of Lord Richmond's study. He entered when the earl bade him to come.

"Ah, Darcy, I am pleased you are here." He stopped and narrowed his eyes for a moment, then began to chuckle. "You were correct, Nicholas." He opened the top drawer of his desk, withdrew what appeared to be a bank note, and placed it on the far corner.

Hatton, who was sitting in the nearby chair, leaned forward and slapped the paper before drawing it towards himself. "I told you he would fall before the New Year."

Darcy stood stunned. "You were wagering on me?"

"More specifically, on how long you would take to propose to my cousin," said Hatton, wagging a finger. "Thank you, Darcy. In appreciation for you winning me twenty pounds, I shall pour you a glass of brandy."

"My brandy!" Lord Richmond crossed his arms over his chest, though the side of his lip twitching contradicted his affected anger.

"Since I am to inherit, what is yours will eventually be mine, so..." Hatton could not even finish the statement before he began laughing. "I cannot even..."

"Thank goodness for that," said Lord Richmond, chuckling. "Do not look so shocked, Darcy. I often tell Hatton that I am not dead yet when we discuss estate matters. I do so in jest, but this is the first time he has attempted to turn the joke around on me. Do sit down. You have my consent and blessing to marry Lizzybeth. I shall not torment you for sport."

"That is it?" This was too simple.

"I have no need to enquire of your income or your prospects. Your eyes give away your love for my granddaughter, which has grown since the two of you resolved your differences, and I know my Lizzybeth. She may have questioned her feelings at first, but her heart is as much yours as yours is hers. Your father will have taught you well to honour your wife with your marriage settlement. I have no concerns. My wife and I agreed when we first saw you together what an excellent match you would make. You have only proven us correct."

Hatton handed him a glass. "It will be good to have her so close."

"You must stay for dinner," said the earl. "We shall announce your engagement then."

The grandfather and grandson were speaking in such a way his mind was spinning to keep up. "Colonel Fitzwilliam just returned from Dover—"

"Capital! Invite him too. Pen him a note and a footman will run it down." The earl passed a piece of paper across the desk and gestured to his pen and inkwell. As soon as Darcy had written a short message, he folded the missive, and Hatton located a footman to take it.

"Now, have the two of you discussed when you will wed?"

His attention jolted back to Lord Richmond while he scratched the back of his neck. "No, we have not spoken of that yet." Well, he could not very well say they spoke little of the ceremony and indulged in more of what came after.

Nicholas almost cackled. "I would wager Darcy wishes to wed before we are too far into the Season. The matchmaking mamas will all weep that such an eligible bachelor is off the marriage market."

At a knock, the earl bid the person come. When Lady Richmond entered, he stepped around the desk. "What brings you to my study, my dear?"

"I have heard rumour in the house that we are having guests for dinner. I came to discover if what I have been told is true so I can speak to Mrs. Taylor about the menu."

"We had invited Darcy, which would mean Georgiana would join us, of course. A note was only just sent to include the colonel in our party should he like to come."

"You should notify your housekeeper you will not be dining at home," said the countess, looking at him.

"I asked my cousin to inform her."

"Good man." She glanced around to each man in the room, then turned her gaze upon her husband. "I do not object, but the three of you are far more cheerful than is your wont. What is it that has you all smiling, particularly Fitzwilliam? I cannot remember seeing his dimples so prominently displayed since he was a young lad and his father gave him his first horse."

That day was perhaps one of the happiest in his memory—until today. Why should he not display his contentment upon his countenance? His cousin oft times complained of his dour expression. Was this not an improvement?

"That will have to wait until dinner," said Lord Richmond.

Hatton lifted his glass as though toasting. "Grandpapa wishes to make a formal announcement."

Lady Richmond looked back at her husband, then she clapped her hands together. "You have proposed! I knew you would, did I not, Hugh? I am so pleased. Why wait to announce such joyous news! The girls and I could be discussing wedding plans." She bustled over to him, took his hands, and kissed his cheek. "I could not ask for a better husband for our Lizzybeth.

We have a wedding to plan! Have you and Lizzybeth decided upon a date?"

"I only asked during our walk and had not thought to discuss that without you." They were too busy celebrating their betrothal, not that Lady Richmond needed to know that part. What he would not give to have Elizabeth alone for another quarter hour! It had not been long, and his arms already ached at her absence.

"That is no matter. We can do so this evening, but I need to go speak to Mrs. Taylor about the menus first." Like a whirlwind, Lady Richmond patted him on the cheek and departed, murmuring while she ticked items off on her fingers.

The earl rubbed his forehead. "I shall not sleep well until Lizzybeth is wed, so pray, do not delay on our account. We shall miss her when she is living with you, but as Nicholas has said, she will be closer than before so we shall see her more often."

What could he mean? Would worry keep him from his rest or was it some other factor? "I do not understand."

"My wife, man. She will toss and turn and speak of the blasted arrangements in her sleep until all is said and done. When Bennet and Sophie became engaged, it was the same. My wife, who has a great deal of good sense and does not succumb to fits of nerves, never stopped planning—even in her sleep."

Hatton did not seem to react to the earl's comment, which was surprising. It was not common practice for couples of their sphere to share a bed every night. His parents had, and he hoped to, should Elizabeth not object, but if others partook of the practice, they never spoke of it.

"Perhaps we should join the ladies," said Hatton. "Grandmamma will not refrain from announcing the engagement to them, and I am certain Darcy would care to be there for his sister."

"Yes, I would." He rose and followed the earl and Hatton to the drawing room where the countess already had Elizabeth in an embrace, the Misses Montford and Georgiana wrapped around his betrothed from the sides and behind.

Lord Richmond laughed and shook his head. "Now that is a sight."

When the group drew apart, Elizabeth wiped her eyes with her handkerchief. He was by her side in a moment. "Are you well?"

"Yes, very much so. My grandmother was sharing her heartfelt wishes for us, and I found her words very touching.

Georgiana threw her arms around him. "I am so excited. I have always wanted a sister, and now I shall have two."

"We have three more sisters," said Miss Jane with a smile.

"Though they are quite different. Mary prefers sermons to Radcliffe, while Kitty and Lydia are more concerned with officers than reading or accomplishments. Papa calls the three of them the silliest girls in England."

"Forgive me, but that is not charitable of him," said Georgiana, who glanced at Miss Jane with a wary look.

Lord Richmond sat in his usual chair and crossed his ankle over his knee. "Speaking of your father and sisters, would you like to invite them? I am certain you would like your father to be present."

She crossed her arms over her chest and tapped her foot. "You know well that he has not written me once since I arrived. I have sent him three letters: one when we arrived, one after your visit to Hertfordshire, and one last week. I suppose I shall continue to try, but if he will not respond, I shall not wait for him to come around."

Darcy took her hand and led her to sit near him on the settee. "What if we journey to Longbourn so you may speak to him? Richmond, you would come with us, would you not?"

"For your happiness, Lizzybeth, I would certainly visit Longbourn with you, though I fear my presence may do more harm than good since I last spoke to Bennet."

"I could go in your stead," said Hatton, who set his hand upon his grandfather's shoulder. "He would know I speak for you." But would Hatton command the same respect from Mr. Bennet as not only his former father but also an earl?

Lord Richmond patted his grandson's hand. "I appreciate your offer, but I believe I should be the one to accompany Lizzybeth. We should have a date settled before we proffer the invitation. Tomorrow is Sunday, so I propose we go Monday. We shall leave when the sun rises and return that afternoon. Would that suit you, Darcy?"

"It would. What of you, Miss Elizabeth?"

"I appreciate your willingness, but are you certain you both want to call on my father? I knew he would be upset at us not returning. This silence from him is unnerving. As for the date, my wish is to be wed before the crowds arrive in London for the Season."

"A vague answer indeed," said Miss Amelia. "For Parliament shall return not long after Twelfth Night. The next group will arrive in the beginning of February, and London will be teeming with those in town for the Season by March."

"It will be quicker to order a gown from Madame Morisot at our next appointment, which thankfully, is on Tuesday for all of you. I thought we could go to the drapers tomorrow morning, but I can delay until Monday before the modiste so you may join us, Lizzybeth."

"Thank you, Gran."

"Most betrothals are a month long, so why should they not wed in January?" asked Hatton. "Lizzy could order her wedding clothes before most return for the Season, and she would take part in the Season as Mrs. Darcy."

After a discussion of guests other than Mr. Bennet, the date was set for the 19th of January, which was three weeks hence rather than a month, but he would not complain of the brevity. After what occurred in his study, it might be prudent for them to be wed before the temptation of her became too much.

Richard was announced by Mr. Gideon just before the housekeeper notified the countess that dinner was ready to be served. "Pray, forgive me. I had barely arrived from Dover when the note came from Darcy, so I refreshed myself and changed for dinner."

"Quite understandable," said Lady Richmond. "We are pleased you could celebrate with us."

"Celebrate?" Richard chuckled and handed Darcy a box he had requested in his letter. "Now I understand why you asked me to retrieve this from your safe. Congratulations, Cousin." Richard followed Lord and Lady Richmond to the dining room with the Misses Montford while Hatton walked with Georgiana on his arm.

He received that usual jolt when Elizabeth's palm rested in the crook of his elbow while he opened the box and held the ring where she could see it. How often had he touched the pink sapphire in the centre while it graced his mother's finger? "I thought this would be your betrothal gift. If you do not like it, I have other rings that belonged to my mother and grandmother—"

"'Tis gorgeous, Fitzwilliam. Would you put in on my finger?" She wiggled her fingers in front of them while she bounced on her toes.

"You will need to stop moving until I can slide it over the tip." The ring fit on the index finger of her right hand without needing to be altered.

"Are the both of you coming?" When they both started, Georgiana stood in the doorway. "Oh! I have seen that ring in portraits of my mother. I believe she wore it on the same finger. It suits you perfectly."

"Thank you."

"Come! We are famished!" cried Richard from inside.

After Darcy kissed the ring on Elizabeth's finger, he set her hand back upon his arm and led her into the dining room behind his sister. No one could ruin his good spirits today—not even his cousin's teasing, which he was certain to endure before the evening was complete. Would Elizabeth agree to embroider his cousin's mouth closed? As much as he would enjoy the prospect, somehow, he doubted it.

As soon as Georgiana retired, Richard refilled his brandy. "I would never have thought you one to anticipate your vows."

"What nonsense are you speaking of?"

"You made Miss Elizabeth the offer of your hand, then brought her here without a chaperon of any sort. I thought it odd your study door was locked. You never lock it since you keep any item of value in the safe. After I consulted with Higgins, I witnessed Miss Elizabeth come down the last of the stairs before she awaited you in the music room. You followed two or three minutes after her. Do know I noticed the blush of her lips when I greeted her. I admit I was stunned when you used Georgiana as an excuse."

He exhaled heavily and began bouncing his foot. "You are mistaken, and I would appreciate if you never spoke of this to her or anyone else."

"You know I would not, Cousin, but what if she falls with child?"

"She will not since we did not anticipate our vows." Richard's insufferable crooked grin made him pinch the bridge of his nose. "I admit we broke with propriety, but I did not take her, and I shall not until we are wed. We truly returned to have chocolate with Georgiana, which would not have necessitated the footmen from Richmond House, but learnt upon our arrival that Georgiana had been invited by Miss Jane to Richmond House for tea while we were walking in Hyde Park. We knew we should not be alone, but as before, when my lips touched hers, I was gone. I am uncertain how I maintained enough control to keep matters from going further." His first error had been tasting her kisses behind the draperies in the music room. When she drew close to him and her orange blossom scent surrounded him, he could think of nothing else. How was he supposed to resist?

"The two of you will be wed in less than a month. You need to keep yourself under better regulation. Rein it in." Richard was telling him nothing he did not know. Why state the obvious?

"What have you heard of Bingley since Dorset's ball?" At least Richard changed the subject on his own!

After he told him of Bingley's request for an introduction to the earl, he shook his head. "I have not heard of him since."

"Let us hope he does not become more desperate than he already is."

He could only agree. The next few weeks needed to pass smoothly so he could claim Elizabeth as his bride. Nothing could interfere, especially Bingley and his debts!

Chapter 19

Her grandfather held her hand as his carriage made its way through Meryton. Many of those walking through the small market town stopped and watched since such a grand equipage was rare to pass through during its journey. Meryton was off the main roads, and although a post coach stopped at the inn, the local populace saw little out of the ordinary on most days. Still, many just continued to the shops or on their way, oblivious to their presence.

Elizabeth pointed through the window. "Aunt...Mrs. Philips is speaking to Mrs. Goulding in her garden."

"Is that Mrs. Bennet's sister?" Her grandfather ducked down a little in order to see.

"She is and just like her in temper. You cannot sneeze in Meryton without Mrs. Philips knowing and informing the entire town." As they passed the turn to Lucas Lodge and Netherfield, she pointed them out to her grandfather as well. He had been to Longbourn before but speaking and giving her mind another occupation other than thinking about what was to come aided with her nervous energy. She would burst if she did not preoccupy herself with some task.

When they pulled before Longbourn, Mr. Darcy helped her alight and offered her his arm, which she gratefully took. A commotion of noise could be heard from the front parlour where Lydia, Kitty, and Mrs. Bennet all peered through the windows with wide eyes.

"I would say your carriage has been noticed," she said, withholding a sigh. Their reaction was hardly unexpected. It was the same with Mr. Bingley's equipage when Miss Bingley and Mrs. Hurst once called.

An unknown maid answered the door, and when her grandfather handed over his card and requested an audience with her father, the woman regarded him with enormous eyes before she hurried in the direction of the library. She returned soon after. "I'm very sorry, my lord. He is not at home." Her eyes were trained to the side, and she shifted on her feet.

"'Tis no matter. I am here to see my father." Where the sudden fire within her originated, who knew, but she marched past the maid to the library door and strode inside without knocking.

"What is the meaning—" His tirade ended as quickly as it began when he noticed her standing before his desk.

"Did the maid not make mention that my grandfather was accompanied by your daughter and Mr. Darcy? She was informed. I can only assume since you have not responded once to my letters that you are avoiding me now too. Will you also refuse Jane's visit should she come to Longbourn?"

"Elizabeth—"

"Do not attempt to placate me. You singled me out from my sisters and invited me into this room to discuss books and what was written in the paper. Was this for nothing more than your own entertainment? Now that I am living with my grandparents, am I useless to you?"

Her father stood, his chair screeching along the floor. "Do not dare speak to me this way, Elizabeth Abigail. I am—"

"The man who has allowed his wife to belittle me for years, to put her own daughters and Jane, because of her beauty, above me. I have defended you to Grandpapa, made excuses for Mrs. Bennet. I came today to tell you I am betrothed to Mr. Darcy and to ask you to give me away." Fitzwilliam took one of her hands and squeezed which was far from appropriate yet needed more than he could know.

Her father pointed at Fitzwilliam, his countenance riddled with disgust. "You are engaged to *him*, a man you claimed to detest? You *have* changed. You are not my Lizzy. Obviously, your grandparents have wooed you with their money and the balls and parties you could attend, the gowns you could purchase—such as the one you are wearing now—"

"You know little of your own daughter if you believe what you say," said Fitzwilliam in a low and dangerous tone. "I apologised for my unguarded and untrue words at the assembly and my arrogance. Your daughter is a lady worthy of being pleased, and I set out to court her—"

"When you learnt of her connexions and whatever fortune *he* has set up for her." Her father threw up his arm at her grandfather, his face red and his voice rough.

"Think that if you must," said her grandfather in a calm but firm tone. "The truth is you allowed my granddaughter to be chased by Mr. Collins and allowed it to go so far as a proposal for your own entertainment." Her father opened his mouth, but her grandfather stepped closer. "Do not deny it. You could not have missed his marked attentions. Lizzybeth has described them to us. He did all in his power to be close to her during his time in this house, and in your selfishness, you allowed your daughter's discomfort to continue."

"Do not forget Bingley," said Fitzwilliam.

"Yes," said her father, "God forbid my daughter become attached to a man of five thousand a year. I thought you his friend, but by your behaviour in our neighbourhood, I should have surmised your fickle nature."

Fitzwilliam gave a wry chuckle. "Fickle nature, indeed. I told you on our last call how Bingley was often in and out of love. We have since discovered he is more than forty thousand pounds in debt and attempting to sell his most profitable mill to pay the lady he owes—his paramour. When he asked my advice, he gave the impression of one quite desperate. If he has even one hundred pounds of the one hundred thousand his father left him, I should be shocked. He has attempted to force his company on your eldest daughter and requested my aid in the endeavour. While I do believe he enjoys your daughter's company, he would not be seeking to court her were it not for her fortune."

"My grandfather informed us both he had reason to believe Mr. Bingley a poor choice for Jane. I watched the gentleman with my own eyes enter the cardroom at the Duke of Dorset's ball, as well as chase us down after the morning service on Christmas. He is not what he seems, Papa."

Her grandfather stepped to her side. "My investigators have confirmed what Darcy has said. His coffers are empty, and he owes his mistress a great deal of money. Is that the gentleman you wish for your daughter?"

Papa scoffed. "And how would a woman have access to such large sums of money? This is balderdash."

"Lady Jemima is not your usual sort of lady," said Grandpapa. "Her father despises her mother, and the girl has always been a pawn between them. She is exceedingly spoilt. When her father put fifty thousand into an account and gave her free reign over the funds, people thought him mad. No one expected her to increase that sum. She is shrewd with her money and an accomplished gambler, if one can call someone who risks their purse in such a way accomplished. I assure you we speak the truth."

"Lizzy, do not fall for their lies. Return to Longbourn where you belong. I shall speak to your mother—"

"She is not my mother," she said, blinking madly at the sting of tears. "You married her when I was so very young and have called her my mother for years, but that does not make her my mother. A mother loves and cares for her daughters. She saw Jane's beauty and gentle nature and favoured her while I was scolded for preferring to spend my days out of doors, scraping my knees, and ripping my gowns when I attempted to climb whatever tree John Lucas and David Goulding dared me to climb."

Her grandfather took her free hand. "I suspect you resembled your mother too greatly as well, which made Mrs. Bennet jealous. He once had a portrait of her in here, but I noticed during my last visit it had been removed."

Papa slammed his fist upon his desk. "You poisoned her against my wife!"

"Your wife has done naught to earn her respect and affection. We only helped her to see for herself that Mrs. Bennet has never treated her as a beloved daughter, and therefore owed no loyalty to a woman who decided Lizzybeth was less than those around her. She deserved better, Bennet, even *you* cannot deny that. In your idleness, you have let your house go. You were a different man once—a good man."

"I am a man who lost his wife and son, and now, you would have me lose the only parts of Sophie I have remaining."

"You have not lost us, Papa. If you would visit and write, you would still be a part of our lives. Jane and I do care for you and miss you. I came to ask you to my wedding."

Her father shook his head. "Not while you do their bidding." He punctuated "their" with a jab at her grandfather.

She straightened as tall as she could. "Grandpapa, I have done what I came to do. I now wish to leave." Without another word, she turned on her heel and departed the room. She had to get out of the house before she burst into huge wracking sobs. How had she held it in for this long?

"There you are!" Mrs. Bennet stood in the doorway to the parlour. "I had not been told you returned. Where is my Jane?"

"Jane is in London with my grandmother."

Lydia shoved past her mother and propped her hands on her hips, standing far too close. "Mama! Look at her gown! No gentlemen ever look at her. Why should she have such an expensive travelling gown? I want it!"

Her hand brushed down the bodice to her stomach and stopped, pressing against the shaking within. "Lydia, stop behaving like a child. My grandmother bought me this gown, and you have no right to it."

"Well, that's not up to you now, is it?" Mrs. Bennet's chin was raised, and her nostrils flared.

Grandpapa and Fitzwilliam stepped to either side of her. "I should say it is, Mrs. Bennet. You should have your immature and spoilt daughter step back from my granddaughter."

"You are that man who was here a fortnight ago. The one who refused to speak to me in my own home. It is not as though you are some grand and titled gentleman and better than us."

"Mrs. Bennet." Her father stepped beside her grandfather. "I may never have told you of my Sophie's parents, but this gentleman is her father, Hugh Montford, the Earl of Richmond. Jane is at his London home and Lizzy will be returning there forthwith. Neither will be returning to this house."

"La! Why is Mr. Darcy here?" Her youngest sister twirled a curl from behind her ear around her finger while she sneered in Fitzwilliam's direction.

"He is my betrothed," said Elizabeth in as strong a voice as she could manage.

Lydia burst into gales of laughter, making her flinch. "What a joke! They must be forcing them. He would never desire to marry Lizzy. He said she was merely tolerable and not handsome. Though I say better her than me. I would not wish for someone so prideful."

Elizabeth pulled from her grandfather's hand on her arm and stood toe to toe with Lydia. "He is more than you could aspire to with your unchecked behaviour. No reasonable officer or gentleman wants a wife who flirts shamelessly with every man in the room. You are not even out, yet you rub your chest on men's arms in the same manner as those ladies wearing rouge on Drury Lane. It is mortifying." Mrs. Bennet gasped, but Elizabeth never heard what was said since she pushed past the girl, hastened through the front door, and climbed into the carriage. The servant did not even have time to offer his hand to help her inside.

She should have known better than to come. First, her father ridiculed her choice, Mrs. Bennet suggested she would give Lydia her new gown, then Lydia thought her betrothal to Fitzwilliam a worthy of a fit of raucous giggles. How had she survived Longbourn such as it was for all of those years? She had spent a prodigious amount of time in the gardens, visiting tenants, and rambling the estate. Had she begun those pursuits to avoid those parts of her life that would have made her miserable?

Her grandfather stepped inside and took her hand as he sat across from her. "Do not let them disturb your equanimity. They are not worthy of you, my girl. You will live a grand life and have no need to see Mrs. Bennet or her silly daughters ever again."

Elizabeth delivered her set down and quit the room with a dignity he would not have expected given what had just occurred. Darcy had to purse his lips to prevent himself from laughing at the scene before him, though the earl showed no such restraint. "Who knew she would have observed so much walking into and out of the Theatre Royal?" He bid no one good day. He merely departed.

Darcy turned his hat in his hand. "Mr. Bennet, I hope you know it is not too late. Your daughter is a generous and forgiving lady. A well-worded letter would go far to repair the damage wrought upon your relationship. She loves you, or we would not have come all this way for her to request your presence at our nuptials."

"You forced Mr. Bingley to leave Hertfordshire and abandon my Jane," said Mrs. Bennet as he stepped towards the door.

He stopped and glared as best he could at the insipid woman. "Miss Bingley and Mrs. Hurst were not fond of your connexions, madam, and persuaded him to give up Netherfield. I would not expect his return. He has gambled his fortune away and is in arrears. I would be surprised if he has not retrenched to Scarborough with his aunt by Easter." He almost turned to leave, but instead, drew a hairsbreadth closer to Mrs. Bennet. "Miss Montford, Mr. Bennet's eldest daughter, deserves better than Bingley. Lord Richmond is quite attentive towards such matters. He would never have allowed Miss Elizabeth's marriage to Mr. Collins—and he would have had the final say. Your husband holds no such power. As for

Elizabeth, Lord Richmond and I both will ensure you never torment her again."

"I *said* that is enough, Mr. Darcy!" cried Mr. Bennet. He said "enough?" When had he done so? Darcy had never heard him utter one word much less make a demand. "You will receive no part of Elizabeth's one thousand pounds!"

Darcy pivoted around. "I have no need for it. Your daughter will have a generous settlement and all the pin money she requires, which I would have done even if she came to me without a penny. No child of ours will suffer the neglect of nothing set aside for their futures. I suggest you take Miss Elizabeth's and Miss Montford's portions and split them between your three remaining daughters. They will have more need of it. Good day, sir." With that, he followed the earl, his jaw paining him from how tight it was set.

When he entered the carriage, Lord Richmond was holding Elizabeth's hand and murmuring to her. How he wanted to take her in his arms and hold her until she knew she would never be treated thus again. He would love and respect her for the rest of their lives.

He sat beside Lord Richmond, who rapped his walking stick on the ceiling of the carriage. When they were underway, the earl nudged him. "Sit with my granddaughter. She needs you."

He could not be serious? How was he supposed to comfort Elizabeth with her grandfather sitting across the carriage?

"Stop thinking, Darcy. I am less concerned with propriety at the moment than my Lizzybeth. I can tell her she is loved and be there for her, but at the moment, I believe you would be more effective than me."

Carefully, he shifted across to sit beside Elizabeth and took her hand. "Elizabeth, dearest, look at me." He tipped her chin up as a tear landed upon her cheek and rolled towards her chin. She choked out a sob and fell against his chest, nuzzling into his great coat. He glanced at the earl, who did no more than close every curtain but the one closest to him, which he stared out of as though he were the sole occupant of the carriage.

Darcy wrapped his arms around Elizabeth. "Shh." He rubbed his hand up and down her back and kissed the crown of her head. "I love you." She sniffled and nestled herself closer. They remained thus until her breathing evened. With care, he shifted her so he could sit comfortably for the remainder of their travel and sighed. His head was beginning to throb. He needed to stop grinding his teeth.

"I assume you set down Mrs. Bennet as well?" The earl spoke in soft tones, no doubt to keep from waking his granddaughter.

"I wish I had said more. Naught will come of my words or Elizabeth's, but I cannot deny that I am glad they were said. Mr. Bennet threatened to withhold some one thousand pounds he has set aside for her."

Lord Richmond shook his head. "I believe Mrs. Bennet's settlement set aside one thousand for each of her girls, and Bennet set aside a matching sum for both Janey and Lizzybeth. As far as I am concerned, he may keep his paltry excuse for a fortune. They have no need of it."

The tightness in his neck eased some. "That is good since I told him to save it and split it amongst his remaining daughters."

"I am saddened by Bennet's behaviour, but after today's debacle, perhaps it is for the best the girls to be done with Longbourn forever."

"Would you keep Mr. Bennet from them?"

"No, I could never deny him completely, but should Jane want him at her wedding, I shall pen a letter. We shall not journey to Longbourn. They will never set foot in that house again."

Chapter 20

Three days had passed since their trip to Longbourn, and while Elizabeth was still quiet, she seemed to be rallying. She had not shied away from joining her family in the drawing room, and she had never refused a call from Darcy, nor had she refused a walk outside. This morning, her head rested against his arm while they walked in Hyde Park with a sigh.

"Are you well, my love?"

"I am thankful the cold weather keeps most people indoors and allows us some semblance of privacy."

"Other than Matthew and Michael," he said with a smile while he touched his cheek to her crown.

She glanced behind them at the footmen and situated herself back as she had been before. "They shall not interfere unless you take me in your arms and kiss me senseless, which is unfortunate, since I should dearly love for you to do so."

He breathed through the heat that travelled through his body at her words. "You do not know what that does to me. If I had not tasted your kisses, you would not tempt me so, but your lips, your tongue, and the way you whimper when we kiss— Pray, speak of gowns, lace, or some other frivolity before I drag you from the path and away from your grandfather's footmen. I am certain there are some evergreen trees somewhere in this blasted park that could conceal us." He feigned searching for such a place. When she laughed, his chest lightened.

"Jane and I have been talking in the evenings of what happened at Longbourn."

"I hope speaking of it and your sister's counsel were of aid." His fist ached to hit Mr. Bennet in the teeth, even if he refrained from doing so when they were last face to face.

"She remembers more of when we returned to Longbourn after Papa's marriage, how Mrs. Bennet insisted we call her Mama. Since my sister is not much older than me, her memories are vague, but apparently, I refused to do as Mrs. Bennet wished and would run into the gardens or the stable and hide for hours to escape her. When I was old enough, my father would bring me into his library. I also began my walks and taking books to Oakham Mount or a few other haunts where I would spend the day. Mrs. Hill would make me a pack with some bread, fruit, and muffins to take with me. I also spoke to the Hills before they departed London for Yorkshire. Mrs. Hill helped me put a great deal into perspective. I am pleased they will have a cottage at Richmond for the rest of their lives."

He peered over his shoulder. The footmen were watching their environs, so he bestowed a quick kiss on the crown of her head. "May I ask the point of your reflections? I am certain your talks are of benefit, but are you seeking some specific information in them?"

"During the embarrassing behaviour of Mrs. Bennet and Lydia, I caught myself questioning why I never considered Longbourn unbearable in the past. Jane and I are both considering how Longbourn has made us who we are. While I ran and hid from the problems at home, Jane ignored the bad until all she could see was the good, which is why she never noticed Miss Bingley's and Mrs. Hurst's duplicity."

Her theory had merit. The experiences of an individual could influence their character, so how could those influences not form their traits? "And in situations where you could not run or hide, you learnt to laugh."

She looked up at him, her chin propped near his shoulder in the most adorable way. "I suppose so. I had yet to consider my reaction to you. That was not as simple as avoiding Mrs.

Bennet's overbearing manner. When you entered the assembly, you stood so tall above most of the people surrounding you. I saw a handsome gentleman who made my insides flutter."

"I did? So soon?" What a fool he had been!

"From that first night. After, I convinced myself those feelings stemmed from my pointed dislike of you. I have caught myself wondering if I had not been Lord Richmond's granddaughter, would we have found ourselves at this same place? Would we be betrothed and this content with each other?"

He squeezed his eyes closed for but a moment. "I would like to think we would. You cannot know how much you consumed my thoughts after departing Hertfordshire. I was already halfway to being in love with you."

"Charlotte will be wed next week. She said in her last letter that if I was not to wed, she planned to invite me to Hunsford for Easter. Is that not near your aunt's estate?"

"It is, and Richard and I often visit during Easter to help Lady Catherine. She is overbearing to the steward, so we ensure those improvements for tenants she refuses to consider are implemented."

"So, perhaps we would have met again," she said, returning her temple to his arm. "You could have joined me on my morning walks where you begged me to forgive you for the assembly—"

"And unable to wait, I offered you my hand before we both departed." He cleared his throat and blinked. He could not bear the thought of his life without her for even a few days much less months. "I should like to think we would have found our way to each other."

"I am not to attend Charlotte's wedding."

He glanced down at the top of her bonnet, but naught could be seen to speak of her feelings on the matter. "Whyever not?"

"Mr. Collins has declared me an ungrateful child and grasping to believe I am worthy of the nephew of his esteemed patroness. My family will also be in attendance, and she wishes for no discord. I do not begrudge her the decision. Mr. Collins will likely feel free to express his unwanted and ludicrous opinions while Mrs. Bennet does not withhold her complaints and ire at my last visit."

"I had not thought of it in such a way. Your consideration of her is admirable. Most would feel the exclusion to be an insult."

"No, she explained her situation well." When they stood in front of Richmond House once more, she lifted her head from his arm. "I wish we could spend the afternoon in your study."

"We have a little over a fortnight until we can do so without censure. Your grandparents' offer to have Georgiana stay with them for the beginning of the Season was very kind. We shall not have to worry about abandoning her for the day."

"She and Jane have become quite attached. I am certain she has told Jane everything of Ramsgate, which Jane will not breathe to anyone. Georgiana needed to speak of her feelings, and I must admit, my elder sister was the perfect choice." Mr. Gideon opened the door with a smile.

"I agree. I know we need to go in, but I am not ready to give you up just yet."

"So, do not," she said simply as they stepped into the hall. "Perhaps Grandpapa would enjoy a chess match."

"I believe he would enjoy watching you trounce me soundly once more."

"If you are speaking of chess, then yes, I would." Lord Richmond stood in the doorway of the drawing room, beaming. "Have you enjoyed your walk in the cold? Mrs. Taylor should soon bring tea and chocolate which will do a great deal to warm you."

Darcy followed her grandfather towards his study with mixed emotions. He could never bemoan more time with Elizabeth, yet he craved to be alone with her. Even with her grandfather present, the carriage ride spent holding his intended had fulfilled him in a way nothing else ever had. He appreciated Lord Richmond allowing him to give her comfort, but she still needed him to hold her.

When they reached the study, her grandfather took Elizabeth in his embrace and kissed her temple. "Do you want to defeat Darcy first, then challenge me, or would you prefer I do the honours?"

She arched that one eyebrow. You played him first last time. I should like to have my turn." A gleam in her eye almost made him step back from her. What was that look? Could she understand how much of a distraction she had proven to be last time?

As soon as their tea and her chocolate were poured, and sitting where they could partake of it, they began their match, Lord Richmond sitting to the side of the table so he could watch. This time, however, Darcy kept his eyes on the board and avoided watching those mannerisms he found so enthralling during their last game.

After a good bit of back and forth, he made a play that had her scrambling to gain the upper hand once again. He picked up his queen to put Elizabeth's king in check and began to set it down when something grazed from the top of his boot to the inside of his thigh, an inch or two up from his knee. With a start, he looked down to where a set of delicate stockinged toes rubbed up and down the inside of his thigh. Meanwhile, the little minx lifted her head from where she had it propped on her hand.

"Is aught amiss, Fitzwilliam?" She spoke with such innocence. Thankfully, her foot was not so far her grandfather might notice.

He coughed. "No, I merely thought of a different move and need a moment to decide what strategy I will employ." How had his maiden fiancée learnt to muddle his brain so effectively? He set the piece down and shifted back in his chair. "Check."

With an abrupt giggle, she shifted her king forward one space and took his queen. Damn! He had meant to put it one space back.

"I hope you are not becoming ill, Darcy. You are a bit flushed," said Lord Richmond, a crooked smile tugging at his lips.

"No, I am well. Thank you." What else was he supposed to say? He could not very well tell Lord Richmond the antics of his granddaughter, could he? That was it! If he somehow survived this afternoon, he was going to make Elizabeth pay!

"Good morning, Mr. Higgins. I have come for Miss Darcy. She is to accompany us to Madame Morisot's shop this morning."

"Good morning, Miss Elizabeth," said the stiff butler with a slight bow as her footmen walked around the outside of the house to the servants' entrance. "Miss Darcy has yet to come down, but if you like, you may wait for her in the drawing room." After he took her redingote, gloves, and bonnet, he showed her into the drawing room they usually used when calling upon Georgiana, when they were not using the music room, that is.

She blew out a noisy breath and began a circuit of the room, pausing at this or that, looking at portraits, and examining the prospect from the window into Hyde Park. Georgiana had been told their appointment was at ten. Could she have forgotten? Of course, she was early—a half hour early by the clock chiming in the hall.

"What are you about, Elizabeth?" came a low but exceedingly familiar voice behind her. His tone enticing her to step back into his embrace, alas the door was wide open.

"I am awaiting your sister. She is to accompany us for fittings and to select patterns for more gowns. My grandmother is determined we are not to lack for anything this Season, even if I am already betrothed." Gran had not had many opportunities to shop for her or Jane. She was making up for the past in a matter of weeks instead of over time.

"I see. As I understand it, Georgiana had intended to be down for breakfast about now but overslept and will be another half hour. Perhaps you would prefer to wait in the library. You could read a book until she comes down." He took her hand. As they crossed the hall, he pointed towards the library. "Miss Elizabeth will be awaiting Miss Darcy in the library."

If Mr. Higgins was shocked, he gave no hint of it. "Very good, sir."

He brought her into the library, kissed her hand, and started back out the way they came. "Wait! Are you not staying with me?"

A dimple appeared, then disappeared as his lips twitched. "Now, that would not be appropriate, Miss Elizabeth."

She stood agape as he departed. He had wished to know what she was about, but perhaps she should be asking what was *he* about? With a huff, she walked along the shelves, her fingers trailing the spines, though her mind was wherever Fitzwilliam was. Where had he gone?

Something grabbed her hand and pulled her into a different room, pressing her against the door when it was closed. "Did you really believe I would just leave you in there alone?"

"What is this room?" There were shelves lining the walls and a desk to one end, but no fireplace or any of the comfortable furniture or decorations of his study.

"'Tis an office for a librarian."

"You have a librarian?"

"No, my grandfather thought perhaps one would be needed, but neither my father nor I have required one." He wrapped his arms around her and trailed his nose from her earlobe down her neck. "Now, my beautiful and mischievous betrothed, I wish to know where you learnt that little move you distracted me with during chess." She had started to laugh, but he suckled that place at the base of her neck—the one that made her pant and squirm.

"I shall tell you nothing." Her voice was breathy. Why could she not disguise how weak he made her?

"That is too bad, because I dearly want to know." Her bodice was suddenly loose, and Fitzwilliam's eyes held hers while his fingers slipped under her stays. His lips found hers and left no part of her mouth wanting while he rolled and pinched her nipple. A whimper bubbled up from her throat while she lost herself, drowning in the needy burn sweeping her body.

He softened his kiss while his hand withdrew from her stays. He drew away and she cried out in protest. "Where are you going?"

"You will not tell me, so I thought to return to my business."

"You cannot be serious? You would leave me here like this?" How would she explain her unbuttoned gown? His wicked grin was enough to make her clench her hands to keep from throwing herself into his arms.

"Where did you learn it?"

She crossed her arms over her chest with a huff. "One day, while I was out on one of my rambles, I happened upon a Longbourn maid and groom who were...well, they were in an intimate situation. They were clothed, but she raised her knee between his legs and rubbed him while they kissed. I could not very well do that while we were sitting with my grandfather, but I wondered if I could distract you from winning by rubbing the inside of your leg with my toes."

"And you knew I would be helpless to retaliate because of your grandfather."

She gave a one-shouldered shrug. "I suspected."

He stepped forward, and her arms fell while her body arched a bit, eager for his embrace. "Georgiana will not be down for another twenty minutes." His lips found hers again, cradling and caressing them before deepening the kiss, making her head spin. How could he take control over her body with merely a few kisses and touches? She loved every bit, but it only made her look forward to their wedding night more.

He trailed little kisses down her neck while she tugged her arms from her sleeves so her gown would not be in his way. She needed his fingers on her bare flesh. Once she removed the impediment of her petticoats and revealed her stays, he gazed into her eyes while he drew down the material over her breast, tracing circles around the centre. "You are so beautiful."

His gaze never left hers as he took the tip in his mouth, making her knees buckle. Without difficulty, he lifted her and placed her atop the desk while he continued to worship her breast.

She tore at his buttons on his waistcoat and topcoat until she had them open, slipping her hands around his sides. He sucked air through his teeth as his hands slid up her legs to her rear and pulled her so her core was pressed snugly against his hips.

He was so strong and the feel of the muscles under his shirt and the way they moved only served to excite her further. Her legs trembled and tiny gasps filled the air as he ground against her, increasing that mysterious ache that had bloomed and began to spread to every part of her.

While he nipped at her neck, his fingers grazed along the tops of her stockings and the muscles of her thighs clenched. How had they reached this point so quickly? Her entire body screamed for him to touch her where she ached for him.

"Fitzwilliam, touch me."

"I am."

"No." She took his hand and steered it where she wanted him. He stared into her eyes as his fingers tentatively slid along the seam.

"We should not be going this far." He breathed heavily and the muscles of his back were bunched under her palm.

"Are we anticipating our vows?"

He shook his head. "No, not yet, but touching you in this manner makes it increasingly difficult to stop before that happens."

"I trust you." And she did. She would trust him with her life.

He buried his face into her neck while his fingers explored between her legs. At a spark of pleasure, she gasped, which made him concentrate his efforts in that place. One of his talented fingers eased inside her, and some force she could not explain made her move with his efforts, doubling the sensation.

The muscles of his neck were bunched and corded when he lifted his head, his gaze meeting hers. Their eyes held, not wavering, though as her eyes fought to remain open, her arms wrapped tightly around him. She needed him to be her anchor in this storm. The swells increased, buffeting her with their intensity until they dragged her under, and he claimed her mouth, swallowing her cries as she broke apart in his arms. He coaxed every wave possible from her until she all but collapsed in his embrace. His kisses softened and became sweeter, less consuming until he withdrew and pressed his forehead to hers. "Life will be a misery until we are wed. I thought knowing your kiss was temptation itself, but this will be a torture to ignore."

"You claim there is more? I feel as though I shall expire from what we have done. How am I to survive what is to come? His low chuckle enticed her to kiss his neck. He moaned out her name and moved so they were once again face to face.

"Your grandmother should explain that before we are wed."

She traced the line of his jaw, cupping his cheek in her palm. "I want you to tell me."

"Elizabeth," he whispered, his eyes pleading. "You hold entirely too much sway over me."

"I do not want my grandmother's explanation. I want to know what you envision—how you see our future."

His hand covered hers. "When we are wed, we shall have no need for nightgowns or dressing gowns when we retire, and I shall kiss and love every part of you until neither of us can bear it any longer."

The ache that had momentarily subsided began to bloom once again between her legs. "What happens then?"

He guided her hand to a hardness in his breeches. "Then I put this part of myself inside you where I touched you and join with you. I have been told the first time can hurt for a lady, but I hope it will not."

"Is that all of it?" If the act was anything similar to the pleasures they just experienced, she would have no complaints!

He shook his head. "No, but I shall show you then. It is hard to describe, but I hope we both shall have that very same release you did."

She guided his hand back to where the ache had bloomed once again. "Touch me again, Fitzwilliam."

"Elizabeth..." His mouth claimed hers as he hiked her skirts out of the way and swallowed her moans and whimpers and eventually cries when those fingers set her aflame. As soon as she sagged against him, he held her until their breathing calmed, then helped her from the desk and turned her around. "We need to right ourselves before Georgiana comes searching for you."

"What of my hair? Tate is quite specific when she does it, and I cannot recreate the look."

"I managed to keep my hands out of it, so it is not mussed, unlike your gown and your red lips." He traced along her neck while watching with an intense gaze where his fingers touched.

"What is it?" She tilted her head to afford him a better view.

"Only a few red marks. I did not bruise you, but we should hope they fade soon, or your grandmother will know what we have been up to."

Her complexion reddened. "That would not be good." She would not want to explain to her grandmother their activities. How would she ever look her grandmother in the eye again? After determining the library was clear, they slipped from the office and Elizabeth crossed her arms over her chest.

"Relax," he said softly before he disappeared into his study.

No more than five minutes passed before Georgiana entered, fiddling in her reticule. "Forgive me. My maid brought me toast and tea while she arranged my hair, so I have no need for breakfast." While Georgiana spoke, Elizabeth dropped her arms to her side and attempted not to fidget. When she finally looked up, Georgiana gasped. "Lizzy!"

She grabbed Elizabeth's hand and dragged her into Fitzwilliam's study. "What have you done?"

"We only kissed a little," said Elizabeth, flaring her eyes at Fitzwilliam. He had best not disagree!

With her lips pressed into a thin line, Georgiana glared at her brother while pulling on Elizabeth's arm. "Come, my maid will need to press your gown, and we shall put some cool cloths on your neck, lest your grandparents know you and my brother could not keep your lips off each other."

When they entered the dressing room, she traced the pink splotch on the base of her neck, and her blushed lips. "Do not fret. My maid is discreet. We shall have you put to rights in but a moment. In the future, you should not be alone in a room with my brother until you are wed. I never would have guessed he was so little to be trusted."

Elizabeth kept her mouth sealed tight while Georgiana helped her with the buttons. She could never confess that she was to be trusted less than Fitzwilliam. If it were in her hands, she would anticipate their vows and not regret a single moment. They could not be wed soon enough.

Chapter 21

All of London, such as it was until the Season, must have turned out for Viscount Bradbury's Twelfth Night Masquerade. Fitzwilliam despised few things more than a crush, and at the moment, he struggled to help Elizabeth through the throng without her being bumped and jostled. What was the purpose in dancing? You could not very well dance when you were packed so tightly you could not move.

Elizabeth's merry laugh rang through the room as they honoured their partners. When she took his hand for the turn, she squeezed it. "You will have no more teeth left if you continue to grind them as you are."

He could not but smile at her happy countenance, at least what he could see of it with the mask. "I cannot be pleased at an event such as this. In the host's need to feel important, he has made the event miserable for all who attend. We could have enjoyed ourselves at Richmond House or Darcy House without being suffocated in this crush."

Two partners down, Miss Jane smiled as she danced with his cousin, and Miss Amelia was beside her with Sir Anthony. The gentlemen of their party had discussed the need to keep an eye on the ladies this evening. Lady Richmond, who had called on the hostess earlier in the week, had expressed concern over the estimated number of guests. No one knew if Bingley had been invited, but he had attended the masquerade in the past. It was not far-fetched to believe he would come tonight.

"Do you see Jane?"

"I do, and before you enquire, no, I have not seen Bingley."

"It would be difficult to locate him with everyone in masks." Which had been their biggest concern.

Someone barrelled into him from behind, and he turned to glare at the lady, who appeared to have almost fallen. She straightened, then shrank back into the crowd with an apology. He yanked the bottom of his topcoat. "This is interminable."

Elizabeth took his hand and tugged him from the line. She paused and whispered to Jane, who awaited his cousin's turn with the lady beside her. Her sister nodded, and Elizabeth took his hand once more and led him towards the back of the room. "Where are we going?"

She bit her lip as she drew him behind a heavy drapery and into a corridor. "You will see."

"How do you know where you are going?"

"I called on the viscountess with Gran. She brought us from the drawing room into the ballroom to boast of the preparations." She slipped inside a room, which had a low fire burning in the grate, and closed the door behind him.

"What are we doing, Elizabeth?"

"We are restoring your good humour, but you must not wrinkle my gown. I do not have your sister's maid to press it for me." She hooked her finger above the top button of his topcoat and pulled him into the darkest corner of the room. Her fingers threaded into the hair at his nape as she drew his face closer.

"What of your set with Richard? When you are missing, your family will worry."

"I told Jane we were going outside to view the performers, and she should remain with the colonel." The viscount and viscountess always hired entertainment from Astley's Amphitheatre who juggled, ate fire, and twisted themselves into odd shapes in the gardens during the revelry inside. "Stop thinking and kiss me, Fitzwilliam."

Good God, she would be the death of him! He could not refuse. Unable to restrain himself, he claimed her lips without holding back, pulling off his gloves and letting them drop at his feet. The skin of her chest above the seed pearls trimming her amaranth silk gown was soft as he traced the swell of each of her breasts, revelling in the hitch of her breathing at his touch. He concentrated those efforts to her chest, her upper back, the small portion of her arm not covered by her gown or her gloves—anywhere but her gown.

She flattened his hand over her breast and moaned, making him stiffen to keep from pushing her against the wall and sliding his hand under her skirts. They needed to marry. The more he kissed her, the more his body screamed for her, and the more his heart pained him when he departed Richmond House without her. Every part of him was too far gone to be rational.

Time faded as he lost himself in the sweetness of her kiss and her passionate responses to his caresses. His lips were faithfully examining a particular spot at the base of her neck, suckling with as little pressure as possible so as not to mark her, when the door opened, and they both stilled.

"Where are you taking me? Release me! I insist you return me to my grandparents at once!"

"'Tis Jane," whispered Elizabeth against his cheek.

"I mean no harm. I only wish to speak with you, but no one will allow it. Your grandparents, Lord Hatton—even Darcy— are conspiring to keep me away from you." Bingley!

"I asked you to release me, Mr. Bingley!"

"Stay here," Darcy said softly. Without pause, he turned on his heel, strode directly to Bingley, and struck him across the jaw with his fist, sending the younger man to the floor while Jane gasped with a cry. In the dim light of the drawing room, Bingley had never seen him coming, but Jane had never spoken with such force in his presence before either. She had done better than he would have expected given her usual calm demeanour.

Bingley scrambled away from him with his hand clutching his cheek. "What the hell! Darcy?"

"The lady told you to let her go. What are you doing, Bingley? You were told the earl would never sanction a match between you and Miss Montford. Are you so addled and desperate that you want to force the matter? Do you believe this will bring you happiness?"

The younger man pulled himself to his feet. "I love her, and you and her family are keeping her from me!"

Darcy half-laughed, half-scoffed. "You love her? Is that why you have had Lady Jemima as your paramour? No, if you harboured such great feelings for Miss Montford, you would not keep a lover. She would be enough for you."

When he glanced over at Miss Jane, Elizabeth was persuading her towards the door. "Take her to your grandparents and remain with them until I return."

As soon as the door closed behind them, Bingley hastened closer. "You do not understand. I am in a serious predicament, and I have not the funds to clear my debts."

"And Lord Richmond will not hand Miss Montford's fortune to you without a marriage settlement. He is a shrewd gentleman and will not have his granddaughter go unprotected. You must find another way. What of selling your mill? You could give the mill to those you are indebted to."

"They do not wish to be tainted by the stench of trade, and the first few offers have been lower than what I can accept."

"Do you have any choice but to accept them?" He was in denial of his situation, that much was evident.

Bingley began to sob. "I cannot lose it all!"

Darcy grabbed him by the arm and dragged him towards the ballroom, peeking out and stopping a footman. After a quiet exchange, the servant aided him in removing Bingley from the home and into his own carriage.

"What of Caroline?"

"I assume Mr. and Mrs. Hurst are inside somewhere?"

"Yes." He hiccoughed and slumped into the squabs. Was he in his cups as well?

"Send the carriage back. I am certain the Hursts and your sister can manage themselves. If you truly wish to discuss a way out of your predicament, come to Darcy House on the morrow and we shall speak of it."

"You will loan me the money?"

He shook his head. "No, but we can take stock of your assets and help you devise the best way to repay your debts."

"What a friend you are," said Bingley with a sneer. "Little good that will do me. Damn you, Darcy." He cried out to the driver to "move on," and Darcy just managed to close the door before the carriage moved forward, disappearing into the mist of the chill London night.

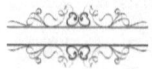

"Mr. Darcy will not hurt him, will he?" asked Jane, almost tripping over her own feet to keep up with Elizabeth's hurried pace.

"I believe he struck him to force Mr. Bingley to release you, dearest. With you away from the situation, he should have no need to do so again. Come." She slipped out from the heavy drapery arm in arm with Jane and wove through the throng towards the statue of Hercules where her grandparents had last stood.

"Miss Montford! There you are!" The colonel hurried forward. "Forgive me. One moment your hand was on my arm and the next, you had disappeared."

"Lizzy! Where is Darcy?" said Nicholas as they approached.

When she reached her grandfather, she motioned him closer. "Mr. Bingley attempted to take Jane to a drawing room, and Fitzwilliam struck him to force him to release her hand." Nicholas leaned in, his jaw working after she said Mr. Bingley's name.

"Bingley is here?" asked the colonel.

"He was when I left him with your cousin."

"Where are they now?" asked Nicholas.

"If you duck behind the drapery over there, the second door on the left."

Her grandfather's eyebrows lifted at her, making her cheeks heat, before he, the colonel, and Nicholas hastened in the direction she pointed. Could he have surmised what she and Fitzwilliam were doing before they caught Mr. Bingley up to no good?

She glanced about them, then approached her grandmother. "Where is Amelia?"

"She is dancing with Mr. Grey. He is a lovely gentleman who owns a rather respectable estate not too far from Richmond Castle. How was your dance with Mr. Darcy?"

"As good as one could expect considering the number of people in the room. A lady stumbled into him, so we did not finish the second dance."

With a smile, she patted Elizabeth's hand. "Fitzwilliam has never enjoyed crowds. I was not surprised when I noticed you leaving the line for the refreshment table." Her grandmother tilted her head down a little, and she could not hold her gaze. She had been naïve to think one of her grandparents would not notice. "Do not accept any further offers to dance," said her grandmother. "I shall be surprised if we stay long after the gentlemen return. Your grandfather will want the two of you safe and sound at Richmond House. This crush makes keeping an eye on you girls exceedingly difficult."

When her grandfather returned, Fitzwilliam had joined them. While her grandfather whispered to her grandmother, Fitzwilliam moved to her side and offered his arm. "We are departing. We shall discuss what occurred in the carriage."

Jane was on Colonel Fitzwilliam's arm, and once Amelia returned, Nicholas ensured his sister was accounted for. Their equipages were situated to make an easy departure, as her grandfather preferred. Fitzwilliam, the colonel, Jane, and she all entered the one carriage while her grandparents and cousins boarded the second.

"Lizzy, what were you and Mr. Darcy doing in that drawing room?"

"Jane!" she said in a high-pitched tone while the colonel began to chuckle. Jane glanced between each of them. Fitzwilliam stared directly out of the window without distraction, the colonel's shoulders still shook with mirth, and she pressed her palms to her cheeks. Would they ever cool?

"Lizzy!" Her sister covered her mouth with her hand.

"It was nothing so scandalous, and we shall be wed in less than a fortnight. Besides, if we had not been there, where would you be?"

Jane exhaled heavily. "That has not escaped my notice. I am merely surprised you would be so bold as to hide away during a ball with your intended. Was Mr. Bingley well when you left him, Mr. Darcy? He appeared a little in his cups when he was bringing me to the drawing room. He stumbled twice between the drapery and the door."

With a sigh, Fitzwilliam removed his hat and raked a hand through his hair. "I do believe he was drunk. If you are concerned that I struck him again, I had no need of it after he released you. I attempted to persuade him to accept my aid, but when I refused his request of a loan, he became belligerent. He as much as admitted he is in dire straits."

"Perhaps we should speak to Hurst," said the colonel.

"Mr. Hurst is in a worse state than Bingley more often than not. I cannot see him being of much help."

"Do not thrash yourself for this, Darcy. If you loan him the funds, he will not amend his ways. He could have changed when Lady Jemima took over his debts for him, but he did not. He would become like a leech, bleeding you dry."

Fitzwilliam tapped his fist on his thigh. "I considered offering him money for but a second when he called requesting the introduction to Richmond. When he refused to confess the extent of his debt, I knew he had lost it all, every pound his father left him down to the pence. That was when I knew he was too far gone. I cannot dig him from the hole he has made, and he would only use the money to continue his gaming and put himself further into debt."

"Poor Mr. Bingley," said Jane.

No one said another word until they pulled up to Richmond House and alighted. Mr. Darcy and the colonel closed themselves into the study with her grandfather and Nicholas, no doubt to speak of what had occurred and what, if any, steps should be taken. But what could be done?

The colonel and Fitzwilliam stayed for a light supper of cold meats, bread, potatoes, and cake before they departed, and the family retired for the evening. Not long after Tate finished preparing her for bed, a knock came from the door, startling her. When she peered into the corridor, Grandmamma awaited her.

"I thought we should talk, dearest."

Elizabeth withheld a groan. Why could they not forget what occurred in the drawing room? Well, her part of it, anyway.

"Would you like some sherry, Gran?" she asked as she let her in.

"I forgot Mrs. Taylor now puts sherry in your sitting rooms. You have grown so quickly. At times, I forget you are a child no longer. It does not help that you have been reminding me frequently as of late."

Elizabeth poured her grandmother's sherry. A glass of brandy would be of great aid in enduring this conversation! When she handed Gran the glass, her grandmother frowned. "You will not drink with me?"

"I am not fond of sherry, Gran."

Her lips twisted. "Give me one moment." She departed for a few minutes, returning with a glass of what could only be brandy. "I should throttle your grandfather for giving you the palate for such an unladylike spirit."

"I never liked sherry. Grandpapa allowed me to take a sip of his brandy when I was fifteen, and I much preferred the flavour."

"Next you will tell me you enjoy his whiskey too."

Elizabeth feigned a great interest in the contents of her glass. "I shall not if you do not wish it."

"Oh, for Heaven's sakes. That man! If he was not such a dear to me, I could be very cross with him." Her grandmother exhaled and took her free hand. "I saw you slip away with Fitzwilliam this evening, and if you caught Mr. Bingley with

Janey in the drawing room, I am assuming you showed Fitzwilliam the way. To my knowledge, he is not friends with the viscount and has never been beyond the ballroom—if he has even been to one of their balls before."

Elizabeth cheeks burned as though they were on fire. "Gran—"

"Do not be embarrassed. Many a betrothed couple has hidden themselves away at some point to steal a kiss. Your grandfather and I managed to lose ourselves in the maze at Richmond while my parents and I were visiting, and I—"

"Grandmamma! You?"

"Why not? I was young and in love like you once upon a time. Since you are to wed, I should explain what occurs in the marriage bed, but despite what my mother told me, I found I only needed to trust your grandfather. The specifics only served to make me more nervous. So, if you have any questions, I shall answer them, regardless of what they are."

Did she have any questions? She had no need for more than the information Fitzwilliam shared with her. Their courtship may not have been long, but she loved and trusted him implicitly. Her grandmother's wisdom seemed perfect for her situation as well.

"Lizzybeth, is he kind?" her grandmother asked, drawing her attention back to her.

She started. Why would he not be? "Yes, he is always kind."

"And he does not press?"

She took a deep draw of the brandy and swallowed, letting the burn bolster her. "I believe I am the one who presses." Good Lord, she would not be able to look her grandmother in the face for days!

Her grandmother smiled and held her sherry in both hands that rested in her lap. "Dearest, a wife who enjoys her husband is a blessing in a marriage—just do not be too forward before you are wed. He is but a man. You may not believe me, but you will remember this time with fondness, so do not rush matters. I am trusting you to leave some parts of what occurs between a man and a woman for your wedding night. After all, you will be married before you know it.

"Now, as I have not heard what occurred in that drawing room, you must tell me."

Elizabeth inhaled sharply, choking on her brandy. "I beg your pardon?"

"With Mr. Bingley." Grandmamma giggled and rolled her eyes. "You need not tell me what was happening before. If you had a question, I would answer, but I have no desire to know unless you have some need I must address. Do you understand?"

"Yes, Gran."

"Good, now tell me what that despicable boy did."

Chapter 22

"I appreciate your company for this." Richard walked beside him down the corridor in White's that led to the gaming rooms.

"Whilst I would have preferred to sit in your library and drink your brandy, Darcy, I would never leave you to such a chore on your own. That said, are you certain he is here?"

"Hurst was in his cups, Mrs. Hurst was as useless as ever, and Miss Bingley was unsure of where he was, though she was quite curious as to why I requested the information. Hurst did mumble 'White's,' which is why we are here." Miss Bingley also clung to his arm and tittered in a way that sent a shudder up his spine. Had she not heard of his engagement?

Richard scoffed. "I can imagine."

The card room was smoky and dark, as it always was, and he squinted in an effort to see to the edges of the large room. In the back left corner, a shock of light hair stood out, so he tapped Richard with the back of his hand and pointed. His cousin nodded.

When they approached, Bingley wore a wide grin while he studied his cards. Good Lord, did the man not know how to dissemble? The entire table was certain to know he held a good hand with that countenance.

Bingley indeed won when the round ended and pulled his winnings in front of him while Darcy walked around beside him. "Have you come to take me home?" he asked.

"This is not the answer to your problems."

His young friend turned his head and looked up at him. "On the contrary, I am up ten thousand. If my good fortune continues, I shall pay what I owe, then never step foot in another card room again."

"And if you should lose it all?" asked Richard.

"You brought Colonel Fitzwilliam?" Bingley rolled his eyes and shook his head. "I shall stop if I begin to lose. I do possess some restraint."

Richard levelled a hard stare at Darcy. Yes, yes. He did understand that if Bingley could stop himself, he would not be in such debt, but what was he to do? Was it prudent to drag the man away when he was winning? Even if he could pay back a small amount, he would be better off than he was now.

The next hand was dealt, and Bingley's wide grin dropped with the force of a heavy stone. It was all Darcy could do not to cover his own face with his hands. Bingley should have never stepped foot in a card room in the first place. When the round played out, he lost six hundred pounds.

"Come," said Richard. "Quit while you still have winnings for your purse."

Bingley scowled and pushed forward his wager. "I lost but one hand. You know one hand does not call an end to the evening." The next deal was just as dismal, but instead of folding, Bingley played it out to the bitter end, losing another seven hundred and fifty.

With a hand under Bingley's arm, Darcy hauled him to his feet. "We are departing *now*. Gentlemen, if you would settle with our friend so he may leave."

Lord Marbury stood with a glare. "I do not think your friend wishes to leave just yet."

Richard, who was thankfully still in his uniform, set his hand on his sabre. "I have official business with this man. Would you stand in the way of the crown?"

The earl flinched and coughed. "No, of course not. I had not realised."

Without delay, the gentlemen settled and handed Bingley their notes. Much to their surprise, he did not argue but willingly walked out to the street, blinking when the brightness of day hit his face. "I would have quit on my own after another loss."

"If you could cease losing on your own, you would not need us to pull you out," said Richard with a drawl. He had never cared for Bingley, and he detested those who wasted their lives away in the gaming hells of Pall Mall.

"How did you get into White's without a membership?"

"Lord Marbury has brought me as a guest on several occasions. He is very affable."

Affable? That was not the Lord Marbury he knew. "Lord Marbury is as kind as a rabid dog. How much did you lose to him in the card rooms during the Season? I am assuming Lady Jemima covered your debts with him. If so, she did you a great favour. He is not known for his tolerance for those who are indebted to him. Having you as his guest at White's allowed him to win more from you, do you not see?" Bingley huffed and climbed into Darcy's waiting carriage.

"Let us be done with this," said Richard. "I am ready for that brandy."

They took Bingley to the bank and assisted him in claiming the funds, ensuring Bingley arranged an order for the winnings to be passed to Lady Jemima's accounts. After they ensured the younger man was returned home, he and Richard were quiet until they reached the study at Darcy House.

His cousin immediately moved to pour himself a drink. "You will not be able to save him from himself, you know."

"I am to be wed in four days. I merely thought if I could ensure his well-being for the moment..." He scrubbed his face and sank into a chair. This was wearying.

"He will not remain," said Richard. "Whether tomorrow, in a week, or even later this evening, he will return to some gaming hell in a vain effort to pay his debts. He is a grown man, not a child, and you are not his nurse. You cannot keep him from falling further into poverty no matter how hard you try. He will dig himself into a deeper hole, and you can do naught to prevent it."

"You have your life ahead of you with a new wife and, eventually, children. Miss Elizabeth suits you well and makes you happy. I could not be more pleased for you. As difficult as it may be, you must leave Bingley behind, or he will drag you down with him. You cannot afford to have the impost takers[3] coming to your door in an effort to collect what he owes."

"You are right. I know you are."

The door to his study flew open and Mr. Higgins, accompanied by Matthew, one of Lord Richmond's footmen, stood in the door panting heavily. "Pardon me, Mr. Darcy, but I thought you'd want to know. Lady Catherine attempted to call upon Richmond House, but when she was denied entry by Mr. Gideon, she began pounding upon the door and demanding to be let in loud enough to attract the attention of that half of the street. With all the uproar, Miss Darcy insisted upon sending for you."

"Good Lord," said Richard under his breath. "I suppose our aunt had word of your upcoming nuptials and decided to attempt an end to the affair by demanding you are betrothed to Anne."

He made to stand, setting his glass upon the side table. "I have told her I shall never marry Anne. I have said the same to Anne, and I mentioned it once more when I wrote them of my intention to wed Elizabeth. Only my aunt would have the presumption to journey to London and demand entry to the home of an earl to make her point." After giving Matthew a few coins, Higgins whisked him away.

"Did you expect Lady Catherine to learn humility? Father says she was humiliated when she was forced to wed Sir Lewis de Bourgh. The experience only soured her temper further."

"She was forced?" He paused in putting on his coat and stared. "How have I never heard of it?"

"Since Sir Lewis is dead, likely no one thought to make mention of the tale. My father was bitterly complaining one night after three glasses of brandy when he spoke of it. Being the good son that I am, I offered him another glass and asked what he meant. He told me the entire tale." His cousin chuckled, and as they hastened to Richmond House, told him the entirety of the story.

He winced when his aunt's screech became audible. "Good God! What could she be thinking?"

"Richmond's neighbours will be gossiping of this scene for months." They approached the grand lady from behind while she continued to bang upon the door with the side of her closed fist.

"Lady Catherine! Just what do you think you are doing?" said Darcy in as stern a voice as he could.

She whirled around and straightened. "Darcy! I heard a report of a most alarming nature and journeyed hither to see it dispelled."

"Then you must return with us to Darcy House where we can speak of this further. You do not want to be on the tongues of Mayfair when calls are made on the morrow."

The grand dame glanced up and down the street. "At this time of year? No one has returned to town as yet. It would be most unfashionable to remain in London for Christmastide. Of course, I would not expect the Earl of Richmond and his wife to observe such matters, but *I* am quite attentive to them.

"I have heard you are to wed his granddaughter, a lady of questionable family when you do not consider her grandparents, but that would mean little if you were not intended for Anne—"

Darcy clenched his hands into fists at his sides. Why was she still spouting these delusions? "I have told you, on no less than four occasions, that I had no intentions of offering for Anne. She is sickly, and I am certain she would prefer not to wed me, though she would never speak against your wishes."

"Nonsense! It was the dearest wish of your mother—"

"To force a union as content as your own?" he asked. "I doubt that. You were dancing with Sir Lewis when your gown ripped, but he denied so much as tripping upon the hem. Meanwhile, you insisted it was him. I wonder; I never knew Sir Lewis to tell falsehoods, so who did ruin your gown?"

Lady Catherine gasped, clutching her chest with such ferocity one might have thought she was having a fit of her heart—if they did not know her as he did. "How dare you! I was the best Sir Lewis could have managed at his age, and the decoration at Rosings was atrocious. Rosings would not be what it is now if not for me!

"Nephew, you and Anne are destined for one another." Her tone was less strident, and she held her hands before her in a placating manner. "The arts and allurements of this lady have, in a moment of infatuation, made you forget what you owe yourself and all your family."

"Hah!" barked his cousin. "I assure you neither my parents nor Milton expect Darcy to wed Anne, and neither do I. Georgiana has begged him not to marry your daughter—"

"She is too young to understand—"

"Not another word." He stepped closer and leaned forward until he was almost nose to nose with Lady Catherine. "I will *never* wed Anne. I love Miss Elizabeth Montford, and she loves me. We shall be wed, regardless of your wishes. Your demands have no bearing on my decisions. If you wished for Anne to wed to keep the estate in the family, you should have planned for Richard. He and Anne have always been good friends. They could have quite the companionship." Lady Catherine's complexion turned almost to a deep shade of puce before he stopped speaking.

"Companionship! What a preposterous notion! A couple need not be friends to find contentment. They also do not require love. The purpose of marriage is to unite families and wealth. What wealth would Richard bring? He would be a leech upon our coffers." His cousin made an odd noise through his nose, but he ignored the sound.

"Well, you may bluster and complain as much as you like, I shall not be swayed by your vitriol."

"Then I know how I must act," she said. "I will end this travesty by legal means if I must."

Richard burst into great gales of laughter, taking Lady Catherine aback. "How will you manage that? You do know that the Richmond earldom is significantly wealthier than you. When you combine their wealth with that of Darcy, they have the means to hire the best legal minds and fight you until you have nothing left."

Lady Catherine slammed her walking stick against the pavement with such force, it was surprising it was not split in two. "I will be a laughingstock! It is well known in London of their betrothal."

"You may have freely spoken of an engagement, but I assure you, madam, I spoke as freely of it being a most treasured wish on your part. Lady Richmond herself has had your rumours mentioned in front of her, and she has been of great aid in dispelling the gossip as have many of my friends and their wives. Lady Fitzwilliam has even denied the existence of your plans. You may act as you see fit, but I assure you, the alliance you seek between me and your daughter will never happen."

The longer he spoke, the more Lady Catherine spluttered, and the dark hue of her complexion became darker. With an indistinguishable sound which echoed through the park, she bustled back towards her carriage, her walking stick swinging with violent motions. "I am most seriously displeased. I take no leave of you, you ungrateful wretch. After your insult of Anne, you are no longer welcome at Rosings. You deserve no such attention from me."

When her carriage pulled away, Richard clapped him on the shoulder. "Do you think she will attempt to prevent your wedding?"

"She has little time to do so. Did not your parents arrive in town yesterday?"

"They did." Richard nodded with a wide grin. "I shall pen a note to my father. He has been the only person who could ever put a stopper in Lady Catherine's plans and would despise the gossip she would cause by attempting to carry out her threats."

"Mr. Darcy, Colonel Fitzwilliam, I thank you for ridding us of that nuisance. Lord and Lady Richmond have asked me to invite you into the music room for tea." Both men startled at Mr. Gideon's voice. When had he opened the door?

"Capital, indeed," said Richard, who required no further invitation and stepped inside.

"Thank you, Mr. Gideon. I must apologise for the commotion caused by my aunt. The incessant pounding was surely not a pleasant sound."

"The family and Sir Anthony moved to the music room as it is to the rear of the house where the banging was not as loud, then Miss Montford and Miss Darcy played a lovely duet, which helped greatly to drown out the sound."

As his cousin handed the butler his hat, he shook his head. "Did the earl refuse her entry? I do not know how you would remove her from the house once she was inside. She would need to be carried out."

"If you will pardon my frankness, sir, the earl pulled me aside when Mr. Darcy began courting Miss Elizabeth. He gave strict instructions that if Lady Catherine de Bourgh ever applied to call on the ladies or demanded an audience with him, she was to be told the family would not receive her."

"I am assuming she took great offense to being refused." She had been denied when attempting to call on a family three years ago and had complained of the slight for months. How many houses had she informed in an attempt at vengeance?

When Mr. Gideon announced them, all in the music room were smiling and laughing, a stark contrast to what had occurred outside only moments before. After greeting his betrothed with a kiss to her knuckles. He sought out Lord Richmond.

"I must apologise for my aunt. She has no restraint it seems."

The earl clapped him on the shoulder. "Do not let it disturb you. I expected her visit as well as the ensuing tantrum when she was not allowed to vent her spleen. I had a missive prepared for Lord Fitzwilliam that was sent, but you managed to dispatch her before he arrived."

Sir Anthony approached and shook his hand. "Darcy, I hope you were uninjured in battle."

He allowed a slight smile at Sir Anthony's quip. While not great friends, they had been acquainted at Oxford. "I have come through unscathed, though I am uncertain as to whether I was the victor."

"Perhaps we require a preventative action in the event your aunt is not through," said Sir Anthony with a slight cock of his head. "I know I have heard rumours of a betrothal over the years, as well as your denial. Why not spread Lady Catherine's actions? Shame her back to Kent like a dog with its tail between its legs."

Lord Richmond clapped his hands together. "Oh, ho! A splendid idea."

"What is a splendid idea?" asked Hatton.

"I am not sure." Darcy winced. His aunt's ire could be merciless.

"I say we go to White's for whiskey and gossip like old ladies," said Sir Anthony. "What say you?"

Richard approached with his brow furrowed. "We are to go to White's? I thought we were having tea."

"Are you objecting to whiskey over tea?" asked Darcy.

"No, indeed." Richard held his hands up as if he had been accused of a dreadful act.

The earl straightened after explaining to Hatton the plan at hand. "I shall have my carriage pulled around."

"I rode my horse over," said Sir Anthony, "so I shall follow. If you will excuse me, I shall take my leave of the ladies." When the baronet left the group, he spoke to Elizabeth, Lady Richmond, and Georgiana before taking his leave of the Misses Montfords, who were sipping tea near the fire.

Darcy was easily distracted when Elizabeth approached, stepping away from her cousin and his for a modicum of privacy. "You are leaving so soon?"

"I fear I must, but if I do not return today, I shall call tomorrow. I promise."

The smile he adored peeked through her pout. "I suppose I must forgive you this once." She spoke with an affected air and one of her eyebrows lifted.

"I would much prefer to sip tea with you than drink whiskey at White's. Do not ever doubt where my heart lies. I choose you. I shall always choose you."

As he bowed over her hand and kissed her knuckles, her thumb sneaked a caress to his cheek. "I never held any doubt."

Chapter 23

A melia tilted her head to the side while she gazed at Elizabeth, her hands clasped at her chest. "Oh, Lizzy, the pink silk is stunning." Elizabeth adjusted the bodice. The colour was lovely, and it was perfect that Fitzwilliam had selected it. Hopefully, he would be as pleased as Amelia.

"My brother will love that you saved the fabric from his Christmas gift for your wedding gown," said Georgiana. "He has enquired several times since our trip to Madame Morisot if you had received the gown. I believe he has been quite eager to see you wear it."

"Then I look forward to his reaction when I enter the drawing room." She truly did. This was the first gown where she had not detested the fittings.

"Your betrothal gift matches the colour as well," said Jane while Tate tugged a little at the skirt. Elizabeth splayed her hand against her stomach. The colour of the stone did indeed complement the shade of the gown.

The maid bustled away at a knock upon the door. "My lady, the earl is requesting a word in private."

Her grandmother's brows drew a bit towards the middle. "I shall return in a moment."

As her grandmother hurried out, Georgiana clasped her hands together. "I am so excited. My brother has been alone for so long. He deserves to be happy. I have oft times worried what would happen if I were to wed one day. Pemberley needs a family under its roof, filling its walls with happiness and laughter. It is too large for him alone."

"Girls, I need to speak to Lizzybeth. Will you give us some privacy?" Her grandmother's countenance was tight, and her lips were pulled into a fine line. What could her grandfather have said to cause such an alteration in her grandmother's mood? Elizabeth tightened her hands to keep them from trembling. Nothing terrible could have occurred, could it? How would she and Fitzwilliam manage if their nuptials needed to be delayed?

Amelia and Georgiana kissed her cheek while Jane gave her one last embrace before they departed. Her maid disappeared through the servants' door. When they were alone, Grandmamma took her hands.

"Dearest, your father is downstairs and wishes to speak with you."

Her trembling ceased. "Papa is here? I cannot credit it. Since Jane and I have become old enough to travel with servants he has not come to either Richmond House or Castle." After what occurred on their last trip to Longbourn, she had not expected him at all. He was not one to admit he had erred, and he had no way to prevent her wedding—at least that was what her grandfather had claimed on more than one occasion.

"You have smiled and behaved as though his behaviour has not been of consequence, yet I am certain it has pained you."

She threw up her hands, then let them drop to her sides. "Of course it has, but I cannot dwell upon what happened at Longbourn, whether it was years ago or a few days ago. I am not one to wallow, and I decided the evening of our return that Papa and Mrs. Bennet would not cause one more moment of misery for me."

Her grandmother nodded. "I can understand. Nevertheless, your father is now downstairs and desires a word, and your grandfather wants to know if you will speak to him." What should she do? Perhaps she should disregard him as he had her for so many years. No, that was unfair. He had brought her into his library to minimise her time with Mrs. Bennet; he just never exerted himself to do more.

"Grandpapa will remain, will he not?"

"After what occurred on your last visit to Longbourn, I doubt he would consider leaving the room, particularly if you desire his presence."

"Very well. I shall see him, but I want to do so now. Today is my wedding, and I intend to be happy. I do not want to be mired down in what I cannot change."

"Well said, my dear," said her grandmother.

When she made to go, her grandfather awaited her outside of her rooms. "I was certain you would not wish to delay."

"Let us see what my father wants."

Her grandfather remained beside her during the walk to the drawing room and closed the door behind them when they entered. Papa, who had been standing near the fire, turned and clasped his hands behind his back. "You could not meet me alone? Really, Richmond, is this necessary?"

"I requested his presence." She stood as tall as possible. It would not do to show one hint of intimidation. "I hope my sisters are well." Her grandfather stepped over to the window and regarded the prospect. His unspoken message was clear. He would not interfere unless she had need of him.

"They are as silly—" He inhaled deeply. "Forgive me. It took a few days for the truth of your words and the way I have failed both you and Jane to settle in my mind, but I *have* tried since to be better. They are all well. I have convinced Mary to read Dante in the hopes of turning her from sermons to literature. I thought a more gradual approach to be prudent. She will have her theology, and I can discuss the content with her as she reads. She was requesting a copy of Fordyce's sermons. Can you imagine?" He gave a stilted chuckle.

"Kitty and Lydia now have a governess. I am uncertain as to how I will pay her in the long term, but I have discussed with my steward some changes to our planting. Sir William wants to breed my stallion to one of his mares. He has offered me a generous amount. Your grandfather gave that horse to me when you were young. I have had people request breedings in the past, but I never wanted the bother."

"If you will pardon my interruption," said her grandfather, "that horse has excellent bloodlines, and his sire is no longer living. I would be interested in breeding several of my mares to him should you allow it. I am certain Darcy would as well. He could indeed bring you some handsome breeding fees."

Her father gave a little startle. "How fascinating. I do not know why I never considered it before.

"Before I forget, Kitty and Lydia's governess requires them to read a certain amount each day. They have borrowed a few of your books from your bedchamber. I have told them they must return them; that you will want them at some time."

She shook her head. "They can have them. Most of what I would wish to keep I brought with me." She never left much of value lest Lydia and Mrs. Bennet take it while she was gone.

"You would not want your books? You have read them each more than once. What if you want to read them again?"

"The library at Darcy House is extensive, and I have been told it is nothing to that of Pemberley. I doubt I shall lack for books to read, and if I do, I have no question that Mr. Darcy will purchase them for me. He has joined Nicholas, Grandpapa, and I on a trip to Hatchard's and has shown a great love for books and reading."

Her father nodded. "I am glad to hear the two of you share interests."

"He is an excellent man. We all judged him unfairly in Hertfordshire. I have now witnessed his behaviour amongst friends as well as at a ball. His manner at the assembly was unease combined with our neighbours whispering of his ten thousand a year, and he apologised for his comment, which he has even claimed he should not have made. I have witnessed how uncomfortable he is in large groups of people. You should have seen him at the Twelfth Night Masquerade. The crush was a misery for him. Grandpapa has noticed such behaviour from him in the past too."

Her grandfather turned and smiled. "I have indeed."

This was all well and good, but had he come to chat of the happenings at Longbourn or had he some other motive? "Why have you come, Papa? I had not expected to see you today."

"I hoped to see you wed. I realise I have made a mess of many things over the years. Mrs. Bennet's unchecked behaviour being most of those mistakes."

Her grandfather coughed then tapped his chest with the thumb end of his fist. "I beg your pardon."

"You have every right to be angry with me for how she behaved. I knew she wanted you and Jane to call her Mama, and she told you to do so when you were little. You were always a spirited child, and I should not have been surprised that you attempted to defy her. I was not aware she took the gowns you had received from your grandparents and gave them to Lydia. I know it is too little too late, but I have taken those from Lydia. They still have some use—"

"I do not want them." Her grandmother had purchased so many gowns and had mentioned Fitzwilliam would need to purchase her more for the Season. She had no use for those that were reminders of such unwanted memories. She blinked madly at the sting in her eyes. "I journeyed to Longbourn to request you come, and you insulted me and my betrothed in response. Today, I am marrying the man I have come to realise suits me in every way. Neither of us wants this day to result in conflict of any kind, so if you are intent on that, pray, depart now—"

"I just want to be here—to try to make some amends," said her father.

She nodded and took measured breaths in an attempt to maintain her equanimity. "I do not object to your remaining, but two others have a say in whether you stay. First and foremost, my grandfather has a say as this is his home."

Her grandfather turned from the window to face them both. "This decision is yours, Lizzybeth. I shall not interfere unless you wish it or it is required for your protection."

"And second is Mr. Darcy. You insulted him at Longbourn. This day is his as well, and I shall not make a decision without allowing his opinion on the matter. When he arrives, you must apologise to him for what you said and speak to him. I am certain he will defer to me on this matter, yet I will give him his say."

Her father opened his mouth, his expression hard, but at the last moment, he made an abrupt halt, relaxed, and cleared his throat. "Very well." Obviously, he had thought better of what he was going to say, but she would never enquire as to why. She had no desire to hear any more hateful words than he had already said.

"Good. Now, I was enjoying the company of Jane, Amelia, and Miss Darcy before I was interrupted for this. I should like to return. If you will excuse me."

When she glanced at her grandfather, he gave a barely perceptible dip to his chin, his lips upturned just enough for someone who knew him well to distinguish. With his unspoken approval, she departed the room without looking back.

Darcy arrived at Richmond House with a case of nerves the likes of which he had never experienced. He was to wed Elizabeth today, and everything had to be perfect. She had endured enough of late. Her peace of mind was his utmost priority from this day forward.

When Mr. Gideon admitted him and Richard to the house, the butler smiled, but not in his usual relaxed manner. The air was thick and tense. "Sir, if you will follow me," said the man after they had removed their coats and hats.

Mr. Gideon took them to the earl's study and announced them. As soon as they stepped inside, Darcy stiffened. Why was Mr. Bennet here? After the man's reception to their betrothal at Longbourn, he had not expected him to come to Richmond House today or even Darcy House in the future. What could this mean?"

"Well, do not stand there with your jaw hanging open," said Lord Richmond. "Come inside. You must be apprised of what has occurred this morning."

"Is everyone well?" asked Richard as Mr. Gideon closed the door behind them.

"Yes, we have merely had a surprise guest. Colonel Richard Fitzwilliam, may I present Mr. Henry Bennet, father of the Misses Jane and Elizabeth Montford."

Richard did not bow as Mr. Bennet had but stepped over to the brandy. "May I? I would be pleased to pour you a generous helping as well."

The earl clapped a hand to Richard's shoulder and pulled him back. "Bennet, the colonel is Darcy's cousin and the second son of the Earl Fitzwilliam."

Mr. Bennet did not bow again in greeting. "Mr. Darcy, I am deeply regretful of the hurtful words I said to both you and my daughter when you visited Longbourn. I was intemperate and wrong, and I apologise. The two of you had journeyed to invite me to your nuptials today, and I do hope you will allow me to stay and witness the happy event."

It was all Darcy could do to school his features. Mr. Bennet was begging his forgiveness and hoping to attend their wedding? What had come over the man? "I appreciate your apology, but I admit to being perplexed as to why you are speaking to me of this. Should not your application be made to your daughter?"

The man shifted on his feet and cleared his throat. "I did. She has said I may remain provided I offer you an apology for my behaviour, and you agree to my presence."

Richard chuckled under his breath. "Good on Miss Elizabeth. Have I said of late how much I like your betrothed, Darcy?"

With his hand still on Richard's shoulder, the earl lifted his eyebrows. "What do you think? If you wish to speak with Lizzybeth first, I can have her brought to the library, but she was firm that you had the final say."

He inhaled and stretched his arms down at his sides to relieve some of the tension caused by Mr. Bennet's sudden appearance. "If Elizabeth has given you leave to remain, I shall not go against her wishes, but I must say, if you interrupt or behave in such a way that causes her unhappiness, I will not hesitate to see you thrown from this house."

"And I would not stop him," said Lord Richmond.

"By the expression on Mr. Gideon's countenance when I arrived, I am certain he would enjoy seeing me thrown onto the street," said Mr. Bennet.

"My wife hires loyal servants. We have yet to hear rumours of what occurs in this household, but we cannot keep them from gossiping amongst themselves, and much of what they speak of is to ensure the house runs efficiently. The footmen should know which guests are to be refused if they are answering the door in place of Mr. Gideon.

"Now, should you wish to speak to Jane before the ceremony, I can have her brought down from upstairs."

Mr. Bennet's gaze darted between the three of them. "That would be agreeable. Thank you." The earl poked his head from the room before Mr. Bennet departed, a footman guiding him to the green drawing room.

As soon as the door was closed, Darcy's shoulders released the painful tightness he had been holding since he walked into the study. "Elizabeth wants him here?" He was not shocked, but he had to be certain.

"My assumption is she wants no regrets," said Lord Richmond. "I am uncertain of her wishes going forward, and she said nothing of him giving her away. He has not mentioned it either."

Richard scoffed. "He likely understands he has ruined his opportunity for that honour. Given Miss Elizabeth insisted he beg Darcy's forgiveness and request his permission to attend, Mr. Bennet has been left in no doubt of his current standing with his own child."

"He has no one but himself to blame." Darcy pointed to the brandy. "Forgive me, but after that conversation, I do believe I should like a taste if you do not object."

Lord Richmond poured them each a small measure. "My granddaughter would never forgive me if I put you in your cups, but just enough to toast your nuptials." They clinked glasses, then Darcy took down the entirety in one gulp. Mr. Bennet would be present at his wedding. One thing was certain, the man had best not say one word to upset Elizabeth. Darcy would not tolerate it, and neither would Lord Richmond. Elizabeth deserved every happiness life had to offer—and from this day forward, he would do all in his power to ensure she had no reason to repine.

Chapter 24

His heart swelled at his wife's small hand resting in the crook of his arm. Thanks to a special license procured by Lord Richmond and the attendance of only their family, their wedding was completed with little fuss and no interruptions—other than the unexpected arrival of Mr. Bennet, that is. He would never forget when Elizabeth entered the drawing room on her grandfather's arm. The realisation that she had saved the fabric he had given her for Christmas to make her wedding gown was a welcome surprise. What an unexpected way for her to demonstrate her love for him than to use his gift for such a special day.

Lady Richmond planned a sumptuous and elegant breakfast, and at the first opportunity, he made their excuses and swept Elizabeth away. They now walked the small distance down Park Lane to Darcy House blessedly alone. He was struggling to keep himself under good regulation. After all, this would be her first time entering as Mrs. Darcy. Mrs. Darcy! How well that sounded.

They were not far from the house when Elizabeth rested her head just below his shoulder, his arm hugged to her side. "Are you tired, my love?"

"No, simply indulging in what I could not with Michael and Matthew following behind us."

His expression was surely beaming. "I find I cannot complain one bit. Since we departed, I have been expecting them to chase us down to return you to Richmond House. I cannot credit that we are truly alone, that we are allowed to be alone."

"As much as we can be walking down Park Lane during the middle of the day," she said in a teasing tone.

"I see but one person who is way down on the opposite end." He pointed over his shoulder.

Higgins opened the door when they approached, and they handed off their coats and hats once they were inside the warmth of the house. "What should you like to do now that we are home?" Home! This was indeed her home after today. How long would the excitement of their newly wed state remain? He would be content if it never disappeared, though it was unlikely. How many long-married gentlemen were continually giddy when their wives entered their home?

As soon as the servants left them to themselves, she bit her bottom lip in the way he loved and took his hand, leading him upstairs.

"I do not object, but do you know where you are taking me?"

"No, but I thought you may be of aid." When they were at the top of the stairs, she looked over her shoulder and lifted her eyebrow. "I have been in your chambers but once, and you claimed I had no need to view the mistress's before we were wed. So, I am unsure of where I am going. Which way should I turn for the family wing?"

"Turn right." He allowed her to pull him along until they reached the end where he pulled her back against his chest. "This door is to your bedchamber, this is to our sitting room, and this is my bedchamber. Which way should you like to enter?" He had pointed to each door in succession before his hand returned to her stomach, his nose caressing the line of her neck to where it met her shoulder.

She leaned into him. "I do not want to sit in the drawing room, the library, or the music room where we take tea and sit at a proper distance. Your arms are where I want to be."

His lips brushed the shell of her ear. "We could close the door to any of those rooms and be alone."

After a swat to his hand, she turned in his arms. "I am certain we could, but that is not what I wish."

He took her hand and drew her behind him into his bedchamber, dismissing Jameson who stood at the ready. Once she was seated on the settee, he poured a glass of brandy for each of them, handing her one before he sat beside her. Her boots were removed and laid on the floor to the side of her dainty stocking-clad feet. She took a sip of her drink, then placed the glass on the side table and turned her back to him. "Pray, unfasten my gown."

He burst into a fit of coughs as he inhaled the brandy. "You are serious?"

"Yes," she said, looking over her shoulder. "I had thought we would relax together. You may be able to relax wearing your suit, but I cannot do so in stays."

"I can fetch your maid if you would prefer," he said as he freed the first button. His fingers trembled a little, making the task difficult. How was he supposed to do this without touching her? He was desperate for her but did not want to press so soon after arriving home. Would she even be amenable to retiring so early in the day?

"Unless you have some objection to a few buttons, I have no need of Tate." As soon as the long row of buttons was open, she stood, removed her gown, her petticoats, and her stays, laying them over a nearby chair. She returned to the settee in her chemise, which showed her figure to perfection when she briefly passed in front of the fire. She drew up the fabric when she sat down and tucked her legs to her side upon the cushion. God help him! Was that flash of pale pink the ribbon at the top of her stocking?

He cleared his throat. "Pray, one moment. I require Jameson." He did not look back as he hastened into his dressing room where his valet startled from departing through the servants' doorway. "I need my boots and coats removed." He began fumbling at the cravat, his fingers useless in loosening the blasted knot. "Pray, make haste, man!"

"Sir, if you will allow me."

He lifted his chin while his valet untied the material with nimble fingers. As soon as Darcy had his topcoat and waistcoat unbuttoned, Jameson tugged the tight coat off. His boots were removed without delay before he thanked the man and hastened back to his bedchamber. Thankfully, his valet had not thought to offer him a nightgown. With his current state, he would not be removing his breeches in front of anyone but Elizabeth. That would be mortifying! "Forgive me."

"You appear much more at ease," she said with an endearing smile. At ease? He was anything but at ease. His brandy called to be drawn down in one long drink to quell the nerves in his gut. And he had thought himself nervous when he arrived at Richmond House this morning!

She reached out and touched the chest hair at the opening of his lawn shirt before sliding her hand to the back of his neck and pulling him to her for a kiss. Her tongue swiped at his lips, and he groaned and lifted her to straddle him as he deepened their kiss. During their courtship, she had taken the initiative for small matters, her doing so in this manner surprised him, though he was far from complaining. Why would he do such a thing? Particularly, when all he wished was to hold her and touch her. Calm! He needed calm.

After a moment, Elizabeth drew back and one by one pulled the pins from her hair, dropping them on the side table as her long ebony locks fell around her shoulders. Good God, he was holding on by a thread, and she was about to fulfil one of his most long-held fantasies. How many times had he wondered about the length of her hair? How it would appear spread upon his pillow? He shifted in his seat as his breeches tightened.

When her lips found his, he lost himself in the sweetness of her kiss while he slid his fingers along the top edge of her stockings—along the softest skin he could have imagined and pressing her hips forward to meet his. This was madness! He had not considered that she would be so willing to consummate their vows so soon. She had never been shy, by any means, but if she was nervous at this moment, her behaviour did not reflect it while he surely trembled from head to toe.

Without breaking their connection, he stood and carried her to the bed, lying her down beneath him. Her kisses were maddening, but he could no sooner give them up than sever a limb. Meanwhile, her fingers trailed down his sides and up his back, driving him further out of his mind. How was he supposed to think with her touching him as she was? He needed to keep his wits about him lest he frighten her, or worse, hurt her, but how was he to maintain control when she was urging him on as she was? She was shredding his restraint with every touch of her fingers and subtle writhe of her body.

He wrenched himself free and stood. His gaze held hers as he lifted her leg, untied her garter, then slowly peeled off her stockings one by one, his lips and tongue trailing down the bare flesh revealed by their removal.

When he returned to the cradle of her body, she welcomed him with open arms. His hands, meanwhile, wandered over every inch of her legs and her buttocks while he loved her mouth. Unable to resist the lure of her luscious body, his lips left hers to kiss a path down to a peaked nipple that puckered the fabric of her chemise. His gaze held hers as he drew the taut peak into his mouth and suckled it through the soft muslin, making her gasp then moan. Her lax jaw and hooded eyes while she watched him only increased his urgency. He would never maintain control if she continued encouraging him as she was. How long had it been since he first imagined her thus? This was infinitely better than the fantasy had ever been!

His fingers found their way between her legs while his lips returned to hers. She whimpered into his mouth as he stroked that place that had given her such pleasure before. He slipped a finger inside as he caressed her from within as well. He had kissed her to keep her quiet in his study, but in the privacy of their rooms, he longed to watch her fall apart, to hear the cries fall from her lips when she peaked. After he shifted to the side, their gazes held until she began to climb to the highest of summits. When she fell into her bliss, her breathing caught, and her eyes fluttered closed as she cried out. It was the most incredible sight he had ever seen, and he needed more.

He drew her chemise up around her belly, exposing her from the waist down, and worshipped her stomach, her sides, the insides of her thighs. All the while, her fingers combed through his hair while she writhed beneath him. When he covered her most intimate place with his mouth, a sharp gasp filled the room, and her fingers tightened in his hair, causing a sting while she whimpered. Those noises were more beautiful than the finest symphony. How was he to survive this? The answer was simple. He would not. She would render him senseless with hardly any effort on her part, and he would welcome every moment of the exquisite torture. He brought her to another release, then trailed tiny kisses upon her body until he could claim her mouth once again.

He caressed her hair back from her face. "Elizabeth, are you certain you are ready?"

She pushed him from her and removed her chemise, revealing her entire body. He stilled and drank in the gorgeous sight of her—her hair tousled and a bit wild, her lips swollen and red, and her eyes looking upon him with such love, he was undone.

"Yes. God, yes. I want this now." When she began pulling his shirt from his breeches, he helped until he was bare from the waist up.

"You are not scared?"

"A little, but I trust you." Her palm pressed to his stomach while she kissed his chest, her innocent attempts to please him burning him like a branding iron. He buried his face in her hair and inhaled her orange blossom scent. How he loved her! She was the very air he breathed, and she was finally his.

"Dearest." He stepped back, unfastened his fall, and removed his breeches while she watched, her lip trapped in her teeth. She was well aware what that expression did to him. He had mentioned it, had he not?

He climbed over her, shifting her further onto the mattress so his legs were not hanging off the edge, and settled over her. "You feel so..." he said on a groan. "I do not know how to make this good for you."

Her palm cradled his cheek. "What we have done thus far has been lovely. I do not doubt that if completing the act is not as wonderful today, it will be with time. Make me yours, Fitzwilliam."

With care, he began to enter her a little at a time, while watching her countenance for any hint of discomfort. She gasped and a tear tracked down her temple. "Elizabeth?" He stopped and gritted his teeth.

"Do not stop. I promise I am well. I just have never felt so close to you as I do now. I am so full."

He seated himself fully and buried his face in her neck. How would he not expire from this? He had thought himself undone before, but it was nothing to this moment, buried inside her and enveloped in her heat. Her hips moved, and he grabbed her side. "No, I beg of you. This will be over far too soon if you do not give me a moment."

A moan accompanied her wicked hands as they slid down his lower back and pressed against his rear. "I need you, Fitzwilliam. You cannot know how I ache for you."

At her plea, he gritted his teeth and rocked in and out, loving her in a way he had craved for so long. She was perfect— so warm and so tight. Blood rushed through his ears and blocked out everything around them while he was consumed by every inch of her body against his, her small gasps, the hitches in her breathing, and those other sounds that made him spiral higher and higher.

Her legs lifted around his hips and one leg wrapped around him. The pleasure became so intense, he could do nothing but let his release wash over him, bellowing into her neck and the pillow below.

When he had gathered his wits, he attempted to lift himself, but she wrapped her arms around him. "Pray, stay with me."

"I am too heavy, my love."

"No, you are perfect."

"I shall not go but allow me this." He drew up so he could see her face, his elbow on the mattress and his head propped on his hand. "You are well?"

"I am exceedingly well. Do we ever have to leave our rooms? I believe I should like to remain thus forever."

"With Georgiana at your grandparents' house and Richard at Montague House with his parents, we need not leave our chambers for some time if we do not wish it." He dipped down and kissed her neck, brushing his nose against the soft flesh. "I waited so long to find you."

"You were the love I never expected," she said. "I have always said I would never marry but teach Jane's many children to play the pianoforte very poorly indeed."

"You are too full of wit and beauty to have never wed."

"Not all consider wit to be a necessary accomplishment for a wife."

He smiled. For him, it was the most important. "Which shows how perfect your accomplishments are to be my wife."

They kissed and talked until he rolled them over, holding her to him in such a way to keep their connection. With a wicked grin, she trailed her tongue down his chest in a manner similar to what he had done earlier. She nipped along his ribs which made him lift his hips. "Elizabeth, if you do not stop—"

Her kiss prevented him from completing his statement, so he sat up with her astride him, and wrapped his arms around her and helping her with a rhythm pleasing to them both. Perhaps there was some method of them never leaving these rooms again. After all, he could never object to loving her so forever.

"Mr. Darcy."

Darcy startled awake with a gasp. The bedcurtains were closed, ensuring very little light filtered into their secluded haven. Elizabeth's supple body was partially atop his, her arm wrapped around his chest and one knee bent over his lower stomach. His painful erection pressed against the sheets, begging for relief. It seemed he would never have enough of her. Certainly not a quality to bemoan in a wife.

"Mr. Darcy." He blinked and turned to face the bedcurtains. Had someone just touched his wrist? One of his arms was wrapped around Elizabeth, but the other hung through the gap.

"Mr. Darcy," came the voice once again. Jameson? What time was it, and why was his valet waking him? He was under specific orders not to come unless called.

With extreme care, he slid out from under Elizabeth and ensured she was covered before opening the curtain just enough to reveal Jameson on the other side, a chamberstick held in his hand. "What time is it?"

"Almost midnight, sir."

"This must be urgent indeed if you are waking me at this hour on my wedding night." He scrubbed his face in an effort to wake further.

"Yes, sir. A servant from Mr. Bingley's household is downstairs. He claims Mr. Bingley has been shot. Naught was said of how, but your presence is requested at the Bingley home."

His stomach dropped. "Good God. Get my clothes ready. I shall be in my dressing room directly."

"Yes, sir."

"Fitzwilliam," said Elizabeth in a breathy but sleepy voice. "What is it?"

"I am not certain as yet, but I need to see Bingley. One of his servants is downstairs and very insistent I go to Grosvenor

Square." He had no desire to alarm her. He needed to be aware of the situation first.

"Should I accompany you?" She sat up, covering her breasts with the sheet, presenting a picture he was loath to part from.

"No, I am unsure of what awaits me. You should remain here where I know you are safe."

"Safe? Fitzwilliam, what has happened? Why would you worry so for my safety?"

Why had he said safe? He should have known better. Now she would fret for him. "'Tis no more than a precaution. Besides, now that you are my wife, Miss Bingley, if she is there, will not be pleasant. I would prefer you remain here. I want you well rested for my return." After a grin, he gave her a short but passionate kiss. "I love you."

"I love you too," she said with a palm to his cheek.

Without looking back, he stood and departed for his dressing room. They had only been wed an evening, why did his chest hurt so to leave her? His heart was heavy as he closed the door behind him. It was better this way since he could not know what awaited him at Bingley's. He would not have her abused by Miss Bingley, or worse, harmed by someone intent on injuring Bingley further.

Chapter 25

Bingley's servant, a boy really, led him out to Hurst's carriage that waited along the kerb. Once Darcy was inside, the servant made to close the door, but Darcy put a hand upon it to stop him. "No, I want to know what has happened. You will sit in here and tell me."

When the boy climbed inside, he peered around the interior before he sat. "Beggin' your pardon, sir, but I'm never allowed inside."

He rapped upon the wall behind him since he had no walking stick. "I understand. What is your name?"

"I am Samuel."

"What do you do in Mr. Bingley's household."

"I am a footboy in the kitchens, tendin' the fires and carryin' what needs carryin'."

"I am certain you do excellent work. What can you tell me of Mr. Bingley?"

"He looked positively dreadful, sir. They brought him through the kitchens. Blood be everywhere, and he was gaspin' for breath." They? Who were they?

"Who brought him?"

Samuel shrugged. "Don't know. The doc was sent for. Mr. Hurst sent me for you before he showed."

"Do you know where Mr. Bingley was shot?" Do not say stomach.

"Looked like the chest but can't know for certain. Blood was all over 'em."

He squeezed his eyes closed and covered them before steeling himself and resuming a more neutral expression. "Who in the family knows of this?"

"Mr. Hurst, sir. Miss Bingley and Mrs. Hurst had retired already. I remember when Miss Bingley's maid returned to the kitchens, grumblin' of the lady. She's always grumblin'." The boy nodded with wide eyes. He had to be no older than ten. Most footboys were eight or nine.

The carriage slowed and stopped, and the boy scrambled out to place the step. After Darcy alighted, he stared up at the façade of the house. He dreaded what awaited him when he stepped through that door. A chest wound? Bingley's condition could be nothing but grave indeed.

As he approached the front, the door opened wide to allow him entry. Hurst was descending the stairs as he began removing his coat. "Thank God you are here."

"Is he alive?"

"He clings to life, but by a hair." As soon as the butler disappeared through the servants' entrance, Hurst stepped closer. "I simply cannot fathom what has occurred for him to have taken part in a duel." He said the last in an urgent yet lower tone. Bingley had oft times mentioned their servants held no loyalty thanks to Miss Bingley's horrid treatment of them.

"He has not mentioned his debts?"

"Debts?" Hurst's countenance was taken aback. "He has not mentioned much to me of personal matters in the last two years. Blasted Caroline has made this house a misery." Darcy could not prevent his eyebrows from lifting. He had never heard Hurst speak so and had not seen him sober in a year at least. Had the shock of Bingley's arrival sobered him or had he, for once, not endeavoured to lose himself in brandy and port.

"We should remove ourselves somewhere more private," said Darcy glancing around him.

"Yes, of course. Follow me." Hurst led him up the stairs and to the left to a sitting room. He pointed to the adjoining door. "Bingley is through there should you wish to see him. A physician and surgeon are with him now, so pray, first tell me of this debt." After a long sigh, Darcy explained all he knew from Bingley's liaison with Lady Jemima to her covering his debts at the gaming tables.

During the recitation, Hurst stumbled into a chair and held himself up with his hands to his thighs. "Blast! Now more of what has been said makes sense. Bingley was muttering 'Jemima' when I first saw him; his driver had brought him to the mews and through the servants' passages so as not to disturb his sisters, then he had his valet fetch me. After sending for you and for help, I interviewed the driver. He could not tell me much. Bingley had asked to be taken to Hammersmith. Apparently, the duel was to occur at sunset since dusk is so much later at this time of year. He said the gentleman Bingley duelled was dressed well, and they called him 'your grace.' I am willing to wager the gentleman was the Duke of Dorset."

"I would have to agree."

"Do you know the extent of his indebtedness?" How was he supposed to convey such bad tidings—or at least bad tidings as far as he knew?

"I had heard of him owing forty thousand."

"Forty thousand!" Hurst shot from the chair and began to pace. "Why would the dullard be so stupid? He could afford to pay such a debt, even though it would lower his income."

"I have no proof, but after dragging him from White's one day, the manner in which he spoke led Colonel Fitzwilliam and I to believe he has lost the entirety of his inheritance."

Hurst punched the wall. "So help me! If he lost Caroline's fortune, I may kill him myself. I had a betrothal arranged for her three years ago, but she insisted on holding out for you—"

His hands shot up before him, palms out. He never considered nor would ever consider Miss Bingley. "I was wed this morning."

"Yes, we heard the rumours of your betrothal. You should know Caroline was livid—is livid. She spent three days in her bedchamber after more than one call confirmed your engagement. The servants wanted naught to do with her, and her maid quit. Do you know how difficult it was for my wife to hire a new maid? Caroline has developed a reputation amongst the servants of London. Few will even come to our door anymore. That said, if you desire to escape this house from the servants' entrance, we can arrange it.

"As for a marriage, she has her sights set far too high. If she were more agreeable, perhaps a gentleman of means might consider her, but too many know of her mean-spirited gossip and her avarice. They will not take her."

"Forgive my bluntness, but you are aware your wife's name is associated with her sister's." Hurst may flay him for it, but it begged to be mentioned.

"Unfortunately, I am, which is another reason I want Caroline married and away from us. Louisa was not this way when we first wed, and I hope the removal of her sister's influence may return her to the lady she was. I want Caroline married and gone. I cannot continue drinking as I have, and her very presence is enough to put a glass in my hand. The gout has been interminable." He could understand Miss Bingley driving a man to the bottle. He had often joined Bingley for a glass of port—or three—after her more trying behaviour.

"I recently found another gentleman who is willing to wed Caroline for her fortune," said Hurst. "He is in possession of a small estate in Northumberland and hopes to purchase a parcel of land adjacent to his own."

"He wants to increase the size of his estate then?" A smart investment if one was profitable off the land.

"Yes, he is a sheep farmer, and does well—very well. Caroline will be incensed. He is willing to journey to London to marry her but does not take part in the Season. They would return to Northumberland as soon as the nuptials are over and done. She is six and twenty and will be on the shelf if she does not accept that this is the only offer that will ever be made to her."

A creaking made them both turn as two men entered from the door connecting the sitting room to Bingley's chambers. Their lips were drawn into fine lines, and they shared a glance before the taller of the two cleared his throat. "Mr. Hurst, after some time consulting over the wound in your brother's chest, we have determined it is not prudent to remove the ball."

"Not prudent?" said Hurst, crossing his arms over his chest.

"Sir, when I sent for Mr. Walters, I did say I was unsure if the bullet could be removed."

"Upon further examination," continued the man who could only be Mr. Walters. "The ball broke a rib, entering and possibly passing through the lung and lodging near the heart. Too much damage has been wrought by the shell alone without tearing apart his chest in a futile attempt to remove it. We are trained to set breaks, amputate limbs, and lance boils. I have removed bullets from the shoulder and closed wounds, but I would never attempt to saw open a man's chest. If the bullet did not kill him, I most certainly would."

Hurst paled more and more as the surgeon explained himself. "I had not considered it in such a way."

"If the bullet had lodged closer to the surface, between the ribs for example, I could have removed it with little effort. As it is, I fear you must prepare yourself for the worst. A miracle would need to occur for him to survive."

Darcy squeezed his eyes closed and exhaled in an audible breath. "I cannot imagine his agony. Does some remedy exist to ease his pain?" When he opened his eyes, Hurst had sunk into a chair with his head in his hands. "And do you know how long he may live in his current state?"

The physician nodded. "I have been called for a few cases such as these. I have found dampening a strip of cloth with laudanum and placing it in the patient's cheek to be beneficial. His teeth are clenched shut with the pain, so he cannot choke on it. Though he is not awake and cannot be given liquids, he is swallowing so should be ingesting some of the elixir with his saliva. I cannot guarantee it will alleviate all his pain, but he should find some relief. As to your second query, I am uncertain as to his longevity. Since neither of us were on the scene when he was shot, we do not know how much blood was lost. He does continue to bleed, so he could bleed to death, or his breathing may be an issue since we believe the ball to have entered his lung. In either case, I do not expect him to linger for long—he may survive until the morrow, but I am inclined to doubt it."

"Thank you," said Darcy when Hurst did not respond. "I am certain you wish to return home. If you can instruct us on what needs to be done, we can make do until he..." He gulped and shuddered.

"I have instructed the maid on how to give him more laudanum. She and his valet are both with him to ensure the cloth does not find its way into his throat. Such a complication is unlikely, but I prefer to take every possibility into account."

"I thank you for your aid and your honesty." Hurst hauled himself up from his chair. "The footman in the hall will show you to the door and retrieve your coats and hats."

After both men departed, Darcy ran his fingers through his hair. "Is your wife aware of his condition?"

Hurst shook his head. "No, I thought it best to wait until the physician examined him. Was there no surgeon at this blasted duel? Does not the Code Duello demand one?"

"I want to know the coward who was his second. Why did he not accompany Bingley here and give you an accounting of what occurred?" He turned his back to Hurst while he breathed to manage the restlessness within. "You should inform your wife. If she wakes in the morning to find him dead, she may not forgive you. The two of you should then discuss how to tell Miss Bingley."

"I will go to my wife now," said Hurst. "Will you wait with us? I am already indebted to you for coming on your wedding night, and I do realise I am asking a great deal—"

"Elizabeth will understand. I wish to look in on him, so I shall do so while you are gone."

Once Hurst dragged his feet through the door, Darcy swallowed the bile that had risen into his throat as he pressed open the door to Bingley's bedchamber. His friend lay on his back, covered to his shoulders with the coverlet, his skin pale and bluish-tinged. His eyelids were squeezed closed and his breathing laboured. A scrap of cloth hung from one side of his mouth.

"Good evening, Mr. Chambers." The valet's eyes flared, surely at being addressed by name, but how many times had Bingley told some bawdy joke he had heard from his valet? Chambers was a name known well to him.

The maid sitting at the bedside stood and curtseyed, and Bingley's valet bowed. "'Tis a sad day, Mr. Darcy. He would be glad you are here. He thought highly of you, sir."

"May we speak privately?" he asked the valet. After the man said few words to the maid, she curtseyed again and departed.

"I am certain I know what you are to ask of me. I knew some of his affairs, but not all, mind you. You are aware of some—he mentioned you removing him from White's."

"I know he owes a substantial sum to Lady Jemima, his lover."

Chambers nostrils flared. "From what he told me, they have not been lovers in a couple of months, but while they were together, no wrong could be said of her. I think he was flattered she singled him out, her being the daughter of a duke."

"You challenged his relationship with her?" That would have been brave of his servant to do so.

"Not directly. I asked questions I hoped would open his eyes. If he had answered them honestly to himself, he would have seen his error in dallying with the daughter of someone so high-born. He is a good man. I had no wish for him to be hurt."

"Do you know how the duke came to challenge him?" The answer would seem obvious, but the question begged answering.

"A few days ago, the duke caught him with the lady—if you can call her that. You may know Mr. Bingley had a small house left to him by his father in Cheapside. Miss Bingley refused to live in that part of town, so my master purchased this house. Since it was not leased of late, he met Lady Jemima at the house in Cheapside. I am not certain how the duke knew of their arrangement, but he burst in while they were arguing and demanded satisfaction. Mr. Bingley was quite agitated when he arrived home afterwards. He had offered to marry her, but the duke refused to be associated with a man so lately linked to trade and who owed his daughter such a disreputable sum." The duke would never have consented to her marrying his friend. Dorset was concerned greatly with appearances and the stench of trade still lingered on Bingley's fashionable, well-tailored suits.

He clasped his hands behind his back while he stared at Bingley. "Was the lady willing to marry him?"

"I do not know. He said the duke's men removed her from the house without delay. She may not have had the chance to accept or refuse. You should know Mr. Bingley made a comment—well, I believe they met because the lady is with child."

"Good God." How would Hurst react to such tidings? Lady Jemima could be married to a man in need of an heir, or the child would be passed off to a foundling home or a tenant family to avoid the shame. "Do you have any idea who his second was?"

"My master mentioned Lord Marbury. I cannot imagine him asking anyone else. He would be too ashamed to request it of you. He thought too well of you."

The door flew open, and Mrs. Hurst ran to the bedside, pressing her palm to her brother's forehead. "Charlie? Oh, dearest, what have you done?"

Hurst came to his side. "I had not had the opportunity to speak to Chambers. Have you learnt anything useful?"

"A great deal more than we knew ten minutes ago."

Chapter 26

Darcy scrubbed his face with a weary exhale. What time was it? He had been at Bingley's for an eternity. The sounds of servants bustling through the house filtered through the door, so it must be nearly morning. How he longed to be in his bed with Elizabeth held tightly in his arms. This was interminable.

Poor Bingley had taken his last breaths only moments after Mrs. Hurst rushed into the bedchamber. He had given a weak gurgling cough while his eyes fluttered though his lids never opened. He had attempted several laboured inhales, but the breaths stopped before they filled his chest. Mrs. Hurst moaned when her brother let out an exhale that seemed to go on forever. When he stilled, she fell over his body and wept.

He had aided Hurst in penning letters to Bingley's elderly aunt in Scarborough, Hurst's family, as well as a few friends. A nub of black sealing wax had been found in the very back of the desk, likely from the elder Mr. Bingley's death three years prior. The missives would be sent off in the post as soon as London awoke for the day.

A note had also been sent to Darcy House for Tate to deliver to Elizabeth when she woke. He would never have her worry when he could put her mind at ease, and she would be concerned when he had yet to return.

Hurst dropped Bingley's ledger upon the desk and rubbed his palm across his forehead. "Naught but five thousand remains. Thankfully, it appears Caroline's fortune is untouched. I have penned a response to the gentleman I spoke of in Northumberland. Perhaps he would be willing to travel to Scarborough. The wedding would need to be a small, private affair since we are in mourning."

"What of Miss Bingley's opinion on the matter?" Not that he cared, but if she objected, the nuptials would be impossible.

"She has no choice. You read Bingley's will." They had found the document while searching for the sealing wax. "She has her fortune, and he said that unless I was willing to take her in, she had to marry to receive the funds. He could be an addle pate, but he was not ignorant of her behaviour or habits. I often heard him lament of her overspending her pin money."

At a knock, Hurst strode to the door and admitted a footman who glanced at Darcy before he cleared his throat. "Forgive the interruption, sir, but a man from the Duke of Dorset's home is at the servants' entrance, requesting an audience with whomever is responsible for Mr. Bingley's estate."

His stomach dropped while Hurst paled and appeared about to faint. "Pray, bring him here without alerting Mrs. Hurst or anyone else in the household. We will hear what he has to say." The footman departed after a dip of his chin.

"Do you think he wishes to collect on Bingley's debt? I can offer him the five thousand remaining in the account, but without selling the factories, I have naught to give him."

"Let us see why he is here before we panic."

They both started when the footman brought in a man wearing a well-tailored suit. Darcy stood while he stared at this caller. This was no servant. He had met him before—years before—but he knew him. "You are Lord Cranfield. You are the duke's heir." He was the Baron Cranfield.

"Yes, Mr. Darcy, we met at Oxford. Your cousin Milton introduced us. I must beg your forgiveness, but talk of what has occurred will, no doubt, be all over London when calls are made, and I thought it best to keep our meeting as concealed as possible."

"I understand. Since we are hardly holding to propriety, may I present Mr. Reginald Hurst, Mr. Bingley's brother."

Cranfield gave a slight bow. "I should like to continue with this open discourse we have begun if you will allow it."

Hurst nodded, and Darcy followed suit. "I believe we can agree that would be the most prudent."

"The duke was clearly enraged at learning of the relationship of Mr. Bingley and his daughter as well as the great debt Mr. Bingley owed her before the duel."

"I would wager she gained a great deal from him before then as well," said Hurst. "He has the paltry sum of five thousand remaining, so I am afraid, that is all I can offer at this time to repay his debts—unless the duke desires a mill in Yorkshire."

The baron raised a hand. "Pray, I understand your frustration. While I am his heir, I do not care for my cousin much at all, and Lady Jemima has been raised to be spoilt indeed. The duke did wish to make some attempt at collecting the debt, though he would never accept a mill in lieu of the money. I, however, proposed another solution that I do hope will meet with your approval."

After a glance at Hurst, Darcy waved at the baron as though gesturing him forward. "We are listening."

"I do not know what Mr. Bingley said of his relationship with my cousin, but she is in a scandalous state. When the duke interrupted them in Cheapside, they were arguing over what would become of the babe. You see, she felt it quicken the day prior. Mr. Bingley had insisted they should wed, but despite her being of age, Jemima knew her father would ensure it never came to pass. Neither could financially withstand the legal challenges the duke would wage."

"Good Lord," said Hurst.

"You wish Hurst and his wife to take the child and the debt will be repaid." It was the only solution that made sense. The duke would wish the child as far from himself as possible while exerting as little of himself to rid his house of the scandal.

"Yes," said Cranfield. "Should Mr. Hurst agree, Jemima would journey north. The expectation would be for you to arrange lodgings for her until the birth. Once the child is born, she would return to her father, and you would do with the babe as you see fit."

Darcy straightened and wagged a finger. "If a boy, he could be your ward, Hurst. You could use the five thousand left and any funds from the mills to see him educated, all the while recognizing him as Bingley's. You would need to claim his natural mother was from some other county so as to not implicate Lady Jemima, but he could inherit the mills. He would have a better future than most born in his situation."

"Exactly," said Cranfield. "Or, if a girl, the mills could be sold, and the funds placed into the account with the five thousand to pay for her upbringing and to aid her in making a suitable match."

"That is quite generous." Hurst's tone was faint. "Forgive me. I had not expected this. My wife and I have yet to have a child, so I am certain she would be overjoyed to raise her niece or nephew. I have a small estate in Scotland, left to me by an uncle. We could journey north with Lady Jemima after my brother's funeral. Once the babe is born, she can depart, and we would assume responsibility for the child."

"Could we have it in writing that the duke will not seek redress for the debt owed to his daughter?" Darcy did not trust Dorset.

Cranfield removed a folded paper from his coat. "I had my cousin draw this up in the event we struck a bargain."

He watched while Hurst scanned the paper. "I am satisfied. How will we contact you?"

"I have a messenger I trust implicitly. On the morrow, my wife and I are to remove Lady Jemima from London and take her to the duke's cottage in the Lake District. If you will write your direction, we can coordinate when you will take her to Scotland and when we are to retrieve her."

"The Lakes?" asked Darcy in a slightly high tone. This was not the season to take in the lakes, which would make it ideal.

"Yes, I thought it the best place. Few will be in that part of the country this time of year, and we can keep her secluded. I would be surprised if Dorset does not have a husband for her within a few months of the child's birth. He views her deception and the taking of a tradesman as a lover as the deepest of betrayals. Her accounts will be added to her fortune to secure a suitable match."

Darcy winced. The duke's idea of a suitable match would not resemble his, and that sum of money would attract the worst of fortune hunters. She would be wed to a peer, but who was likely in as much debt, if not more, than Bingley was. "Do you agree with him?"

With a sigh, Cranfield motioned to a chair.

"Yes. Pray, sit." said Hurst. "Forgive me."

"I am certain you have had little sleep, and you are dealing with trying circumstances. The servants in the kitchens were speaking of Bingley's death. I am sorry. I did not know him well, but he seemed a cheerful sort."

"He was." Darcy cleared the lump choking him from his throat. He had no time for emotion at the moment.

"As for my cousin's dictates, no, I do not agree with him. I have mentioned I would be pleased to act in his stead in the matter, but he has yet to agree. He *has* indicated the desire to wash his hands of her, so I shall try again before we depart for the north. A good friend of mine inherited his estate from a distant cousin six months ago. The finances have been a nightmare, and I travelled to Shropshire to be of aid to him. He is a good sort, not prone to gaming, drink, or vice. I would reserve part of her fortune for her settlement and allow him to use the remainder to shore up his estate and put things to rights. By the time she would end her confinement, he would be nearly out of mourning. I only need to convince Dorset."

"I wish you luck." Hurst was being gracious given the circumstances. Cranfield may not have killed Bingley, but he was negotiating in Dorset's stead.

"Thank you," said Cranfield. "For what it is worth, Jemima cared for him. She has confided in my wife and has said he was the first person who did not ingratiate himself to her or attempt to use her to improve his associations. He was nothing more than a happy gentleman who noticed her discomfort with one of her father's friends and claimed a dance so she could escape. She said she stood up with him, then he walked her to the refreshment table and wished her well. They saw each other at a couple of balls after, and Jemima claims she initiated the affair. She regrets their relationship cost him so greatly—the extent of how much he had lost was not known to her until he was unable to pay. She hoped ending matters with him would keep him from following her to the cardrooms, but those habits had become fixed.

"I do not anticipate informing her of his death. She will be overwrought. It was she who insisted we request you take the child. Her father would just as soon hand the whelp off to a foundling home, but Jemima threatened to make her shame public to force his hand.

"I hope you will not judge her too harshly. Her parents' feud has taken its toll over the years. Jemima has lived in an unhappy home where her mother and father both used her to take revenge upon the other. My object in arranging a marriage for her is to remove her from their influence. Perhaps she may find some semblance of contentment. She claimed to feel so when in Bingley's company."

Cranfield stood and glanced about him. "I should return to Dorset and give him the news. I also have yet to arrange for our travel to The Lakes." Hurst made his way to the desk and penned a few lines before handing the paper to Cranfield, who looked it over and nodded. "Very good. Do you have a plan for the funeral?"

"A cart will leave this evening with my brother's body. My wife, her sister, and I shall depart the day after. We hope to have the funeral the day after our arrival. I do have a matter of business I must see to before I depart Scarborough, but I hope to have that accomplished within a fortnight."

"We should be able to conceal Jemima's condition for another month, maybe two. The sooner you could collect her, the better."

"I agree," said Hurst as Darcy stood. The bell was rung, and a servant arrived promptly to show Cranfield out the way he entered so as to remain concealed from those on the street.

"I should depart as well, unless you have further need of me." He longed for home. Miss Bingley's voice had not filtered through the house as yet, but his body screamed to be as far from this house as possible before it did.

"No, I am indebted to you, Darcy," said Hurst. "I know you and I have never spoken much, but I appreciate your coming when you did. I could not have managed the arrangements without you—or dealt with Lord Cranfield so well."

Darcy shook his head. "Cranfield's offer, or should I say Lady Jemima's request—made sense. If she made such a threat to her father, I would say she cared for Bingley, at least. I hope you and your wife take some solace in that."

"Maybe in time. Maybe spending time with her in Scotland will be of aid."

"I hope so. At the very least, the child will be a blessing. It is not often a child born in such circumstances can be considered as much." He clapped him on the shoulder. "I am certain you will be an excellent father to him."

Hurst sniffed and blinked. "I shall do my best."

Darcy crept upstairs and into his dressing room where his Jameson awaited him with a hot bath in the tub. "I had not expected a bath."

"Mrs. Newnham sent a note to Mr. Bingley's requesting some warning before you were to depart. She wanted the water waiting for you upon your return."

"Pray, thank her for me. Her efficiency is quite welcome after such a long night."

His valet gave a slight bow. "May I enquire after Mr. Bingley? We have all prayed he is well."

"I am afraid he died. The bullet entered his chest, and his injuries were too severe." After removing his clothes, he startled when the door opened, and Elizabeth tore into the room. She stopped upon noticing his valet and crossed her arms over her chest.

"Ring should you need me," said his valet who departed with haste.

"I heard your voice. I can return to the bedchamber should you wish it."

Her hair cascaded down around her shoulders, her ebony locks contrasting sharply with the white shift...no, that was his shirt she wore, which hung to almost the floor with her toes peeking from beneath the hem. His feet led him forward until she was in his embrace where she belonged. Her arms wrapped around him.

"I was worried when you had not returned."

"Did you not receive my note?"

"Tate brought it after I rang for her."

He kissed her crown, buried his face in her neck and lifted her into his arms, carrying her to the tub. When he sank into the warmth of the water, she gasped. "Fitzwilliam, I am still wearing your shirt."

When he lifted his head, she frowned and wiped his cheeks, which were damp. Had he been crying? "What has happened? Last night, you said you were needed at Mr. Bingley's, but if you said why, I do not remember."

He shook his head. "Not right now." His fingers trailed down her cheeks and her chest until it reached where the peak of her breast could be seen through the wet cotton. "You are beautiful." After he removed the shirt, he pulled her to him. He needed her warmth. He was so cold—so very cold.

Chapter 27

E lizabeth's fingers combed through his hair, and she peppered kisses to his temple, his ear, and his cheek. What could have happened? With the debts Mr. Bingley owed, she could only assume the worst, and her husband's behaviour confirmed whatever occurred must have been dreadful. He would not be so distressed over a mere argument. What could have sent him to Grosvenor Square in the middle of the night?

All she could do was hold him and soothe him until the water cooled. "Fitzwilliam, come. We need to get out. We will take a chill if we remain thus." When he lifted his face, he blinked as if he had just awoken from a heavy sleep. She kissed him sweetly and cradled his cheeks in her palms. He was loved and well, and she would ensure he was aware of that fact. He would certainly speak of whatever troubled him when he was able.

She lifted herself from the tub and began to dab at her arms with the soft towelling. The water splashed in the bathtub behind her as he rose, and she made to reach for a second towel to pass to him when Fitzwilliam's warmth pressed firmly against her backside, making her gasp.

His lips found the curve where her neck met her shoulder and began to suckle, which never failed to send a jolt straight between her legs. How could a simple kiss wreak such havoc? She could hardly credit it.

A palm to her belly kept her hips flush to his while his other cupped her breast and squeezed. She needed to touch him, but in this position, she was quite limited in her reach. One hand threaded through his hair at his nape, keeping him from ceasing those attentions that were so pleasing, while the other covered his hand on her belly, lacing her fingers with his. He needed her, and she would not deny him. Whatever comfort she could provide, she would offer without one ounce of hesitation, and this was certainly no hardship. She wanted him as much as he wanted her.

She was melting against him and helpless to stop, but how could she get closer? Her head dropped against his shoulder, and she guided his mouth to hers, kissing him with all the passion he was stirring within her. His lips were not gentle or caressing but sought to devour her whole as his hand found its way between her legs. Her knees buckled when a finger slid inside, and he began to manipulate her in such a way she could do no more than anchor herself to him to keep herself from collapsing to the floor.

He swallowed her cries but never ceased those caresses that made her senseless and more wanton that she had ever been in her life. If she could have, she would have begged him to never stop—to give her more and more until she crumbled into tiny pieces in her passion.

He suckled hard at the base of her neck as he pinched her nipple, sending her over the edge as her loud cry filled the room. Those wicked fingers never ceasing until she stopped falling and some semblance of awareness trickled back.

She barely registered when he lifted her limp body and set her upon a hard surface. When he drew her hips forward, he entered her effortlessly as she gave a sharp inhale. "Fitzwilliam."

"Am I hurting you?" His chest heaved, and he gritted his teeth. He was asking if she was in pain? He was the one who appeared to be suffering.

"No. Pray, do not stop." His body released some of its tension under her fingertips as he began to move within her, his hands on her lower back guiding her to meet every delicious thrust of his hips. How could he know where to touch her to make her so needy for him? Mrs. Bennet complained loudly of the duties of a wife, but how could an intimacy this pleasurable cause complaints? Or perhaps it was the love she held for Fitzwilliam that made it so perfect.

Her heart was indeed full of him. So much so she had to be closer—to feel him against every part of her—so she wrapped her legs around his waist as he buried his face into her neck. Their bodies moved together in a rhythm as she tightened her hold upon him when her traitorous body threatened to go limp.

As they continued to love one another, whatever he had set her upon began to strike the wall loudly with their movement but that was soon lost to her as she began to climb towards Elysium once again. He moaned and began to make inaudible noises which only served to quicken her ascent while she could do no more than hold tighter to him and beg him for more. That newly familiar sensation lit within her and spread, and her head dropped back as she cried his name over and over until the unbearable pleasure carried her to the absolute peak, then set her adrift to float back to earth. His bellowed cries joined hers as he almost struggled to continue, and he stumbled, requiring a hand to the surface to remain standing.

They both panted as they recovered, her eyes prickling and blurring with tears. How she loved him! Would they have found one another sooner if they had both put aside their discomfort and prejudices during their first meeting? It was useless to speculate. They had not lost years or decades to their foolishness, but maybe weeks.

When he drew his face from her shoulder, his eyebrows drew together in the middle when his gaze met her face. "Forgive me. I lost myself in you and became too rough."

"No," she said quickly, holding him so he could not withdraw from her. "You needed me and the comfort I could provide. Do not dare apologise for being so caught up in our love that you forget to hold yourself back. You did not hurt me. On the contrary, you filled my heart and brought me such pleasure, I do not know how to put it into words."

He pressed his forehead to hers. "Are you in earnest?"

She took his face in her hands. "Did you not hear my cries? I promise they were not of pain. You touched me in such a way you had to feel what you were doing to me. I could never hide that from you."

"So you are saying that, on occasion, you desire to be taken on the serpentine chest in my dressing room." One side of his lips tugged upwards. The infuriating man was teasing her.

"To tell the truth, I had no idea what I was sitting on until you told me. I hope your valet is not waiting just outside. He may never touch the furniture in here again if he knew what we had done on it."

He lifted her into his arms and brought her to his bed, settling her into the covers before lying beside her. His fingers toyed with a long curl. He wrapped it around his finger, then let it unwind.

"Why do you not tell me what happened at Mr. Bingley's?"

"I wanted time with you before I had to recount that nightmare. When I left you last night, I had received word that Hurst required my assistance. You see, the duke finally discovered Bingley's relationship with Lady Jemima and challenged him—"

"To a duel? Oh!" She rolled to her side and covered his hand with hers. Facing each other in the warmth of the coverlet, he told her what he had found upon his arrival at Mr.

Bingley's Grosvenor Square home, what he learnt from his friend's valet, and finally, of Mr. Bingley's death and the discussion with Baron Cranfield.

"I am grieved indeed," she said when his story concluded. "Poor Mr. and Mrs. Hurst to be caught so unawares. I hope they will be kind guardians to the child. Too many children carry the stigma of their birth when they committed no sin but that of being born."

"Bingley once told me that Mrs. Hurst grew closer to Miss Bingley and her husband turned more to drink when a babe had not come within two years of their marriage. With Miss Bingley in Northumberland, I can only assume the child may help repair the damage wrought to their marriage by their disappointment and Miss Bingley's presence."

"I believe having Miss Bingley in a home of her own may be beneficial as well. Living with that lady for any longer than Jane and I stayed at Netherfield would be a trial. When we departed for Longbourn, I rejoiced at leaving. The tension was too great."

"Am I included in the cause of your tension?"

She opened her mouth, but what to say? He was, but she had learnt so much more about his character and his heart. She would never find him trying now. "I—"

He leaned in and kissed her on the lips. "Do not worry. We had no understanding of one another then. If we had known, I am certain matters would have been much different."

"You were teasing me?"

"I tried," he said, "but I fear I am not quite proficient at it this morning. I have not slept."

With gentle fingers, she combed his hair back from his eyes. "Then you must rest."

"What will you do?" His eyes fluttered. He was exhausted. How had she not noticed before?

"I am certain your housekeeper and Tate can ensure I am fed and entertained until you wake."

"We need to speak of Bingley's funeral. The Hursts plan to leave tomorrow for Scarborough." He could barely keep his eyes open.

"Shh, we can go if you wish it, but sleep. We can make arrangements when you wake if need be." If he was like her, he would only be able to sleep for so long. She could never wile away the day after a ball in bed. Instead, she would awaken in a few hours, tired but unable to rest further.

She watched him sleep for a while, tracing his features with her eyes. As much as she wanted to remain with him, she would ache or have a headache if she slept the day away, so she rose and went to her dressing room where she rang for Tate.

Her maid dressed her with her usual efficiency before she went downstairs. She peeked into each of the drawing rooms before she turned a corner and startled. "Oh!" said she and Mrs. Newnham at the same time.

"Mrs. Darcy! I had not meant to startle you. Forgive me. Mr. Jameson said he did not expect you or the master to be downstairs soon, so I was ensuring the maids cleaned as they ought."

"Which is why this house is always beautiful. Thank you. After his late night at the Bingleys, Mr. Darcy is sleeping while I am not tired at all, so I thought to entertain myself until he wakes. We could discuss household matters if you have the time."

"Of course," said the housekeeper with a nod. "Are you hungry? I know Mrs. Bunting has been waiting for some word of breakfast for you and the master."

"I do not expect her to go to a great deal of trouble for just me. A muffin and tea would suit me well. If you would join me, we could speak over tea."

The housekeeper's eyes widened a little before she nodded again. "Very good. I shall have it brought to your parlour, and I shall bring the household accounts. The former Mrs. Darcy often met with me in that room. Should you like to change it in the future, you need only say so."

She followed Mrs. Newnham into a comfortably appointed room with a table and chairs in the corner near the window facing the back of the house. When the draperies were shifted to the side, a small garden with a trellis and beds all dormant for the winter hinted at a lovely view come spring and summer. "This should work quite well. Thank you."

"I shall return soon." With that, the housekeeper departed while Elizabeth stared out the window. A small bird pecked then scratched at the ground before pecking again, seeking some food she could not see from where she was.

"Forgive me for the interruption, Mrs. Darcy."

When she turned, Mr. Higgins stood in the doorway. "Do not trouble yourself. I was only waiting on Mrs. Newnham. Is there something you required?"

"Despite the knocker being down, Mrs. Hurst is in the blue drawing room. She is insistent it is important, and after the events of last night, I thought you would want to admit her."

"Yes," she said more abruptly than she intended. "I shall speak to her. Pray, apologise to Mrs. Newnham and request tea brought to the drawing room. I do not know if the lady shall remain for long but I am of the opinion refreshments could never go amiss" She followed him into the hall, and he gestured towards a room to her right, then closed the door behind her when she entered.

After they both curtseyed, she gestured to the chairs near the fire. "Mrs. Hurst, may I say how sorry I was to hear of Mr. Bingley's death. He was a happy and genial fellow. I know you will miss him dearly."

"Thank you, Mrs. Darcy. He was an excellent brother and always kind. I cannot recall a word he ever said in anger."

"And I can well believe that as the absolute truth by what I saw of him."

Mrs. Hurst fidgeted with the ribbons of her reticule and shifted in her chair. "My husband mentioned you and Mr. Darcy may attend the funeral in Scarborough."

"Yes, he mentioned as much to me before he retired."

"May I speak freely? I admit I am uncertain how to say this without being rude."

"Yes, of course. Whatever you need, do not hesitate to ask. Your brother and my husband were friends for some time. I am certain he would wish us to be of service to you and your family during this time." She could only assume, but why would he not? Despite Mr. Bingley's problems before his death, he was still Fitzwilliam's friend. Otherwise, he would have never tried to help him.

"Perhaps I should explain. When my sister woke this morning, I went to her bedchamber to speak to her of Charles. She denied the possibility when I told her of his death and unleashed her ire upon me for even suggesting such a thing, accusing me of some horrid joke. In her fury, Caroline hastened to his bedchamber in her dressing gown and threw open the door where she discovered his body. Thankfully, his valet had already cleaned and dressed him before retiring himself. I cannot imagine what she would have done had she found him as he had been only hours prior."

The lady cleared her throat, blinked a few times, and breathed. "She became overwrought and began beating poor Charles's body."

Elizabeth covered her heart with her hand. She had never liked Miss Bingley, but she would never have wished anyone so much grief. "I hope she was able to be calmed."

"My husband offered her a glass of sherry, which was of aid. I am unsure of how much you know of my brother's finances or his...his..."

"Because he pursued Jane after we arrived in town, and after the happenings of last night, I do know of his debts, of the Duke of Dorset's daughter, and of your future ward—" After a light knock, a maid entered and placed a tea service on the table before she departed. "I thought tea might be beneficial. I am also not above drinking brandy this early should you require it." Elizabeth raised one eyebrow, almost earning a crooked smile from Mrs. Hurst.

"I appreciate the offer of tea, but I believe I will accept that glass of brandy if you do not mind."

With a glass in each of their hands, she relaxed back into her chair. "Now, what is it you require from us?"

Mrs. Hurst swallowed a large gulp and covered her mouth. "Pardon me. Since you seem to be aware, my husband is arranging for Caroline to marry a gentleman from Northumberland. He sent an express today to confirm matters as well as request the nuptials happen as soon as can be. My sister is displeased..." She took another sizeable drink of the brandy. "I should not say displeased, for it is worse. She is in a fury the likes of which I have never seen. Reginald told her you and Mr. Darcy wed yesterday, but she is insistent he is mistaken. Upon learning of my brother's debt, she became irate and began blaming your husband for Charles's death. With her current state, we believe it best that you and Mr. Darcy do not attend his funeral. We fear she will be unpleasant to you both should you come to Scarborough. My husband penned a letter explaining to your husband should you require it."

She took the note from Mrs. Hurst and sighed. "He will be disappointed not to farewell his friend, I am certain, but we can only thank you for your honesty in the situation. Neither of us would wish to make the funeral more difficult for either of you."

"I shall pass along your kind words to my husband. We shall not return to London due to mourning and shall seclude ourselves in Scotland until summer at the very least."

"I understand. I hope you find some solace in your new niece or nephew."

Mrs. Hurst stifled a sob, then fanned her face with her hand to compose herself. "I shall enjoy having a baby in the house. My husband is consulting with the solicitors this morning regarding my brother's will. He had left the entirety to Reginald as we understand the document. We hope it remains unchanged for the sake of the child." She looked into her glass and back at Elizabeth. "Forgive me for my rudeness in Hertfordshire. I have been unhappy for some time, and I should not have tried to make myself feel better by belittling others. I am appreciative of your being so agreeable today. I do not deserve it."

"How could I turn you away? Perhaps when you return to London next Season, or if we invite you to Pemberley this summer, we can begin again?" She had no reason to dislike the lady before her, who was greatly altered when compared to the Mrs. Hurst of Hertfordshire.

"I shall send our direction when we reach Scotland, then. I thank you, Mrs. Darcy." She set her empty glass on the table beside her chair and stood. "I must truly return home. We gave Caroline a liberal dose of laudanum, but I should be present in case she awakens."

"I do hope all goes well with your journey, Mrs. Hurst."

"Thank you."

After Elizabeth walked Mrs. Hurst to the door, she sagged a little. What a terrible time for the Bingleys and Hursts. She could do naught until Fitzwilliam woke, so she set off to find Mrs. Newnham. It was time for tea and household accounts until Fitzwilliam woke.

Chapter 28

A fortnight later...

When he entered her dressing room, Elizabeth stood in front of the mirror, smoothing the front of her gown, and watching him in the glass. "You stay where you are, Fitzwilliam Darcy."

He pressed his hand to his chest and attempted his best expression of innocence. "Me? What have I done of late?" Her smiling maid curtseyed and chuckled as she departed the room.

His wife planted her hands on her hips. "What have you...? You know very well why you are guilty, and I refuse to call Tate back to this room once again to repair the damage you have wrought. She had to press my gown and let my hair down to arrange it—again. It could also not have escaped her notice that it is Sunday, and we have missed church entirely. We must appear the worst of heathens." He had not been able to resist. When he stepped into her dressing room a half hour ago, she was bedecked in her wedding gown, her cheeks rosy, and her lips slightly red from their earlier love making. What sane man would deny himself the pleasure of her embrace? Even now, his fingers itched to free the buttons so he could drown himself in the treasures hidden within.

"She is paid handsomely for her service as well as her discretion, which given her history with you, she certainly holds our privacy as dear as I do." He took a step forward, but she held up a hand.

"No, you keep your distance. We may have missed this morning's service, but we will not miss Sunday breakfast with my grandparents. They are expecting us, and it would be rude to be late, especially as Georgiana has not seen us in a fortnight."

She kept her hand up while she made for the door, hastening out as he began to follow. Her legs carried her with brisk steps to the stairs, and when she reached the hall, Tate awaited her with a pearl-coloured redingote.

Higgins and her maid departed as soon as his coat and hat were in place, and he stepped close beside her and brushed his lips against her temple. "You are not angry, are you?"

Her hand took his elbow, and she tugged him out to the pavement where she turned right to walk down Park Lane. "Of course, I am not angry. I am as guilty as you are. Once I am in your arms, I cannot deny you. If we were to ever depart, I could not let you near me lest we remain in our chambers all day. The servants must think me the worst of wantons."

He laughed, making her regard him with lifted eyebrows and her jaw slightly agape.

"You think me humorous?" she asked, her pitch somewhat high.

"Yes, if you must know. Those who claim ladies wanton for enjoying their husband's attentions do not have a marriage based on love. If we are contented, our servants will benefit from serving in a happy home. I am certain Tate would wish for you to have a joyful marriage. After all, she has known you since you were quite young. Her look as she departed your dressing room carried no derision, only good spirits."

"You should have seen her expression of shock when she arrived after I rang for her. She did press her lips together after I threatened her not to say a word."

"If I had been on my own after Bingley's death, I would have spent too much time in my study, drinking brandy and port and mired in guilt and sadness over his end. I am exceedingly thankful I have had you as a distraction."

"A distraction?"

He covered her hand with his. "A most welcome distraction, who I am pleased will distract me for the rest of our lives." He would never consider that she could go before him. He could not even think of the notion. It was too much to bear.

"When you wish it, you can be entirely too charming. How am I to ever be upset with you?"

"Do you want to be upset with me?" He laughed at her low growl as they stepped to the door of Richmond House, and he rapped upon the door with the knocker.

Mr. Gideon beamed when his gaze set upon them. "Mr. Darcy, Mrs. Darcy, I am pleased to welcome you to Richmond House."

"Thank you, Mr. Gideon. It is good to see you looking so well." Elizabeth untied the ribbon of her bonnet and passed it to a maid.

The butler nodded while he helped Darcy with his coat. "I am well, miss. This house has been quiet without you. Miss Darcy does add a bit of liveliness—though not nearly as much as you."

"There you two are," said Lady Richmond from the doorway of the drawing room. "I began to wonder whether I would need to send a footman to retrieve you."

With a hand to Elizabeth's back, he stepped forward and bowed. "'Tis my fault we are late. I had not realised the time."

Lady Richmond glanced between them and pursed her lips. "I am certain that is true."

As soon as they entered, Elizabeth hurried forward and kissed the ladies' cheeks, then greeted Hatton and her grandfather.

Sunday breakfast was, as usual, a boisterous affair, and when Lord Richmond stood at the end of the meal and insisted upon Elizabeth's presence in his study with the gentlemen, her grandmother did no more than roll her eyes. "Do as you will. She is wed, and I daresay Fitzwilliam has no care that she drinks brandy with the men since he knew of the habit before he proposed."

"It simply provides me more time with her, which I cannot repine."

No sooner had the study door closed behind them, than Hatton poured himself a glass of brandy. "Have you heard from Mr. Hurst since their journey to Scarborough?"

"I had a letter from him but two days ago," he said. "Miss Bingley is no more. She is Mrs. Burton now and has joined her husband in Northumberland."

"That alone is a relief," said Hatton. "While she had her cap set at you, she was not selective in her prey. She followed me some at a few balls last Season. Now, she is one less lamprey I need worry over."

"Nicholas! A lamprey—really?" Elizabeth took a small helping of brandy from her grandfather and sat in her usual chair by the fire. "Mr. and Mrs. Hurst are to spend the coming months in Scotland. Mrs. Hurst's letter said they would be departing on the morrow."

"You are corresponding with Mrs. Hurst?" Her grandfather's eyebrows were high on his forehead.

"She came to Darcy House and spoke to me after Mr. Bingley's death. I do believe the two of us could be friends in time." Darcy loved that she toed off her slippers and curled her feet under her.

"They will take the child, then?" The earl dipped his chin and peered at Darcy over his glasses as he handed him his brandy.

"Yes, they are anticipating raising him. The solicitors confirmed the inheritance was left first for any children born to

Bingley, then the Hursts should no children exist. As it is, Hurst will be the trustee until the child is old enough to run the businesses himself, or should it be a girl, he will sell the mills and put the funds into an account for her."

The earl nodded. "A prudent move. The child will be fortunate to have a living, or a fortune set aside for its future."

"'Tis a shame you missed church this morning, Lizzy," said Hatton with an impish grin. "You missed Sir Anthony joining us and sitting with Amelia."

Elizabeth shot up to sit straight as can be in her chair. "He did! How did she react? She has professed since she came out that they are no more than friends, but there is something in his looks. I have always believed him to carry a tendre for her."

Lord Richmond shrugged. "She behaved as she always does, as though he is any one of us. He does not seem deterred, however."

"He walked her to the carriage." Nicholas raised his eyebrows with that ridiculous grin still upon his countenance.

"I wager you are champing at the bit to tease her over it." Darcy leaned against the arm of his chair, which brought him a hair closer to Elizabeth. Why could she not sit on the settee? Then he could sit beside her and take her hand.

Hatton gave an incredulous bark. "Why would I not tease her, Darcy? She is my younger sister. I have a duty to torment her mercilessly."

"Careful," said Richmond. "You may come to regret that duty one day. Do not forget that you will need to marry to secure an heir."

"Perhaps I shall court a lady without any hint of attachment, then elope to evade such scrutiny."

Elizabeth laughed. How could such a merry noise calm him?

"Why do you laugh so, Cousin?"

"Grandmamma would never forgive you, and if you believe none of us would tease you upon your return, you are sorely mistaken. The retribution you would suffer would be endless. On second thought, pray, elope. Amelia and I should love to hold that over your head for the rest of your days."

Hatton took a sizeable mouthful of his brandy with a sour expression. "I cannot win in this family."

"You have teased Lizzybeth without fail since you discovered her history with Darcy. Why should she give you quarter when you have enjoyed yourself immensely at her expense?"

After downing the last of his brandy, Hatton set his glass upon the table and rose. "I shall go sit with the ladies. Perhaps they will be more accommodating."

"Ha! I would not count on it," said Richmond. "Your grandmother will only pester you over selecting a wife. I do know how you take pleasure in those lectures." Hatton still departed with a wave of his hand, though he never looked back.

Elizabeth's lips curved. "So, Sir Anthony has taken an interest in Amelia? He has danced with her for several Seasons. Why wait until now?"

Lord Richmond sighed and wagged his knee back and forth while he stared into his glass for a moment. "Sir Anthony is a sensible fellow. His father, however, was not. Thankfully, I do not think he left Dereham Hall too much in arrears, so Sir Anthony was able to pay the debts. He is finally turning a profit from the estate and feels prepared for the expense of a wife and family."

"He is sensible indeed." Darcy could only be impressed at the course the baronet had taken. Had he inherited a similar situation, he would do much the same.

"Yes," said Lord Richmond. "He showed an interest in Amelia upon her coming out but never requested to call due to his financial situation. At balls, he contented himself with speaking with her during a set or over a glass of punch at the refreshment table. While he enjoyed her company and liked her upon their first acquaintance, he mentioned that the years since her coming out have served to make her more attractive as a potential wife. She has matured and gained confidence, qualities he admires."

Elizabeth nodded. "I have to agree with him. She was so timid when she came out, not as much as Georgiana, but she was overwhelmed with the sudden attention she received."

"She was, and unfortunately, the gentlemen who came to call were more interested in a connection to the earldom than her as a lady of worth. Their conversation was insipid and dull. She bore their efforts well, but I was thankful when they all gradually ceased to call. It was for the best. Sir Anthony is a good match for her. He enjoys music and takes pleasure in riding, which you know Amelia adores. She joins Nicholas and I on our early morning runs on Rotten Row. Your grandmother does not know that. She would have an apoplexy should she discover Amelia's penchant for racing. I thought to have her join us on the fox hunt this summer if she does not wed."

"It's not as though you take her out when Rotten Row is crowded and dangerous during the peak hours of the day." Darcy often rode Rotten Row before those who flooded the avenue arrived.

"I give him credit for his patience," said Elizabeth. "I hope she gives him the opportunity to win her heart. She has become quite set in her ways, and well... stubborn, though I would never say that to her."

Her grandfather smiled and scratched his cheek. "She has become like your grandmother. Do you not recognise the same glint in her eye not to mention the same steely recalcitrance?"

"As I recall, my father mentioned that Grandmamma enjoyed riding when she was younger."

"You had just been born when she took a fall. After, she proclaimed that grandmothers do not ride horses, and her beloved mare became a pet. She spoilt that horse. The grooms declared her impossible to ride after a while. She would roll whenever one of them tried to mount her."

Darcy laughed. "What did you do with her?"

"Her bloodlines were impeccable, so she bore a number of babies who made me a substantial sum. Amelia's stallion is one of her offspring. He is an excellent mount."

The longer the day wore on, the more restless Darcy became. How would they endure the Season if he could not bear to sit in a room with Elizabeth and not touch her in some way? Would another week cure him of this preoccupation, or would he suffer from this for months, or even years?

When they arrived home and had shed their coats and hats, he took her hand and dragged her into his study. He pulled her into his lap and placed delicate nips along the swell of her breasts. "Lord, but I missed you."

"I have been at your side for the entire afternoon," she said almost breathless.

"But I could not touch you in front of your grandparents."

She caressed her fingers along his cheeks while they held one another's gazes. "You held my hand in front of them. They did not object. After all, I have seen them do the same often." He buried his face into her neck, tasting the soft skin under her ear and relishing her shiver in response.

"What will we do when Georgiana returns in a fortnight?" she said with a smile. "We cannot leave her to her own devices every day."

"Mrs. Annesley will keep her preoccupied."

Her throaty laugh only served to fuel his ardour. "You must see to estate business and the accounts lest Pemberley fall into ruin."

"I have an exceedingly capable steward."

He turned her in his arms, so she straddled his lap, his fingers digging into the flesh of her hips as he guided her.

"Fitzwilliam," she breathed. "Love me."

He smiled against her cheek. "Always."

The End

Acknowledgements

I cannot finish a book without thanking those who helped me get this one ready for publication! To Debbie for betaing, Gail W. for giving it a quick going over, to Marie and Patty for proofreading, and finally, to Carol for the last read through.

I couldn't do what I do without the support of my husband, children, and friends. My love to you all.

My biggest thanks to my fans. Your wonderful comments and re-reads make it possible for me to get these stories out of my head instead of existing in a constant loop in my head.

Thank you all!

About the Author

L.L. Diamond is more commonly known as Leslie to her friends and Mom to her three kids. A native of Louisiana, she spent the majority of her life living within an hour of New Orleans before following her husband all over as a military wife. Louisiana, Mississippi, California, Texas, New Mexico, Nebraska, England, Missouri, and now Maryland have all been called home along the way.

Aside from mother and writer, Leslie considers herself a perpetual student. She has degrees in biology and studio art but will devour any subject of interest simply for the knowledge. Her most recent endeavors have included certifications to coach swimming and a number of fitness certifications. As an artist, her concentration is in graphic design, but watercolor is her medium of choice with one of her watercolors featured on the cover of her second book, *A Matter of Chance*. She is also a member of the Jane Austen Society of North America. Leslie also plays flute and piano, but much like *Pride and Prejudice's* Elizabeth Bennet, she is always in need of practice!

Check out these other titles by
L.L. Diamond

Regency
Rain and Retribution
An Unwavering Trust
The Earl's Conquest
Particular Intentions
Particular Attachments
Undoing
Agony and Hope
His Perfect Gift
That Perfect Someone
An Endeavour to be Worthy

Modern

A Matter of Chance
Unwrapping Mr. Darcy
It's Always Been You
It's Always Been Us
It's Always Been You and Me
He's Always Been the One
Confined with Mr. Darcy

Sci-fi/Fantasy Romance
The Peculiarity of Mr. Darcy's Mirror

[1] Shakespeare, William. *As You Like It.* Act 1, scene 2, 97–106. 1600.

[2] Regent's Punch - A punch named for Prinny. The receipt called for two bottles of Madeira, three of champagne, one of Curacao and hock, one pint of rum and one quart of brandy. Four pounds of oranges, lemons and raisins sweetened with sugar candy flavoured two bottles of seltzer water which was added to the mix. The "receipt" recommended green tea to dilute the concoction rather than brandy. Laudermilk, Sharon & Hamlin, Teresa L. *The Regency Companion.* Garland Publishing (1989). Pg. 165.

[3] Impost takers - usurers who attend the gaming tables and lend money at great premiums. Grose, Captain (Francis). *Dictionary of the Vulgar Tongue. 1811.* Ikon Classics. 2004.

www.ingramcontent.com/pod-product-compliance
Lightning Source LLC
Chambersburg PA
CBHW020405260626
47156CB00007B/2238

* 9 7 8 1 9 6 0 0 5 7 0 0 6 *